MODERN SOVIET SHORT STORIES

MODERN SOVIET SHORT STORIES, selected, translated and introduced by George Reavey, offers some *twenty-five* stories by *twenty-four* outstanding Russian writers of the Soviet period. The stories include hitherto unpublished stories by Maxim Gorky, Andrey Biely, and Boris Pasternak.

The stories included in this volume range from the early 1920's to the late 1960's. They therefore cover some forty years of Russian literary development in the Soviet Union and, besides the literary qualities of the individual stories, they also reveal many different aspects of Soviet reality in war and in peace. They contain humor as well as tragedy, human frailty as well as wilful assertion, doubt and perplexity as well as dogmatic simplification. They deal with human problems in the background of a political machine. But above all they reveal the dilemma of the individual caught in the vast and merciless processes of social transformation. Reading these stories and the human destinies they exemplify, one also becomes acutely aware of the conflict between the new and old, the dynamic of Soviet life and the tug of the older Russian traditions. Here and there, one is made aware, too, of the attraction exercised by Western modes of thought and the Western way of life. Far from being cast in one mold, the stories offer a variety of approach, style, technique and content. In fact, paradoxically enough, the general impression gleaned from these stories is one of variety.

The collection contains, besides such well-known authors as Maxim Gorky, Sholokhov, Alexey Tolstoy, Babel, Zamyatin, Olesha, and Boris Pasternak, the less well known but vastly important Andrey Biely, who is undoubtedly one of the most original writers and novelists of the 20th century. Included also are younger authors like Dudintsev and Kochetov of recent controversial fame, as well as two women poets and prose writers, Vera Inber and Olga Bergoltz, as well as other contemporary figures like Panferov, Paustovsky and Ehrenburg.

GEORGE REAVEY

comes from a North of Ireland family in which a tradition of poetry and music was cultivated. As a poet, Reavey first began to publish while at Cambridge University where he was one of the founders of the review *Experiment,* whose contributors included William Empson, Kathleen Raine, Richard Eberhart, J. Bronowski, and T. H. White.

He divided the 1930's equally between Paris and London, and was widely published in both cities. In Paris, he became a close friend of the Irish poets Denis Devlin and Samuel Beckett and the French poet, Paul Eluard. When he founded the Europa Press, he published Beckett's poems (*Echo's Bones,* 1935) and also edited, translated and published Eluard's *Thorns of Thunder: Selected Poems* (London, 1936). He met Dylan Thomas in 1932, and was the first to acquire the rights of Thomas's 16 short stories *(The Burning Baby)* in 1937.

Since his first book, *Faust's Metamorphoses* (1932), Reavey has published five books of poems, of which *The Colours of Memory* (Grove Press, 1956) was the last.

George Reavey is also an eminent scholar of Russian Literature. He was Deputy Press Attaché at the British Embassy in Moscow (1942-1945), where he also personally met Boris Pasternak with whom he had corresponded since 1931 and whose poems he has been translating and publishing since 1930. In 1959 Reavey translated Pasternak's short novel, *The Last Summer* (Noonday). He has lectured on Russian Literature and Affairs at the Universities of Manchester, London and Oxford as well as in the United States. He is also the author of *Soviet Literature Today* (Yale University Press) and the translator of various Russian classics. At present George Reavey is Professor at C. W. Post College (Long Island University).

Principal Works —

Poetry: Faust's Metamorphoses
Nostradam
Signes d'Adieu
Quixotic Perquisitions
The Colours of Memory

Criticism, Translation, etc.

Soviet Literature
Soviet Literature Today
Dead Souls by Gogol
Fathers and Sons by Turgenev
The Last Summer by Pasternak
The Silver Dove by Andrey Biely
The Poetry of Boris Pasternak

MODERN
SOVIET
SHORT
STORIES

SELECTED AND TRANSLATED
BY GEORGE REAVEY

WITH AN INTRODUCTION
AND BIOGRAPHICAL
NOTES

THE UNIVERSAL LIBRARY
GROSSET & DUNLAP
NEW YORK

Contents

INTRODUCTION

Forty Years of Writing in Soviet Russia

IN THE PAST FORTY YEARS Russian writers have produced many interesting, valid and even notable comments on man's involvement in himself, the life around him, and the historical framework of his time. Some of them have likewise commented either passionately or ironically upon the forcible impact of that dynamic framework upon them. One of them, indeed, wrote: "Why then don't I feel passion, exaltation, awe, in the presence of this glory? I am filled with hatred. He is a statesman, a Communist. He is building a new world. And the glory in this new world glows when a new salami is delivered by a salami man. I do not understand this glory. What is the meaning of it? The lives of great men, the shrines, history—these did not tell me of such glory. . . . Does this mean that the nature of glory has changed? Has this happened everywhere or only in this country, where a new world is being built?" That was Olesha in his *Envy*. "Where are the eagles and the trumpets?" T. S. Eliot seems to have asked a similar question.

After all, what is literature if not a form of artistic comment (through the appropriate medium) about man and his human situation as seen through the color-feelings of the prism of the imagination. The elements involved—those of subject and object, time and form, feeling and idea, the one and the many, personal inclination and social requirement, individual life and history, fact and imagination, I and You, are all these not diverse enough to guarantee some variety of expression in outlook, mode and language, even—or because—history is knocking at the door? Each has a choice of being either tragic or comic on the steps of the scaffold. He has the choice too of keeping mum or talking like a machine.

Variety and choice have not been lacking in Russian literature in the post-Revolutionary period, if we consider and confront such diverse writers as Maxim Gorky and Andrey Biely, Zamyatin and Zoschenko, Alexey Tolstoy and Michael Prishvin, Alexander Grin and Vsevolod Ivanov, Boris Pilnyak and Sholokhov, Isaac Babel and Valentin Katayev, Paustovsky and Dudintsev, Vera Inber and Panferov, Bergoltz and Kochetov, Tendryakov and Pasternak, Ehrenburg and Olesha. All these writers have written or are still writing in the Soviet period of Russian literature. Yet how different they are in substance and form, in life and death. Some of them, like Gorky and Prishvin, had served their early literary apprenticeship long before the Revolution; others, like Babel and Pilnyak, "vanished" in the 1930's; others again have died very recently, like Pasternak and Panferov; but many are still active or just emerging into the literary limelight. Between them they give, if not an exhaustive, then at least a fairly representative panorama of some of the best and more serious Russian writing in the period 1920-61.

If I stress variety, it is because there has been a tendency to accept unconsciously Soviet propaganda and its emphasis on a monolithic appearance at its face value, and by a reverse process to attribute to the literature of the Soviet period those same characteristics of solid unity, monolithic structure, identity of views and monotony of style. This is, however, far from being the case. The many controversies, critical polemics and communications will tend to bear this out. But, on the other hand, I am also far from denying that there has been a great deal of dull, gray, uniform and monotonous matter written, published and propagated. But many writers in the Soviet Union are themselves well aware of this fact, and highly critical of it.

I have naturally tried to avoid the stereotype, though not always the typical or what is significant of its kind in a particular phase of development. Thus, the Vsevolod Ivanov and the Alexey Tolstoy stories here included may be said to be typical of the 1920's, though in very different ways, of the initial, post-Civil-War stage of Soviet literature: the Ivanov story, *The Desert of Toub-Koy*, is typical of a newly emerging writer of talent with a sense of modern structure and style as applied to a heightened but fundamentally simple war theme; and the Tolstoy story, *The Viper*, is typical of an older writer's analysis of a more complex psychological and historical situation in the same period. Both stories are rooted in what might be called Soviet reality, but they cannot be described as either propagandist or uniform; and they are certainly distinct in structure, style and point of view. If we add to them a story each by Babel, Grin and Olesha, these differences between writers of the same period will become even more pronounced, because we shall also have variety of theme. Themes: public and domestic, realistic and fantastic, warlike and constructive, peaceful and destructive, youth and old age, commissar and bureaucrat, industrial executive and the superfluous man, to name only a few.

It might of course be argued that the first decade of Soviet literature was indeed the most varied and richest, and the least exposed to a numbing, thoroughly organized control, as well as the closest in time to the more complex pre-Revolutionary scene. There is a great deal in this argument. And did not Boris Pasternak, in referring to what came after, say: "During the last years of Mayakovsky's life, when all poetry had ceased, either his or anybody else's, when Essenin had hanged himself, when, to put it more simply, literature had stopped—for even the beginning of *And Quiet Flows the Don* and the first works of Pilnyak and Babel, Fedin and Vsevolod Ivanov, were poetry." The anti-intellectual 1930's under Stalin, even if they introduced the measuring-and-whipping rod of Socialist Realism and almost obliterated literature by over-organizing it, yet introduce certain new themes such as those of industrial effort, collective farm drives and life, and party management, which could and did become the mainspring of a new type of character and his background in the short story and the novel. There is of course nothing wrong in the theme itself or in any theme, for that matter; it all depends on the treatment and the quality of the writer. But under Stalin, and right up to his death—

except for two or three years of war—the treatment became as it were by higher command increasingly stereotyped, and the main hero of literature ever more obviously Stalin himself as the omniscient and all-effective man of steel and party ruler. On this forge were made to bend even the staunchest literary adherents of "the line" like Fadeyev; and a good many writers with no such ambition simply ceased to write or were denied publication not only in the '30s but also between 1946 and 1953. A number of writers in this last category such as Zoschenko, Olesha and Pasternak, are to be found included in this volume, though this of course is not the main reason for their inclusion.

Since I have not been guided in my selection here by strictly documentary and chronological motives, but rather by my own taste and the limitations of space, I have preferred to sacrifice the even balance of the decades to a seesaw-like confrontation of the 1920's and the 1950's as the two most creatively lively phases of the Soviet period. As a result, the intervening decades, if judged only statistically, will appear perhaps unjustifiably shrunk or barren. But I am consoled for this by the thought that the Soviet 1930's have already received enough notoriety; and that some of the best works of that period in the industrial and collective farm vein were novels such as Gladkov's *Energy* and Katayev's *Speed Up, Time!*, Panferov's *Brusski* and Sholokhov's *Seeds of Tomorrow* (Vol. I of *Virgin Soil Upturned*), which had already made their impact long ago and had familiarized us with this type of fiction. On the other hand, we have not been so familiar with rather different types of story-telling as still practised in the 1930's by Prishvin and Pasternak among others. Thus Michael Prishvin, with an eye always on nature rather than industry, can write about the pleasures of shooting game and the agonies of training a bird dog. Similarly, Boris Pasternak, who has always done the unexpected, is to be found publishing his highly poetic *The Last Summer: A Tale* in 1934 (incidentally, his last published prose book in the Soviet Union) and then writing an unpublished novel *The Year 1905* during the worst days of the Stalinist terror. Miraculously several distinct and complete episodes from this novel were somehow published at the time, and two of them are included in this volume. The importance of *The Troubled Days* episode, for example, lies not only in the fact that it is a hitherto unpublished piece of Pasternak's in a somewhat different and more realistic vein than his earlier work, such as *The Last Summer: A Tale*, but that it also forms a definite link in characters and incidents with the later and now internationally famous novel *Doctor Zhivago* (Part I).[1] We can also draw the moral from this, that we cannot judge a decade or an epoch only by the more obvious and most propagated examples of its art, which is also unfortunately and increasingly the case in the West.

In the same way, I have not included any stories of the World War II period or of the succeeding Iron Curtain years until 1953. Not because there was nothing at all to merit attention during that time, but rather because the atmosphere after Stalin's death becomes on the whole less sinister, cynical and hypocritical, and the story-telling on the whole freer, more critical, and more sincere; and, as a result, more interesting and varied. This is the period of Ehrenburg's *The Thaw* and his later autobiography, *People, Years and Life*, Pasternak's *Doctor Zhivago*, some poems of which *were* published in the Soviet Union, Dudintsev's *Not By Bread Alone* and *A New Year's Fable*, Paustovsky's *Great Expectations*, Tendryakov's *Ace, Three, Seven* and other novellas, as well as a number of works by other authors, which have all helped to change the literary climate in quality, content and spiritual mood. Not that everything is beautiful all at once. But there has been a marked literary upsurge as compared with the preceding twenty years, but not perhaps as compared with the 1920's from the purely literary point of view of awareness of form and style. There is every ground for believing that this upsurge would have come ten years earlier, in the immediate postwar period, if it had not been artificially restrained and restricted by Zhdanov's intervention in literary affairs in 1946 and the subsequent so-called "anti-cosmopolitan" drive, which was in essence anti-Western. Under Malenkov and then Khrushchev a somewhat broader view has fortunately prevailed despite the anti-"revisionist" controversy of 1957 and the anti-Zhivago agitation of 1958. This broader view has allowed, within certain limitations of course, greater familiar-

[1] For a more detailed article on *The Troubled Days* and its relation to *Doctor Zhivago*, see *Portfolio IV* (December, 1960).

ity with both the Occident and the Orient and, within measure again, a somewhat greater freedom of expression in both content and form, opinion and critical judgment. This is evident not only in the more recent works of Ehrenburg, but also in the stories of Dudintsev and Tendryakov, the novels of Kochetov and the autobiographical works of Paustovsky, but also in some of the most recent war novels, like Simonov's *The Living and the Dead* (1960). In this novel, Simonov is far more objectively critical of the conduct of the first phase of the war up to the siege of Moscow than he could possibly have been under Stalin. Simonov in his novel admits all those elements and episodes of panic, confusion and miscalculation which, as Sholokhov has also shown in his last book, *Harvest on the Don*, led to such enormous waste of human energy and life. In fact, on the basis of the latest works by Simonov and Sholokhov, Kochetov and Dudintsev, Panova and Tendryakov, I would venture to suggest that we are witnessing the beginnings of a new critical realism, involving a deeper probing into character and motive, into the background and mainsprings of human behavior whatever external label it may wear. In the same way, Sholokhov's *They Fought for their Country* gives an equally realistic picture of the war—a picture touched here and there with humor as the episode "During the Retreat" demonstrates.

If I have not confined myself so far to mentioning only short stories, and have illustrated my argument by frequent reference also to novels and autobiographical works, it is because I have been attempting to define the freer tone and the possibilities of this new stage in the development of Soviet fiction as a whole, of which the short story is a vital branch. But, though I am concerned in this collection mainly with the short story, I have resorted on a few occasions to episodes from novels where I thought they could throw some additional light on the changing background of debatable problems. Needless to say, I do not believe that "everything in the garden is rosy." The ideologist still keeps a wary eye on his less solidly rooted brother. There are still polemics and controversies, threats and accusations, but the professional troublemaker, the informer, and the career bureaucrat, are themselves beginning to be held up to ridicule or contempt by some of the writers in their stories and novels. Nor is the party man as such sacrosanct. The once obligatory abrupt man of iron is out of fashion, and so is the bureaucrat-by-rote. The new model appears to be a man who can combine firmness with human understanding. But there is still every possibility for conflict, since all these types have to co-exist and snipe at each other. It is still a dog-and-cat life, some on the offensive, others on the defensive, and the majority somewhere in between. Life is still political, but it is also human. There are the "great causes," but there is also domestic life. Domestic life has problems, that has been admitted too. And so has extra-domestic life. Important executives can lose their wives and get drunk and commit suicide. The vice-President of the Painter's Union can take a week off and indulge himself in an affair (see "Love and Art" by Panferov). There are the egotists and the more socially minded. The nihilists, jazz-fans, flighty girls, unhappy wives, disappointed inventors—all these besides the many varieties of the level-headed and the active, the patriots and the pushers, the callous and the snobs, the sentimental and the feeling, the atheists and the religious, the depraved and the virtuous, the cowardly and the heroic. All the human states in fact, operating sometimes without the ubiquitous conscience of the party. Indeed, with this and that, and the domestic note, a semblance of humanity seems to have reappeared. But it is perhaps significant that the ideological diehards still continue to think this an inadmissible weakness. And there are critics like the one who argued in December, 1960, that Soviet youth was being detrimentally affected by Western, and especially American, influence, and that it was time to put a halt to these influences. Thus, there are currents and crosscurrents; but that is not so bad, as long as there is no absolute dictatorship in ideas as they apply to the arts.

The short story has a long and honorable lineage. Its history cannot be explored here. It is a fundamental genre, easier to appreciate than to master, very exacting in economy and demanding patient craft as well as verve. Homer, poet that he was and blind, certainly had one inner eye trained upon the craft of story-telling. So had Chaucer. The story often went with poetry. But in the age of prose, the story became a cycle of prose stories and then the novel. But romantic poets like Poe also wrote mystery stories, and one can still use a poem like *The Raven* at some remove to weave a modern fable like Dudintsev's.

Once upon a time in the age of Poe also began the life and history of the modern Russian short story. It began with Alexander Pushkin (1799-1837) and Nikolai Gogol (1809-52). Pushkin, the grand initiator of literary Russian and of practically all genres in Russian verse and prose, had also turned to the short story and the novella (his novel before this, *Evgenyi Onegin*, was written in verse somewhat in the manner of *Don Juan*). But Pushkin, the poet, as the founding father of Russian literature, had a strong intuition as to the importance of prose in the 19th century, and he worked hard in his last few years to develop every possible prose genre, from the short story to the family novel, the historical narrative and the historical novel. We all remember his *Captain's Daughter* and *The Ace of Spades*. Although this latter story has in it a streak of romantic fantasy, Pushkin proved on the whole to be a realist in prose; and he always insisted on a clear distinction between the language and manner of poetry and prose. Not so, of course, all writers. Some prefer to write ornate prose—imaged and emphatically rhythmical prose, like Dylan Thomas for example, and Baudelaire, and Gogol. Gogol's prose in his stories (*Evenings in Bikanka, The Overcoat*) and his novel (*Dead Souls*), coupled with his strange fantasy, even stranger psychology and his grotesque, unearthly realism, was not only a continuation, but also a new departure. Thus, at the very beginning of Russian literary prose, two very different possibilities became open to the even greater novelists who were to succeed. Pushkin's prose heritage was taken up and developed by Turgenev and Leo Tolstoy; Gogol's, by Dostoyevsky and, later, by Andrey Biely. Turgenev and Tolstoy were of course classical and psychological realists. Tolstoy especially pushed psychological analysis to a great depth while yet preserving a balance of subjective and objective forces. Of him James Joyce could write in April, 1935: "In my opinion *How Much Land Does A Man Need* is the greatest story that the literature of the world knows. I used to like also very much *Masters and Servants* in spite of a little propaganda in it."

When the slogan of Socialist Realism was officially adopted as the platform for Soviet writers in 1932, it was laid down that the work should be "Socialist" in content, national in form, and realistic in method. Tolstoy's method of psychological realism, rather than subject matter, became the model for the technical handling of fiction. In theory this slogan rules to this day, and Sholokhov is considered to be its greatest Soviet exponent. But if we examine Soviet literature, we shall see that not all of it can be labelled Socialist Realism, and certainly nothing or little before 1933, though the Stalinist critics began to insist that Gorky's novel *Mother* was in fact the original of the species. The Soviet critics themselves from decade to decade have had rather varying notions as to what really constitutes Socialist Realism, and the debate on this subject goes on to this day. Dudintsev and Kochetov in their novels were, in their different ways, probably trying to write within this framework, but that did not prevent a controversy. In his *A New Year's Fable* (1960), Dudintsev is certainly trying something else: his owl might be out of Poe, while his satire of the "science bureaucrats" is something else again. Tendryakov's stories, too, have given rise to some heated polemical exchanges between offending and defending critics. Thus, one critic has maintained that Tendryakov lacks "the organic feeling of being contemporary" and "constantly avoids a radical presentation of the problem." This rather veiled and abstract language really implies that Tendryakov has departed from the content of Socialist Realism or, in other words, that his work lacks a clear "party" argument or conclusion. Another argument that has been used against him is that he is mainly preoccupied in his stories with "everyday, average types," "the simple Soviet man" in fact, rather than with "selected men of high qualities" (i.e. "active communists," presumably). The same critic takes to task authors, who show a "compassionate interest in people of so-called perspective-less professions." Another critic defends an author's right to describe "ordinary people" despite "distrust of the ordinary" among certain critics. This debate over Tendryakov's work should help to illuminate the type of discussion that is still roused by writers who appear to have dropped any ideological interpretation of their characters and seem to rely on "realism" pure and simple. Zoschenko's "disgrace" in 1946 had been due to rather similar criticisms, but, in a different atmosphere, he was penalized quite severely by expulsion from the Writer's Union. Fortunately he was rehabilitated after Stalin's death, and his works, or most of them, are now available again.

If we go back to Gogol's prose, that second line of development, we shall see that Dostoyevsky took from Gogol some of his psychological preoccupations and his play with irrational factors, as well as his interest in the small and frustrated personality (*The Overcoat*). *Poor Folk* and *Notes from the Underground* come from this parentage. But Dostoyevsky did not elaborate on Gogol's prose style. He was too busy being a reporter of "warring ideas." That was left to another, later writer, the truly remarkable Andrey Biely, who emerged in the first decade of the 20th century. To Biely, the symbolist, the word in itself as a root and also a symbol of multiple meanings, meant a great deal. He was interested in the concept of relativity, in dynamic structure, in rhythm, in the principle of association, in all the devices of poetry including alliteration, in puns, irony and humor. He believed with Heraclitus that the world was fluid, that men were on the edge of catastrophe, that a bomb might explode at any moment or a flood might burst through a wall and engulf the "cube" in which man chose to live. Biely was symptomatic of a sort of universal sense of unrest, and he constructed a prose to suit this feeling. As Pasternak notes, his prose altered the whole literary atmosphere prior to the Revolution. His impact on many of his contemporaries, and on some of the more talented young Soviet writers, was tremendous. He broke up the classical novel; and, without knowing his work—novels like *The Silver Dove, Petersburg*, and *Kotik Letayev*—it is hard to understand what happened to a great deal of Russian prose, especially in the 1920's. Writers like Pilnyak, Olesha, even Pasternak felt his influence. The structure of *Doctor Zhivago* seems to owe something to Biely. It is this school of prose, of "distorted forms" and "twisted language," as its critical opponents have often called it, that has suffered most in the Soviet period by being denied publication or serious criticism even though it produced some of the brightest talents. The force of Biely's impact may be judged from the fact that, as late as 1946, Zhdanov still ranted against him as a ghost that was troubling the dovecots of Socialist Realism. Biely of course had certain elements in common with James Joyce, though there was never any direct connection between them. They were parallel phenomena, independent of each other but linked in time, erecting each of them his own monument in rainbow prose.

I have left much unsaid, but the biographical notes accompanying the stories by individual authors will help to fill in some of the gaps. We leave Soviet literature, much of it dealing with violence, to its new and, we hope, peaceful decade, during which the pursuits of peace will assist the efflorescence of a grander literature, which will not neglect the front of domesticity, nor show contempt for the humble "ordinary" man. And if a romantic, heroic gesture be needed in the manner of the early Gorky who said, "Man! How proud that sounds!", let that call sound for Biely, too, whom by that time the masses likewise should have learnt to read and enjoy.

George Reavey

MAXIM GORKY

The Nightingale

THE PADDLE STEAMER was proceeding on its way between Kazan and Kozlovka.

It was quiet and fresh on the Volga. Evening was falling. A lilac-colored mist was beginning to envelop the hilly bank of the river; the opposite bank of meadowland had been flooded and pushed far back to the horizon. In places, green islets of submerged trees rose above the water. The noise of the paddles sounded dully in the damp, thick air heavy with the fragrance of fresh foliage. A broad band of foaming water stretched behind the steamer, and waves were sent rolling towards both banks. The sunset was burning down ahead of the steamer, and night was catching up in the rear. Here and there in the darkening sky stars kindled faintly.

A group of first-class passengers on the promenade deck was muted to a minor key under the influence of the melancholy evening, which was nascent on the river. There were four passengers seated there: an old man, tall and stooping, wearing a soft, wide-brimmed hat, the brim of which overshadowed the whole of his face, including the beard; beside him sat a young lady, wrapped closely in a gray shawl, staring dreamily out of her blue eyes at the hilly, wooded bank. Not far from them, on the same bench, sat another pair—a dry-looking gentleman in a gray overcoat and a buxom, shapely lady with regular features and large dark eyes. The gentleman next to her, who was nervously twisting his carefully trimmed French beard, leaned forward slightly and seemed to twitch. The lady, on the other hand, had settled against the back of the bench and sat there as immobile as a statue. The old man, gripping his cane with both hands and resting his chin on them, hunched himself forward and stared fixedly at the deck.

They were all silent.

The steamer shuddered as it moved forward rapidly. Somewhere below could be heard the intrusive clatter of dishes, the trampling of feet and peals of laughter; and, from the stern, floated a subdued, almost sighing song, which was lost every now and again in all the noises that had blended into one smooth, monotonous wave of abrupt and incomplete sounds.

"A bit fresh, isn't it. . . . Shouldn't we go down to our cabins, eh?" the old man suggested, raising his head.

In the meantime, floating from somewhere a good way off, came a strange, husky whistling that resembled a yearning, long restrained sigh from some small but powerful and very passionate breast.

The passengers raised their heads.

"A nightingale!" the old man exclaimed with a laugh.

"A little early, isn't it!"

"Let's stay and listen, papa . . ." the young lady suggested.

"As you wish. You may stay here, and they have no objection either," he answered, rising. "But I'll be off. After all, nightingales are not my . . ." But, leaving his sentence unfinished, the old man sat down again.

The nightingale's ringing, joyful, nerve-stirring trill rang and lilted through the air. The notes rushed so fast, so impetuously one after the other, that it seemed the songster was afraid he would have no time to say everything he wanted to say in his song. Nervously quivering roulades were suddenly interrupted by husky, sighing sounds, somehow very descriptive of a deeply yearning, impassioned heart. Once more the feverish *pizzicato* spattered through the air, vanishing abruptly and giving place to a minor melody, interrupted in its turn by a sort of crackling sound as if the singer were smacking his lips at his own song.

Everything on the steamer grew hushed. Every noise, except

for the monotonous thud of the paddle wheels, had vanished somewhere.

The song poured out and ruled both the river and the passengers, who listened to it in silence. The young lady smiled dreamily; the married lady's face lost something of its seriousness and
strictness. The old man sighed and said:

"There we have it, the playful and fantastic wisdom of nature!
A small, useless bird is endowed with such a wealth of tone . . .
but the cow, though a useful animal, is capable only of uttering a
single, unpleasant mooing tone. We have become so accustomed
to these peculiarities that we fail to notice them, and regard them
all as in the order of things. And yet we cannot help noticing that,
both in our life and in nature, men find the crude and ugly
useful, whereas, what is beautiful and enjoyable . . . touching to
the soul . . . man finds useless."

"Don't talk, papa . . . I can't hear!" the daughter exclaimed
tartly, shrugging her shoulders.

The father smiled skeptically and growled again:

"Well, listen, listen. . . . But you must agree that, if cows sang
like nightingales, it wouldn't be at all bad, eh? Or maybe we would
not then appreciate the cows singing and would be in raptures over
something far cruder and much worse? As one of the Goncourt
brothers has said, only the rare is beautiful. That is true, perhaps. . . . But all of us human beings would probably turn out
to be very poor judges of the truly beautiful if its eternal ideal
were revealed to us and we were able to compare it with what we
now consider to be beautiful. . . . For, if we examine the matter
closely, we have no eternal ideal. We ourselves have created the
models . . . but we are not eternal; and all our creations cannot
be eternal."

"Do stop it, papa!" the daughter implored.

"All right . . . all right . . . I'll keep quiet! But he's stopped
too . . . that rapsodist of love. . . . Have you had your fill?
Well, shall we go down to the cabins?"

"Let's sit here a little longer . . ." the married lady said slowly
in a hushed voice.

The nightingale was still singing. But now his song had grown

faint and dying. . . . The sunset had burnt out. The waters of the
Volga had grown dark and solid-looking. The moon was climbing;
and the hilly bank cast dark shadows upon the calm surface. There
was the gleam of a bonfire in the hollow of a hill, and the crimson
band of the reflected fire sparkled and quivered on the river. It
was wonderfully quiet. . . .

The nightingale's song broke off. . . .

A sailor appeared on the promenade deck.

For a while he shuffled about on one spot; then he removed his
leather cap, looked at the passengers and resolutely approached
them.

"You wouldn't like to hear the nightingale, would you?" He inquired rather awkwardly for some reason.

"What's that?" the old man asked squeamishly with a wry expression.

"The nightingale, if you wish? . . . There's a boy here . . .
who whistles like a regular nightingale . . . God's truth!" the
sailor explained, backing away from the old man's piercing scru-
tiny.

"Bring him along . . ." the married lady said curtly. The man
beside her began to shift nervously on the bench.

"Is it necessary, Nina?" he demanded, frowning sourly.

The young lady stared at the sailor with wide-open eyes.

"Would you want me to bring him?" the sailor asked again.

"Yes, of course . . . I told you so," the lady snapped angrily.

"He'll come by himself!" the sailor clarified and then disappeared.

"The devil knows what this is!" the old man explained, raising
his brows. "Some sort of a boy who whistles like a regular nightingale. . . . We heard him already, believing he was a real nightingale and, listening to him, one of us began philosophizing. . . .
What a wild fowl!" And he shook his head reproachfully, feeling
embarrassed by this wild fowl.

A boy of about fourteen appeared on deck.

He was wearing a jacket, narrow trousers and, on his head, a
new, visored cap tipped slightly to one side. His freckled face,
his rolling gait, his thick, short fingers and his sun-bleached yel-

low hair, proclaimed him to be a villager. He approached the group, removed his visored cap, bowed, shook his head and, leaving it uncovered, silently began to fidget with the visor as if trying to straighten it. . . . The passengers also scrutinized him in silence. There was a puzzled look in the young lady's eyes. The boy's gray eyes swept boldly over their faces.

"Would you have me whistle?" he asked.

"Was it you whistling just now like a nightingale?" the old man inquired.

"Yes, me. The barman had asked me. . . ."

"Is that all you do . . . whistle?"

"Exactly so. . . . I board the steamer and travel as far as Kazan. . . . Then I do the return trip from Kazan. . . ."

"Well, then let's hear you whistle, please!"

"I don't want to hear it," the young lady said in a low voice.

The boy looked at her, puzzled.

"Who taught you this?" the married lady asked the boy in a husky contralto.

"Why, I myself . . . I was a herdsboy . . . I come from hereabouts," he said, waving his hand vaguely towards the river bank, "from a village . . . I'd be minding the herd and listening all day to all sorts of birds. . . . So I began whistling to the birds myself . . . well, and so I learnt little by little. . . . I can whistle like a siskin . . . the robin, too. . . . But that's not as rousing as the nightingale. And I've become such a good hand at the nightingale that I even take in the hunters. I'll sit in the bushes and let rip! Just like a real bird, honest!"

As he talked, the boy's face glowed with the proud awareness of his mastery and the vanity of an artist.

"When I became such a good hand at it," he went on, "there were village folk who said: 'Just go on, Misha, don't stop. Just go on whistling. . . . You might please the gentry who travel by steamer. Maybe you'll get somewhere. So off I went. . . . Then I started riding on these here steamers. . . . It's not too bad, I get on. At times they give so much money, my eyes pop. Money's cheap to the gentry. . . ."

He broke off, realizing that he had said too much, and then asked bashfully:

"Would you have me whistle now?"

A silence of several seconds ensued before the married lady commanded curtly:

"Whistle!"

The boy threw the cap at his feet, put his fingers to his mouth and arched his throat. . . . For some reason his face was smiling, but he took some time to begin. First, he pulled his fingers out of his mouth, wiped his lips, snorted and made all kinds of grimaces.

At last the yearning, sighing whistling resounded again. It rang out and died away. And then suddenly the full lilting trill of a nightingale's roulade rang out in the air. The young lady quivered and sighed sadly. . . . The married lady smiled glumly and contemptuously; her companion hunched himself and grimaced nervously; and the old man stared seriously and intently at the boy's face. This latter had turned very red and swollen from the effort; but his dilated eyes remained dull and inexpressive and did not illumine him in any way. The "nightingale" crackled, trilled and, throbbing, stopped for an instant and then renewed its singing, calling . . . and sighing nostalgically. The imitation was remarkably exact.

"Papa, tell him . . . to stop," the young lady said in a low voice. She suddenly rose and walked away, looking pale and with tears in her eyes.

"Enough!" the old man said with a wave of his hand.

The "nightingale" broke off his song, wiped his lips with his hand, picked up the visored cap and held it out towards the old man's hand. There was a rustling of paper. . . .

"My humble thanks!" The boy said and quickly disappeared, descending somewhere downstairs. The lady followed him with her eyes and smiled ironically. Her companion growled something to himself and raised the collar of his overcoat. . . . The night deepened, growing thicker and darker. The water looked black now. The banks of the river were lost in the shadow. But the stars were already gleaming in the sky and, as before, the water churned monotonously beneath the paddle-wheels of the steamer.

"An artist!" The old man exclaimed, changing his position. "Another victim of the public. . . . That's how it is—the public will swallow anything—just as it swallows Swift and Offenbach, Heine and 'the glib pen' from Grub Street. Everything gives the public pleasure . . . the weight lifting of a circus strong man and a virtuoso playing the violin. And yet the public is no pig in the Gogol manner—no, it's a more intelligent animal; all the more intelligent because it is bigger. It is not particular about who serves it or how . . . but it knows how to enjoy the very process of being served. . . . It feels flattered when it observes that a man is ready to do anything in order to merit its attention . . . to twist himself into any shape for the sake of the public's dime and its attention. The public loves to feel itself lord over the personality . . ."

But apparently the others were not listening to him, for nobody answered.

"But if that sailor had not come," he began again after a pause, "we would have remained convinced that we had heard a bird famed by the poets rather than a scrubby little village lad, a pretender. H'm . . . yes! To learn the truth is not so great a pleasure . . . when the illusion is more beautiful."

"Let's go," the lady said, rising. They all got up and went to their cabins.

"Lena is probably weeping by now . . . she's such a nervous girl," the old man added. "But that's all right. . . . Gradually she must get used to the trifling, foolish pranks of life. . . . She'll find it easier to deal with larger and more serious issues. . . . Why are you trembling, Sonya? Is it the chill?"

"No, it's nothing. Don't worry," the lady replied softly. Her nervous companion glanced indifferently at her through his colorless and ironically screwed up eyes. Then they all disappeared behind the cabin door.

The moon, ascending, cast her reflections upon the dark waters; and, gleaming faintly, they quivered on the vacillating surface of the waves.

In the distance quivering points of light appeared.

A feeling of sadness hung over the drowsy river.

ANDREY BIELY

The Gropings of Cosmoses

From KOTIK LETAYEV

"O sing not those fearful songs." F. TYUTCHEV

1. THE UNIVERSE

I was always gazing out of windows:

impressively, the gestures of stone in long lines, in walls, and in sooty chimneys, thrust up by the mounds of roofs under a cloud seeping into the sky, addressed me; a cat sat on a chimney; and towards it strode a chimney sweep, carrying a short ladder and some pulleys; down below, the roadway grinned noisily, showing its rows of hard white cobblestones; the roadway was delirious with the multiple rumbling

. . . rrr . . . rrr . . . rrr . . .

of cartwheels and carriages, down below there in the crevices: in the midst of measureless passages and streets, all leading to a dead end, to the universal, windowless wall with a drainpipe, the crater of which yawned into nowhere and out of which, on rainy days, a celestial flood would gush; the crater gaped into an abyss, beside which sat a beggar in tatters, drawing attention to his horrible sores; there, a little dog, too, rubbed its hairless back against the edge of the

8

drainpipe; and the dog whimpered there—over the abyss.

Pavements, asphalt, parquet floors, party-walls, blind alleys—all these formed a vast mound, a mound that was the world, and that world was called "Moscow"; in the center of a vast, empty globe, Moscow hung suspended upon the asphalt, the parquet floors and the party-walls; we lived within that globe, which was the sky; it had small windows which opened and let in the air; and, in charge of it all, was the police inspector of the Prichistensky district, who dwelt in the watchtower and who, with a globe raised aloft, informed us that he was in good fettle and that the "world" was still hanging unhindered. Our particular apartment ended in a blind wall; if a hole were made in that wall, then the celestial flood would burst in; there would be an inundation; whitemaned waves would foam over the cobblestones and "Moscow" would brim over like . . . a barrel.

Meanwhile, behind the blind wall, outside the world, a neighbor had been living for a long time: Christofor Christoforovich Pompoul. His writing desk hung heavily down in the gloom directly behind our wall, and the four casters of his armchair glittered into nothingness. In that armchair, Pompoul would be ensconced with with some very big book; and with that book he would bang on our wall; between the arms of his chair, his striped belly would grumble and thunder its deliriums; there was a flash of fires in his belly; and the day would come when he would burst to pieces and bombard our wall with his fragments; then a black hole would form; and the flood would gush through it.

2. POMPOUL

Christofor Christoforovich bore a remarkable resemblance to . . . a sideboard and, though he lived outside the world, beyond the blind wall, he ventured into the "world."

If one were to squeeze our yellow dining room sideboard hard enough, it would bulge in the middle; a bulging would be the result, and, as a consequence, we should have a sideboard with a bulging belly: bulging into nowhere and nothing. We should also hear the ear-splitting rumbles of plates splintering inside the sideboard; and that would be Pompoul.

Of Pompoul it was said at home that he was always collecting some sort of *data;* he threw himself into London for *statistical data;* and *London,* as I knew, was a *landau* (we had seen a *landau* on the Arbat). And I pictured Christofor Christoforovich Pompoul chasing all day long after *statistical data* in London; that is; driving about all day long in a *landau* (searching through it all the time). Pompoul with a pair of yellow side-whiskers and wearing everything striped; and stripes, I thought to myself, represented the true image of life: according to *statistical data.*

At night, contrary to everything, he began to live behind our wall: outside the world. . . .

Later, I came to know his room; later, I understood: he had begun to live there in the midst of a multitude of very loud objects, and he pottered about there in a state of confusion; and he would take down volume after volume from the shelves of a very large library. And he made a great din, knocking the volumes against the shelves in a pillar of book dust; it seemed to me then that someone lived there. One could hear the tread of an oak-stumping step in the corridor, coming from behind the wall; and I could feel. The wall did not divide me from that step; accordingly: Pompoul would appear by my bedside; Pompoul with a bulky book in his hand; and I thought: now here comes Pompoul: and, indeed, out of the universal void, dull, ghostly thuds tarabanged: Pompoul was pounding the dust, and that made our oaken sideboard bulge in alarm.

3. HE BREAKS FOUR-WHEELERS

Once we went for a walk in the springtime; it was frightening. Above us, a stout, slow-limbed man was climbing down.

"Look out! It's Pompoul!"

Christofor Christoforovich Pompoul broke the axles of four-wheelers: he'd lie in ambush for a cabby and then throw himself at him, straight into *London.* The axle would break; the cabby would swear; whenever I saw Pompoul descending and tapping with his yellow cane, I immediately thought of Prohor, the fast, dandy cab-driver; I would want to run ahead and bang the cab-door in front of Pompoul and shout in the street:

"Look out!"

"Pompoul's coming down. . . ."

"Save yourselves, cabbies! . . ."

The cabbies would often scatter in all directions from him. Wherever Christofor Christoforovich passed through the street, tapping the curbstones with his yellow cane, there it would empty: not a single four-wheeler would show in sight; but there would always be plenty of them round the corner, where they would bide their time till the yellow-tousled Pompoul had passed by; and, afterwards, they would roll again, rumbling, over the white hard cobbles.

"Take me, sir!"

"Please. . . ."

Sometimes a four-wheeler would suddenly dash round the corner; and go speeding into the depths of the Arbat, away from Pompoul.

Christofor Christoforovich was aware of this and, squatting in concealment behind the wall of a side street, he panted horribly; and with a striped handkerchief wiped the sweat from his strong-boned brow. And, behold, a four-wheeler would come rolling along. Pompoul would quiver at the sight and crawl on all fours to the corner at the crossroads, and then jump into the four-wheeler with an incredibly huge leap: striped belly and all; and that was how Pompoul, on a broken axle, drove about in "London"; and there he collected *data*.

"Yes, you know, Christofor Christoforovich does break four-wheelers. . . ."

Thus papa would bring to a conclusion his fanciful tale (dimly I remember it), laughing mischievously and his spectacles glittering; I believed it, but mamma would grow angry; she disliked fantasy.

"You musn't prevent me telling lies," papa would say to her. "If you don't like it, don't listen. . . ."

4. LEO TOLSTOY

Dimly I remember: Leo Tolstoy listening to papa's fantasies and loving them.

Leo Tolstoy? Who was he?

I had no notion of "stoutness" (or was it "Tolstoyanism"): well, it might have been a calling like that of a prelate, a priest or a mathematician; and where prelates abound, there stoutness is around; thus I would have replied then to the misplaced query about Tolstoy. If I had known at that time that University towns existed everywhere, then I would have replied that each town should have its own mathematician, governor, prelate and . . . a Leo Tolstoy; I did, however, know one town (it was said that we would visit it), and that town was "Klin."

Every town is "Klin."

At that time I too saw something of one, Leo Tolstoy: he came to visit papa; he sat in a red armchair; they brought me in and said:

"Here is Lev Nicolaievich . . ."

I do not recall him well. He took me in his arms; but I do remember very vividly: the grains of dust on the gray Tolstoyan knees; and the enormous beard which tickled my little forehead.

These beards, I thought, must be the leonine manes of the "Tolstoys"; and I thought of: papa's fantasies, the axle of the four-wheelers, Pompoul, the Kostroma peasant and the prophet Magdy; papa it was who had told about the "peasant" and "Magdy." To all the Moscow cabbies—and papa's fame reverberated in all the late-night taverns of Moscow—the cabbies, collecting there, passed on his tales: of the "peasant" and "Magdy."

Some time later, I remember, a sleigh came dashing out of a blizzard; it was papa being rushed along in a sleigh, wearing a volumunous raccoon coat. Out of it protruded a high fur hat, a pair of spectacles, and a pair of whiskers. Papa, clasping a briefcase to his chest with a rather ragged fur sleeve, would be roaring with laughter while the driver rumbled:

"And the Kostroma peasant?" . . .

"Ha, ha, ha. . . ."

And the sleigh would dash away.

I once met a cabbie (six or seven years ago); he was a bent old man, but he recognized me:

"How should I not remember you? You were Kotik. . . ."

"Why, yes, of course; I remember the master, your father. Ha-ha-ha. . . . Michael Vassilievich it was. . . . He liked his joke. . . . You'd say to him: Shall I drive you to Mohavaya Street? And he'd start telling you a story: all about the peasant and the devil."

"He didn't look down on plain folk. . . . He tried his best." . . .

"May he live in eternal memory. . . ."

5. PROFESSORS

Suspiciously, I greeted the guests, the Professors and the Directors of various State Gymnasiums, because I knew something about them:

all of them were Ornaments; and, moreover, all of them were Statues; they decorated the Empire; that I had heard from both auntie Dotya and granny; and of their being "strongbrowed," I had heard from uncle Yersh: with their foreheads they pounded walls; and everyone else told me that a "Professor" was a foundation,

that is, a sort of founding stone; and I construed for myself the image

of the "Empire," that is, of some sort of institution like the Treasury: of a colonnade or, perhaps, a cornice propped up by a strong, very strong skull; and then it became clear that a Professor

descends

from a cornice.

And already thoughts began

to gnaw at me: of the abnormality of a "Professor's" corporeal composition. The inexpressible, chimerical stirrings of consciousness in a Professor's body must be truly terrifying, for somehow he was something so-so and yet not quite so. In trepidation I recall how I used to stare into their bloodless morose faces; yes, their foreheads were ponderous and stone-pale; their tread stoneheavy; and their voices the grating of a spade on cobblestone. . . .

Professors and "lecturers"—

—a glorious gang of them (from all the Moscow cornices) would sometimes congregate at our house; and they would plump themselves down on the red armchairs of the drawing room; vociferous smokemountains would rise;

tapping an armchair with his finger, Grohotunko wove his delations; and his branching denunciations,

but I did not understand; and I shuddered

from the meaningless froth of thundering words and the lurking horrors of the "Professorial life"; and ancient deliriums would raise their head:

the "Professor" in person was a groping into another universe, where everything was still molten and where the Professor carried his deliriums; and there he would be rushing like the old hag had once rushed about; the *old hag* was his wife. My godmother, Malinovskaya, was an old hag—a female Professor. Very often a Professor was an old man.

I was afraid of old men and old hags.

EVGENYI ZAMYATIN

Mamai

IN THE EVENINGS and at night there were no more houses left in Petersburg: only six-storied stone ships. The ships, solitary six-storied worlds, scudded along the stone waves in the midst of other solitary, six-storied worlds; the ships beamed with the lights of numberless cabins into the tumultuous ocean of streets. The cabins, of course, held no ordinary lodgers, but passengers. As on board ship, they were all distantly acquainted; they were all citizens of a six-storied republic besieged by the nocturnal ocean.

The passengers of stone ship No. 40 scudded in the evenings through that part of the Petersburg Ocean which can be located on the map under the name of Lachtinska Street. Ossip, formerly a porter but now Citizen Malafeyev, stood by the gangway, peering through his spectacles into the dark beyond whence, at rare intervals, the waves cast up now one, now another, of the passengers. Citizen Malafeyev would pull them out of the gloom, all wet and covered with snow and, adjusting his spectacles, he would apportion the respect due to each; the source of this respect seemed somehow to be connected by a complicated mechanism with his spectacles.

Now he turned around, like a severe schoolmaster with spectacles on the end of his nose, for the benefit of Piotr Pietrovitch Mamai.

15

"Your wife, Piotr Pietrovitch, has been expecting you for dinner for quite a while now. Why so late?"

And with that the spectacles settled down defensively in their saddle. The next passenger, a long-nosed fellow from No. 25, arrived in a car. How awkward! This long-nosed one was a problem: "sir" wouldn't do, and "comrade" was a little awkward. How could he get around it? . . .

"Ah, mister-comrade Milnik! Nasty weather. . . . Mister-comrade Milnik. . . ."

Then finally, the spectacles shot up to his forehead; Elisei Eliseivitch was stepping aboard.

"Well, thank God! Everything all right? Fur coat and all, aren't you afraid of losing it? Allow me—I'll brush it. . . ."

Elisei Eliseivitch, the *upravdom*,* was also captain of the ship. Elisei Eliseivitch was one of those gloomy Atlases who, stooping and wrinkled with suffering, seemed to support the cornice of the Hermitage on Millionaya Street.

That day the cornice evidently weighed even heavier. Elisei Eliseivitch was puffing and blowing:

"Send word to all the apartments . . . quick . . . meeting . . . in the communal room. . . ."

"Lord! Elisei Eliseivitch, is there some new . . . complication?"

But no answer was necessary: a glance at that tortured forehead, at those heavily burdened shoulders, sufficed. Citizen Malafeyev, ingeniously balancing his spectacles, ran to rouse the passengers. His tocsin knock on the doors sounded like the Archangel's trumpet: embraces congealed, quarrels froze in rigid puffs of breath, soup-spoons hung suspended on their way to the mouth.

Piotr Pietrovitch Mamai was eating soup. Or, to be more exact, he was being rigorously fed by his wife. Buddha-like, she throned it on the armchair—mighty, merciful and multi-breasted. Buddha-like, she nourished on soup the terrestrial man of her creation.

"Now, do hurry up, Pietienka, the soup will get cold. How often must I repeat: I won't have you read at table. . . ."

"Yes, Alienka, yes, immediately, yes, immediately. . . . It's the

* House manager.

sixth edition. Do you realize that? The sixth edition of Bogdano-
vitch's *Dushenka!* In 1812, at the time of the French invasion, the
whole edition was burned, and only three copies . . . And this
is the fourth. Do you realize it?"

The Mamai* of 1917, unlike his warlike namesake of the
thirteenth century, only conquered books. As a sturdy ten-year-
old lad he had learned the Ten Commandments, to play at nibs,
and had been fed by his mother: as a bald-headed boy of some
forty years of age, he worked in an insurance company, found
pleasure exclusively in books and was fed by his wife.

He swallowed a spoonful of soup as a sacrifice to Buddha; then
once more, the terrestrial man in his preoccupation forgot the
vision in the marriage ring and tenderly felt and caressed every
letter of the book.

"An exact rendering of the first edition. . . . With the approval of the Censorship Committee. What a nice darling н, on
two stout little legs. . . ."

"Well, Petia, what's the meaning of this? I've been shouting at
you, and you're still reading. Deaf? You must be deaf. There's
somebody knocking."

Piotr Pietrovitch made for the hall as fast as his legs would
carry him. At the door he was confronted by a pair of spectacles
on the end of a nose.

"Elisei Eliseivitch has called a meeting. Hurry up."

"What a nuisance! One just settles down to a book. . . . And
what's the matter now?" There were tears in the bald-headed
boy's voice.

"I've no idea. Only hurry up. . . ." The cabin door banged
and the spectacles hurried away.

Clearly all was not well on board. The ship had, perhaps, lost
its bearings; or, again, an invisible leak might have sprung, and
perhaps the distressing ocean of the streets was already threaten-
ing to burst in. Somewhere above, to the right and to the left,
alarming staccato knocks resounded on the cabin doors; somewhere, on dim-lit landings, sounded the muffled undertones of
conversations; and there was patter of quickly descending feet—
of feet making for the common cabin, the house clubroom.

* A famous Mongol khan and conqueror.

There the vaulted sky looked ruffled with stormy clouds of tobacco smoke. A stifling, calorific silence hung in the air, broken occasionally by scarcely-audible whispers. Elisei Eliseivitch rang a bell, stooped forward, frowned—his shoulders could be heard cracking in the darkness—raised the cornice of the invisible Hermitage and let it fall with a crash on the heads below.

"Gentlemen. According to reliable information, there will be a house-search tonight."

The scraping and shuffling of chairs; a few heads shot out of the mass of protruding fingers with rings, warts, ribbons, and side-whiskers. And from the tobacco clouds a downpour fell on the stooping Atlas:

"No, allow me! We'll be obliged. . . . How? And the paper money? . . . Elisei Eliseivitch, I suggest that the gates . . . Books, that's the surest place, books. . . ."

Stooping stiffly, Elisei Eliseivitch bore the downpour. And without even turning his head (perhaps it would not turn now), he addressed Ossip:

"Ossip, whose turn is it to go on guard tonight?"

Amid the silence, Ossip's finger traced a fatal scribble on the wall: the finger set in motion not letters, but Mamai's heavy bookshelves.

"It's Citizen Mamai's turn next, Citizen Malafeyev."

"All right. Take the revolvers. And if anybody attempts to enter . . . without a warrant . . ."

Ship No. 40 scudded through the stormy seas of Lachtinska Street. It rolled and groaned as the snow thrashed the gleaming cabin-windows; there was an invisible leak somewhere in the hold, and there was no certainty that the ship would weather the stormy night and reach a morning harbor or that it would not go down. In the rapidly emptying communal room, passengers swarmed around the petrified captain.

"Elisei Eliseivitch, what if they search through our pockets as well? But surely they won't do that."

"Elisei Eliseivitch, what if I hang up my notes with the toilet-paper?"

The passengers then rushed to their various cabins. Their behavior in the cabins was unusual: they crawled over the floor;

their hands explored under the cupboards; they peeped with awe
inside a plaster-cast head of Tolstoy; they unhooked some ancient
frame, from which their grandmother had smiled tranquilly for
the last fifty years.

The terrestrial man-dwarf Mamai stood face to face with his
Buddha and hid his eyes from the omniscient terrifying eye. His
arms were perfect strangers to him—just short penguin wings.
His hands had been his great embarrassment for the last forty
years, and if they had not embarrassed him then, he might, perhaps, have spoken and unburdened himself—it was all so terrifying and unthinkable. . . .

"I can't think why you're so frightened! Even your nose has
turned white! What does it matter to us? What thousands have
we got?"

God knows, if the Mamai of thirteen hundred and something
had possessed hands as strange and awkward, the same secret
and the same wife, he might, perhaps, have acted as did the
Mamai of nineteen-seventeen. Somewhere, from some corner, in
the menacing silence, the scratching of a mouse sounded. The
eyes of the Mamai of nineteen-seventeen flew at full speed in the
direction of the mouse-hole, and then he stammered out:

"I have . . . that is . . . we have, four thousand two hundred."

"What? You? Where did you get it?"

"I . . . I . . . little by little. . . . I was afraid to ask you so
often. . . ."

"What? You mean you stole it? You deceived me, you mean?
And I, unfortunate creature, I thought . . . but Pietienka, dear,
how. . . . Ah, what a wretched creature I am!"

"It was for books. . . . I . . ."

"I know these books in skirts! Don't talk to me!"

The ten-year-old Mamai had once only in his life been beaten
by his mother; he had turned on the tap of the newly kindled
samovar and let the water run out, the samovar had become unsoldered, and the tap drooped sadly to one side. And now, for the
second time in his life, Mamai felt his head gripped as in a vice
under his mother's arm, his trousers had been let down, and . . .

But suddenly, with a boyish sense of cunning, Mamai found a

way of glossing over the sadly drooping tap—the four thousand and two hundred. He said plaintively:

"It's time for me to go on guard till four. With a revolver. And Elisei Eliseivitch said that if anybody attempted to enter without a warrant. . . ."

Instantly the multi-breasted, benevolent mother replaced the lightning-menacing Buddha.

"Lord! Have they all gone mad? It's all Elisei Eliseivitch's fault. Take care! And don't really take it into your head to . . ."

"No-no, I'll just—er—keep it in my pocket. Do you think I ever could? I wouldn't harm a fly. . . ."

He spoke the truth, for if a fly ever happened to fall into his glass, Mamai would always pick it up carefully, blow on it and let it go . . . fly away! No . . . there was nothing to be afraid of.

But the four thousand two hundred.

Then the Buddha spoke once more:

"What a plague you are! But where will you hide your loot,—no, not a word, please,—loot, yes. . . ."

Books? The galoshes in the hall? The lavatory paper? The samovar pipe? The lining of his hat? The rug with the pale blue knight hanging in the bedroom? The partially opened and damp umbrella? A stamped envelope clearly addressed to an imaginary commissar, Comrade Goldebayev, carelessly left on the table? . . . No, too dangerous. . . . Finally, toward midnight, it was decided to concentrate all hope in the finest of psychlogical calculations: they would search everywhere except near the entrance door, where there was a loose parquet square. The square artfully raised with a paper knife. The stolen four thousand ("Not a word, please!") was enveloped in waxed biscuit paper ("It may very likely be damp under the entrance door"), and the four thousand were interred under the square.

Ship No. 40 was all a-quiver, on tiptoe, a-whisper. The portholes gleamed feverishly into the dark ocean of streets; and on the fifth, second, and third floors curtains were raised and shadows flitted across the bright panes. No, not a thing was to be seen. However, there were two of them down in the yard, and they would sound the warning when it began. . . .

Below, with his spectacles perched on the end of his nose, stood Citizen Malafeyev, meditating.

"By nature, I'm a peaceful, kindly soul, but it's hard living in these evil times. Let's see, I thought to myself, I'd take a trip home to Ostaskhov. I arrived . . . and the international situation . . . well, you can't imagine anything worse. Everybody at everybody else's throat—no better than wolves. No life for me, that. I'm a peaceful soul. . . ."

Thus spoke the peaceful man, holding a revolver in his hand— with six deaths tightly packed in the six bullets.

"But how did you manage in the Japanese war, Ossip? You had to kill then."

"Well, in war. . . . War is, of course, another matter."

"And you used the bayonet, too?"

"On occasions. . . . It's like pricking a melon, a bit hard at first, when it's the rind, and then—in it goes all right, very easy."

At the mention of the melon, Mamai felt cold shivers go down his back.

"And I . . . I wouldn't do it for anything. Even if it meant my immediate death!"

"You wait! When you see it close, you'll think different. . . ."

Silence. White snow-flies were flying around the lamp. Suddenly, in the distance, they heard the long-drawn-out crack of a rifle-shot; then again silence, and the snow-flies. Thank God, four o'clock! They will not come now. The guard will be changed in a moment, and then he would go back to the cabin, to sleep. . . .

On the wall of the Mamayev bedroom, the pale-blue, chequered knight swung his pale-blue sword and paused; a human sacrifice was being offered before the eyes of the knight.

Lady Mamai, all-embracing, multi-breasted, Buddha-like, sat throned in the heights of the white linen clouds. Her appearance said that she had finished the creation of the world that very day and that she was very satisfied with everything; even with this little man, in spite of his four thousand two hundred. The little man stood resignedly by the bed; he looked frozen and red-nosed, and he had short, stranger-like, penguin-wing arms.

"Well, get in, get in. . . ."

The pale-blue knight half shut his eyes. It was distressingly obvious that the little man would cross himself, stretch out his arms and dive into bed head-forward as into water.

Ship No. 40 weathered the storm and put in at the morning harbor. The passengers were hastily pulling out their business portfolios and baskets with provisions, and were hurrying ashore past Ossip's spectacles. The ship was in port, but only till evening; then it would have to cross the ocean again.

Stooping, Elisei Eliseivitch bore the cornice of the invisible Hermitage past Ossip, and crashed it down on him as he went by:

"You may count on it for sure tonight. You had better warn them."

But a whole day had to be lived through before night. And the passengers wandered perplexedly about that strange, unfamiliar city—Petersburg. In some ways so like—and yet so unlike—the Petersburg from which they had sailed almost a year ago. Sailed where to? God only knows. And would they ever return? Strange, frozen waves of stone and snow; hills and valleys; Australian aborigines, clad in strange rags, with rifles slung over their shoulders on strings; and outlandish customs too—calls made by night in the manner of Walter Scott's Rob Roy. And here are the outskirts with drops of blood branded in the snow. No, no, this was not Petersburg.

Mamai wandered along the unfamiliar outskirts among the Australian aborigines. His penguin winglets embarrassed him; his head drooped, like the tap of the unsoldered samovar; and, on his left, downtrodden heel, a hard snow *globus hystericus* made every step a torture.

But he suddenly lifted his head; his feet danced along like a twenty-five-year-old's; poppies bloomed in his cheeks, for, from a shop-window, there smiled on Mamai—

"Hey, look where you're going!" Swarthy aborigines pushed by him with enormous sacks of grain slung over their shoulders.

Mamai jumped out of their way, without taking his eyes off the window; and, as soon as they had gone by, he was back at the window again, where there smiled—

"Yes, for the sake of this, one might steal or deceive or do anything."

From the window there smiled, temptingly and voluptuously uncovered, a book of the time of Catherine the Great: *A Portrait Descriptive of the Beauties of Saint Petersburg*. With a seemingly negligent gesture of feminine wile, it allowed him a glimpse of its interior—a warm hollow between two supple, marble-blue pages.

Mamai had fallen in love like a twenty-two-year-old. He used to go to the Zagorodnyi every day and, looking silently into the window, sing serenades. He could not sleep at night and deluded himself: he pretended he could not sleep because a mouse was gnawing somewhere under the door. He went out every morning, and every morning the same square by the entrance door used to thrill him sweetly. Mamai's fortune lay buried under that square, at once so near and so far. But what was he to do now that the truth about the four thousand had been revealed?

On the fourth day, gripping his heart, like a sparrow, in his fist, Mamai penetrated through the familiar door on the Zagorodnyi. Behind the counter stood the gray-bearded, bushy-browed southerner, in whose captivity "she" pined. His warrior namesake came to life in Mamai, and Mamai bore down bravely upon the southerner.

"Ah, Mr. Mamai! I put something aside for you . . . a long time ago, a long time. . . ."

Gripping the sparrow tighter, Mamai pretended to leaf through the books and to caress them, but he was all back; for there behind his back, in the window, "she" was smiling at him. Picking up a faded copy of an 1835 *Telescope*, Mamai bargained endlessly, and then hopelessly waved his hand. Finally, sniffing along the shelves, he made his way, with circuitous fox-steps, toward the window. Then, casually he asked:

"And how much is this?"

Ah! the sparrow had flown. Hold it! Hold it! The southerner fingered his beard:

"We-ell . . . as a favor . . . a hundred and fifty, to you."

"Hm. . . . Perhaps. . . . (Cheers! Bells! And salvos!) Well, perhaps . . . I'll bring the money tomorrow and take it."

But he still had to face the most terrifying thing—the square at the entrance door. That evening Mamai sat on pins and needles; he must have it, he couldn't, he could, it was unthinkable, possible, impossible, necessary.

The omniscient, merciful and terrible vision-in-the-wedding-ring was drinking tea.

"Why aren't you eating, Pietienka? What's the matter with you. . . . You've been sleeping badly again?"

"Yes, the mice. . . . I don't know. . . ."

"Stop twisting your handkerchief like that! That's something new!"

"I'm not twisting it. . . ."

His tea glass was empty at last; not a glass, but a bottomless, forty-bucket barrel. The Buddha, in the kitchen, was accepting sacrificial offerings from the cook. Mamai was left alone in the study.

Just before the beat of twelve, Mamai was himself ticking the minutes like a clock. He then swallowed a mouthful of air, listened, tiptoed to the writing-desk and picked up the paper knife. Then, like a gnome, he squatted down feverishly by the entrance door. An icy dew beaded his bald head: he inserted the dagger under the parquet square, levered it, and . . . then uttered a desperate howl.

At the howl, the Buddha thundered in from the kitchen and saw at her feet a turnip of a bald head, a crouching gnome with a dagger, and, below him, a small heap of nibbled paper.

"The four thousand . . . the mice . . . Ah, there, there he is! There!"

Merciless and cruel as the Mamai of thirteen hundred and some-thing, the Mamai of nineteen-seventeen sprang from his haunches and leaped, brandishing his dagger, toward the corner by the door where the mouse had run after escaping from under the parquet square. Mamai bloodthirstily stabbed his enemy. A melon —hard at first, because of the rind; then easy and—stop: the wooden parquet square, and the end.

VSEVOLOD IVANOV

The Desert of Toub-Koy

HEY, YOU STUBBORN GRASSES! No horse, no stone even, has strength to crush or crunch such grass. And does that not explain why the mountain cliffs are so crumbly, brittle as the teeth of horses crumbling impotently against the grasses of Toub-Koy?

And over all this, as far as the very glaciers, a sky lowers, yellow as the sands of Toub-Koy.

And the stars upon it are, one might say, the scobs of the dry dung of spring-bucks.

But is that really so? For no one can tell whether there are any stars at all on that dirty yellow, color-of-moldering-straw, skinflint sky.

But, notwithstanding, there had come, braving these stubborn grasses, these sands, from somewhere in Tumien, through the Ural and other steppes, to Comrade Omiehin's partisan detachment, the agitator, demonstrator and talker generally, Ievdokim Pietrovitch Glushkov.

His alabaster, girlish complexion was more astonishing than his phraseology, which put to shame that of fifty newspapers. No desert sun could have ruffled that tender skin; and, without any pretence of blushing, he boasted of his rhetoric and especially of his method of agitating.

25

He had brought his belongings on three donkeys. The first, nicknamed "Commander," carried a machine gun in "good working order," according to regulations. The other two carried a "Cocq" film-camera, and, in a variegated Turkman sack, several round boxes of film.

Glushkov's feet were bare, cracked, and chapped; and, for some reason, he let his trousers drag so that the turn-ups were clogged with thick yellow dust, just as if he had intentionally strewn a lot of sand there.

He stood at attention in front of Comrade Omiehin, and his face shone so pink he might have come from the glaciers.

"The secret of my astonishing effect on the masses depends on the explanations I give of the events of the antecedent social order and on the demonstration of the above-mentioned events and love dramas on the screen by means of ordinary household electric installations, and the machine, worked by hand, called 'Cocq' which, in Russian, means victory."

"Victory?" questioned Omiehin. And he stared at the hills of Toub-Koy, at the glaciers that alone cleft the sky. There the White detachments had vanished, without leaving a trace.

"Of victory there can be no doubt," answered Glushkov, his teeth shining whiter than his alabaster face.

"That may be," said Omiehin. "We're not against bourgeois culture, if there's any sense in it. . . . Let's see what you've got."

Omiehin's detachment had been scouring the dunes of Mongolia for over a year now; and for the last ten months the horses had been crunching the stubborn grasses of the steppe, and Comrade Omiehin had begun to forget many things.

Taking a few strides, he stopped and stared at the three exhausted donkeys, at the fat gadflies buzzing around them, and at Glushkov, who was unpacking his "Cocq" camera on a piece of felt.

"So, you've got something about love?"

"Preferably about love, comrade."

"Pity. Death would be more suitable."

"We'll make the necessary adaptations."

Only the glaciers, gleaming with hatred of the heat, only the glaciers cleft the sky. The hills of Toub-Koy were high and ringing.

As he strode off to his tent, Omiehin muttered hoarsely: "We'll do all the adapting, if necessary."

II

In the middle of the reel, when the smooth and oily ne'er-do-well had confessed his love for the lady in the long train while his rival, a malodorous, bald-headed villain, was playing Peeping Tom behind a curtain, and when Glushkov had just mentally put the finishing touches to one of his amazing speeches, a dozen of which would have sufficed to bring the old world down in ruins, an auxiliary force of Ufim Tartars, who had arrived by secret tracks, galloped up to the detachment.

The screen grew dark; the partisans roared "Hurrah"; and Lukashka, the Cossack, swiftly cut a mare's throat with his curved knife. In honor of the guest, the liquor-stills were washed as thoroughly as though they were intended for the preparation of medicine; and, in accordance with the custom of the steppe, Omiehin, with his own fingers, placed the first morsel of roasted goat into the mouth of Maxim Semeonovitch Paleyka, the commander of the Tartar detachment.

"I place myself under your direct command," Paleyka announced, quickly swallowing the morsel.

"Eat your fill," Omiehin answered, moving the dish nearer. "In connection with the picture, I would remark that, from the point of view of human utility, love calls up a feeling of self-pity."

"That doesn't follow . . ." Paleyka replied. "Life does not prevent loving, and especially giving birth. And what is life without birth! My idea is to have only one woman. Or, to put it figuratively and by way of allegory—a woman that would hang around your neck and not leave go."

"I don't approve of that," Omiehin protested.

It was on the tip of his tongue to question Paleyka about his bourgeois origin, but at that moment a mountain-horn sang out with a sound so slender it might have been evaporating in the air, which was as dry as flame.

The riders leaped on their horses.

The Cossack Lukashka, who had cut down the mare, led in two Kirghiz. In their fear, trying to sit straight in the saddle after the Russian manner, they said that the *ak-rus* (white people from the glaciers) were outflanking Omiehin's detachment and were driving off the Kirghiz flocks on the way; and that the tribal chiefs were getting ready to cut down the *djataks*.

"We're *djataks* ourselves," they said. "Take us in. We came of our own free will."

"*Djatak* means poor man," Glushkov translated for his own benefit. "Essential to note it and make use of it in my speech when I finish my film demonstration. . . ."

The days here are as dry as the wind, and the boredom of life in these parts is drier and simpler than the wind, and the wind buries the ends of life with coarse yellow sand.

Thus, three more partisans had set out in the morning to gather fuel, and had failed to return.

In the vale of Kaiga, guards remained to watch over the reserve of horses, the empty tents, the three donkeys pasturing by the *saksauls*,* and the agitator Glushkov who, out of boredom, was sleeping on a stone near his reel of film.

The guards were telling tales of priests' wives and workers. An unslaked nostalgia for a woman's body dripped from their lips, and Glushkov woke at the question:

"You don't say there are women like that outside films? We must assume that they've all had their throats slit. If not—we'll finish the job. Why put on such airs, you bitches, when we're all suffering here, eh?"

Glushkov awoke. He felt hot and uncomfortable in his soiled clothes. He fingered his hot and perspiring belly and thought to himself: was it really wise of him to exhibit such "ribs" in the desert. And with a curse, unusual for him, he added:

"I'll cut the above-mentioned section from the reel."

At that very moment, on one of the dark tracks, a horse shied with a clatter of hoofs.

---

* A cactus-like bush that grows in Turkestan.

The dark-cherry light of a resinous chip then lighted up Omiehin's rugged chin, the blood on the horse's hoofs and a man's chest, cut in a star-shaped wound. The horse's hoof had sunk to the fetlock in the man's chest.

It was one of three partisans who had gone to gather fuel that morning.

In these parts, coarse sand buried the ends of a man's life.

Paleyka adjusted the straps of his revolver and said quietly to Omiehin:

"I suggest we put the corpse aside and take no prisoners."

His words fluttered from mane to mane, from fur cap to fur cap, like the indistinct sound of cartridges being inserted into the breach.

"No prisoners."

"Ex—actly," whispered the last man of the detachment, looking over his shoulder into the impenetrable darkness. "Ex—actly. No prisoners."

In the battle near the mountain village Tatchi, as you know, Colonel Kanashivili was killed, seventy-three of the ataman's followers were cut down, and Kanashivili's brother was made prisoner.

The mountain torrent took no prisoners. Water becomes turbid from blood only in songs, and the mists in the mountains remained as multitudinous as ever.

"Shoot him!" Paleyka ordered, without looking at the prisoner. Paleyka was unsuccessfully groping for his matches, for he had not smoked all night, and it was of course more agreeable to hold a cigarette than a sword in one's hand.

"Comrade. . . ."

Omiehin struck a match for him. Such attention surprised Paleyka, and he even bowed:

"Thank you, Comrade Omiehin."

Omiehin struck another match, and, holding the tiny, burning splinter in his hand, said:

"But, comrade, in so far as she is a woman, and not the brother. . . ."

Paleyka groped again for his matches.

"I suggest we shoot her in half an hour. I'll question her myself. So, it's not the brother, but the wife?" he asked Omiehin for some reason.

The latter shook his head, and Paleyka lowered his head.

"And the wife . . . can also be shot."

"She, too," confirmed Omiehin. And then Paleyka suddenly felt that his cigarette was pulling at last.

It was dawn. Friday. The Tartars were skillfully slaughtering the mares; and with as great assurance, with as great daring, the glaciers of Toub-Koy glittered as if their glitter were the source of their happiness.

III

"We've questioned her. She doesn't need a guard; her clay hut's so strong, you only have to touch it, and it will crumble and crush her. There'd be no time even to finish her off with a bullet. The houses they build nowadays! Pottery's harder. She knows what she's in for."

Paleyka liked talking about the Great War. He used to recount how, at the taking of Lvov, a black-haired Magyar girl had fallen in love with him for his bravery, and how he had wished to marry her. The marriage did not take place because the army abandoned Lvov, but she had made him a present of a dozen bright blue silk handkerchiefs.

He would then pull out one of these handkerchiefs and, if need be, bury his nose in it.

And so it happened now; he fumbled for the handkerchief, and his riding-breeches spread out over the stone he was sitting on.

"You've questioned her, Maxim Semeonovitch?"

Paleyka raised his handkerchief. Five Tartars were waiting behind Omiehin, lazily shuffling their feet.

"As to questioning, I've questioned her. I must warn you, however, that the Georgian in question is not the wife, but the sister of Kanashivili. She's called Helena, and is a virgin into the bargain. She has agreed to give us exhaustive information about the bandit bands and to show us the outflanking tracks and all the bandits' liaisons with the town."

By the firmness with which Paleyka uttered the last sentence,

Omiehin realized that he was lying. A wave of hate flowed from his lips to his ears, then fell on his neck, and it seemed to him as if he were retracting.

"I agree to postponing the execution. I'll finish questioning her myself, Comrade Paleyka."

"Very well. As you are an old hand in political affairs, and have made a thorough study of them during your prolonged stay in the steppe . . . haven't you any links with the town, if one were to dispatch her there?"

The red flag was the only link and, as it was, the winds and the rains had worn it thin.

Eccentric Paleyka, blue as a spring sky your soul!

Omiehin went up to the decrepit Kirghiz clay hut. Several partisans were peeping through round holes that had been bored in the back wall of the hut, and were pushing for places, swearing and plucking each other forcibly by the sleeves.

"Devil, what the hell are you doing? You've ripped my sleeve off! You can sew it on now!"

"And you've stuck your head in, like a bug. Hey, you're all red with the blood you gorged. Give the others a chance. . . ."

A lean peasant, wan as the old shabby soldier's coat he was wearing, was firmly shouldering his way between two sturdy Tartars. The sides of his soldier's coat, as they hung down over his tightly belted waist, entirely hid the wide thong with its twisted ends, and his elbows stuck into the Tartars' sides.

"Just a peep, brothers, with one eye," the sickly looking fellow begged. "Just one peep, won't you. . . ."

Another barefooted, slender, nimble fellow in a short coat, to which he had managed to give the appearance of a natty caftan, slipped like an eel between two smooth round backs and found a peephole for himself right under the peasant's elbow. The caftan-wearer's dry feet scraped inaudibly against the Tartars' heavy boots.

He gave a squeal of delight.

"Ai, what a waman! . . . Does nothing but pownder and pownder herself."

A roar of laughter came from the crowd.

"You don't say; she's still powndering herself? There's a hag for you, she's doing it for the third day now. Another woman, were she a Russian, wouldn't have dried her tears yet, but this one doesn't care a damn. . . ."

"She's a Pole."

"Maybe a Jewess, only a white one."

"They say her husband's a general. But they didn't catch him."

"What does she want a husband for? He wasn't with the detachment at all. She managed herself, like a commander. A devil of a woman, in trousers, with a dagger, and a painted face. . . ."

A fresh band of would-be observers pressed toward the peepholes, pulling at each other's elbows. One old bullet-riddled soldier's coat tore and hung in a fold to the ground. Its owner, without so much as turning, found the guilty one's head with his fist. The latter's forage cap tilted over his eyes. Furious, he began hitting out wildly in the crush around him. Gray soldiers' coats blended in one cursing, swaying, and dishevelled heap.

Omiehin, who had long been reluctantly watching the soldiers, strode up, his hand on his heavy pistol.

"Stop there. You're not a fly! Where are you crawling? Where are the sentries? Get out of the way there, I tell you."

The peasants broke apart as if come unstuck, and a pungent odor of perspiration hit Omiehin.

"She hasn't stopped powndering herself," came a hoarse whisper from behind.

Omiehin made his way past the partisans and looked for a peephole at his own level.

He could find no peephole at that level. He looked around.

"Where does one look here?"

"Try a little lower, brother. A little lower."

Omiehin discontentedly pulled his forage cap on a little tighter and, bending almost double, peeped in. He saw nothing at first; the narrow window-pane near the ceiling gave but little light. The hut was quite empty. It smelled of ash. Finally, he could distinguish two dirty strips of pine-tree benches or, rather, one long narrow bench and sitting upon it a woman in a white Circassian costume. Two plaits hung straight down her back. The plaits looked green. The face could not be seen, for it was turned toward the light of the window. On her knees lay a white fur cap. A round mirror had sunk deeply into the smoothly combed lambskin of the cap. Nearby, on a block of wood, stood a round, sky-blue flat box. The woman held a powder-puff in her hands. She was moving it over her face and twisting her head in front of the mirror. Her face was gradually turning away from Omiehin. He had evidently leaned too heavily, for the decrepit wall of clay brick gave a dry crack. The woman quickly gathered her legs in their black patent-leather boots under the bench and looked around. There was an ever-stronger whiff of moist ash. Her gray eyes, glowing with hate, explored the wall. Her eyebrows hung low over her eyes; or was it her eyelashes that reached her brows?

"Ssss . . . swine . . ." she hissed rather than said.

A pale, burned out, lifeless, introspective face, not easy to approach. Roving, aggressive eyes.

Omiehin turned away from the peephole and shuddered, as if those impetuous, lightning-bearing insects had run across his chest.

Paleyka's hand closed in a firm, friendly grip on his shoulder. His fingers were dirty and untidy as a ragged broom.

"Have you questioned her?"

"Just going to," answered Omiehin.

"We might dispatch her with a letter. The men are undesirably excited. You've noticed that, Alexei Pietrovitch?"

Omiehin, pursing his wide mouth, quickly answered:

"It seems, Comrade Paleyka, that you're taking a greater interest in her than . . . Her shop's here; she won't go much farther than her powder-box. Yes. . . . It's no good talking to her. I'll question her. I'll question her. . . ." Omiehin repeated.

Their voices were low, carrying little farther than their compressed lips and short breathing, but the prisoner's ear was keen. She pressed herself with her whole body against the wall of the hut. And her body was so hot and flaming! The shaggy gray wall absorbed and inhaled her heat, and grew quite warm. Very warm. It would not be at all surprising if the warmth she communicated would reach and touch the faces of the men standing near. The cheeks of one of them flushed, and then his ears caught fire.

"I don't agree with you. As military commander, I should be absolutely the first to learn any information she has to give."

Paleyka, of a sudden, turned sharply, military fashion, saluted silently and strode away, skirting the tents.

Omiehin shouted in his wake:

"Hold on, Maxim! We must thrash out any misunderstanding. Believe me. . . ."

These last words he muttered already in his stride, as he threw back with his knees the long folds of his soldier's coat.

"We'll talk it over in the forest," Paleyka tossed over his shoulder.

"In the forest?"

"In the forest. It's not convenient here."

IV

Omiehin threw his army coat on a *saksaoul* shrub. A pale-blue bird, a stranger apparently to the region, flew out from under the shrub.

A good spot for a grave, he thought.

Paleyka strode ahead, waving his arms in a loose, unsoldierly way.

. . . He may take it into his head to go as far as the hills. And if not to the hills, to the very crags of Kagi. That's five miles, no less. And five miles, in good language, is a dog's run.

There was smoke of fires in the valley. The horses of the partisans tore off the blades of grass as though they were branches. The hills looked like tents in which Death might have been sleeping.

The glaciers alone cleft the sky.

The glaciers laughed coldly at the desert.

. . . "Is he really making for the hills?"

. . . "You won't reach them, brother; not in this melancholy waste."

. . . We all of us fall short of our destination. There was another summer in Petersburg, where there are no hills and where the sea is kept in check by smooth cliffs of men's fashioning.

But even there a desert wind blows, sweeping through the streets and parching lips that are already dry. In Labyagyi, my native country, a bird will lead its yellow fledgelings from among the stones to the clear waters. I have not seen them. Books reminded me of this. Petersburg tracks are straight and level, and I haven't gone very far, after all, in my nostalgia. . . .

Paleyka, exhausted, fell prostrate on the ground.

The *saksaoul* bit into the thin cloth with its sharp thorns and tore at the prostrate body. Warm rain, thought the shrub with displeasure.

Omiehin, all out of breath, halted beside him. His lips were crisp as bark. Omiehin might have been eating cork all his life.

"You, I see, Maxim, are really. . . ." he would like to have said, but as always, when about to venture on a speech, he shuffled his feet and bent up the sole of his right foot.

"It happens," he pronounced.

Such stillness succeeded his words that, from a neighboring shrub, some four inches from the stalk, a bluish mouse suddenly leaped out. "Iukhtach" they call it, which means greedy. Its slightly hooked nose looked musing and solemn.

Paleyka raised himself on his elbows and silently pulled out his gun. His mouth gaped; one of his teeth had apparently outgrown the others and was, into the bargain, the yellowest of all.

He turned his perspiring head toward Omiehin and said:

"Fire!"

Omiehin made to retreat, but Paleyka took aim while Omiehin whispered:

"Good God, Maxim Semeonovitch, why should I fire at you?"

"At the mouse, not at me. Whoever hits it, will get *her*. Fire in God's name!"

"You're mad! I've never shot at mice with a gun."

"Fire! I'm counting two. Whoever hits it, takes her. Our revolvers have different bores. Fire, I tell you."

The mouse pricked up its ears, raised its tail, took a breath, and got ready to run . . . suddenly, losing awareness of himself, Omiehin whispered:

"Count!"

V

The woman lay on a bench, her fur cap spread under her head.
When Paleyka sprang into the hut and hurriedly bolted the door,
she raised herself quickly and sat up, gripping the edge of the
bench with her hands.

"I'll scream. What do you want?"

Paleyka, without replying, struck a match, lit a small candle-
end, and looked around for a place to set it down. The woman
narrowed her eyes as if about to try and escape, but then, instead,
she quickly bent his arm at the elbow and said:

"Stand like that!"

She carefully pulled out of the pocket of her blouse a round
mirror and from the side-pocket of her skirt a powder-box, and,
opening the blue box, she began to powder herself, without so
much as a glance at Paleyka, who was standing motionless, holding the light for her.

When her nose had grown whiter than her face, she touched
her lips slightly with a lipstick and then smiled with an onerous
lightness.

"That's better."

She put away the powder and lipstick and glanced at Paleyka.
The mirror remained in her hands. She stretched herself and,
bringing the mirror up once more to her nose, brushed Paleyka's
chest with her hand.

"Stand off."

Paleyka—though not in response to her hand, which had
merely flicked him like a bee—stepped back.

The candle flashed its reflection in the mirror. He wished to
blow the candle out, but his lips had gone dry.

She sat down again and set the mirror on her knees.

"Well, are you going to be as dumb as you were the last time?
What do you really want of me? I know where you are sending
me in the morning, but I won't tell you anything. Not that I know
anything."

She reflected for a moment. Something—it might almost have
been a water-spider—flickered over her cheek. That particular
spider had a droll name—*msia*.

"I'd like to leave something behind me . . ."

"To me?"

"Not to you at all, but generally. I think my plaits would do. Let them live on. . . . I love them."

She laid her two plaits together on her breast and played with their downy ends.

"She's cunning," Paleyka thought angrily, feeling the insistent moisture of emotion in his nose.

Then he said in a low voice:

"Won't you ask anything more serious? You might have something else to say."

"How funny! But this is very serious. . . ."

"But surely you could count on me in the way of, let us suppose, some slight help. In the last resort, we could scrape along somehow."

"Help. . . . Pshaw! And besides . . . you must understand. Whoever serves or generally acts in some way or other with boors loses all his nobility. I don't accept services from those who are deprived of nobility. You'd better go now. I have no more need of you. Thanks for the candle-end. Yes, now one more thing: let me do my hair for tomorrow, for there won't be time then. Will you hold the candle for me?"

Quietly, and with a gesture as studied as her words, the woman began to undo her hair.

Paleyka quickly set down the candle-end on the floor. His big, unwieldy shadow flashed over the wall, then broke apart near the ceiling. Then it became transformed into a log. He sat down beside the woman and, without giving her time to collect herself, caught her hands.

"Help? Yes? Fie, how disgusting, even the thought of it. Go away. And you dare touch me; your hands are filthy. Look, your nails are broken, short, yellow . . . like cigarette-butts. . . ."

She wiped her plump hands disgustedly on the skirt of her Circassian coat. The mirror suddenly slipped from her knees and fell on the floor, breaking in two.

The woman looked in a frightened way at the splinters and, picking them up as if she could not believe her eyes, looked at herself and burst out crying, stamping her feet and shouting shrilly:

"There's only sorrow, misfortune, and loss from you! I hate you, I hate you! Get out! I know you'll shoot me tomorrow, I know . . . but there was no need to break the mirror!"

She threw herself on the bench and, gathering her knees under her and burying her head in her fur cap, began sobbing. Her plaits, hanging down to the floor, jerked, quivered, and stealthily unplaited themselves.

"There's a devil for you!" said Paleyka hoarsely. His throat was parched as if it were lined with blotting-paper. "There's a devil! She's sorry for her mirror. Superstition, that's all it is."

He grew silent. His fingers found the handkerchief in his pocket. It was his last madyar handkerchief. A little frayed at the edges. Paleyka would never possess such handkerchiefs again. No such tuneful love again. It was the end of it.

"I'll leave it with you."

The woman kept silent.

"I'll leave it here, by your side. My bride gave it to me. No doubt, she's dead by now. I'm not suggesting you should love me, but just in case . . . if you should feel any sympathy for me, then hang it up where I can see it. As I see it, you should have a long life ahead of you because, according to certain calculations, I propose postponing your execution."

"I am wearing boots, but not trousers yet. Will you put that handkerchief out of the way?"

Paleyka stubbornly walked up to the bench, meticulously spread out the handkerchief and, banging the door tightly, said sternly to the two Tartar guards:

"Keep your eyes peeled. She's a bitch."

One of the Tartars merely spat over the edge of his lips.

"We know."

He raised his rifle and spat again.

"We know everything, commander."

Omiehin sat up on his plank-bed when Paleyka entered.

"How was she?"

"Not bad."

"Did you talk?"

Paleyka, with a sweep of his bushy eyebrows, roared with laughter.

"You have a lucky way with women, Comrade Paleyka. Hi, hi! a lucky way. I'm no mean shot myself, and I missed to make you happy. And what did I miss—a mouse. She was willing? . . ."

"Of course."

"Women are scum. We killed her brother, slaughtered a good few of her friends, and here she is on the fourth day . . . You can marry her now. But we'll have a lot of bother with her."

"What bother? We'll send her off to her destination."

"And what about you, Comrade Paleyka?"

"I've had my fun—that's enough."

"Yes . . . both good and bad. A lucky way you have with women, Comrade Paleyka."

"Yes, a lucky way," sighed Paleyka.

The sands do not cool in a night, unlike the heart. The sands spread themselves over the entire desert just as blood spreads through the whole body. Who will shelter the *saksaouls* from the whirlwinds? Clouds of sand whirl around the *saksaouls*.

VI

The plank-bed was harder than a saddle. The army coat had impossible seams. Not seams, but cables. By morning, the body would be covered in red weals, the imprints of thick coarse seams. He wished he could have placed the tailor responsible with his tenderest spot upon those seams. He would have enjoyed seeing the tailor twist, groan, and scratch himself. But it was not only the seams that made one scratch oneself. As he tossed, Omiehin muttered:

"Seams . . . lice. . . ."

Still, there would have been no harm done in calling the tailor to order to make him sew more accurately. I regret to inform you, but . . .

"The devil take this life! You sit like a louse on a frying pan— grease all around and nothing to eat. If one had a woman at least as a prop against this life."

"The commissar's already sleeping behind that wall. Snoring like a boar, for sure. . . ."

But Omiehin was listening.

"Not a breath from him. Means he's content."

"Eh, drat him, I've got his mark!"

He pulled out his tobacco pouch, and smoked a pipe. He lay down again, covering himself with a fold of his coat. Inside it was as stifling as in a retail shop. A patrol galloped past. He had slept for years on that coat and had not felt cramped, but now . . . He suddenly recalled the fragrance of the Bogorodsky grass. Five wishes to be wished at that smell, if it were sensed in a dream by a maiden. . . . Here came the patrol again. Better think of ploughing. Ploughing on a hot spring morning. Ploughing . . . pause . . . power . . . plunder . . . and lust. . . .

When bored he used to read a dictionary of foreign words, all of which were Russian. . . . "Foreign" had been printed to help the sales. Funny.

. . . An Easter-cake kind of night. With the smell of Easter baking in the air. A moon probably and strange mountains. The moon here makes of every day an Easter. . . .

He threw off his soldier's coat. The buttons struck sharply on the wall. Omiehin pulled out his boots from under the bed cover.

"I'll go and inspect the sentries."

Trying not to clink with his spurs, he began to pull on his boots.

Then he distinctly heard a woman scream and the roar of several voices; a shot rang out, but strangely enough, it did not re-echo in the mountains. As in a dream, where an echo can never be heard.

Omiehin stumbled over the threshold.

A lantern flickered by the hut, and a partisan kept knocking against the glass with a hurriedly girded sword. An unheard-of gabble of voices rose there. Dogs howled in the brushwood beyond the camp.

"Quiet, there! Will you . . ."

A partisan in an ample caftan caught hold of his hand, laughingly pointed to three Tartars and shouted in his ear as loudly as if shots were still being fired:

"Just look at them . . . look at those mugs. They were hot. . . ."

"What's the matter, lads, eh?"

In a corner of the hut the woman was sobbing, holding in one hand a knife and in the other her fur cap. She was probably ashamed of being seen in tears, and that is why she squealed in an unbearably high-pitched voice:

"Monsters, executioners! Today it was the commissar, and now it's the whole pack. . . . Shoot me, but stop tormenting me! Do it this minute! Reptiles!"

Omiehin, unfastening his holster, glanced at a stooping Tartar, one of the sentinels.

"Well . . . ?"

The Tartar stood at attention. His face suddenly flushed, and his temples grew puffed. He looked around at the others.

"No woman. Bore it four months when Ufa went away, no woman. She'll be shot tomorrow any case. The commissar had his fun, we too must have little-little fun. He . . ."

The Tartar pointed plaintively to his straggly beard, over which blood was dripping.

"He knife—straight here, began stabbing me. Why we have no woman?"

The partisan in the caftan guffawed.

"That mug, brother, look, that mug! Wants a woman! Suffer, cur, suffer as the Revolution suffers you, eh?"

And in a perfect transport of delight he slapped his rifle against his boots.

"They let off a squib to impress her. . . . We'd better lock her in."

"Lock her in," Omiehin said irritably. "Bar and bolt. You keep guard for a while." He motioned to the caftan-bearer.

The latter, for some reason, unsheathed his sword and froze to the spot; only his teeth grinned in the dark, and they could be seen, so it seemed, a good ten yards away from the hut where Omiehin had withdrawn with the Tartars and Paleyka.

The stones upon which the lanterns stood were warm and seemed to be perspiring. An ill-flavored wind slightly ruffled the folds of the soldiers' coats.

"In so far . . ." began Omiehin, fixing the stone.

A candle was dripping and there wasn't a fool to right it, and as a result, Omiehin felt increasing irritation.

"In so far as the commanding force of our famous partisan detachment has failed to do its duty by not finishing with her at once, and as her continued presence among us will disgrace our detachment altogether, I find it obsolutely necessary to pronounce—without further delay—the revolutionary sentence. In the absence of mitigating circumstances in the anarchist behaviour of the sentinels Gadeyin, Alim Kashi, and Zakia Kazimbaev, they are sentenced to the utmost penalty; but taking into account their lack of awareness, the sentence will be accounted conditional. Until the execution, they are to keep guard over the citizeness . . . and thereby wash away their guilt. Otherwise—the devil take them. Understand! Any objections? Has anyone any objections?"

"None," said Paleyka.

With his eyes still fixed on the stone, Omiehin said to the Tartars:

"You're condemned conditionally to be shot. To your places and no nonsense on guard. Understand?"

The Tartars suddenly fell back, catching hold of each other's hands.

"Well?"

"Eh, understand, Alexei Pietrovitch, eh?"

The stooping Tartar bowed low, almost to the ground.

"Eh. . . ."

"I take the liberty to report," said Paleyka. "They may not have understood. Perhaps I'd better explain?"

"No explanations. They're not asking for mercy. It's clear."

VII

In the morning, tracks were found leading from the hut toward the hills. Four horses had galloped and, on the lightest mount, on Paleyka's dun-colored ambler, on the outside of the other three, Helena Kanashivili herself had apparently ridden.

There are all sorts of events in life, just as there is every kind of water in rivers, but Omiehin saw a very turbid world that morning. He sat in the saddle, sticking out a pair of long, dry legs, and looked on irritably as Paleyka picked a horse for himself out of the drove.

"What are you going to do about it?" he shouted. "Looks as if you'd slept with that woman badly, for she's beat it. You must have made a bad job of it."

Paleyka, with a yell, struck his whip into the drove. The horses scattered, a clatter of hoofs rang out behind the tent, and Paleyka rode out on an unsaddled horse.

"Commander . . . want to ride without a saddle? You're not a gadfly. Give him a saddle."

The Tartars caught Paleyka as he dismounted.

"I'll give you my saddle for luck," said Omiehin. "But not the horse. You'd let it slip through your fingers."

Six riders galloped after Paleyka.

Paleyka dashed on alone, off the beaten track, stumbling over bushes, stones, and ditches. His horse, as he tugged at the curb, began to rear, twisting and, turning on the same spot, even attempted to throw off a rider whose wishes it did not comprehend.

It was as if Paleyka were pursuing the runaways and, at the same time, riding away from Omiehin.

Nevertheless, Omiehin caught up with him at the sharp bend of a mountain track, near the mountain Ai-ol. Swinging around at the clatter of hoofs, Paleyka yelled out:

"They'll kill us like cockroaches, Alexei Pietrovitch. There are four of them."

Omiehin sat in his saddle as safely as over a book, over the dictionary of foreign words he so heartily despised. His legs were pressed firmly into the horse's flanks, and he looked square, blunt, and dull.

Six miles from the camp, they perceived the corpse of the runaway guard, Alim Kashi, lying a few paces away from the tracks. His skull had been cleft with a sword. The blade had slipped deeper and had cut open his jacket, revealing a hollow, tubercular chest.

"It only needs a woman," said Omiehin, without getting off his horse. "I think he must have refused to go into the hills with

them. He refused to become a traitor to the working class. Bury
him, or the wolves will make short work of him."

Arid, wind-swept cliffs showed darkly in the distance. The
riders had to squeeze their horses' flanks strongly with their
knees, till the blood came, to make them summon their remaining reserve of strength.

By the Agatov cliff, they found the prostrate bodies of the
partisan horse and its rider—the guard Gadeyin. He was a handsome, six-foot lad, gay and fond of laughter. His twisted arms
were entangled in the bridle. The deformed head of his horse
lay beside him.

Gadeyin was still alive.

He raised his numbed eyelids and almost inaudibly, as if with
his eyelids, asked Omiehin:

"Come to shoot? Pity I ran from your bullet. One's own was
surer. He says—let's run, he'll kill, we'll be shot anyway. Kashi
says—let's run. Zakia says—let's run, we'll be shot all the same.
Ha, where's a Tartar to run from his own rifle? . . . Ha . . .
Zakia no woman. Zakia ran. Zakia shot me in head, as woman ask.
Don't shoot me in the face, Alexei Pietrovitch, shoot straight in
the heart."

"Yes," said Omiehin, gathering up his reins, "it will be soon
over. Very likely he didn't understand the meaning of 'conditionally.' What does conditionally mean?" he flung back.

A forward lad from Penza straightened himself in the saddle.

"Conditionally—means, Comrade Commissar, those who ought
to be shot, but who were taken pity on, because they were fine
fellows."

The nearest hill was covered to the waist with a skirt of brushwood; then it became naked and craggy. A horse was pasturing
among the bushes. Lifting up its swollen lips, it gaily plucked the
prickly grass. The arrival of men did not alarm it.

It had rested and refreshed itself, and neighed joyously. In
advance, some distance away from the horse, a corpse lay face
downward on the stony track. It had dug its dirty fingers into a
crevice in the stone.

Four revolver bullets had been plugged into its back, neck, and
head. All absolutely unnecessarily and aimlessly.

"That's a woman's work," Omiehin commented.

From that point the track of a single horse continued.

Omiehin glanced at the mountains. The brushwood came to an end, revealing naked stone. A mountain village showed gray somewhere among the high snows. Smoke spiraled among the crags. The rocks wafted an eternal heat.

Omiehin pulled his left rein and, himself, swung to the right. "Enough! We'll get plugged ourselves farther on. About turn, comrade. Take the horse. Pity about your ambler, Maxim Semeonovitch, but God grant we'll catch her one day."

Behind his back he heard Paleyka whisper:

"Did you notice, comrade—that last one had clutched her hair. . . ."

"What about it?"

"And he was the ugliest of the lot. Zakia, who killed them all. He just had time to clutch her by the hair. . . ."

Omiehin reined in his horse and, drawing level with Paleyka, bent over him so that he could smell the odor of kumiss and goat's cheese.

"Well, and even if he did clutch her hair. . . . One ought to pull such women by the hair and not get killed."

VIII

They rode in silence as far as the torrent, which flowed in the near vicinity of the camp. When the hoofs had startled the handmade wooden bridge and when the water seemed to whirl even faster, Paleyka caught up with Omiehin. Holding on to the bow of his saddle, he muttered:

"It was all lies I told you, Alexei Pietrovitch, sheer lies. She may be his wife, his sister perhaps . . . or a Polish spy. I did not sleep with her. Nothing happened. And it's a pity you missed the mouse. Better I'd missed it. I only made her a present of the blue handkerchief."

"Well?"

"So that she might show it, if she had any sympathetic inclinations, but she . . ."

Omiehin suddenly turned heavily in the saddle and shouted with what looked like disappointment:

"And she took it?"

Paleyka's dry cheekbones flushed hotly; the bridle slipped out of his hand, and he lied:

"She burned it. She showed me the ashes after the Tartars. The ashes. How much ash is there from silk? As much as from a cigarette."

A viscous warmth filled Omiehin's veins. He felt sleepy; his stirrup dragged and felt uncomfortable.

"The devil take her," he said lazily. "We must make out a protocol and have it all in order. I'd like to see the hut again in the daylight, and see how they got out. A pity about the Tartars. . . ."

Paleyka's blue handkerchief was nailed to the door of the hut, just by the cramp-iron.

"So," said Omiehin musingly, looking on as Paleyka grabbed at the handkerchief hurriedly and without even getting off his horse, "so, she's had her laugh at us, the bitch. If I meet her, six bullets won't be enough."

Riding off a short distance he halted, looked at Paleyka, shook his head and, suddenly leaping down from his horse, strode toward his tent. A partisan, who was passing by, caught hold of the horse's bridle.

That evening, Omiehin took down his rifle, reloaded it, and, for some reason, though he liked the clink of spurs, pulled the spurs off his boots.

The rifle seemed unusually heavy; the night, unbearably sultry. The only tolerable thing was that the gloom had blotted out the hills.

He sat down not far from the bridge across the torrent. There seemed to be less water. And it wafted a fragrant mountain odor.

It was the second night Omiehin had not slept, and that was why everything tasted salt to him. His temples felt swollen, and the night gloom seemed intolerably endless.

Under his feet he seemed to hear the patter-patter of tiny pebbles, sharp as needles. The fires of the camp went out, and soon the returning patrol crossed the bridge. The peasants were laughing loudly, and one of them threw a handful of mountain-nuts into the torrent.

Omiehin sat like this for a long time. A cramping pain in his veins gripped his legs. He had laid the rifle aside. Somewhere in the sky a yellow-green spot of dawn flashed, and then he heard the muffled beat of hoofs.

The rider, coming from the direction of the camp, slowly neared the bridge. He halted for a short while and then, in a loud whisper, urged on his mount. The horse struck out sharply with its hoofs.

"You—Paleyka?" challenged Omiehin.

The rider started and exclaimed unnaturally loudly:

"I!"

"Lift your head higher. I'll show you where to run."

Omiehin, according to regulations, hugged the butt of his rifle firmly to his shoulder.

The horse shied at the shot, took two jumps, and galloped off with an empty saddle back to the camp.

Omiehin turned over the corpse and, from a side-pocket, pulled out a packet enveloped in a blue madyar handkerchief. It contained a little money and Paleyka's documents. He threw both the documents and the money into the water after the corpse; the handkerchief he thrust into his pocket.

Then, for no apparent reason, he lit a fire. Lighting a cigarette, he spread out the handkerchief in front of him. He then picked up a flaming branch and stuck it through the middle of the handkerchief. There was a smell of smoldering; with the same stick, Omiehin threw the handkerchief into the fire. To the staff secretary who came up, he said:

"Today I'd like to see the end of the picture that the Tartars interrupted. It would be interesting to know what moral came of their love."

"You can't see the end, Comrade Commissar," the secretary replied.

"Why can't I see the end?"

"Because it's two weeks already since the demonstrator, Comrade Glushkov, took another road, with your permission changing his donkeys for horses because the donkeys, as you know, were eaten by the wolves for want of looking after."

"Two weeks?"

"Exactly so."

"My! how life runs. Life runs straight . . ." but he did not finish saying how exactly his life ran. Comrade Omiehin did not finish. He only smiled.

Stone in the mountains is dull and stingy. Gay and green is the earth under it. The flame of the sun grew dim in the mountains, and the clouds, like ashes on a man's fire, covered the stones.

But the grass was near to hand. Hey, you stubborn grasses! There is no crunching, no crushing you. And yet, over these stubborn grasses, over these sands, from somewhere in Tumien, across the Ural and other steppes, through Comrade Omiehin's detachment, the agitator, demonstrator and talker generally, Ievdokim Pietrovitch Glushkov made his way on further.

ALEXANDER GRIN

The Loquacious Goblin

*"I stood by the window, humming a
song about Anna. . . ."* H. HORNUNG

A HOUSE GOBLIN suffering from toothache: isn't that slander
against a creature who has so many witches and sorcerers at his
command that he can safely gobble sugar by the barrel? But that's
how it was, a fact. There he was, a small, sad-looking goblin
sitting by the cold range, which had long forgotten what a fire was
like. Rhythmically shaking his disheveled head, he held his bandaged cheek, moaning piteously like a child, and his red, turbid
eyes reflected suffering.

Rain was pouring. I had entered this deserted house to shelter
from the downpour and had suddenly caught sight of him who
had forgotten that he should vanish. . . .

"It doesn't matter now," he said in the voice of an agitated
parrot. "It doesn't matter now, for no one will believe that you
have seen me anyhow."

Making a pair of horns with my fingers to ward off the evil
eye just in case, I replied:

"Don't be afraid. I won't shoot you with a silver bullet, nor
will I pronounce an incantation. But why are you here? The
house is empty."

49

"Oi-oi. And yet I find it hard to quit this spot," the little goblin explained. "Now listen. I'll tell you everything. So be it. As it is, my teeth are aching. It's a relief to talk. It eases the pain . . . oi! My dear fellow, it was all a question of a single hour, and that is why I got stuck here. My people . . ."—here he sighed plaintively—"my people, well, in a word, our people, after they departed, have been grooming their horses' tails for quite a while on the other side of the hills, but I just can't get away because I must understand what happened.

"Just look at the holes in the ceiling and the cracked walls, and then imagine to yourself this place all neat with shining copper vessels, white transparent curtains, and the house as full of flowers as the forest; a brightly polished floor; and the range, on which you are sitting as on a cold gravestone, all redhot with the dinner simmering in pots and exuding an appetizing aroma.

"There were quarries, granite quarries in the vicinity. A married couple, a rare pair, inhabited the house. The husband's name was Philip, and his wife was called Annie. She was twenty, and he was twenty-five. Now, if this pleases you, she was just like this." Here the goblin plucked a tiny wildflower, which had sprung up out of the earth accumulated through the years in a crack on the windowsill, and demonstratively presented it to me. "I liked the husband too, but I was fonder of her, for she was more than just a good housekeeper; we goblins find great relish in what links people closer to us. Well, she used to try and catch fish in the stream with her bare hands, and she also used to tap on the big stone that stands at the crossroads and listen for long moments to the ever fainter ringing sound it made, and she used to laugh on seeing a yellow patch of sunlight on a wall. Don't be so surprised: there is a magic in all this, the fine knowledge of a beautiful soul; but only we, the cloven-footed, are able to detect its signs. Ordinary folk are so unperceptive.

" 'Annie,' the husband would cry out joyfully whenever he returned at dinnertime from the quarry, where he held a job in the office, 'I am not alone! I have Ralph with me.' But the joke was repeated so often that Annie, smiling and unperturbed, would only lay the table for two. Annie and Philip always met as if they were discovering each other for the first time. She would run towards him and he would carry her back in his arms.

"In the evening he would pull out a batch of letters from his old friend Ralph, in whose company he had spent part of his life before marriage, and he would read the letters aloud to Annie, who, propping her head with her hands, listened to the familiar words about the sea and the glittering, wonderful sunbeams on the far side of our vast country, about volcanoes and pearl-fishing, tempests and conflicts in the shadow of huge forests. And each word rang out to her like the stone that sang so long and ringingly at the crossroads when she tapped it.

" 'He will arrive soon,' Philip would say. 'He will come to visit us as soon as his three-masted schooner, the *Sinbad*, berths in the harbor at Gress. To reach our place takes only an hour by train and then an hour more from the station.'

"Sometimes Annie would show interest in some aspect of Ralph's life; and Philip would begin to tell her enthusiastically about Ralph's daring, his peculiarities, his magnanimity and his strange destiny, reminiscent of a fairy tale: his early poverty, his gold strike, his purchase of a schooner, and all the lacework of legendary exploit woven of ship's tackle, sea foam, gambling and trade, peril and discovery. Eternal gambling. Eternal excitement. Eternal music of sea shore and sea wave.

"I never heard them quarrel, and I hear everything. I never saw them exchange a cold glance, and I see everything. 'I feel sleepy,' Annie would say at night, and he would carry her to the bed, laying her down and wrapping her up like a child. Falling asleep, she would say: 'Phil, who is that whispering in the tops of the trees? Who is that walking on the roof? Whose face is it I see in the stream beside mine?' And he would answer in a troubled way, peering into her half-closed eyes: 'It's a raven walking on the roof; the wind in the trees; pebbles glittering in the stream. Sleep now and don't walk about barefoot.'

"Then he would sit down at the table to finish his routine report; afterwards, he would wash, arrange the logs and go to bed, falling asleep at once and always forgetting everything he dreamt. He never tapped on the singing stone that stood at the crossroads, where the fairies wove astonishing carpets from grains of dust and moonbeams.

2

"Well, listen . . . There isn't much more for me to tell about the three people who put me, the goblin, into such a quandary. One sunny, fully flowering day, Philip, with a notebook in his hand, was marking off piles of granite; and Annie, in the meantime, was returning with purchases from the station. As usual, she stopped by her stone and, as always, made it sing out by tapping it with a key. The stone was a fragment of ancient rock, about half as tall as herself. When one tapped it, the stone would sing out, ringing fainter and fainter; but, when one thought that it had stopped ringing, it was enough to apply one's ear to it to be able still to detect a barely audible voice inside the mass.

"Our forest paths are veritable gardens. Their beauty grips the heart. The flowers and the branches above one's head peer through their fingers at the sun, which changes in color, for the eyes quickly tire of it and begin to wander aimlessly. The white sand reflected the yellow, chalky and somber green hues. On a day such as that cold water was the best thing.

"Annie halted, listening to the forest singing in her breast. Then she began to tap on the stone, breaking into a smile whenever a new wave of ringing sound imposed itself upon the fading sound. Thus she amused herself, imagining that no one could see her; but then, suddenly, a man came striding round the corner of the path and approached her. His steps sounded softer and softer, and finally he stopped. Annie, continuing to smile, glanced at him without being startled or without stepping back. It was as if he had always stood there.

"He was swarthy, very swarthy, and the sea had left upon his face the imprint of a scurrying wave. But it was a beautiful face, reflecting a soul at once desperate and tender. His dark eyes gazed at Annie, darkening and gleaming more intensely; and Annie's luminous eyes shone gently back.

"As you have rightly concluded, I always followed her about, for there were snakes in that forest.

"The stone had long grown silent, but this man and this woman still gazed at each other without uttering a word. Then he held out his hand, and slowly she offered her own, and their hands joined them together. Then he took her head carefully, so carefully that I was afraid to breathe, and kissed her on the lips. Her eyes closed.

"They moved apart then, and the stone stood between them as before. Suddenly Philip appeared, striding towards them. Annie, catching sight of him, hastened to meet him:

" 'Here's Ralph. He has arrived.' "

" 'Yes, he has,' Philip said, unable even to shout for joy. Finally he tossed his hat in the air and embraced the new arrival. 'Ralph, you have already met Annie. It is she.' His rugged, generous face glowed from the excitement of the meeting. 'You will stay with us, Ralph; we shall show you everything. And we'll talk to our heart's content. Ralph, dear friend, my wife also has been awaiting your arrival.'

"Annie placed her hand on her husband's shoulder and directed her frankest, warmest and purest glance at him and then, without changing her expression, gazed at Ralph as if he were as close to her as her husband.

" 'I'll be back soon,' Ralph said. 'Phil, I wasn't sure of your address. I thought I was on the wrong track and therefore I left my luggage at the station. I'll go back and fetch it now.'

"They agreed on the details and separated," the goblin said. "That is all I know. But I can't understand it. Perhaps you will explain to me."

"Did Ralph return?" I asked.

"They waited for him, but he only wrote them a note from the station to say he had met an acquaintance who had offered him a profitable deal."

"And what happened to them?"

"They died . . . died long ago . . . some thirty years back. She drank some cold water on a hot day. She caught a chill to begin with. His hair was half-gray when he followed the coffin. Then he disappeared. It was rumored that he had locked himself up in a room with a brazier. But that's not the point. . . . My teeth are still aching, and still I don't understand . . ."

"And that's how it will remain," I replied politely, shaking his shaggy, unwashed paw in farewell. "Only we, five-fingered folk, can read the signs of the human heart. Goblins are so unperceptive."

VERA INBER

Maya

IT WAS A TOWN on the southern shore of the Black Sea. A small town. It had an old Genovese fortress, consisting now mostly of rubble, pollen and lizards. There was, however, a coffee house on this spot, where a century-old glucine dropped its petals into the coffee cups as it crawled up the steep cliff. There was a market place in the town too, which was stocked in the summer with fresh turbot and ripe peaches. The new corn there showed attractive wisps of gray hair and fine small kernels: the rest of it was enveloped in tender green husks. The town also had a movie house and two or three official institutions, but every street finally gave on the sea—and everything else seemed trifling compared to this. On a sandy beach many nets were spread out, and a number of boats were resting on their back or belly on the sand. Now and again a wave would run up the sand and, hissing, vanish again.

At night the town, bathed in moonlight, resembled a drowsing fish. The roof tiles glittered like fish scales; the vineyards, like long narrow fishtails, were lost in the distance, and the wind played with them. At that point of the shore, where a fish-head should have been seen, one lonely eye only gleamed—the lamp of the museum curator.

The town did have a museum.

At sunset the fishermen's wives snared busily among themselves. They were black from the sun and wore bright red aprons; and when they bunched themselves together, they reminded one from afar of a crust of black rye bread with a slice of tomato.

As they waited for their husbands and cooked their meal, the women gossiped among other things about old Stavraki, the present curator of the museum, formerly a wealthy man and reputedly the grandson of a smuggler. There was no doubt at all but that his grandfather, old Nicholas Stavraki, had engaged in smuggling and had done a trade in duty free tobacco. He had had a windfall besides: he had inherited a pile when his then partner, a Russian merchant, was drowned while fumbling with a sail . . . But God alone knew how that sail had looked in reality: it may well have worn a black beard and wide trousers, and its name may well have been Nicholas Stavraki.

Nothing was known for certain, but ever since that time wealth had showered upon Nicholas Stavraki. He had built a fine spacious house for himself and had spread upon the tables and the divans all sorts of strange objects imported from abroad. Among them was a Persian shawl, white and pink like rose in the snow.

Adrian, the son of Nicholas, did nothing reprehensible. He lived in a large city—in Odessa. There he kept a shop, where he sold canaries and coral. He made a terrific amount of money at this. As to his son and heir, also called Adrian, he did not even look at the shop. He sold it and began trading in fruit, but he employed a manager and abstained from doing business himself. He traveled abroad, lived there for a long while, but never married. Then, returning to his native town, he reconstructed his grandfather's house and settled there till the end of his days. He not only rebuilt the house, but also embellished it to an unheard-of degree . . . His grandfather's shawl was no longer alone: it now had a whole collection of companions, shawls of the same design and all Persian. In addition, the house was now full of paintings, statues, antique furniture, lace and precious stones—in a word, everything that wealthy man could allow himself.

Young Stavraki lived in this way until he, too, became an old man.

But then came the Revolution.

A decree was published making beautiful objects the public property, but no one was allowed to take them home. They were all to be placed in a special house, which was to be called a museum; and on Sundays and even weekdays except Mondays, everyone would have the right to look at these objects but not to touch them. In this way, Adrian Stavraki's house was turned into a museum, and the former proprietor became the museum curator. For his personal use, he was allotted a corner room, which had formerly contained a large white statue representing a nude girl with a mirror.

The daughter of the old shop keeper Diamando was given a place near the main staircase where she issued tickets to museum visitors even though the entry was free. On Sundays and weekdays except Mondays every one could convince himself that old Stavraki was a good guardian of the people's property, that not one of the Persian shawls had been eaten by moths, that none of the daggers had become tarnished, and that the statue of the nude girl, washed clean with a bast-wisp, gleamed for all it was worth.

2

It was Sunday, and the museum was especially crowded. Diamando's daughter was almost torn apart as she distributed tickets and relieved the visitors of their umbrellas, canes and even pipes. This last rule had been very strictly enforced ever since Christo, the fisherman, had halted in front of a painting of the Italian school.

"A rotten boat, that!" He had exclaimed. "I'll be damned if anyone could row it against the wind out near promontory! The stern is much too low!"

And, saying this, he had knocked his pipe so hard against the old canvas, that a hole appeared on the smooth surface of the sea. At this, Pavel Zuyev, a young Russian lad and a Komsomol, turned to him reproachfully:

"We thought you were 'conscious,' comrade Christo, but you

have proved yourself to the contrary. Who would dream of touching an art object even with his finger? That must never be done."
Pondering and scratching the back of his head, he added thoughtfully: "But the stern is really no good."

Thus, taking into account past experience, visitors' pipes were
now taken away at the entry.

Adrian Adrianovich Stavraki, disturbed by the unruly flood of
beauty lovers, entered, contrary to his habit, the spacious square
room with windows giving on the sea. This had been the former
dining room and now it was the show place of the museum,
with Pompeian frescoes lining the walls and a bronze Renais-
sance lamp hanging from the ceiling. Adrain Adrianovich's corpulent figure in a tussore jacket, his graying beard and frowning
bespectacled eyes—all this produced an embarrassing effect on
the visitors. Dorochka, the weaver, who had arrived with an
excursion group—a tanned, impetuous and brilliant sportswoman,
who had smashed all the records in the All-Union swimming
competitions—stood before a canvas depicting a woman holding
a babe and wearing stiff dress, plaited hair woven with pearls.

"Just look at that dress . . ." she exclaimed. "What devilish
work it entailed! They didn't like bathing in those days. Of
course, they led a parasitical sort of ilfe. But . . ."

She examined the face closely and detected the shade of a
smile and then added in a whisper:

"But she's beautiful all the same."

Christo, the fisherman, this time without his pipe, confirmed
this:

"A beautiful woman and, what is more, a kind one. You can
see that by the way she is holding the child."

Just at that moment Adrian Adrianovich passed by. Dorochka
stopped talking.

A visiting pioneer stood at another wall before a cast of Michael
Angelo's David. He stood there with his legs wide apart and his
hands behind his back. His cap was pushed back and there was a
knotted red tie over his chest. Finally, he snapped his fingers.

"A talented old man!" he exclaimed.

"Who?" Adrian Adrianovich inquired, disbelieving his ears.

But the pioneer was less easily embarrassed than Dorochka, the weaver.

"Michael Angelo, of course," he replied. "Look at his chap's biceps! And his legs! Do you know, if he started running, he'd beat everyone over any distance even with a handicap."

3

Sunday was at an end. The last and most insistent visitor, who came to the museum every evening to stare persistently at the black-eyed ticket woman, had also departed. Adrian Adrianovich was relaxing in a chair in his corner room. Peacefully the sea and the moonlight were pouring in through the wide open window. In the glass bookcase the book spines glimmered gold. A rose was unfolding in a Venetian goblet on the writing table.

One-eyed Afanasy, the museum guard, who also served as Adrian Adrianovich's cook, laundress and maid, brought in on a tray a supper of boiled cream in a flat earthernware dish, a fritter, butter, and a portion of honeycomb on a vineleaf. A fine supper this, which not even an ancient Greek would have spurned. In addition, Afanasy had delivered several letters—a stamped catch, which the sea of life had now splashed upon Old Adrian Stavraki's table.

Adrian Adrianovich ate without haste and examined his correspondence. Both the moonlight and the lamp lighted his hair and his broad shoulders.

The letters were of little interest. Two or three were from his colleagues, museum people like himself. One of them was offering him an ancient Novgorod icon (he had several of them already) in exchange for an antique funerary urn, no later than 400 B.C. Another asked his advice as to how best to preserve rolls of parchment from drying. And much else in the same spirit. There was a letter from the "center"—not a letter really, but an official instruction from the *Narcompross*.[1] But here, at last, was a real letter. It was an old friend writing from Paris, a poet, who was freezing in exile. The poet wrote: "As you know, despite my austere appearance, I was always a gallant man with

[1] *NARCOMPROSS*—The People's Commissariat for Education.

the ladies. There are only two ladies, only two, I cannot bear.
The first is Lady Death; the second, Our Lady the Revolution.
With the first I am fortunately only acquainted by hearsay. But,
as for the second . . ."

Adrian Adrianovich nodded his head in sign of agreement.
The moon floated calmly over the sea, spilling silver and black
over a small yacht at anchor opposite the second grade school.

There was yet another letter. The address was scrawled faintly
on a cheap and unexpressive envelope. Adrian Adrianovich tore
open the envelope and read: "Dear, darling uncle!"

He paused: "uncle"—whose uncle was he? Then he remembered. He really did have a niece. Her name was Aglaia. Something had happened to her. He recalled. She had married a communist. And what did she want now, this Aglaia, who had a
gentle profile like that of the Byzantine Empress Theodora. She
had given no sign of life for so long, but now here she was
writing to him. It seems she had been unwell (that was under-
standable, of course). Her husband had been sent to Siberia to
plant cooperatives, but she and the children were in need of sea
air. So she had remembered her dear, darling uncle, and thought
that he would not refuse her hospitality. She was waiting now
for an answering telegram.

Adrian Adrianovich pondered at length over this. On the one
hand, this would naturally mean the waste of a summer; on the
other, Aglaia had been such an entertaining little darling of a
child . . . She adored fruit and fairy tales. On seeing a coconut
one day, she had said:

"Why doesn't it bounce if it's a ball? But if it's a monkey,
where's the tail?"

Adrian Adrianovich proceeded to wake Afanasy, who was
sleeping in his closet under the stairs where the moonlight
stabbed, like a dagger, through a narrow slit of a window. He
gave Afanasy a note, some money and following instructions:

"Take these to the telegraph office tomorrow morning." And
departing, he added: "And put in order the spare room where the
frames are kept."

4

Kostya, the cabman, had the only cab in town furnished with rubber tires. Now he drove up to the porch with the expected guests. First, out of the depths of the cab, he pulled out a pale, unknown woman with a child in her arms, then a large valise followed by a smaller one. Finally, Aglaia herself leapt down from the high footboard. She looked exactly the same as on the day when she had first seen the coconut. Aglaia had the same tiny nose, upon which three freckles of varied size were disposed like the holes on a knib. Aglaia still had the same chestnut mane of hair and the eyes of a Byzantine Empress.

"How do you do, uncle," exclaimed the pale, unknown woman (not Aglaia). "Uncle, you don't recognize me? I am Aglaia. And here is my daughter—she's six; and this is my son, eleven months old, and he has three teeth."

Adrian Adrianovich, with the help of Afanasy, conducted his guests into the house, made them feel at home and then finally, when they had washed and refreshed themselves, treated them to a late dinner in his corner room. The infant with the three teeth, exhausted by the journey, had already fallen asleep on a chair. Adrian Adrianovich, while talking with the real Aglaia, kept looking at her daughter, who so much resembled the young Theodora. Theodora kept silent while stuffing a mutton chop between her cheeks. Children will always be children. They always adore fruit and fairy tales. And this fruit and these tales were immutable. Aglaia, for example, adored oranges above all. And, thus, Adrian Adrianovich, picking a large golden globe from a dish, offered it to Aglaia's daughter.

"I like apples better," the young girl answered in a ringing voice.

Adrian Adrianovich was amazed.

"Why so?" he asked. "An orange is tastier."

"But an apple is harder, and one can bite on it. An orange chews itself somehow," Aglaia's daughter announced with great self-confidence and, avoiding the orange, she picked for herself a firm blushing apple.

The table was cleared. Afanasy, managing the broom with

difficulty, swept the floor. Aglaia, after briefly sketching her life over the past few years and outlining the situation of the co-operative in Siberia, retired to her room to feed the infant son on semolina gruel. Adrian Adrianovich was left alone in his room with his second niece.

As often happens in the South in early spring, the sunset looked rather austere. A strong breeze had made the sea bristle, and it was now covered with short, spiteful waves. The wind banged the doors, shook the jasmine bushes in the garden and, finally, biding the sunset, cast the first spatter of rain drops at the windows. The shades were pulled down, and it was decided to light a fire.

The logs were brought in. They were kindled in the fireplace, and the fire raged as fiercely as it had probably raged on those smuggling nights of Nicholas Stavraki, and, earlier still—in all the hearths of the land. Adrian Adrianovich decided it was time to acquaint himself more intimately with his new female relation. He squatted in front of the fire. Her face showed that she had recovered from the journey, had eaten well, was content with life and inclined to friendly conversation.

"Well, my child," Adrian Adrianovich began, picking up the poker and sitting down also on the rug, "let's have a chat. I don't even know your name."

"Maya. And I know they call you Adrian and also Adrianovich. But I shall call you grandpa."

"Yes, call me that, my child. Maya—what a beautiful and imposing name that is. In Hindu it means dream or illusion. . . . If you don't have a handkerchief, my dear, take mine."

"No, not dream, but the First of May, and not in Hindu but in Russian."

"First of May . . . I see. And how old are you, Maya, my girl? Mama told me, but I've forgotten."

"I'm six. I'm three years younger than the Revolution, but I'm growing up together with it. And how old are you, grandpa?"

"Sixty-one," Adrian Adrianovich replied obediently, and then he asked irritably: "And who told you about yourself and the Revolution?"

"Papa told me. He knows everything. And do you know what our little boy is called? His name is Rem."

"Excellent!" Adrian Adrianovich exclaimed, with a sigh of relief, striking a charred log. "Now we only need a Romulus. I only hope he was not nurtured by a she-wolf?"

"No, we had a goat, because we lived outside the town. But, grandpa, what does Romulus mean?"

"What does it mean?"

"Yes. Out of what words? Rem means: Revolution, Electrification, Metallurgy. But Romulus—where is that from?"

"Maya," Adrian Adrianovich asked in complete despair, "do you like fairy tales?"

"Very much," Maya answered. "About how a boy went to the town of Tashkent for bread."[1]

"No, little girl, that's just a story."

A strong gust of wind careered over the house. A dark wind was blowing, and the sea was getting rough. In the room a fire was burning. A splendid setting it was for the pearl that was a fairy tale, sprung from the sea-shell of folk wisdom.

"Listen, Maya," Adrian Adrianovich began, "I'll tell you a fairy tale now or, to be more exact, a myth."

"And what is a myth?" Maya immediately inquired.

"A myth is a tale too, but a very very old one and therefore all the more beautiful. Sit closer to me and . . . do take my hand-kerchief."

Maya fastened her rounded eyes on Adrian Adrianovich, who began the tale:

"Long, long ago," Adrian Adrianovich started, "there lived a little girl by the name of Proserpine. She was an enchanting little girl. If we ever go together to Paris, I shall show Proserpine as the artist Moreau has represented her: with black curly hair and a smooth skin, holding a pomegranate in her hands, and with lips that remind one of a burst pomegranate. One day it happened that Proserpine and her companions were gathering some white flowers in a meadow . . ."

[1] An early Soviet novel, *Tashkent, City of Bread* by A. Neverov (1886-1923), tells of a small boy's wanderings in search of bread during the famine.

"Daisies?" Maya asked.

"No, not daisies. They were probably narcissus. Only they were larger and more fragrant than our present ones. As she walked along, she saw more and more flowers. Leaving her companions behind, Proserpine moved further and further away. . . . Then suddenly . . ." Here Adrian Adrianovich rose, pushing his armchair aside, and drew a line with the poker on the floor. "Just try and picture the scene: let the footstool be Proserpine; and the flowers on the rug, real flowers. Then suddenly—there, by the bookcase—the earth gapes open and, in a chariot drawn by horses breathing fire, Pluto appears—Pluto who—there below (hereupon Adrian Adrianovich tapped the floor with the poker) —had a kingdom of his own. Pluto snatched Proserpine as he would a flower, and the earth closed over them."

"Pluto lived in a cellar?" Maya asked in a sinking voice.

"No, not in a cellar, but under the ground. He had his own estate there. Everything there was like it was on earth, but the sun never shone there and the rain never fell as it is doing here now."

"Go on, tell me more," Maya urged him.

"Aha!" Adrian Adrianovich thought spitefully, putting the armchair back in its place. "So you want more? I can see that the Tashkent boy has rather faded in your imagination."

"Proserpine had a mother—Ceres by name," he picked up the tale. "This wise and inexhaustibly abundant woman had charge of all the plants on the earth. Learning of Proserpine's misfortune, she flew off in search of her."

"In an aeroplane?" Maya inquired.

"No, on foot. But she discovered nothing. Then, taking off her rich cloak woven with ears of wheat and putting on rags instead, she journeyed to foreign parts. But, since no creature on earth would reveal to her the secret of Proserpine's disappearance, she resolved to punish the earth by depriving it of all flowers and plants. And for a whole year there were none."

"And what about apples?"

"Of course not."

"And what did people eat?"

"H'm . . . Probably canned food purchased in cooperatives.

But, listen further. . . . Ceres journeyed on and on until she came to a strange kingdom. In those days everything was simple, and she was immediately brought to the palace. And there was great celebration going on there; for a long expected son had just been born to the King and Queen, and the mother Queen was trying to find for him a . . ."

"Goat?"

"No, a wet nurse. When Ceres entered the royal chambers, her face and imposing carriage amazed everyone. Her tresses were as thick and heavy as a sheaf of wheat, and the folds of her tunic looked the furrows made by a wooden plow. As for her eyes, they were as deep as water. The Queen at once sensed that all living things would flourish under the care of those eyes, and so she suggested to Ceres that she raise up her son. And Ceres agreed on one condition . . ."

"Maya," Aglaia could be heard calling out just then, "it's time for bed. I'm exhausted as it is. Remik's been terribly difficult: it's either his fourth tooth cutting or he caught cold, I don't know."

"No, no," Maya implored. "I must know the condition. I can't go to bed now."

"Five minutes more!" Adrian Adrianovich yelled in the direction of the other room. "In five minutes by the watch I'll bring her to you. . . . Well, here we are. Ceres agreed on one condition, that neither the father, nor the mother, nor any other relative, should oversee her or give her any advice. She must be given complete freedom. Thus it was decided. Time passed. The boy was already beginning to walk, and he looked healthier, handsomer and more full of life than any other boy in the kingdom. He was never ill and never had a cold. He smiled even when his teeth began to cut."

"I don't believe it," Maya said.

"I assure it was so. Then the mother Queen decided she must spy and find out the means by which this marvelous good health was attained."

"Through sport," Maya answered. "Papa says . . ."

"Be silent." Adrian Adrianovich interrupted her. "Once late at night, when everyone had gone to bed, the Queen, taking off her shoes, crept stealthily to the door of the nursery. And what did she see there?"

"What? Well, what?"

"There was a fire burning in the nursery hearth. The mound of coal gleamed like a heap of gold coins, just like the fire over there. Ceres undressed the child and examined his body very carefully. The naked child, white as foam, stared at the fire, and its flames were reflected in the dark pupils of his eyes. Then Ceres approached the fire, scraped the live coals apart and placed the child upon them as upon a heap of sand."

"Ah!" Maya cried out in a whisper.

"Yes. And the boy merely laughed. He was happy. But the Queen, at the sight of her son in the fire, let out a loud cry. And, as if in response, the boy began feeling the pain and yelling desperately."

"How? I don't understand."

"It was a magic treatment. We must not forget that Ceres was a goddess. She wished to make of the boy an invulnerable hero, and he had already reached the stage where, for example, he could feel no pain from the heat. But no mortal eye was supposed to behold this. The mother spoilt it all."

"An invulnerable hero . . ." Maya repeated dreamily. "But the mother spoilt it all. But what is a goddess?"

"The five minutes are up!" Aglaia declared, appearing on the threshold. "I insist that you go to bed at once. It's very late already. Remik has fallen asleep at last. He's worn the life out of me."

"Come on, Maya, come on," Adrian Adrianovich urged, getting up. "We've given our word."

"And Pro . . . serpine? What happened to her?"

"I'll tell you the rest tomorrow if you're still interested."

"I am interested."

Maya walked slowly to the door. Her movements were uncertain, her eyes wide open. Apparently she saw before her a distant hearth, a royal child, a cloak of woven wheat, a whirlpool of unaccustomed images in which she was drowning. She stopped on the threshold and asked:

"You will tell me the rest tomorrow?"

"Without fail."

"But tell me just one more thing today: was it all true or not?"

Thereupon, the wise old man, defending his own childhood with his breast, gave the child an ambiguous answer:

"It's a myth, Maya," he replied. "A myth. It all happened so long ago that no one knows exactly whether it really happened or not. Sleep soundly, my little girl."

5

The bad weather came to an end. The menacing cloud, quivering with heat lightnings, passed beyond the horizon, and a slender, waning moon rose above the sea. The moist jasmine bushes were besprinkled with heavy, richly fragrant diamonds.

Arian Adrianovich was falling asleep on an old divan, which served him as a bed. The dying embers in the fireplace crackled slightly. The sparse smoke of the moon could be perceived through the now uncurtained window. Sleep approached nearer and nearer to the old divan. It touched the old man's wrists, it touched the pillows, it touched the gray hair, and Adrian Adrianovich was sound asleep. He dreamt of a rye field, which was at the same time the sea. Then, like a winged cloak, a cloud passed above him. Suddenly, lightning leapt from that cloud. He heard a terrifying peal of thunder and a terrible cry.

Adrian Adrianovich opened his eyes. In front of the fireplace stood Maya, trembling and weeping, looking like a white blotch in her long nightgown. Behind her was Aglaia, paler than she had been in the daytime. Little Rem was howling desperately in his mother's arms. Afanasy, in his night clothes, was quavering in the doorway.

"What . . . what's the matter?" Adrian Adrianovich asked, trying to outshout Rem. "Why are you all here? Afanasy, give me the Valerian drops! Come on, tell me!"

They began speaking all at once.

"Merciful Lord!" Afanasy intoned, searching the shelf. "Why, as I walked down the corridor to check the front door, what did I see, Merciful Lord! Why, there was the young lady dragging her infant brother, and she out of herself. Her eyes were blazing, and into the study she goes. It gave a jolt, it did. I followed them, and here she was putting the infant into the fireplace, just like a log, the Lord be Merciful!"

"I was sleeping," Aglaia sobbed, "when I heard a rustling. I opened my eyes—the children were gone. I ran out and saw Maya's nightshirt disappearing behind the door. I just had time to run in, just at the moment when she . . . Rem . . . into the fireplace. It was lucky the coal had burnt down, leaving almost nothing but ash. His hand, my little boy's hand is paining him. Aa-aa, my baby, my little chick! Ah, you horrid girl!"

"Hold on, hold on, Aglaia," Adrian Adrianovich interrupted. "You musn't do that! Look, she's all trembling . . ."

"I wanted . . . I wanted to make of him . . . an invulnerable hero," Maya said, sobbing, "but mother interfered just as she did before . . ."

Finally, they all went to bed again. Even Rem, who had been bathed in soda, had fallen asleep. The dawn had already touched the sea, and the stars were growing fainter every moment. But Adrian Adrianovich could not sleep.

He was sitting at table and, in the flickering light of the lamp, was writing a letter in reply to his poet friend in Paris.

"Everything changes," he wrote, "even the children. What was good for us is damaging to them. And the other way round. . . ."

The Viper

I

WHEN OLGA VYACHESLAVOVNA ENTERED the kitchen in her satin dressing gown, with her hair uncombed and gloomy face, everyone stopped talking, and only the freshly cleaned primuses, full of kerosene and concealed fury, could be heard hissing. A sense of danger emanated from Olga Vyacheslavovna. One of the lodgers had said this about her:

"There are bitches like her with fingers ready on the trigger . . . One should give them a wide berth, my darling little doves . . ."

Olga Vyacheslavovna, carrying a tin mug and a toothbrush, a rough towel wound round her waist, would march up to the washbasin and wash herself, deluging her dark, clipped head of hair under the tap. When there were women only in the kitchen, she would let drop her wrap to the waist and bathe her shoulders and her but slightly developed teenager's breasts with their brown nipples. Finally, clambering on a stool, she would wash her strong, beautiful legs. One could not help noticing then a long scar across her thigh and, on her back above the shoulder-blade, a pink shining cavity where a bullet had come out; and on her right arm, near the shoulder, a small bluish tattoo mark. Her shapely body was of a swarthy, golden hue.

All these details had been closely studied by the women, who lodged in one of the many apartments of a large house in the Zaryadie quarter. Maria Afanasievna, a seamstress, who deeply hated Olga Vyacheslavovna, used to call her "the branded one." Rosa Abramovna Bezikov, who had a husband in the Siberian tundras and did no work herself, literally felt ill at the sight of Olga Vyacheslavovna. A third woman, Sonya Varentzova or, more familiarly, Lyalechka, a pretty girl who worked in the Mahorka Trust,[1] would abandon her roaring primus and flee the kitchen as soon as she heard Olga Vyacheslavovna coming. It was lucky for Lyalechka that both Maria Afanasievna and Rosa Abramovna were well disposed to her, for, other wise, she would have been obliged to eat burnt gruel every day.

After washing, Olga Vyacheslavovna would stare at the women through her dark, "wild" eyes and then retire to her room at the end of the corridor. She had no primus, and no one could tell how she nourished herself in the morning. Vladimir Lvovich Ponizovsky, a lodger, an ex-officer and now an agent for the purchase and re-sale of antiquities, asserted that she drank brandy in the morning. Everything was possible. But it was more likely that she did own a primus, but that out of sheer misogynism she used it only in her room until such time as the house committee prohibited the practice. Zhuravlev, the head of the committee, was almost murdered when he threatened Olga Vyacheslavovna with court action and eviction if she persisted in infringing the "fire prevention regulations." She threw a blazing primus at him, which he did well to dodge, and shouted such obscenities at him as he had never heard before even on the street during a public holiday. The primus was of course written off.

At ten-thirty in the morning, Olga Vyacheslavovna used to leave the house. On the way to work, she very likely bought herself a sandwich of some sort of "dog's delight" and then had tea in the office. She came home at indefinite hours. She never received any male visitors.

A keyhole inspecion of her room failed to satisfy the general curiosity: bare walls was all one could see—without a single photograph or postcard—and a small revolver hanging over the bed. There were five pieces of furniture: two chairs, a dressing

[1] *Mahorka*—a sort of cheap, very dry tobacco.

table, an iron bedstead and a table by the window. Sometimes the room was tidy, and the shades raised. A small hand-mirror, a comb, two or three phials stood neatly on the peeling dressing table; a pile of books was heaped on the table, and there was also a flower of sorts in a small milk bottle. At other times, everything had been left in an appalling state of disorder: the bed resembled a battle scene, the floor was littered with cigarette butts, and a chamber pot stood in the middle of the room.

"A demobilized soldier, not a woman," Rosa Abramovna would comment in a weak voice.

Peter Semeonich Morsh, a bachelor, who worked at the Medical Supply Center and was a man of regular habits, had once suggested, giggling and his bald pate shining, that they should "smoke her out" by blowing ten grams of iodoform through a paper funnel inserted in the keyhole. "No living creature could bear the poisoned air." But this suggestion was never put into execution—the lodgers were too frightened to attempt it.

In any case, Olga Vyacheslavovna was the butt of daily criticism; petty passions would flare up; and, but for her, the lodgers would have found life extremely dull. Yet not a single eye had probed the deep secret of her life. Even the innocuous Lyalechka's repeated trepidation had remained a mystery.

Lyalechka, when questioned, merely shook her curls and replied with trifles. Lyalechka would have been a film star if it had not been for her nose. "In Paris, they'd make the sweetest thing out of your nose," Rosa Abramovna used to say. "But, O Lord, what's the use of talking about Paris here!" Lyalechka would smile at this as a blush reddened her cheeks and her blue eyes blinked enviously at the very thought. Peter Semeonovich's comment about her was: "Not a bad girl, no fool . . ." But that was only half-true! Lyalechka's strength lay in appearing to be a fool and in unerringly discovering her own style by the age of nineteen. This suggested a subtle and practical mind. Work-weary men, responsible workers, and married men found her very attractive. She evoked a tender smile from the lost depths of the soul. One felt like sitting her down in one's lap and dandling her, so as to forget the bustle and the smell of the city, all the statistics and the rustling papers of the office. Whenever she

sat down primly at the typewriter after wiping her little nose
with a handkerchief, spring seemed to blossom in the gloomy
premises of the Mahorka Trust. Lyalechka was fully aware of
this. But she was harmless and, if Olga Vyacheslavovna really
hated her, there was bound to be a mystery behind it.

On Sunday, at half-past-nine as usual, the door at the end of
the corridor creaked. Lyalechka dropped a saucer and fled from
the kitchen. She could be heard bolting her door and bursting
into sobs. Olga Vyacheslavovna entered the kitchen. A couple of
wrinkles showed about her rigidly tight mouth, her arched brows
were knitted, and her gaunt, gypsylike face looked sickly. A
towel was bound tightly round her waist, slender as a wasp's.
Without blinking an eye, she turned on the tap and began her
ablutions, splashing water on the floor. "And who's going to
wipe it up? We ought to stick her face into it," Maria Roma-
novna wanted to say but held her tongue.

Having dried her wet hair, Olga Vyacheslavovna looked
darkly round the kitchen, staring at the women and squat Peter
Semeonovich Morsh, who had just entered by the back door
with a piece of sifted bread, a bottle of milk and his revolting and
perpetually quivering little dog. His dry lips were parted in a
poisonous smile. Hunched and birdlike, with grizzled beard and
yellow teeth, he seemed to incarnate the quite unshakable principle of "Well, well, live and see." He loved to bring bad news. A
pair of soiled trousers, which he always wore on his morning
errands, hung loosely round his bandy legs.

Then Olga Vyacheslavovna uttered a strange sound as if everything in her throat had burst into this cackling fragment of em-
bittered derision:

"The devil alone knows what this is!" she exclaimed in a low,
intense voice before throwing the towel over her shoulder and
sweeping out. A satisfied grin spread over Morsh's parchmentlike
face.

"From overdrinking, a sudden passion for cleanliness has come
over our house manager," he declared, dropping his dog to the
floor. "He was standing down below on the stairs and affirming
that my dog had filthied the staircase. 'That's its excrement!' he

says. 'If your dog continues these manifestations on the stairs, I shall have to bring you to court.' I answered: 'You are wrong, Zhuravlev, that is not my dog's excrement . . .' And so we argued instead of his sweeping the stairs and my going to work. Such is Russian reality."

At that moment a voice at the end of the corridor was heard exclaiming: "The devil knows what this is!" and a door was banged. The women in the kitchen exchanged glances. Morsh retired to have his tea and to change his trousers for a pair of Sunday best. The pendulum clock in the kitchen showed nine.

At ten o'clock that evening a woman dashed into the militia office. A brown hat, like a helmet, was pushed down over her eyes; the high collar of her coat hid her neck and chin; that part of her face which was visible seemed to be powdered white. The chief militiaman, after scrutinizing her, concluded that it was pallor rather than face-powder, for there was not a drop of blood in her features. The woman, as she pressed with her breast against the edge of the high ink-stained desk, spoke softly but with a sort of agonized despair:

"Go to Pskovsky Street. . . . I don't know what I did there. . . . Now I'll have to die. . . ."

Only then did the chief militiaman notice a small revolver in her blue fist. Leaning over the desk, he gripped the woman's wrist and snatched away the dangerous toy.

"And have you got a permit for carrying fire-arms?" He shouted for some reason. The woman threw back her head to see better and continued to stare vacantly at him.

"Your name and surname? Your address," the chief militiaman demanded more calmly.

"Olga Vyacheslavovna Zotova . . ."

2

Ten years ago, on Prolomnaya Street in Kazan, a fire broke out in the middle of the day in the house of an Old Believer, Vyacheslav Illarionovich Zotov, a merchant of the second guild. On the first floor the firemen found two corpses bound with electric wire: those of Zotov and his wife; and on the top floor they also discovered the unconscious body of their seventeen-year-old daughter Olga, a school girl. Her night-shirt had been ripped in tatters, and her neck and hands bore the marks of finger nails. All the evidence pointed to a desperate struggle. But the bandits evidently had not been able to overpower her or, in their haste to depart, had merely knocked her out with an iron weight attached to a strap.

The firemen failed to save the house, and all of the Zotov possessions were reduced to ash. Olga was removed to a hospital, where a dislocated shoulder was set and the broken skin on her scalp was stitched. She remained unconscious for several days. She first became aware of pain when her bandages were changed. Then she saw a military doctor sitting on the edge of her bed and looking at her benevolently through his spectacles. Impressed by her beauty, the doctor tried to prevent her from moving. But she stretched out her hand to him:

"What savages, what beasts they were, doctor!" she exclaimed, bursting into tears.

A few days later she told him:

"Two of them I did not know. They were wearing army greatcoats. . . . The third I do know. . . . I have even danced with him. . . . Valka, who was at school. . . . I heard them killing papa and mama. . . . There was a crunch of bones. . . . Oh doctor, why would they do it? . . . Doctor, why did it happen! What horrible beasts!"

"Sh . . . Sh . . ." the doctor hissed in alarm, while his eyes grew moist with tears.

No one else visited Olga Zotova in the hospital. Those were troubled times, people had other things to do. Russia was rent by civil war; stable life was cracking and disintegrating; the words of decrees, those white posters, breathed violence and fury wherever one looked. Olga had no alternative but to weep for days on end out of a sense of unbearable pity—in her ears still rang her father's desperate cry: "Don't do it!" and the inhuman howling of her mother, who had never screamed in her life before—from fear of the future, from despair at the unknown forces that were rioting, yelling and shooting in the night outside the hospital windows.

During these days she must have wept a whole lifetime of tears. Her carefree, thoughtless youth had been cut short. Her soul, like a healed wound, was now covered with scars. She was not yet aware of the whole force of her own somber and passionate strength.

One day a man with a bandaged arm sat down beside her on a corridor bench. He was wearing a hospital shirt, underpants and scuffs, and yet, like an iron stove, he radiated a hot, cheery warmth.

Barely audibly he whistled "Little Apple" and tapped time with his bare heels.

His gray, hawklike eyes rolled more than once in the direction of the beautiful girl. His wide, sunburnt face with its unshaved, hairy cheekbones wore an expression of unconcern and even laziness, but his hawklike eyes glinted harshly, even cruelly.

"Are you in the V.D. ward?" he asked indifferently.

Olga failed to understand at first, but then she was filled with indignation.

"I was almost murdered, but escaped. That's why I'm here," she shot back, moving away and dilating her nostrils.

"Oh Lord, what an adventure! There must have been a reason for it. Or was it just bandits? Ah?"

Olga stared at him: how could he speak like that, so casually, as if to relieve his boredom. . . .

"You didn't hear about us, then? The Zotovs on Prolomny Street?"

"So that's it! Yes, I remember now. . . . Well, you're a real fighting girl, you know . . . you didn't give in. . . . (He wrinkled his brow.) Types like them ought to be burned alive, boiled in a cauldron . . . then, perhaps, we'd get somewhere. . . . What low types have suddenly crawled out of the woodwork, more of them than we ever thought possible . . . we're just amazed. It's a darn shame. (His cold eyes scrutinized Olga.) Of course, that's the way you will see the Revolution now—through violence. . . . That's a pity! You come from a family of Old Believers? You believe in God? But never mind, you'll get over that. (He thumped the bench with his fist.) Struggle is what you should believe in."

Olga wanted to say something mean, justified no doubt because of the ruin of the Zotov family, but under this man's ironic, expectant eyes all her thoughts rose and then slumped without finding expression.

"Well, well. . . . A mettlesome horse!" he commented, "a good mixture of Russian blood with a dash of the gypsy. Otherwise you'd live your life like everyone else—watching life through an aspidistra at the window. . . . A bore that!"

"Is it merrier the way things are now?"

"But isn't it merrier? Shouldn't we go on the rampage sometimes and not just keep totaling up accounts on the abacus?"

Olga again grew indignant, but could not say a word. She merely shrugged her shoulders: he was too cocksure. . . .

"You've ruined the whole town," she muttered at last. "You'll ruin the whole of Russia, you shameless men. . . ."

"Not just Russia. . . . We intend to ride our mounts over the whole wide world. . . . Now that the horses have snapped their tethers, maybe it's only the ocean will stop us. . . . Willing or not, you'd better ride with us. . . ."

He grinned, bending towards her, and his teeth glittered with wild joy. Olga felt dizzy. She seemed to have heard those words before; she remembered these grinning white teeth; it was as if her memory had stepped out from the darkness of her blood and the ancient voices of previous generations had shouted: "To horse, mount and ride to your fill, my soul!" She felt dizzy. Then she perceived the man again sitting there in the hospital with a bandaged arm. But now her heart felt both hot and feverish; in some way, this gray-eyed man now seemed very close to her. She scowled and moved to the other end of the bench. But he just whistled and beat time on the floor with his heel.

It had been a brief conversation—to break the monotony of a hospital corridor. The man had whistled and gone his way. Olga had not even asked his name. But when she sat down again on the bench the next day and had glanced into the depths of the stifling corridor, and had earnestly sifted in her mind what she would say that was convincing and clever to shake his self-confidence, and he still failed to appear—instead there were some people on

crutches—then she suddenly realized quite clearly that yesterday's encounter had been a terribly exciting thing to her.

She waited for perhaps another minute before the tears rose to
her eyes at the hurt of waiting while he did not seem to care. . . .
She went back to her ward and lay down, imagining all the most
unjust things about him. But how, in what way, had he troubled
her?

Curiosity tormented her more than the sense of injury. She
wanted to see him again, even if for an instant: what was he like?
There was nothing to him. . . . There were millions of such
fools. A bolshevik, of course. . . . A bandit. . . . And those
eyes of his, the insolence of them. . . . Her maiden pride tortured her too: how could she be thinking of such a man all day
long! Who was he to make her clench her fists!

That night the whole hospital was roused. The doctors and the
stretcher-bearers began running about, dragging bundles. The
frightened patients sat up on their beds. Outside there was thunder of cart wheels and peals of mad cursing. The Czechs were
entering Kazan. The Reds were withdrawing. All who were able
abandoned the hospital. But Olga remained behind, forgotten by
everyone.

At dawn the hospital corridor resounded to the thud of rifle
butts. The big-chested Czechs in neat foreign uniforms had arrived. There was a sound of someone being dragged away and
the voice of the assistant hospital manager was heard howling: "It
was against my will. I am no bolshevik. . . . Let me go. Where
are you taking me?" Two paralytics crawled to the window
giving on the courtyard and whispered bits of information:
"They've taken him to the shed . . . to string him up . . . the
poor fellow . . ."

Olga put on a gray hospital dress and hid her bandage under a
white kerchief. The bells rang festively in the town. The light
was getting stronger. The military bands of the regiments
marching into town could be heard now louder, now fading. The
diminishing thunder of guns rolled on somewhere beyond the
Volga.

Olga walked out of the ward. Round the bend of the corridor

a patrol of two mustachioed Czechs stopped her with sibilant hissing and ordered her to go back. "I'm not a prisoner, I am a Russian," Olga cried out, her eyes flashing. The Czechs laughed and stretched out their hands to pinch her cheek, to chuck her under the chin. . . . There was no point in thrusting herself upon the blades of two lowered bayonets. With quivering nostrils she returned and sat down on her bed. Her teeth were chattering.

The patients were served no tea that morning, and they began to grumble. At dinner time the Czechs rounded up five amputated Red Army men. The paralytics at the window said that the poor fellows had taken to the shed. Then a Russian officer entered the ward; he was tightly belted and wore a pair of side riding breeches resembling a bat's wings. He glanced along the beds, and then his screwed up eyes stopped at Olga. "Zotova?" he asked. "Follow me." He seemed to fly through the air in his riding breeches, and his spurs with their clinking filled the empty corridor.

They had to pass through the courtyard. At that moment, from the porch towards which she was being led, emerged a curly-headed youth in an embroidered Russian shirt who, as he put on his cap in passing, glanced at her sideways and hastened to the gate. . . . Olga stumbled. . . . It seemed to her . . . But it could not be.

She entered the waiting room and sat down near the table, staring at the officer before her. He had a long, crooked face, as if seen in a mirror. He stared back at her through squinting eyes.

"Aren't you ashamed, you, the daughter of a man greatly respected in the town, you, an intelligent girl, aren't you ashamed to associate with scum?" She heard him say in a reproachful voice that stressed the vowels. She made an effort to grasp what he was saying. But a persistent thought prevented her from concentrating. With a sigh, she gripped her knees and began to tell him everything that had happened to her. The officer puffed his cigarette slowly, leaning on an elbow. When she had finished, he turned over a sheet of paper, beneath which lay a penciled note.

"Our information does not quite corroborate your statement," he declared, thoughtfully wrinkling his forehead. "I'd like to hear something from you about your ties with the local bolshevik organization. What?" The corner of his mouth crawled up, and his brows set crookedly.

Olga watched with alarm the ghastly assymetry of his clean-shaven face.

"But you. . . . I don't understand. . . . You've gone mad. . . ."

"I regret, but we have indisputable proof, strange as it may seem. (Holding his cigarette at arms length and rocking himself to and fro, he blew out a whiff of smoke. One could imagine nothing more "society" than this man.) Your sincerity impresses. . . . (A smoke ring.) But push your sincerity to the very end, my dear. By the way, your friends, the Red Army men, died like heroes. (One skewbald eye was now fixed somewhere in the direction of the window, from which could be seen the doors of the shed.) So you are silent? Well, then . . ."

Gripping the arms of his chair, he turned to the Czechs:

"*Bitte*, please . . ."

The Czechs ran up, lifted Olga out of her chair, and passed their hands over her sides and her breasts, their mustaches twitching with satisfaction; they fumbled under her skirt, looking for hidden pockets. The officer rising, watched all this with his dilated, squinting eyes. Olga choked. A blush, a fire of blood spread over her cheeks. She tore herself free and screamed. . . .

"Put her in prison," the officer ordered.

Olga spent two months in prison, first in the common cell and then in solitary confinement. During the first few days, she was almost driven mad by the persistent image of the shed doors, which were propped with a board. She could not sleep; she seemed to feel a rope round her neck whenever she dozed off.

No one questioned or interrogated her. She seemed to have been forgotten. After a while she began to reflect. She might have opened a book: everything was so clear now. The curly-headed man in the embroidered shirt was Valka, the murderer: she had made no mistake. . . . Afraid of being denounced, he had hastened to get the advantage: the pencilled note contained his denunciation. . . .

Nothing prevented Olga from tearing about her cell like a puma: all her passionate requests (through the iron door) to see

the prison chief, the interrogator, the public procurator, were ignored by the grim prison guards. In her state of fenzy, she still
believed in justice and invented fantastic plans for getting hold of
paper and pencil and reporting the whole truth to the higher
authorities, who were as just as God.

One day she was roused by the sound of coarse, staccato voices
and the crash of a door being flung open. Someone had entered
the next-door cell. A bespectacled man was held prisoner there.
All she knew of him was that he coughed harrowingly at night.
Jumping up now, she listened. The voices behind the wall rose to
a shout. They were impatient and pressing. They broke and subsided. Then a groan pierced the silence. It sounded as if pain
were being caused to someone who was trying to control himself
as if in a dentist's chair.

Olga huddled in a corner under the window, her dilated eyes
staring madly into the darkness. She recalled the accounts she
had heard in the common cell of torture. . . . She seemed to see
the upturned, earth-gray face in spectacles, his flabby cheeks
quivering in torment. . . . They were binding his wrists and
ankles with wire so tightly it cut to the bone. . . . "You'll talk,
you'll talk," she seemed to hear. . . . There was the sound of
blows as if a carpet, rather than a man, were being beaten. . . .
He still held his tongue. A blow, another. . . . Suddenly a moaning sound. . . . "Aha! you'll talk now!" Then, no longer a
moaning, but a sickening howl filled the whole prison. . . . Olga
felt that the dust from that terrible carpet had enveloped her;
nausea gripped her heart; her feet began to slide; the stone floor
swayed; and she hit it with the back of her head. . . .

That night, when man tortured man, all her timid hope in justice was buried. But Olga's passionate soul could not remain mute
and inactive. After some black days, when she almost lost her
reason, she suddenly found salvation as she paced the cell diago-
nally: hatred, revenge. . . . Hatred, revenge! Oh, if she could
only get out of here!

Raising her head, she stared at the narrow window; the dusty
windowpanes tinkled softly, and dead, withered spiders swayed
in a cobweb. Somewhere in the distance guns thundered. (It was
the Fifth Red Army advancing on Kazan.) A guard brought the

dinner; sniffling, he glanced sideways at the window; "I've brought you some kalatch, Miss. . . . If you need anything, just bang on the door. . . . With political prisoners we're always. . . ."

The window panes tinkled all day. Outside the cell the guards kept sighing deeply. Olga sat on her bunk, clasping her knees with her hands. She did not touch the food. She felt her heart beating in her knees, and the guns with their thunder pounded outside the windows. At dusk the guard tiptoed in again and whispered: "We've been subjected, but we are always for the people."

Round midnight there was bustle in the prison corridors— doors were banged, menacing shouts were heard. Several white officers and civilians, waving their weapons threateningly, were herding downstairs a crowd of some thirty prisoners. Olga too was dragged out of her cell and pushed down the stairs at a trot. She wriggled like a cat and fought to bite their hands. For a minute, she saw the windy sky in the courtyard square, and the chill of the autumn night filled her lungs. Then, passing through a low doorway, she found herself descending a few stone steps into a damp moldy cellar packed with people. The conical beams of pocket torches swept over the brick walls, the pale faces and the staring eyes. . . . All round people swore desperately. . . . Revolver shots rang out, and it sounded as if the vaults of the cellar had collapsed. . . . Olga hid herself somewhere in the darkness. Then, for an instant, in the light of a torch, she caught sight of Valka's face. . . . Something hot seared her shoulders, and a fiery wheel drilled through her breast, tearing at her back. . . . Stumbling, she fell face down on the moldy floor smelling of mushrooms. . . .

The Fifth Army captured Kazan: the Czechs went off down the Volga on steamers; the white Russian bands dispersed as best they could; and half the population, frightened at the prospect of the Red terror, fled to the other side of the world. For several weeks, these refugees with bundles over their shoulders and sticks in their hands suffered indescribable privations as they wandered along both banks of the Volga, the waters of which had become swollen by the autumn rains. Valka also had cleared out from Kazan.

Contrary to all probability, Olga survived. When the bodies of the executed people were carried out of the prison cellar and laid side by side in the courtyard beneath the dreary, drizzling sky, a cavalryman in an untanned sheepskin coat squatted down beside Olga's body and gently turned her head.

"The girl's still breathing," he cried. "We must go and get a doctor quickly, brothers. . . ."

He was the same lad with the prominent teeth and the hawk-like eyes whom Olga had met in the hospital. He himself carried the girl to the prison hospital and then ran off to try and find amid all the confusion of a captured town, a doctor, "a professor of the old regime, of course." At last he burst into the apartment of one such "professor," arrested him on the spot and, almost frightening him to death, drove him to the hospital on a motor cycle and, pointing finally to the unconscious, bloodless-faced Olga, commanded: "She must live. . . ."

Olga did live. After the bandages and the camphor, she opened her blue eyes. She must have recognized the hawklike eyes fastened upon her. "Come nearer," she pronounced almost inaudibly. When he had come quite close, and was waiting there, she incomprehensibly demanded: "Kiss me. . . ." There were other people grouped round the bed, and it was wartime; the man with the hawk eyes started back, glanced round and exclaimed: "What the devil!" He wouldn't be kissed, but he rearranged her pillows. . . .

Emilyanov was the cavalryman's name, Comrade Emilyanov. Olga learnt that his full name was Dimitry Vassilievich Emilyanov. On hearing this, Olga closed her eyes and moved her lips, repeating "Dimitry Vassilievich."

Emilyanov's regiment was being reformed in Kazan, and he visited Olga every day. "I must say, Olga Vyacheslavovna," he kept repeating to encourage her, "you're as lively as a viper. . . . Get better, and I'll enroll you as an orderly in my squadron. . . ."

Every day he spoke to her of this, and never tired talking, nor she of listening. He used to laugh, displaying his glittering teeth, and her weak lips would break into a tender smile. "We'll cut your hair, and I'll get you a light pair of boots I took from a schoolboy who got killed; in the beginning, of course, I'll strap you to your mount so you don't fall off. . . ."

Olga really was as lively as a viper. After all that had befallen her, she seemed to have nothing left but her eyes. They burned now with a sleepless passion and impatient greed for life.

She had left her past behind her on some far shore. Her father's strict, prosperous household; her school, her sentimental girl friends, the fun of early snows, her girlish enthusiasm for visiting actors, her very normal adoration of her Russian language teacher, Voronov, a plump but handsome man; the "Hertzen circle" at her school and her enthusiastic devotion to her friends in this circle; her reading of foreign novels and her sweet longing for the Nordic heroines—such as do not exist in real life—of Hamsun, and the feverish curiosity excited by Victor Margueritte's novels. . . . Had all this really existed? The new dress for Christmas and her Yuletide infatuation with a student masquerading as Mephistopheles with horns stuffed with cotton-wool and blackened with soot. . . . The fragrance of flowers frozen at 30° Farenheit. . . . The nostalgic silence, the bell ringing at the height of Lent, the crumbling snow already turned muddy in the shopping district. . . . The alarums of spring and its feverish nights. . . . Their country *dacha* at Verkhnyi Uslon, the pine trees, the meadow lands, the shining Volga spread in boundless flood, and the massed clouds on the horizon. . . . All these delights she now remembered only in dreams perhaps, in the moist, tearful warmth of a hospital pillow. . . .

Into these dreams of hers, as she saw it, Valka had burst in with his raging flesh and his five-pound weight on a strap. Valka had been expelled from school for hooliganism; he had volunteered for the Army, but was back in Kazan within a year, wearing a dandy Uhlan uniform and a private's St. George cross. It was said that the police officer Brykin, his father, had petitioned the Army Commander of the region to have his son sent to the front trenches, where he was sure to be killed, since it would be better for his own paternal heart to see his son dead than alive. . . .

Valka was always hungry and thirsty for pleasure, and as bold as
the devil himself. The war taught him all kinds of tricks and he
had learned that blood smelled sour; but it was the Revolution
that untied his hands.

Valka's five-pound weight had smashed to smithereens the
thin, rainbow ice of Olga's dreams. That ice had turned out to be
horribly thin, and yet she had once dreamt of building her happiness upon it; marriage, love, family, a stable and happy household. . . . An abyss had yawned beneath this ice. . . . It broke
—and a rude, passionate life had overwhelmed her in its turbid
waves.

Olga accepted it as such: life was a desperate fight (twice *they*
had done their best to murder her—and had failed; now she
was afraid of nothing), hatred to her heart's content, a crust of
bread for the day and the wild excitement of an, as yet, untested
love—such indeed was life. . . . Whenever Emilyanov sat down
by her bed, she would prop herself on a pillow, grip the edge of
the quilt with her thin fingers and talk to him looking into his
eyes with innocent trust:

"I had always imagined my husband as a blond respectable
man," she would say, "and myself in a pink peignoir; there we'd
be sitting, with our reflections in a nickel coffee pot. And that
was all! And that meant happiness to me. . . . I hate the girl that
I was! I expected happiness, idiot that I was, in a dressing gown
over a coffee pot! What a slut!"

Emilyanov, his fists on his haunches, laughed at her stories.
Olga, without realizing it, strove to pour herself into him. She
had only one desire at that moment—to tear her body away from
the hospital bed. She clipped her hair. Emilyanov obtained for
her a short cavalry sheepskin coat and a pair of blue riding
breeches with red piping and, as he had promised, a pair of small,
elegant goatskin boots.

In November Olga was discharged from the hospital. She had
no relatives or friends left in town. The northern clouds with
their lashing rain and snows, swept over the deserted streets and
the boarded shops. Emilyanov plodded energetically from street
to street through the mud in search of a lodging. Olga plodded
after him a step or so behind in her soaked and now heavy sheepskin coat and the dead schoolboy's boots. Her knees felt weak,

but she would have rather died than not keep up with Dimitry. From the executive committee, he had obtained a chit for living quarters for "comrade Zotov," who had been tortured by the white guards, and was now searching for something out of the ordinary. Finally, he fixed on and requisitioned a large, abandoned mansion with columns and mirrored windows which had belonged to the merchant family of Starobogatov.

The wind, sweeping through the broken windows of the uninhabited house, moved freely about the suite of rooms with painted ceilings and gilded but already ragged furniture. The crystal pendants of the chandeliers tinkled plaintively. The bare maple trees creaked drearily in the garden.

Emilyanov kicked open the French doors.

"Just look! Ah, the devils, they relieved themselves straight on parquet by way of protest. . . ."

In the main drawing room Emilyanov broke up the oak organ, which was the size of the whole wall, and carried the wood into a corner room with divans where he lit a blazing fire in the fireplace.

"You can boil a kettle here, and it's warm and light. . . . They knew how to live, those bourgeois. . . ."

He got hold of a tin kettle, some dried carrot to infuse instead of tea, some groats, lard, potatoes, enough supplies for a couple of weeks; and Olga stayed alone in the dark, empty house, where the wind howled terrifyingly in the chimneys as if the ghosts of the merchants Starobogatov were lamenting their sorrows on the roof beneath the autumn rain. . . .

Olga had plenty of time for reflection. She would sit down on a stool, stare at the fire, where the kettle was beginning to sing, and think of Dimitry: would he come that day? It would be so good if he did—the potatoes were just done. Then she would hear his steps on the echoing parquet; he would enter, cheerful, fierce-eyed, and with him, her life entered too. . . . Unbuckling his revolver and a couple of hand-grenades, and pulling off his damp army coat, he would inquire if all was in order and if she needed anything.

"First of all, get rid of that chest cough of yours and the blood in the saliva. . . . By New Year, you'll be fine. . . ."

Having had his fill of tea, and after rolling a cigarette of mahorka tobacco, he would talk to her about military matters, giving her a vivid description of cavalry actions; and, at times, he would become so excited that it pained to look into his hawklike eyes.

"The Imperialist war was a positional, trench war, because there was no passion, and everyone was dying of boredom," he would argue, standing in the middle of the room with his legs wide apart and his sword drawn from its scabbard. "But the Revolution has created a mounted army. . . . Do you understand? A horse—that's elemental. . . . A cavalry battle—that's the revolutionary surge. . . . Here I am sword in hand, and I cut my way into the ranks of the infantry or gallop at a machine-gun nest. . . . Can the enemy stand firm at the sight of me? No, he can't. . . . And so he flees in panic, and I slash at him. I have wings behind my back. Do you know what a cavalry battle is like? A wall of lava bearing down upon another wall, and no shot fired. . . . A roaring. . . . And you feel drunk. . . . Then comes the clash. . . . And the work begins. . . . A minute, two minutes at the most. . . . The heart can't bear this horror. . . . The enemy's hair stands on end. . . . And so the enemy swings his mount away. . . . All that's left is to slash and to pursue. . . . No prisoners. . . ."

His eyes glittered like steel, and his steel blade whistled through the air. . . . Olga, her back grown chilly from agitation, stared at him, her sharp elbows propped against her knees, her chin pressed against her clenched fists. . . . It seemed to her that, if the whistling blade had slashed her own heart, she would have shouted with joy, so greatly did she now love this man. . . .

But why did he spare her? Was it because he only had a feeling of compassion for her? That he pitied her as an orphan or some abandoned puppy picked up in the street? At times she seemed to catch a quick sideways glance aimed at her, a misty, non-brotherly look. . . . Then the warmth would flood her cheeks, and she would not know where to turn her face, while her pounding heart fell into a dizzy precipice. . . . But no, he would merely pull a Moscow paper from his pocket, sit down in front of the fire and read aloud some feuilleton, in which no

words were spared to "nail down" thoroughly the international
bourgeoisie. . . . "If they don't get them with bullets, they get
them with barnyard language. . . . How they write, the devils!"
he shouted gleefully, stamping his feet. . . .

Winter came. Olga's health improved. One day Emilyanov
arrived before it was light, ordered her to dress and took her to
the parade ground, where he instructed the recruits in the first
elements of cavalry discipline and the handling of horses. At
dawn a soft snow was falling; and there was Olga galloping on the
white parade ground, leaving the sandy marks of hooves behind
her. Emilyanov shouted at her: "You're sitting like a dog on a
fence, you 'mother' you! Lift your toes and don't sprawl!" She
was amused, and the wind whistled joyfully in her ears, intoxicating her heart as the snowflakes melted on her eyelashes.

3

This weak girl had hidden reserves of iron strength: it was
hard to understand where they came from. After a month of
both cavalry and infantry training, she became as taut as a
string, and the frosty wind had brought color to her cheeks. "To
see her for the first time, you'd think a spittle would blow her
over, but she's a regular little devil," the soldiers said. And she
was as handsome as the devil too: the young cavalrymen would
show off before her and the seasoned warriors stopped to ponder
whenever Zotova, tall and slender with a dark cap of comely
hair and her short, tightly-belted, sheepskin coat passed with
clink of spurs through the cheap tobacco smoke of the barracks.

Her slim hands learned to manage a horse dextrously and
sensitively. Her legs, which seemed suitable only for bourgeois
dancing and silk skirts, developed and grew strong; the grip of
her legs especially amazed Emilyanov: she combined steel and
sensitivity; she sat in the saddle like a tick, and her mount obeyed
her like a sheep. She learned to use the sabre. Dashingly she
slashed and pierced but, of course, there was little real force to
her stroke: when slashing with a sabre, the whole weight should
come from the shoulder, but her shoulders were those of a young
girl.

Nor was she slow in the political class. Emilyanov was nervous about her "bourgeois origins"—those were hard times! "Comrade Zotova, what are the aims of the Workers' and Peasants' Red Army?" she was asked. Olga would shoot forward and without hesitation reply: "To fight against bloody capitalism, against the landowners, the priests and the interventionists for the happiness of all laboring people on earth."

Zotova was finally enrolled on active duty in the combat squadron commanded by Emilyanov. In February, the regiment boarded a freight train and was despatched to the Denikin front.

As Olga stood, holding the reins of her mount on the filthy, manure-covered grounds of the railway station, where the echelons had detrained, and stared at the murky, windswept, coal-red and blue conflagration of the spring sunset and heard the distant thunder of guns, then all her recent past rose up in her with all its sense of unforgettable injury and revengeful hatred.

"No smoking! . . . To horse!" Emilyanov's voice rang out. With an easy motion, Olga swung herself into the saddle and her sword knocked against her thigh. "You just try and tear off my shirt now, or to threaten me with a five-pound weight, or push me by the elbows into a cellar!" she exclaimed to herself. "Forward, trot!" came the command. The saddle creaked, the damp wind whistled, eyes stared at the purple murk of the setting sun. . . . "Now that the horses have broken their tethers, only the ocean can stop us," she recalled the comforting refrain of her dear friend's words. . . . Thus began her life of combat.

In the squadron, everyone called Olga "Emilyanov's wife." But she was no wife to him. No one would have believed it; the men would have split their sides laughing had they known that Olga was still a virgin. Both Olga and Emilyanov concealed this fact. To be regarded as his wife was both more simple and comprehensible: no one pawed her, for everyone knew that Emilyanov had a hefty fist, as he had demonstrated on several occasions. Thus the men had a fraternal attitude toward Zotova.

As an orderly, Zotova was constantly to be found beside her squadron commander. During the campaign they shared the same quarters and often the same bed, he sleeping with his head in one direction, and she in the other, each of them wrapped in his own sheepskin cavalry coat.

After their exhausting forced marches of some twenty miles a day, Olga, having attended to her mount and gulped down some food from the big cauldron, would pull off her boots, unbutton the collar of her canvas shirt, and then fall soundly asleep as soon as she had lain down on a bench, stove, or the edge of a bed. She did not hear Emilyanov either going to bed or getting up. He slept like an animal—lightly, one ear always open to the noises of the night.

Emilyanov treated her strictly. He made no distinction between her and the men: in fact, he was even more exacting with her than with them. Only now did she really understand the force behind his hawklike eyes. Only now did she understand the forceful challenge of those eyes—the eyes of a born fighter. During the campaign, he lost his grinning good-nature as well as his superfluous fat. After a night inspection, when he found the mounts in good condition, the men asleep, the outposts and the sentinels in place, Emilyanov would enter the hut, feeling tired and reeking of sweat; he would drop down on a bench and use his last remaining strength to pull off the boots from his swollen feet, but he would often remain sitting there for a while in utter exhaustion with one of his boots partly off. Then he would walk to the bed and gaze for a minute at Olga's wind-beaten, feminine, childlike face flushed hotly in sleep. A mist would spread over his eyes and a tender smile break on his lips. But he would not have condoned any fault of hers.

Zotova was riding one day with a message to the Division Headquarters. Above the steppe, now green, now silver-gray with wormwood, a cloudless May sky trilled with the song of larks. Her mount felt in good fettle and, like an ambler, advanced at a smooth pace. Yellow marmots dashed across their path. On such a morning it was easy to forget the war, that the enemy was pressing and enveloping them, that the Red infantry divisions, refusing to engage, were smashing their railway wagons and retreating to the rear; and that there was hunger in town and revolts in the villages. But spring, as in the past, was adorning the earth with beauty and invading the mind with dreams. And even the horse, sweating excessively because of poor fodder, kept snorting, the rascal, feeling frisky and playful, and turning a lilac eye at the landscape.

Their path skirted a pond, which was partly overgrown with sedge and which reflected a chalk cliff wrinkled on its surface. Olga's mount changed its pace and made towards the water. Olga dismounted, unbridled the horse which, stepping up to its knees in the water, began to drink. But no sooner had the horse swallowed its first gulp than it raised its bald muzzle, and, quivering all over, neighed loudly in alarm. From some willow bushes at the other side of the pond came an answering neigh. Olga hurriedly bridled her mount and leapt into the saddle; staring in that direction, she began to pull her carbine from its case behind her back. Two heads bobbed up in the willow bushes, and then two riders darted out on the shore. They stopped. Olga realized it was a scouting party, but who were they? Reds or whites?

One of the horses lowered its head to shake off a horse-fly; and, when the rider bent down to seize the rein, there was a glitter of gold on his shoulder. . . . "Gee-up!" Olga hit her mount with her scabbard, bent low in the saddle, and the bushes of wormwood and dry burdock flew to meet her. . . . Behind her back she could hear the heavy thud of pursuing hooves. . . . A shot rang out. . . . She looked round: one of the riders was galloping to the right in order to cut her off. His mount, a reddish Don horse, covered the ground like a Borzoi dog. Another shot. Olga let fall her reins and snatched at the carbine. The rider on the Don horse was now galloping some fifty paces behind her. "Stop, stop!" he yelled menacingly, waving his sabre. . . . It was Valka Brykin. Olga recognized him in a flash, and at once she nudged her mount with her leg towards him, leveled her carbine. Her shot flamed vengefully. . . . The Don stallion reared, its head wobbling, and then fell with a thud to the ground on top of its rider. . . . "Valka! Valka!" Olga shouted, wild with joy, but at that very moment the second attacker was upon her from behind. She only caught a glimpse of his long mustaches and then his large eyes boggling with astonishment. "A female!" he exclaimed as his uplifted sabre clinked faintly against her carbine barrel. His mount carried him for-

ward. Olga no longer held the carbine; she must have dropped
it or thrown it away (she could not remember afterwards); but
in her hand she felt the challenging weight of her bared sabre.
A scream burst from her contracted throat; her mount leapt in
pursuit and caught up. She slashed with her blade. The mustachioed rider fell forward on the horse's mane, holding the back
of his head with both hands.

Breathing harshly, Olga's mount carried her over the worm-
wood-covered steppe. She noticed she was still gripping the hilt
of the sabre. With some difficulty she thrust it back into the
scabbard. Then she pulled up her mount; the chalk cliff and the
pond had been left far behind to the left. The steppe looked deserted: no one pursued her, no more shots rang out. The larks
were still trilling in the gaping blue sky, singing as generously
and sweetly as they had done in childhood years. Olga gripped
her shirt at the breast near her throat, trying nervously to control
herself, but she failed: she burst into tears and, weeping, began
to shake in the saddle.

On the way to the Divisional Headquarters, she still kept drying her tears angrily now with one fist, now with the other.

In the squadron, Olga was made to repeat this story a hundred
times. The men roared, wagged their heads and could hardly
keep straight from laughing:

"Oi, I can't take it, brothers, what a circus! The wench put
the lid on a couple of men. . . ."

"Wait, tell us again: you say he came at you from behind and
then suddenly shouted: 'A female!'"

"And how large were his mustaches?"

"And he boggled with astonishment."

"And he wouldn't raise his arm?"

"Not surprising, that!"

"And there and then you slashed him on the head. . . . Oi,
brothers, I'll die laughing. . . . There's a cavalier for you—fell
to bits, he did."

"And what did you do afterwards?"

"What do you mean afterwards?" Olga asked. "I just wiped
my blade and rode on to the division with the message."

There was one serious discomfort about campaign life: Olga could not overcome her sense of modesty. She felt it particularly when, on a hot day, the squadron reached a river or a pond: the men would ride in naked into the water on their unsaddled horses, laughing and yelling amid a rainbow shower of water-drops. But Olga would pick on a secluded spot somewhere behind a bush. The men would shout at her:

"Don't be a fool, girl; tie a rag round you and come in with us!"

Emilyanov watched strictly over the hygiene and cleanliness of his men. "If a cavalryman has a pimple on his buttocks—out he goes, he's no fighter," he would say. "A cavalryman must look after himself more than anyone. . . . If circumstances permit, splash yourself with water from a well both winter and summer, and do fifteen minutes of physical jerks."

Washing at a well was hard for her: she had to get up earlier than the men and run over the chilly dew just as the early morning light was beginning to glimmer in narrow strips through the barred clouds and the mists. One morning she had just pulled up the plaintively creaking pail of icy, strong-smelling water, set it down on the edge and undressed, huddling from cold, when she suddenly felt as if something had noiselessly touched her back.

Swinging round, she saw Dimitry standing on the porch and staring at her closely and strangely. Slowly she moved behind the well and squatted there so that only her unblinking eyes could be seen. If it had been one of the other men, she would have simply shouted out: "What are you staring at, you devil? Look the other way!" But now her voice had grown dry from shame and agitation. Emilyanov shrugged his shoulders, laughed and went away.

It was an insignificant incident, but henceforth everything changed. Everything, even the most simple things, suddenly became complicated. The squadron had halted for the night in a burnt-out village and, as often happened, only one bed was available. That night Olga lay down on the very edge of the bed, on the pungently smelling horse-cloth, and she could not fall asleep for a long time even though she tried to shut her eyes tightly. Even so she did not hear Emilyanov enter. When the crowing cocks woke her, she discovered him asleep on the floor near the door. . . . Their relations were no longer so simple. . . . In conversation, Dimitry frowned and avoided looking at her; she could feel a masked tenseness on his face as well as her own. Yet, all this time, she felt a joyful intoxication.

Until then, Olga had not been involved in a real battle. Her regiment, together with the division, continued their retreat to the North. During the skirmishes she was always at the side of the squadron commander.

But then somewhere at the front something went very wrong; the men spoke of it anxiously and with baited breath. The regiment was ordered to break through the enemy lines, to go round the enemy rear and then cut through the extreme flank of the opposing army.

For the first time Olga heard the word "raid."

The regiment set out at once. Emilyanov's squadron led the vanguard. At nightfall they halted in a forest without unbridling their mounts or lighting a fire. A warm rain spattered the leaves, but in the dark one could not see even an outstretched hand. Olga was sitting on a tree stump, when an affectionate hand was suddenly laid on her shoulder: she guessed who it was, sighed and threw back her head. It was Dimitry bending over her.

"You won't weaken, will you? Well, well, look to yourself. And keep closer to me," he said.

Then a low-voiced command rang out and the men silently mounted their horses. Olga swung round blindly and her stirrup touched Dimitry. For a long time they made their way at a walking pace. The earth squelched under the hooves, and there was the smell of mushrooms. Then patches of misty light broke through the dense darkness—the forest was thinning out. To the right now, quite close, they could see needling flashes of flame and dull explosions rolled over the deciduous forests. Then Emilyanov gave a long drawn out shout of "Draw your sabres, charge!" The wet branches began to whip the men's faces, their mounts jostled each other, snorting, and the riders' knees caught against tree trunks. Then, all at once, a misty, sloping meadow spread out in front of them and shadowy horsemen were galloping over it. Abruptly the solid earth was there no longer. Olga thrust her spurs into the horse's flanks and, gathering its hind quarters, the horse plunged into a river. . . .

The regiment broke through the enemy rear. They galloped in the dark beneath low hanging clouds; the steppe hummed under the hooves of five hundred horses. At a gallop, the buglers blew intermittent blasts on their bugles. Then they were ordered to dismount. Epaulettes and cockades were distributed. Emilyanov gathered the men round him:

"For the purpose of disguise, we are now a composite regiment of the North Caucasian Army of Lieutenant General Baron Wrangel. Do you remember that, you chicks? (The men roared.) Who's that laughing there—you'll get it in the teeth. Silence—I'm no "comrade commander" now, but 'His Honor Sir Captain.' " He lighted a match, which revealed a gold epaulette on his shoulder. "You're not 'comrades' now, but the 'lower ranks.' You'll stand to attention, salute, and use all the proper titles of respect. 'Silence, attent-shun!'—Do you understand? (The whole squadron rumbled: the men stood at attention, saluted and added 'little epithets' to titles such as 'Your Honor.') Now attach your epaulettes, hide the red star in your pocket, and stick the cockade on your caps. . . ."

For three days the disguised regiment galloped in the rear of Wrangel's army. Columns of black smoke rose behind it—railway stations, trains and military supplies were burned and ammunition dumps and water supplies were blown up.

On the fourth day the horses were feeling jaded and began to stumble; it was decided to halt in a remote village. Olga, after attending to her mount, fell asleep then and there in the hay. She was wakened by a woman's loud laugh. A fresh-looking peasant woman with her skirt tucked above the bare calves of her legs was speaking to someone and pointing at Olga: "What a handsome lad!" the woman said, as she hung a pair of cleanly washed underpants to dry in the yard.

When Olga entered the hut, she found Emilyanov sitting there, looking drowsy but cheerful, his legs bare and with down in his hair. It was obviously his underpants that had been washed.

"Sit down, they'll bring us some borstch. Would you like a drop of vodka?" he said, addressing Olga. The same fresh-looking peasant girl entered with a cauldron of borsht, turning her cheek away from the aromatically steaming soup. She plumped down the iron pot in front of Emilyanov and announced with a shrug, "You're just in time, here's the borsht!" she spoke in a thin, sing-song voice that was both pert and cheeky. "I've washed your pants and they'll dry in a jiffy . . ." she went on, eyeing Emil-yanov with the eyes of a lustful bitch.

Emilyanov made sounds of approval as he tasted the soup. He looked somehow softer as he sat there. Olga put her spoon down: she felt in her heart as if she had been bitten by a rabid snake; she felt numb and dropped her eyes. When the girl went out of the door, she caught up with her in the entrance, gripped her by the arm and said in a choking whisper:

"Is it death you're wanting?"

The girl uttered a cry, tore her arm free and ran away. Dimitry glanced several times in a surprised way at Olga. What was biting her? When he climbed into the saddle and saw her fierce darkened eyes, her dilated nostrils and noticed also the plain-haired girl peeping, like a frightened rat from behind the shed, he suddenly understood and burst out laughing, displaying all his white teeth in a grin. As they rode out of the gate, he touched Olga's knee with his own and exclaimed with unexpected tenderness: "Ah, you little fool. . . ."

She almost burst into tears.

On the fifth day, they learnt that a whole Cossack division was launched in pursuit of the disguised Red regiment. They began a rapid retreat, abandoning the exhausted mounts. At nightfall a rearguard battle developed. The regimental flag was handed over to the First Squadron. Without stopping, they galloped into some dark, unlighted village. They beat on the shutters with the hilts of their sabres. Dogs howled, but there was no other sign of life in the vicinity; then the bell in the belfry rang out once and stopped.

Two peasants were brought in. They were as shaggy as two wood sprites and had been found hiding in the straw. Looking at the mounted men, they kept repeating:

"Brothers, dear ones, don't kill us. . . ."

"Is your village for the Whites or for the Soviets?" Emilyanov shouted, bending from his saddle.

"Brothers, dear ones, we don't know ourselves. . . . Everything has been taken from us. We've been robbed and ruined. . . ."

They succeeded nevertheless in extracting from them that, though the village was occupied by no one else, they were expecting Wrangel's Cossacks to arrive and that the Bolsheviks were entrenched beyond the river.

The men of the regiment took off their epaulettes, stuck on their red stars, and crossed the bridge to rejoin their own side. Here they learned that the Whites were advancing furiously along the whole front. The Red forces had orders to defend this bridge to the death. But their ammunition was exhausted: the machine gun belts did not fit, the trenches were full of lice, there was no bread at all, and the Red Army men all looked swollen from eating boiled grain. The men were deserting during the night. Their commissar had died of dysentery.

The regimental commander got into direct touch by telephone with Headquarters, which confirmed the order to defend the bridge to the last drop of blood until the Army could escape encirclement.

"We shan't get out alive," Emilyanov said. He filled two kettles with river water, handed one of them to Olga and, squatting down beside her, stared at the vague outlines of the far river bank. A turbid yellow star hung above the river. For a whole day Wrangel's batteries had battered the Bolshevik trenches with their rapid fire. Then, in the evening, the order arrived to force the bridge, to throw back the Whites from the river and to capture the village.

Olga stared at the turbid, motionless glimmer of the star in the river. It communicated a feeling of sadness.

"Well, Olga, let's go," Dimitry said. "Let's snatch an hour's sleep. For the first time he had called her by her name. The stealthy figures of the soldiers with kettles of water crept out of the bushes and climbed the steep bank: access to the river had been cut off during the day and not a drop of water was left. By now everyone knew about the terrifying order. Many thought this was their last night on earth.

"Kiss me," Olga said sadly and yearningly. Emilyanov set the kettle down carefully, drew her to him by the shoulders as her cap fell off and her eyes closed, and began to kiss her on her eyes, mouth and cheeks.

"I'd make you my wife, Olga, but it can't be done now, you understand that. . . ."

The night attacks were beaten off. The Whites strengthened their defences on the bridge, setting up barbed wire at one end and sweeping it with machine guns. A gray morning rose above the misty river and the damp meadows. The earth continuously spurted up on both banks, making it look as if black bushes were springing up. The air howled and squealed as shrapnel exploded in solid little clouds. Some of the men were stupefied by the noise. Many sprawling bodies lay supine near the bridge. All effort seemed futile. The men could no longer advance against the fire of machine guns.

Then, behind the railway embankment, eight communards rode together under the regimental flag; torn and riddled with shot, the flag looked like a patch of blood in the light of dawn. Two squadrons mounted. The regimental commander said: "We have to die, comrades!" and started off at a walk beneath the flag. Dimitry Emilyanov was the eighth communard. They bared their sabres, spurred their horses and rode out from behind the embankment and, at a heavy gallop, dashed over the echoing wooden boards of the bridge.

As Olga watched, the horse of one of them fell against the railings; then rider and horse plunged into the river from a height of about sixty feet. Seven of them reached the middle of the bridge. One more rolled off his saddle as if asleep. The men in front galloped up to the barbed wire and began hacking at it with their sabres. Then the stalwart flag-bearer began to sway in his saddle and the flag dipped; Emilyanov snatched it up but his mount immediately began to flounder.

The bullets sang hotly. Olga was now galloping along the cracked boards at a dizzy height. The iron supports of the bridge shook and hummed as a hundred and fifty throats roared behind Zotova. Dimitry Emilyanov still stood with legs wide apart by the barbed wire and still holding the flag-staff before him; his face was deathly white and blood drooled from his open mouth. Olga seized the flat as she galloped past. He swayed towards the railing and sat down. The squadrons swept by with waving manes, bent backs, flashing blades.

They burst through to the other side; the enemy took to flight, and the sound of the guns grew fainter. For a long time yet the torn and tattered flag waved here and there over the fields until it was lost behind the white willow trees of the village. By then a broad-faced Red Army lad galloped with it, urging his mount with bare heels and shouting as he waved the flag: "Ride them down, smash them!"

Olga was picked up in the field; she had been stunned by the fall and was badly wounded in the thigh. The men of the squadron were extremely sorry for her and did not know how to tell her that Emilyanov had been killed. The men sent a deputation to the regimental commander to request that Olga be given an award. They debated for a long time what to give her. A cigarette case? But she did not smoke. A watch? But women did not wear watches. Then, one of the men discovered that he possessed a gold brooch of pure gold in the shape of a heart pierced by an arrow. The commander had no objection to this award, but he made this reservation in his citation: "Zotova is to be decorated for her exploit with a gold brooch in the form of an arrow, but the heart, as a bourgeois emblem, must be removed. . . ."

Like a bird rushing through a mad, windy sky and then suddenly falling to earth with broken wings, Olga's whole life of passionate, innocent love, was cut short and broken. She now faced a succession of undesired, oppressive and turbid days.

For a long time she lay in field hospitals, was moved to the rear in delapidated freight cars, almost dying of hunger and freezing beneath her worn army coat. The people around her were mostly bad-tempered strangers. To them, she was just a field case with a number, and there was no one she could consult. It was a gloomy, nauseating life, but death spared her.

When she was discharged from the hospital with her head shaven and looking so gaunt that her army coat and her boots flapped about her as on a skeleton, she first made her way to the railway station where, in the unheated waiting rooms, a crowd of inhuman-looking people lived and froze on the bare floor. Where was she to go? The whole world was like an open field. Finally, she returned to town and presented her documents and her arrow-brooch award to the military commander in charge of the recruiting center. Soon she was despatched with a detachment to fight in Siberia.

The thud of wheels on the rails, the heat of the smoking iron-stove, the thousands and thousands of miles, the soldiers' songs as unending as the journey, the stench and the soiled snow round the barracks, the screeching letters of war posters and the devil knows what other placards and bulletins—all these scraps of paper rustling in the frosty air, the gloomy meetings held within wooden walls in the dusky light of smoking paraffin lamps—and then the endless snows again, the pine trees, the smoking bonfires, the familiar sound of pistons, the gnawing chill, the burnt-out villages, the patches of blood on the snow, and the thousands and thousands of corpses scattered like logs of wood spattered with manure. . . . All these things became confused in her memory and swirled in one long spiral of endless suffering.

Olga was now gaunt and swarthy; she had learnt to drink petrol and to smoke *mahorka;* and, when forced, she could swear no worse than the men. Very few of the men regarded her as a woman; she was too gaunt and spiteful—just like a viper. One night in the barracks a fellow soldier, a homeless, front-line man with large lips, who had been nicknamed "Guban" rolled up to her bunk in a lecherous mood; but, with sudden fury, she hit him so hard on the bridge of the nose with the handle of her revolver that he had to be carted off to hospital. This episode killed all desire even to think of "the little viper."

In spring she found herself in Vladivostock. For the first time in her life, she saw the ocean—blue, dark, and alive. Long manes of foam came rushing impetuously towards the shore; the waves, rising on the horizon and then reaching the shore, dashed against the mole and surged up in a scattered cloud of spray. Olga felt a great longing to sail away on a ship.

The images of her childhood dreams were now revived in her memory; shores with fantastic dreams, mountain peaks, a beam of sunshine shining from an infinite space of clouds and the tranquil journey of a small ship. . . . If only she could steam past the Cape of Good Hope and then sit grieving on a stone by the waters of the Zambezi. . . . All that was just fantasy, of course. No one took her on board. But an old pilot in a secret tavern in the port, mistaking her for a prostitute and in his tearful drunkenness pitying her perished youth, insisted on tatooing an anchor on her hand. "Remember," he said, "this is hope of salvation."

The war ended. In the market place, Olga bought a skirt made of green plush curtain. Then she served in various institutions; as a typist in the Executive Committee, as a secretary in the Forest Administration, or as a female scribe shifted from floor to floor together with her desk.

She did not stay long in any one place; she kept moving from town to town, always nearer to the center of Russia. She had thoughts of revisiting that spot overlooking the river where, after filling a kettle with water, she had last sat together with Dimitry. . . . She would also find that willow bush and the place where they had sat together. . . .

She had not forgotten the past. She lived an austere and lonely life. But gradually the harshness of the war days fell away from her. Olga was becoming a woman again. . . .

5

At the age of twenty-two she had to begin a third life. She pictured what was happening now as something equivalent to harnessing a cavalry horse to peaceful labor. The shaken country was still bristling; men's eyes, still bloodshot, sought what they might destroy; but everywhere already, barricading themselves against the recent past, the white pages of decrees summoned people to repair, to reconstruct, and to build.

Olga read and heard all this, but the task seemed harder than war. The towns, in which she lived, had been destroyed with a savage fury; everything was twisted and crumbled, and nettles grew on the side of burnt-out buildings; men were living under mats. They ate and slept, but the sights of war still troubled their dreams. Creativity went no further than the manufacture of bath switches and primitive clay dishes.

The pages of the decrees summoned people to reconstruct and to create. But with whose hands? Why, with one's own hands—the hands that were still clenched like the talons of a bird of prey. . . . Olga loved to wander about the town streets at sunset, glancing at the suspicious, gloomy faces of the people, faces still furrowed with anger, terror and hate; she was well acquainted with those twitching mouths, those gaping holes in place of the teeth, which had been lost during the war.

They had all been through it—the young boy and the old man. And now they wandered about the filthy town, wearing sour-smelling clothes of sackcloth or of bourgeois curtain material and broken-down shoes, ready at any minute to burst out weeping or to kill. . . .

The pages of decrees told them insistently to create, create, create. . . . All right, but that was more difficult than to blow up a bridge, to sabre a gun-crew or to smash with shrapnel the windows of a factory. . . .

Olga would stop in front of some bright placard on a sagging palisade. Some hand had already crossed with a piece of plaster and scratched an obscene word on it. On the poster she saw incredible faces, waving banners, hundred-storied houses, factory chimneys, smoke curling up to the dancing letters, which spelled out: "Industrialization!" Olga had still preserved all the impressionability of a young girl, and she daydreamed as she stared at the decorative poster: she was excited by the vast scope of the imagined construction.

As the sun went down, its last virulent colors burst through a leaden cloud and set fire to the broken windowpanes in the gaping, abandoned houses. Occasionally a passerby went past, chewing sunflower seeds and spitting them out into the mud of the rutted street, where rusty leaves and the offal of eaten cats lay scattered. Sunflower seeds. . . . Man's leisure now was filled with crunching jaws while the brain stayed dormant in the twilight. The seeds took one back to life as lived before the stone age. Olga clenched her fists—she could not reconcile herself to the quiet, the seeds, the bath switches and the huge waste spaces of this god-forsaken town.

Olga finally succeeded in securing a transfer to Moscow; she arrived there full of determination and self-denial in a plush skirt of curtain material.

Olga took the deprivations of everyday life in her stride; she had seen worse days. For the first few weeks in Moscow she camped anywhere she could; then she was allotted a room in the communal apartment house on Zaryadie. After filling out innumerable questionnaires and petitions, she obtained a job in the Control Department of the Semi-Precious Metals Trust. By this time, she was somewhat abashed by the complexity of all the official forms she had to fill in and the hive-like buzz of the many-storied office buildings. She felt rather like a sparrow, which had landed among the thousand-wheel system of a belfry clock. Her tail was between her legs. She came to work punctually, but was overcome with shyness as she watched, for no effort of her mind seemed capable of judging the utility of copying so many papers. Neither her deftness, nor her impulsive daring, nor her viperish fury, seemed to have any point here. This was a world of typewriters which hammered away with their keys as if in a delirium of typhus, a world of rustling papers and of bossy voices muttering into telephone receivers. It was so unlike the war days, when everything was clear and decisive amid the whistling of bullets, and had a tangible end in view. . . .

Gradually she adapted herself, and her "fur stopped bristling." Working days succeeded each other, uniform and dull. To avoid being drowned in this bureaucratic oblivion, she took on additional social work. To club life she applied the discipline and terminology of the squadron. She had to be restrained from being too sharp.

She received her first reprimand from the assistant manager, who sat to one side of her behind the door to the director's office. Her smoking *mahorka* was the cause.

"I'm surprised at you, comrade Zotova," he said. "You're an interesting woman in general, but you're smelling the place out with *mahorka*. . . . Don't you have any sense of femininity? You should smoke Java."

This trifling remark must have been timely. Olga was discomforted and pained. On leaving the office, she stopped in front of a mirror on the staircase landing, and, for the first time in many years, examined herself as a woman: "Devil take it—a regular scarecrow!" Her worn plush skirt was pulled up higher in front and had been trampled on behind; on her feet was a pair of men's shoes; then a gray satin blouse. . . . How had she allowed this to happen?

Two typists in attractive skirts and pink socks giggled as they glanced at Olga standing there wildly in front of the mirror. All she caught was ". . . enough to frighten a horse . . ." Blood flooded Olga's beautiful gypsy face. One of the typists was Sonechka Varentzova, who lived in the same apartment as Olga.

Several days later the women, who inhabited the apartment in Pskovsky Street in the Zaryadie quarter, were amazed at what Olga did next. Entering the kitchen in the morning, she fixed her glittering eyes, like a viper, on Sonechka Varentzova, who was preparing some gruel. Olga strode up to her and, pointing to her stockings, asked: "Where did you buy those?" Then, lifting up Sonechka's skirt and pointing to her undergarments, she asked again: "And where did you buy those?" Her questions sounded spiteful, as if she were slashing with a sabre.

Sonechka, a gentle girl by nature, was alarmed by her abrupt gestures. Rosa Abramovna came to her help; in a soft voice she explained in detail that these articles could be obtained on the Kuznetzky Most, that women now wore "chemise" dresses, flesh-colored stockings, and so on.

Olga, as she listened, kept nodding her head and repeating: "Yes . . . I understand . . . quite so . . ." Then seizing Sonechka by her tender curly hair, which in no way resembled a horse's mane, she demanded:

"And this—how do you comb it?"

"You must trim it first, my golden one," Rosa Abramovna purred, "short behind, a parting to one side in front. . . ."

Peter Semeonovich Morsh, who had just entered the kitchen, listened and then spat out, his bald pate glistening as usual:

"It's late in the day you're making a transition from war communism, Olga Vyacheslavovna. . . ."

Olga turned on him impetuously (later they said that she gnashed her teeth) and replied quietly but clearly:

"You unslaughtered pig! If I only met you in the field. . . ."

All the employees of the Trust were dumbfounded for a minute when Olga turned up to work in a black silk dress with short sleeves, flesh-colored stockings and a pair of lacquered shoes; her chestnut hair was trimmed and glossy as black-brown fur. She sat down at her desk and bent her head over the papers—her ears were burning.

The assistant manager, a young and naïve fellow, goggled at her as he sat at the madly ringing telephone.

"Hells bells!" he exclaimed. "Where's this from?"

Actually Olga Zotova was strikingly handsome: she had a small graceful face with dark down, eyes deep as the night, long eyelashes, her hands washed clean of ink. In a word, one could say a lot about her. Even the manager himself peeped out of his office and shot his leaden eyes at her:

"A forceful girl," he commented later.

People from other offices ran in to stare at her. They talked of nothing but Olga Zotova's amazing transformation.

After the first moment of confusion, Olga wore this new skin of hers easily and freely, just as she had in the past her school dress or the cavalry helmet, the tightly-laced cavalry coat and the spurs. If the men pressed too much, she dropped her eyelashes, as if veiling her soul, in passing.

At five o'clock on the third day, when Olga had torn off a piece of blotter and, wetting it with saliva, was trying to wipe off an inkstain from her elbow, the assistant manager, Ivan Feodorovich Pedotti, a young man, approached her and told her that they "must have a very serious talk." Olga raising her handsome eyebrows slightly, put on her hat. They went out together.

"It would be simpler to go to my place, just round the corner," Pedotti suggested.

Olga shrugged her shoulder slightly. They went on. Gusts of warm wind stirred the dust. They climbed to the fourth floor. Olga was the first to enter the room and to sit down in a chair.

"Well," she asked, "what is it you wanted to talk about?"

Pedotti flung his briefcase on the bed, rumpled his hair and began to hammer the stale air of the room with his fist.

"Comrade Zotova, we always make a frontal assault on any problem . . . in fighting order. . . . Sexual attraction is a real fact, a natural necessity. . . . It's time to throw all that Romanticism overboard. . . . So that's it. . . . I have explained everything. . . . You understand everything. . . ."

He gripped Olga under the armpits and began pulling her towards him, towards his chest, in which his unsophisticated heart beat furiously as on the edge of a precipice. But he immediately encountered resistance. It was not so easy to drag Zotova from her chair: she was slender but resilient. Without losing her head, calmly almost, Olga gripped both his wrists and twisted them so that he gasped loudly, tried to free himself, and, as she persisted in her torture, cried out:

"You're hurting me, let me go. Go to the devil. . . ."

"You should ask permission before pushing, you fool," she replied.

She let Pedotti go, picked up a *Java* cigarette from the box on the table, lit it and walked out.

Olga tossed in bed all that night. She would get up, smoke by the window and then try again to bury her head in a pillow. She recalled the whole of her former life: her buried past came to life and made her deeply nostalgic. . . . A devilish night this. But why? Why? Was it not possible to live a life as cool as spring water, without all this amorous fever? But she realized with a shudder that life, for all the shaking and pounding it had given her, had not knocked the "nonsense" out of her, and "this" would begin now. . . . There was no way of avoiding it. . . .

Next morning Olga, on her way to washing, heard laughter and Sonechka Varentzova's voice in the kitchen:

"Amazing the airs she puts on. It's revolting even to watch her. . . . But you can't touch her, she's so persniketty. . . . When she filled in the form, she actually called herself 'a maiden.' . . . (Laughter, the hissing of primuses.) But they all say she was just a camp follower to the squadron. . . . You understand? She slept almost with the whole squadron. . . ."

"A clear case of the pox!" Maria Afanasieva, the seamstress, exclaimed.

"But looks like the Baroness Rothschild," said Rosa Abramovna.

"Treat her with caution. I took that viper's measure a long

time ago. . . . She'll make a career for herself before you've
time to blink. . . ." Peter Semeonovich Morsh's bass voice put
in.

"You always exaggerate, Pyotr Semeonovich. . . . Rest assured, you can't make a career with what she's got. . . ." Sonechka Varentzova, and the wrinkles round her mouth, expressed
such contempt that the women began to writhe. But there was
no vituperation this time.

After the incident with Pedotti, who now began to hate Olga
with all the force of his chastened masculine vanity, Zotova
found herself ringed by the silent hostility of the women and the
ironic attitude of the men. They were afraid to quarrel openly
with her. But she could feel their enmity boring into the back of
her head. She was now nicknamed "the viper," "the branded
one," "the wench of the squadron." She could hear the whispers
and see these names on the blotting paper. But, strangely enough,
she took all this nonsense badly, as if it were possible to affirm:
"I'm not as you paint me!"

Dimitry had hit the mark when he called her a gypsy once.
. . . She was depressed to find desire awakening in her, this time
with all the force of maturity. Her virginity was in revolt. But
what was she to do? Bathe herself from head to foot in icy water?
She had already burnt herself too painfully, and to throw herself
into the fire again was terrifying. . . . It was unnecessary, horrible. . . .

Olga had looked at the man a minute only, and her whole being
told her: this is *he*. It was as inexplicable and catastrophic as
running into a bus swinging round a corner.

The large man in the canvas jacket, who had begun to put on
weight, stood on the landing of the stairs reading a wall-news-
paper. Employees were running out of various doors and hurrying past him up and down the stairs. There was a smell of dust
and tobacco. Everything looked normal. With a lazy smile the
man was examining a caricature in the middle of the paper aimed
against the economics director of the Mahorka Trust on the next
floor. Since Olga had also stopped to read the paper, he turned
to her, and, pointing at the caricature (he had a heavy, large and
handsome wrist) said:

"You're in the editorial department, I believe, comrade Zotova. (He had a strong, low voice.) They can draw me with a mane and tail, if they like. . . . But this sort of thing is unnecessary; it's so petty and untalented!"

The caricature showed him with a glass of tea, between two ringing telephones. The wit consisted in suggesting that he liked drinking tea during office hours.

"They were afraid to bite and merely barked like lackeys. . . . Well, and what about tea. . . . In 'nineteen' I used to drink pure alcohol mixed with cocaine just to keep awake. . . ."

Olga glanced into his eyes: they were gray, cool, the color of tired steel; in a way they reminded her of the eyes she had loved and which had closed forever. . . . A clean-shaven face, regular, prominent features, a lazy and knowing smile. She recalled then that, in 'nineteen,' he had been the supplies dictator in Siberia; he had supplied the army, and his name had inspired terror for tens of thousands of miles around. . . . She had pictured men like him with their heads in the clouds. He had dealt with the events and life as with a pack of cards. And here was this man with a briefcase and a tired smile, while the life he had helped to bring about ran past him, elbowing him. . . .

"It isn't so smart to diminish everything in this way," he continued. "You could reduce the whole Revolution to a cheap caricature. . . . The old men have done their bit, they say, and now to the scrap heap with them. We've got our salary, so let's drink beer. . . . Youth's a fine thing, but it's dangerous to cut yourself off from the past. . . . It's an ephemeral thing to live only for today. . . . That's it. . . ."

He went his way. Olga stared at his powerful head, at his broad back, as he ascended slowly the stone steps towards the Mahorka Trust. It seemed to her that he was making an effort not to stoop under the burden of the times. . . . She felt a sharp twinge of compassion. And, as we all know, compassion . . .

At the first opportunity Olga, with a chit from the local committee, ascended to the gloomy offices of the Mahorka Trust and entered the office of the economics director. He was stirring a glass of tea with a spoon; a rich bun lay on his briefcase. A typist was tapping away by the window. Olga was so agitated, she paid no attention to the typist and only saw those steely eyes. He read the chit and signed it. She remained standing.

"That's all, comrade. You may go," he said.

That was really all. When Olga closed the door behind her, she thought she heard the typist giggle. The only thing left for her, she felt, was to lose her reason.

No one would hit her with an iron weight again, no one would shoot her in a cellar; Dimitry would not carry her in his arms again or sit by her bed or promise her a pair of boots that had belonged to a shot schoolboy.

It is better not to recall how Olga spent that night. In the morning, when the lodgers peeped through her keyhole, Pyotr Semeonovich Morsh suggested they might try blowing some ten grams of iodoform into her room. "Our viper's in a rage," the lodgers said in the kitchen. Sonechka Varentzova smiled enigmatically, while her pale blue eyes shone calmly and with a sense of unshakeable security.

It is harder to overcome modesty than the fear of death; but Olga had gone through a battle school. She must act, she was sure of that. To wait for an opportunity, for happiness, to act in a frivolous way by displaying her flesh-colored stocking here or revealing hastily a bare shoulder was not her way. She resolved to approach him directly and tell him everything. Let him then do what he wished with her. . . .

She ran after him several times on the stairs, intending to catch him by the sleeve and say: "I love you, I am dying without you. . . ." But each time he got into his car without even noticing her in a crowd of other employees. . . . It was at this time that she threw the primus at Zotov. The atmosphere of the communal apartment grew electrically tense. Sonechka Varentzova was now very nervous and left the kitchen whenever she heard Olga's steps. Vladimir Lvovich Ponizovsky, the humorist, penetrated into Olga's room with a duplicate key and placed a clothes brush under her mattress, but she slept the night through without noticing anything.

Finally, *he* went home on foot one day (the car was being repaired). Olga caught up with him and hailed him brusquely her mouth and throat were dry. She walked beside him, stepping awkwardly, her elbows protruding and her eyes lowered. The second lasted as long as eternity; she felt both hot and cold, tender and angry. But *he* walked on indifferently, unsmiling and stern. . . .

"What I want to . . ."

"What I want to say is this," he interrupted Olga at once and went on squeamishly. "They've been telling me about you on every side. . . . I'm surprised, yes, yes. . . . You are persecuting me. . . . Your intentions are obvious—please, don't lie, I don't need any explanation. . . . But you've forgotten that I'm no *nepman*[1]. My mouth doesn't water at the sight of every pretty little face. . . . You've shown your good side in social work. My advice to you is to abandon any idea of silk stockings, face powder and such things. You could make a good comrade."

Without bidding her goodbye, he crossed the street where, near a pastry shop, Sonechka Varentzova took him by the hand. Shrugging her shoulders and talking indignantly, she tried to tell him something. Frowning squeamishly, he freed his hand and walked on with her, his head lowered. The fumes from the exhaust pipe of a bus hid them from Olga.

Thus, Sonechka Varentzova had turned out to be the heroine. She it was who kept the economics director of the Mahorka Trust informed of the past and present life of Zotova, "the wench of the squadron." Sonechka was triumphant, but frightened at the same time.

On the Sunday morning we have already described, Sonechka ran back to her room on hearing Olga's door creak, and burst out crying because she found it intolerable to have to live in perpetual fear. Olga, after she had finished bathing, exclaimed twice for some unknown reason: "This is the devil knows what!" She did this once in the kitchen and the second time, in her room. Then she left the building.

The lodgers gathered again in the kitchen: Peter Semeonovich in his Sunday trousers and a new cap with a white crown; Vladimir Lvovich, unshaven and cheerfully drunk. Rosa Abra-

[1] *Nepman*—a Soviet citizen who took advantage of the elated atmosphere of the New Economic Policy in the 1920's.

movna was making plum jam, and Maria Afanasievna was ironing a blouse. They all chattered and joked. Then Sonechka Varentzova reappeared with swollen eyes.

"I can't stand it any more," she declared on the threshold. "It must stop, come to an end. . . . She'll throw vitriol at me. . . ."

Ponizovsky immediately suggested shaving off the bristles of the clothes brush and putting them every day in the viper's bed so that, unable to bear it, she would quit the apartment. Morsh suggested chemical warfare by means of hydrogen sulphide or again with iodoform. These were all masculine fantasies. Only Maria Afanasievna spoke to the point:

"You're extremely secretive, Sonechka, but won't you admit that you have officialized your tie with the director?"

"Yes," Sonechka replied, "we went to the registry office a couple of days ago. I even insisted on a church wedding, but that is impossible for the time being."

"Live a little longer, and we'll see," Morsh croaked, his bald pate glistening.

"What you should do is to wave your marriage certificate in front of that reptile's ugly mug," Maria Afanasievna exclaimed, brandishing her iron.

"Oh, no. . . . Never in the world. . . . I'm frightened. . . . I have a strong sense of foreboding," Sonechka replied.

"We'll stand behind the door . . . you musn't be afraid . . ." they all chimed in."

"We'll stand behind the door, armed with the weapons of the kitchen," Vladimir Lvovich bleated like a lamb in his drunken joy. They persuaded Sonechka.

Olga Vyacheslavovna returned home at eight with an earth-gray face and stooping with exhaustion. She locked herself in and sat down on the bed, dropping her hands on her knees. . . . She was alone, all alone amid this savage, hostile life, lonely as in the hour of her death, and feeling quite unwanted. . . . Since yesterday she had become terribly distraught. She suddenly noticed that she held a revolver in her hand, but she could not remember taking it off the wall. She sat there thinking and staring at the deadly steel toy. . . .

There was a knock on the door. Olga sat up with a start. The knocking sounded louder. She rose and flung open the door. The lodgers skulking behind it drew back—they seemed to be holding brushes and pokers in their hands. Sonechka Varentzova, her face pale, her lips compressed, swept into the room. In a high, cracking voice, she burst out:

"It's absolutely disgraceful—to run after a married man. . . . Here is the marriage certificate. . . . Everyone knows you have venereal disease . . . and that you intend to make a career of it for yourself . . . and through my lawful husband. . . . You're a vile creature! . . . Here's the certificate. . . ."

Olga stared, like a blind woman, at the screaming Sonechka. Then a wave of familiar hatred rolled up and gripped her throat; all her muscles tightened like steel. A howl burst from her throat. . . . Olga Vyacheslavovna pulled the trigger and went on shooting at the white, panic-stricken face in front of her. . . .

15 July 1928

BORIS PILNYAK

With Earth-Soiled Hands

IN THE SUMMER, at the beginning of June, windows in provincial Russian towns should be flung open early in the morning to allow the gently wafted air of June to wander freely through the rooms. The rooms then grow cool and imbued with the greenish light of the linden and maple trees, which grow in the ancient gardens outside. With its foliage, the wild vine on the terrace masks the gold of day. On such days man feels an ally of the earth.

One such morning, the husband was sitting at his writing desk by the open window, in the corner furthest away from the door giving on the terrace. He was engrossed in his papers and thoughts, while his wife, in the gold of the morning, was busy digging in the garden around the flowerbeds disposed among the lilac bushes. Now and then the wife would come walking on the terrace, wearing a three-cornered neckerchief and holding her earth-soiled hands at a distance from her thighs to avoid staining her dress. It is a rare, very rare joy to feel at amity with the earth. It is a very, very rare joy—that of marriage, love, trust and faithfulness. This joy was present in the house, the joy of trust, friendship, love and companionship. This joy is granted only to people of noble thought and design; and these particular people were worthy, simple and hardworking. He was a sociologist and writer; she, an artist; and they had met each other when he was over thirty-five, and she past thirty. There is a joyful form of repose, which tries the muscles: that of digging the soil, planting tobaccos and resin in beds, and plucking all sorts of weeds from the flowerbeds; and a wonderful thing it is to know, as one bends over the soil, that here, in this soil, one has planted something one has sown oneself. Before sitting down to his books, the husband, too, had worked at the flowerbeds beside his wife. The books on the table now stimulated accustomed thoughts, figures, comparisons, quotations, objections, formulae; stimulated genuine labor, that of hours when the eyes of the scientist as well as of the artist grow completely vague, unseeing and completely abstracted from the world beyond the immediate books to hand.

In this state of abstraction, the husband heard a stranger enter the courtyard through the unlocked garden gate, a stranger in a wide-brimmed hat, apparently, and carrying a small valise, apparently. The new arrival announced through the open window that he must see Anna Andreyevna. The husband answered, without raising his head from the papers, that she was in the garden.

In the same state of abstraction, the husband failed to notice how many minutes had passed before his wife came into the room, from the terrace, in the company of the stranger, again holding her earth-soiled hands at a distance from her dress. He did not recall the look on his wife's face. The stranger bowed. The stranger said:

"If you will allow me, I should like to spend a few more minutes alone with Anna."

And Anna added:

"Yes, Paul, I shall take Sergey to my room."

Again the husband failed to notice his wife's face. And again some minutes elapsed, during which eyes are oblivious of the world and the world is made up only of books. Then Anna emerged from her room. Raising his vacant eyes, Paul saw that his wife's hands, which were still earth-soiled, were now twisted in a hopeless gesture, and that her eyes were brimmed with impotent tears. Paul rediscovered the world of objects.

The stranger spoke then. Anna, with her back turned on both of them, stood in the doorway to the terrace. And the gold of day, except for the vine, was cut off by her shoulders.

"Paul Andreyevich," the stranger began and then paused for a long moment. "Paul Andreyevich, we are no thieves, either of us. I am moved by human feelings." Here he stopped to collect his thoughts and to give them a precise form. "I have not seen Anna for thirteen years, and all these thirteen years I have been dreaming and thinking of her. As you know, we parted in Paris when, as a Russian soldier, I fought at the French front. As you know, she spent her youth with me; and, as you know, neither she herself, nor you, have any cause to reproach her. Our globe is still sufficiently large to get lost in. I have now come to Anna after you have already been married to her for eight years. We are now, all of us, very adult people. I had no idea Anna was married."

Before Paul stood a man whose memory they had held sacred during the years of their married life—Anna's first husband, a worthy man; but now he looked aged and grayhaired. As an artist, he had once instructed Anna in the art of painting and a dignified way of life. The elderly man's eyes were kind; they stared at Paul fondly and in perplexity. They could not look otherwise, because there was a unique and beloved woman in the room, and because this man was generous. Paul remembered that he, too, was grizzled, having prematurely turned gray during the years of the Russian tempest; and his eyes were also as generous and perplexed, for they too were naturally given to kindness. The two men now confronting each other were very alike—no wonder Anna loved both of them. Paul's remembrance of what Anna had told him about Sergey as a young and wonderful artist, as a man of sunlit clarity and firm emotions—the remembrance of these accounts now became confused with the image of this kind-looking, elderly man, who was gazing at them with fond and tired eyes. This man had escaped from death. And Paul exclaimed in confusion:

"How you have changed, Sergey . . . Sergey Ivanovich!"

Both men exchanged a very confused smile. Then Paul held out his hand. He gripped and retained it. From the tingling of his spine and the nervous quiver in the region of his shoulder blades, he became aware of himself, Anna and the new arrival. Anna, a pure woman, had loved only these two men in all her life. Anna had respected Sergey's memory, just as he, Paul, had respected the memory of this man, who had once loved his present wife and who, according to a written statement in her possession from a French infantry regiment, had been certified as a Russian artist and a private soldier of this regiment killed in one of the battles at Verdun. Between these three people there existed a particularly mysterious and sacred bond, that of a particularly mysterious and sacred love. Anna's first love had been given to Sergey; her last love had been taken by Paul. Paul respected Sergey's memory. He remembered now that, caring as he did for his wife, he had never once in all the years of their love asked her about her feelings towards Sergey and, preserving his memory, had never compared himself to him. Paul was now holding Sergey's hand. Wife! By the tingling of his spine and the quiver in his shoulders, Paul felt that, as from this moment, he could not even mentally call Anna "his wife," for, as Sergey had said, he was no thief.

He held Sergey's hand for a long while. Sergey's eyes remained immobile.

"Yes, Sergey, I am, of course, no thief," Paul affirmed.

Anna turned towards them. Anna approached them. Her hands, held at a distance from her dress, had grown stiff. Tears brimmed her eyes. Sergey held out his hands to her, palms uppermost. Anna lowered her eyes, and Paul understood that this was a customary gesture of Sergey's, which Anna knew well. He, too, lowered his eyes, just as people drop their eyes shyly when wishing to avoid noticing something they have no desire to see. Anna understood Paul's lowered eyes, and she held out her hands to Paul. Paul did not see this. Anna was left with her hands outstretched.

"I'll go and wash my hands!" Anna cried out.

"Go," said Paul.

"Anna . . . Paul Andreyevich," Sergey began, his lips twitching as though from physical pain, "Anna, darling Anna, if it is your wish, I'll depart at once, forever this time, Annushka. Yes, I've aged a lot, Paul Andreyevich, aged a lot."

Anna, forgetting about her hands, sat down helpless on a chair near the table.

"No, what do you mean, what do you mean?" Paul began.

"Anna has always talked so much and so wonderfully about you. We have photographs of you, and it seemed the image I had . . . no, no, Serezha!" Paul had called Sergey by the name Anna referred to him when reminiscing. "No, wait, Serezha. You have changed only by comparison with the photograph."

Anna's hands, still soiled with earth, were held out to Paul with the same gesture that Sergey had used when holding out his hands to Anna, a gesture borrowed, as Paul understood, from Sergey. Paul now held out both of his hands to Anna and kissed the earth on Anna's hands, kissed the black, damp earth with all the tenderness he felt for this woman. Then he flicked some earth from his lips.

"Yes, yes, our mother earth," he said to himself. "But, Annushka, (here he caught himself calling her by the name Sergey used) I am no thief. I have just realized that I cannot call you my wife—just as Serezha probably can't—until you yourself call me your husband." Paul flicked some more earth from his lips. "How strangely time moves. Now the three of us . . . how shall I put it? What is to me the most wonderful thing in life—you knew it before me, Serezha; and I got to know what you regarded as most holy, your only mystery. But I am at a loss for words."

Anna rose from the chair. For a second she stood motionless. Her will had lost its strength. She went up to Sergey and embraced him. Paul, like Sergey, understood that Anna was protecting Sergey when she held out her hands to Paul; and she was protecting Paul when she went over to Sergey. Leaning her head on Sergey's chest, Anna began speaking:

"I am frightened, Serezha; I am frightened, Paul. How I waited for you, Serezha, after you had gone to the front! How hard I took it when I received in Russia the news of your death! You know how much I loved you. Now you have arrived, I am so glad! No, these are no mere words; you have returned, not just arrived, and I love you. But I also love Paul. I have a son. We have a son, my only son, and I shall have no more children. I am very frightened. I can't think. Do you hear, Paul? I can't think."

Paul approached Anna, embraced Anna and Sergey, leaned his head on Anna's shoulder.

"Annushka," Paul said, calling her as Sergey did and not correcting himself, "Annushka, my love, you know, my love, you know that I, like Serezha, wish you only happiness, happiness only. . . . You know, we are waiting to hear what you will say."

Paul was at a loss for further words because of the great, beautiful, and compassionate love he felt for Anna, because of his gratitude to humanity for the humanity, the humanity, which had created Anna. He fell silent, bowing his head. The universe, with all its gratitude and bitterness, beat in his heart. He wanted to glance at Anna's face, and he did not at once distinguish her features; it was dark in the room, for the day had grown dim outside. Then absent-mindedness, that abstraction from time, which fell upon Paul in the hours of his table work, now gripped all three of them at this hour when the three of them stood there, embracing and arresting time. It was a whitish dusk, that of a white, Russian, June night. The earth had doffed its gold. The room smelled of stocks. There was a twittering of hedge-sparrows in the garden. Anna's face, with its closed eyes, looked helpless. Her hands, still soiled with earth, hung limply over Sergey's shoulders to avoid staining his jacket.

"Night already," Paul exclaimed in surprise. "Annushka, go and wash your hands; they've got earth on them."

Paul took Anna's hands. Tenderly Paul kissed the earth on Anna's hands. Anna's face was happy. She walked to the door on the way to her room to wash the earth from her hands. The windows of the rooms were wide open, and the green evening air wandered about the house. At an hour such as this man is an ally of the earth.

ILYA EHRENBURG

Merry Paolo

THE AIR OF TIFLIS is keen and filled with an old caress. It invites to an easy life in the midst of wine and green leeks. It invites also to an easy death. I have only to remember bright-eyed Paolo, and I begin to smile. I am ready then to believe in you, in myself, and in the gaunt plane trees of the Botanical Gardens, which on this October night are engaged in a disputation with the dull, disgraceful rain.

Paolo was awakened in the early morning by his friend, Chihoshvili, who nervously threw up the blind, letting in the honeylight of the neighboring hills to suffuse the gray walls. Empty bottles, frayed slippers, a candle-end, and a Balzac novel stained with stearin lay in confusion by the bed. Paolo had, perhaps, been drinking wine the evening before? Or had he been reading *La Peau de Chagrin* all night? Chihoshvili, however, had no time for speculation. Sitting down upon the bed, he spread out his hands and said:

"Listen, Paolo, you must leave today. The Kutais letter has fallen into Vanidze's possession. I have just heard about it. If you don't leave today, you will undoubtedly be arrested. You must make haste, Paolo! I have made arrangements with the chauffeur. He will drive you as far as Oguset . . ."

Paolo leaped up and, merrily flapping his bare feet, went over to the window. Bracing himself slightly, he pressed against the obstinate frame. The neighing of mules, the rumble from a nearby stable, the cries of sour-milk traders, poured into the room. Paolo glanced smilingly at the empty bottles and *La Peau de Chagrin*. He breathed in the air greedily, and his hairy chest could be seen rising and falling. Then, at last, he remembered Chihoshvili's fear-inspiring words. He shook his head.

"Vanidze's a dog. But I shall not leave. No, don't try to persuade me! I won't go all the same. I never learned how to play hide-and-seek. It's better not to talk about it. Come and have dinner with me tonight at Anania's."

Chihoshvili pleaded. Paolo, however, was no longer paying any attention. Leaning out of the window, he shouted:

"Hey, friend, bring it along in here! And the freshest you have . . ."

Spreading out a sheet of newspaper, he sliced a large fragrant melon, smelled it, shook the seeds out carefully and, handing half of it to Chihoshvili, began eating it bite by bite.

"Those Balzac heroes lived well: loudly, ambitiously, with a bang! Well, and now I've got to dress!"

He pulled out a fragment of a mirror from underneath a pile of newspapers, breathed on it, and then wiped it with his sleeve. He shaved himself with the greatest care. His fingers smoothed down his cheek as, deftly and a trifle coquettishly, he guided the razor along. But while soaping his chin, he suddenly became lost in thought. The hand with the brush remained poised in the air as though it had been on Sossy's, the barber's, signboard. He continued thinking aloud:

"Do you know, Chihoshvili, they say your mustache goes on growing after you die. How stupid it all is!"

Chihoshvili did not answer. He muttered, with a loud sigh:

"I tell you, Paolo, you must go! Go, quick!"

But Paolo had already recovered his self-possession. He finished shaving. He dressed quickly. He fumbled for a minute, selecting a tie. Which shall it be: the Turkish foulard or the lilac one with the yellow dots? He picked a red foulard with white stripes.

They went out together, but separated immediately. Chihoshvili was in a hurry to go about his business, while Paolo had taken it into his head to go to the "bazaar"; for this was more than an

ordinary day for him. He did not miss a single face or signboard. He smiled at the carriers who, pillowed on their saddles,
were drowsing at the street corners, and he smiled at the nice
watermelons. Passing along the narrow aisles of the bazaar, he
dilated his nostrils as joyfully as a bloodhound. The smell of
leather, sheep's fat and tarragon buoyed up his spirits. He loved
Tiflis—there was no getting away from that. Here he had been
born, here he had lived his thirty-seven years, as simple in their
flower-like unfolding as those merry drawings on the walls of
cellars where wild panthers, milder than kittens, are to be seen
and men with bull's horns, full of "kahetin" wine, in their
hands.

He stopped in at a jeweler's he knew. For a long time he examined a Daghestan rifle, shaking his head disapprovingly: "Ai, ai,
ai! trash for fools!" The jeweler, with a sly smile, pulled out a
dagger from the box.

"Here, if you like . . . Here is one made for you."

Paolo began admiring the fine workmanship. Yes, that was a
dagger! He patted the thick-lipped jeweler on the shoulder:

"No cash . . . In the spring, maybe . . ."

Queer Paolo! Hadn't he understood Chihoshvili's words? He
smiled, and his large horse-teeth glittered in the sun like a Persian necklace. He then went up to the shoemaker Michael and
proceeded to give him a scare: "Hands up, you rich old huckster,
you!" They both laughed. The young simpleton from the cheese-
factory laughed, too, as he stood there on one leg like a stork,
waiting for Michael to mend his heel. The shop had a tarry,
sweaty smell. Michael invited Paolo to taste some grapes.

"Well, do you want your hoofs mended?"

"No, I'll wear them for another three years."

Boys selling corn were bawling. Two cars had collided in the
narrow street, and the drivers were swearing at each other, but
their abuse was as sweet as golden muscat.

It was becoming hot. Paolo strolled toward the main street.
On the way, he stopped at almost every kiosk with fruit syrups
on display. He gazed with awe, like a child, on the slender goblets
filled with the many-colored syrups. He hesitated between the
orange and the purple, and ended up by trying them all: the

cornel was there, the almond, and the grenadine. The syrup was iced, and Paolo half shut his eyes with pleasure. What could be sweeter on a sultry day? A Balzac heroine? A leather love-amulet? A quick, asthmatic sort of death? And Paolo—remembering the stearin-stained volume, felt sad for a moment: Nina . . . of course, he had to say good-by to Nina! But in a second, he was smiling once more, for a fat Armenian woman, who looked like a fish, was rolling toward him, scarcely able to move her short stumps; and in her woven net there was fish from the bazaar.

A queer lot, these Armenians! Why are they so fond of fish! And Paolo went on, laughingly. He had to bow at every step now. The men on the corners were all good friends of his, boon companions. Who was there Paolo did not know? He shook hands with officers, poets and cigarette-vendors. He had a pleasant word for all. With Nivadze, he spoke of the dancer, Tamara, and then of the cunning Englishman; Nivadze was a lady's man and a diplomat. But he merely tickled the stout Nashvili's stomach and groaned caressingly, "Hot, ah!"

Paolo invited some of them to have dinner with him at Anania's: "Come along, there will be music." A few were astonished: what sort of feast was this? Then Paolo would reply, with a cunningly naïve look in his eyes: "It's my name-day."

Suddenly, he saw Vanidze, yes, that very Vanidze of whom Chihoshvili had spoken. Vanidze was walking along, deep in thought. He was swinging his portfolio, and without looking where he was going, bumped into Paolo. Had it not been for this, Paolo probably would have passed him by. He would not have stopped Vanidze; why distress himself or him? For Vanidze, after all, was Paolo's nephew, and they had gone boar-hunting together more than once in those days when Noy Vanidze had managed to get along without a portfolio and Paolo was not in the habit of scribbling crazy notes. But what was to be done now? Vanidze, on the run, swung his portfolio plump into Paolo's side, and Paolo, forgetful of all historic events, laughed out good-naturedly:

"A head-on collision! Well, how's life treating you, Noy?"

Vanidze was painfully embarrassed and at a loss to conceal the fact. Paolo! The one person he did not want to meet that day!

Friendship, good times, love of drink, the same girls, the same stars—all this was a binding tie. But Vanidze was the slave of an idea, hot, dull, like the eyes of a woman who is charming but no longer young, and who is taking leave of a lover as fickle as the wind. That was why Vanidze did not embrace Paolo; but, on the other hand, he did not run away. Instead, he remarked:

"Good day, Paolo. I'm in a hurry, on business."

It would have seemed that, after such a chance meeting, they would have parted. But Paolo was so merry that day, so full of good will for the world, that he would not let go of Vanidze's hand.

"I've been aching to see you, Noy! How long is it since we saw each other last? Yes, four months already. And you are always busy now: business, business. Ah, Noy, Noy, do you remember how we spent that night in the tavern at Passa-ur, where the blind Tartars sang us some stupid song about a blind sultana until we could have wept? That was long ago! No, wait! We only meet once in an age, and right away it's good-by? Busy? Then come and dine at Anania's. It's my name-day today. You don't believe me? You're a queer fellow! Have you made a note of it? You'll come? Be sure, you don't go back on us . . ."

What had led Paolo to invite his mortal enemy to Anania's? It may have been for no reason at all; for he had invited many. Well, they had met, had recalled old times—they had spent more than one night in Passa-ur—well, and so he had invited him to come along. Perhaps, too, he had something in the back of his head. Perhaps, amid the foliage and the mist of wine, he desired to look once more into Destiny's dull eyes?

Vanidze was giving in; he smiled. Good, he will come to Anania's! But he must be running along now—he's late as it is. The Commission . . . the Reports . . .

Paolo was now crossing a bridge. Rafts were swarming about like ducklings on the Kura. Light-heartedness had given way to thoughtfulness. That was probably the effect of the river. Water, be it the sea or the finest of fine rain, teaches man severity and silence. Paolo's eyes were now sad and beautiful. I have seen such eyes on old mules. Paolo did not want to die. He loved these houses by the Kura, the hills and the vines, Balzac novels and bright-colored neckties, and Nina's feet, tiny toy-like feet, which caused even the old carriers to prophesy wonderingly: "Ech dear, you are going to take a tumble!" He loved the magic non-sense of life.

He came to a stop. About him were sheep with branded backs, a staid old car, a cartload of brushwood, the heat, and an intrusive song. Then, Paolo arrogantly began to declaim French verses. He loved that language, perhaps because he had never heard it spoken. It was the language of imaginary heroes. In it, one could easily converse with Nina's photographs, with the rafts on the Kura, with oneself. He repeated some verses about a ship. A buzz gradually filled his ears. He was no longer thinking of Tiflis, nor of Nina's feet, nor of death. He was swimming.

But here was Anania's garden. An end to philosophizing, Paolo! Today, you are alive and merry. You have invited your friends to dinner. Paolo no longer heard the creaking of the riggings. Picking out the coolest bower in the garden, he had a long dis-cussion with Anania about the food with which he was to regale his cherished guests. Trout, chicken, and, of course "shashlyk," and fried cheese. And also, a grilled steak, perhaps? And a dozen fragrant melons? And wine? Anania must not be sparing. For Paolo knew that he had the wonderful bottle of Napareuli hidden in his cellar. Why mix it with sour water!

"Today, I'm going to have a great feast, Anania. You will have to split yourself. Bring on the Napareuli."

All of them came, even Vanidze. Seeing the latter, some frowned. Why had Vanidze been invited? You couldn't breathe free in his presence. But Paolo's good spirits were equal to the occasion. They had not finished with the "shashlyk" when the stout Nashvili started embracing Vanidze. "To the health of our friend, Paolo!" Chihoshvili alone was unable to reconcile him-self to Paolo's strange whim. He did not care to look at Vanidze. Remarking that the heat had given him a nosebleed, he went away in spite of Paolo's efforts to detain him. As he left, he called Paolo to one side:

"In case you change your mind, I'll be waiting for you at Vassa all evening. Remember, the machine is ready. Well, my friend, good-by!"

As he said this, he kissed Paolo sadly on the lips.

When he came back to his guests, Paolo looked pale and grim.

"What is the matter with you, Paolo?"

"Nothing at all! It's the heat! Well, I love Chihoshvili, anyway; he's not a man; he's a lion."

In a moment's time, Paolo had mastered his mood. It was his place to propose the toasts. He was magnificent and eloquent, giving each of the banqueters his due. And though there were many friends and many bottles, and though the Napareuli made one heavy in the head, and the heat did not let up, Paolo rattled on merrily; he seemed to be inspired. He praised the poet, Machradize, for his music, more piercing than all the words in the world, and he went on to compare Machradze's verses to the silence of a mountain morning when a lost shepherd's hopeless laugh is at once a marvelous and terrible thing. He observed of the stout Nashvili that, just as the stone branches on the walls of the Mtsetsky ruins warmed lonely and eccentric men with their eternal wine, so everything in Tiflis, even the typewriters, would die without Nashvili's imagination. Ha, ha! He proclaimed the friendship of one, the bravery of another. He drank the health of old Anania, who kept rosy trout, striped like the dawn, in place of ordinary smelly herrings. He drank to the health of all.

But now, the anxious moment was drawing near. Paolo must lift the goblet in a toast to his nephew, Noy Vanidze. All were smiling, grown sodden with wine, praise and good nature: how they all loved each other! Large bottles, platters with fragrant herbs, empty spits strewed the table; and Anania was already bringing in the melons. Their aroma diffused a meditative sadness. That perfume changed even the stout Nashvili into a silly lover. And there was music, besides! The *zurna** sobbed of Nina, of many Ninas, of all the Ninas, no, of one only. The notes circled like flies, buzzed, stung—there was no escaping them—chase them away and they come back. The melody did not seem to

* Zurna—a sort of primitive oboe.

change: it was always the same, today, yesterday, in the cradle. It was easy to grow mellow here! But Paolo rose, brushing away the flies from his forehead; for there was an endless number of them in the garden. He shouted to the *zurna* player: "One moment my lad!" although the *zurna* player was as old as his song. Paolo began:

"I propose that we now drink the health of our friend, Vanidze. You all know that he is my enemy, but we will not speak of that today. Today, we will drink and laugh. I knew Vanidze when he was a mere lad. Even then, he was a good shot, and he spoke the truth straight to your face without blushing. He's the sort that kills panthers or falls down from high cliffs. This morning, I said in my heart: Vanidze's a dog. I ask your pardon, Noy. You are a good man, hot-tempered and as dry as fate itself. I drink a long life to you; many years, and this is my last glass—for you, Noy!"

There was a sound of laughter and a tinkle of glass. Paolo embraced his nephew, pensively and caressingly. As before, Vanidze's eyes remained dull and oppressive. A silence fell. The banqueters were becoming uncomfortable. Then remembering himself in time, the old man picked up the *zurna;* and the stifling notes once more swarmed around the banqueters. The guests now were grateful; these wordless sounds told of great and important events, of what had happened but a moment back in the sight of all, amid the shrunken bushes and the greasy plates.

The stars were already twinkling when they finished dining; and gazing up at the stars, Paolo walked along the humped street to visit his Nina. He did not stay long with her—time enough only to present her with a bunch of autumn flowers and to kiss her lips, which held a sweet, lacerating fragrance, like the golden muscat of the shoemaker in the bazaar.

"Good-by, Nina! I shall, perhaps, go away very far. For that does not depend on me. People here are like ships—and there are storms. I remember some nice French verses on the subject. But I do not care to talk about verses now. What beautiful feet you have, Nina! And don't be offended. I couldn't have done anything else. For I have only one adviser—my heart. Well, then, good-by, my love!"

He went home. He did not bother to undress, but only lit a candle-end and, opening the volume of Balzac, began to read attentively. He did not lay aside the book till the very minute when a sullen knock echoed up from below. Then, he cried out:

"Come in, the door is not locked!"

None of his friends saw him after that. Two months later Vanidze, meeting the poet Machradze, observed:

"Whatever you may say about it, he died a wonderful death, that Paolo!

"He stood there beaming on all the world. For one second only, he half shut his eyes and cried out in French: 'How stupid it all is, that it should go on growing after death!' I do not know what he was talking about do you? Trees, perhaps? And then, he smiled again, and even said good-by to me. He said, 'Good-by, Noy. I did not deceive you then. I knew you were going to kill me, and yet I was merry. And even now I stand here laughing. Do you know what this is? This, brother, is a merry death!' I was so terrified at these words that I shouted to the others: 'Shoot quick, you bastards!' And he lay there smiling just the same."

Having told the story, Vanidze covered his eyes with his hands and shuddered.

IURY OLESHA

The Cherry Stone

ON SUNDAY I visited Natasha in the country. There were three other guests besides me: two girls and Boris Michailovitch. The girls went off boating on the river in the company of Natasha's brother. We—that is, Natasha, Boris Michailovitch and myself—went for a walk in the wood. In the wood we found a sunlit clearing and lay down. Natasha raised her face and, of a sudden, I found myself gazing at a shiny porcelain saucer.

Natasha treated me as an equal, but she played up to Boris Michailovitch as to an elder. She knew this made me uncomfortable and envious of Boris Michailovitch, and so she kept squeezing my hand and turning to me at every sentence with an interrogative:

"Isn't that so, Fedya?"

And she said this in an oblique kind of way, as if she were asking my pardon.

The droll voice of a bird resounded from a nearby thicket and set us talking of birds. I said that I had never in my life seen a thrush, for example, and asked: "What is a thrush like?"

A bird flew out of the thicket. It flew across the clearing and perched itself on a protruding branch close over our heads. It rested there on the swaying branch and blinked. And I thought that birds' eyes were very ugly; birds had strongly pronounced eyelids and no brows.

127

"What is it?" I asked in a whisper. "A thrush? Is that a thrush?"

No answer. I had my back to them. My miser's look could not follow them; they were enjoying their isolation. I was gazing at the bird. Turning my head, I saw Boris Michailovitch fondling Natasha's cheek. His hand must have been thinking, Let that pretentious fellow watch his bird! But I no longer had eyes for the bird; I was all ears. I heard the smack of a kiss. I did not turn my head, but I caught them in the act all the same; they saw me quiver.

"Is that a thrush?" I asked again.

The bird had vanished. It flew away, high through the tree-tops. It was no easy flight; it flew away, brushing the leaves with its wings.

Natasha was now treating us to cherries. Remembering my childhood, I left one of the cherry stones in my mouth. It rolled around and around in my mouth till it was finally sucked clean and dry. I took it out then—it looked like a piece of wood.

When I left the country, the cherry stone was still in my mouth.

I journeyed through an invisible land.

Here I was back in the city, strolling along. The sun was setting and my steps led me eastward. I accomplished a double journey.

One of my journeys was worthy of more general attention. A passer-by noticed a man strolling along a deserted, overgrown lane. What was happening to this peacefully sauntering man? He saw his own shadow preceding him. This shadow moved on ahead of him, far ahead, with long, faint feet. I cut across some waste-ground: the shadow climbed a brick wall and, suddenly, lost its head. The passer-by did not notice this; I alone saw it. I entered a passageway between two blocks of buildings. The buildings were terribly high, and the passageway was full of shade. The soil here was moldy and yielding, as in an orchard. A wild dog, which was running toward me, made an early detour. We, of course, gave each other a wide berth. I turned around. The entrance shone like a lamp in the distance. The dog was momentarily arrested by a projection at the entrance, but it managed to escape into the waste-ground; and only then could I make out that it had a coat of reddish hue.

All this had come to pass in an invisible land, for in the land of normal observation the facts would have been quite different: a stroller, a stray dog, a sunset, an overgrown waste-ground.

This invisible land is the land of observation and imagination. Here the traveler is never alone on his journey! Two sisters keep him company and lead him by the hand. One sister is called Observation; the other, Imagination.

But what is the conclusion? The conclusion is simply this: I may, contrary to everything, contrary to all established order and society, create within me a world emancipated of all laws except the transparent laws of my own personal impressions. And what may this signify? There are two worlds, we know: an old and a new world. But what sort of world is this? A third world? There are two ways; is this, then, a third way?

Natasha made an appointment, but failed to keep it.

I arrived half an hour before the time.

There was a public clock at the crossroads. It reminded me of a barrel. A barrel, of course! Two flat dials. Two bottoms. "O, empty barrel of time!" the words trembled on my lips.

Natasha ought to have come at half past three.

I waited. But she wouldn't come, of course. Ten past four. . . .

I waited at the tram stop. There was movement all around me. I alone was standing motionless. . . . All the wretches who had lost their bearings spotted me from afar as they might a lighthouse. And then the fun began. A strange woman accosted me.

"Will you be so kind," the stranger said, "as to tell me if Tram Twenty-seven will take me to the Kurdinskaya?"

It would not do for anybody to suspect that I had a rendezvous. They had better think: "This broadly smiling young man has come to this corner to attend to other people's happiness; he will explain everything, direct and comfort us. . . . Let's go to him! To him!"

"Oh yes," I replied, almost swooning with civility. "Tram Twenty-seven will take you to the Kurdinskaya. . . ."

Then I pulled myself together and rushed after the woman.

"No! No! Listen! You must take Tram Sixteen."

But let us forget about the rendezvous. I am not in love.

I'm a kind of genie of the streets. Ho! Flock to me! Flock to me!

Twenty past four. The hour hands joined, and then shot apart at an angle.

"Looks like a fly rubbing its feet. The uneasy fly of time."

How stupid! What is a fly of time?

There was no sign of her; she will not come. Then a Red Army man bore down upon me.

"Tell me," he asked, "where is the Darwin Museum?"

"I don't know. . . . Over there, I think. . . . Excuse me. . . . Excuse me. No, I don't know, comrade I don't know. . . ."

Come on! Whose turn next? Don't be bashful. . . .

A taxi drove up, making a sharp turn. Just look at the driver's contempt for me! He does not even despise me with his whole being, no! He would not stoop to despise me with his whole being. His contempt goes no further than his gloves! Comrade driver, believe me, I'm an amateur; I haven't the slightest idea where to turn your machine. . . .

I'm not here to show people their way. . . . I've got my own business to attend to. This halt of mine is enforced and regrettable! If I smile, it is not because I am good-natured, but because I have a nervous twitch . . . just look!

"Which is the way to the Varsonievsky?" The driver rapped the question over his shoulder.

"Over there, there, and there. . . ." I explained in a fluster.

Thinking it over, why shouldn't I post myself in the middle of the road and apply myself seriously to the job that has been thrust upon me?

Here's a blind man now. This one simply yelled at me! And he pushed me with his cane. . . .

"Is Tram Number Ten in sight?" he asked. "Eh? Ten?"

"No," I reply, almost fondling him. "No, comrade, there's no Ten. Only Two. Ten will be coming along."

Ten minutes have already elapsed since then. What am I waiting for? But, perhaps, she's hurrying along somewhere on wings?

"How late I am, how late!"

The woman has already gone off on Tram Sixteen; the soldier has already entered the cool rooms of the museum; the driver is already tooting along the Varsonievsky; sulkily and pretentiously, the blind man is already clambering on to the front platform, his cane held out in front of him.

They were all satisfied! All happy and content!

But I was still lounging here, aimlessly and smiling.

And people still flocked to me with questions: an old woman, a drunkard, a group of children with a flag. I was already beginning to thrash the air with my arms; I could no longer simply nod my head—with an upward throw of my chin—like a chance passer-by—no! I was already extending my arm with the hand open. . . . In another minute I would grip a baton in my fist.

"Stand back!" I would shout. "Stop! For the Varsonievsky? Turn around, old woman! Go to the right! Stop!"

Behold! I have a whistle between my lips. . . . I'm whistling. . . . I have the right to whistle. . . . Children envy me! Stand back! Aha. . . . Behold! I can stand between two tram-cars. Behold! I stand there, one leg forward, my hands behind my back, propping my ribs with a purple baton.

"Congratulate me, Natasha; I have become a militia-man. . . ."

Then I noticed Abel—my neighbor—standing at a distance watching me.

Natasha will not come, that's obvious. I beckoned Abel.

I: You saw that, Abel?

ABEL: I did. You're crazy.

I: You saw that, Abel? I've become a militia-man.

(*Pause. Another glance in the direction of the clock. Ten to five.*)

I: Nevertheless, it's all beyond you. My metamorphosis into a militia-man took place in an invisible land.

ABEL: Your invisible land is an idealistic delirium.

I: Do you know the greatest miracle of all, Abel? It's the fact that, for some unexplained reason, I figure in this magic land as a militia-man. . . . One might think that I ought to journey through it in peace and dignity as behooves a landowner thereof, and that a prophet's flowering staff ought to gleam in my hand. . . . And just look—I have a militia-man's baton in my hand! What a curious blend of the practical and the imaginary world.

ABEL: (*Preserves silence.*)

I: And even stranger is the fact that the guiding principle of

indivisible love, and none other, has transformed me into a militia-
man.

ABEL: I fail to understand. This must be some sort of Bergson-
ism.

I then made up my mind to bury the cherry stone.

I found a spot and buried it.

Here, I thought, the cherry tree will spring up which I planted
in remembrance of the love I bear Natasha. One day, some five
years from now perhaps, we shall meet, Natasha and I, in the
spring at the foot of this young tree. We shall stand on each
side of it—cherry trees are not very tall—and, standing on tiptoe,
we shall be able to touch the very highest blossom. The sun will
shine down brightly upon us, but spring will still wear a vacant
look, for it will be the time of spring when turbid gutters tempt
children and when this imaginary tree will be about to burst into
flower.

"Natasha," I shall exclaim, "bright and sunlit is the day, and
the wind is blowing, spreading further the brightness of the day.
The wind is rocking my tree, and its lacquered joints creak. Every
flower on it rises and falls, only to rise again, and that is why it
varies in hue from rose to white. That is the kaleidoscope of
spring, Natasha. Do you remember, five years ago you treated me
to cherries? Indivisible love makes of memory an inspired beggar.
To this day I remember the palm of your hand, which was
stained lilac from the cherry juice, and how you made a cornet
of it when spilling out the cherries. I bore away a cherry stone in
my mouth. I planted a tree to commemorate the fact that you did
not love me. Behold, it is flowering now. I can see clearly what a
laughingstock I was then; Boris Michailovitch was the man who
conquered you, but I was a mere dreamer, a child. I was looking
for a thrush while the two of you kissed. I was a romantic.
But behold: a hard, virile tree has sprung from the seed of the
romantic. Do you know that the Japanese believe that cherry
is a man's color? Behold! here stands a squat, strong Japanese tree.
Believe me, Natasha, romanticism is virile, and it should not be
derided. . . . For everything depends on the approach. Had

Boris Michailovitch come upon me squatting in the waste-ground as I buried the cherry stone, he would have sensed once more his supremacy over me, the supremacy of a man over a dreamer. But I was at that instant secreting a shell in the ground. It has burst forth in a blinding explosion. I was hiding a seed in the ground. This tree, Natasha, is my child, begotten of you. Bring here the son Boris Michailovitch gave you. I shall judge if he is as healthy, as clean, as absolute as this tree, fathered by one whom you considered a child."

I had come home from the country. Abel detached himself from the shadow of a wall. Abel is a professional worker. He wears a skullcap, blue socks and sandals. He is shaven, but his cheeks are blue-black. Abel always looks unkempt, as if he were growing a beard. He even gives the impression of having only one cheek, and that a blue-black one. Abel has an eagle nose and a single blue-black cheek.

ABEL: What's been happening to you? As I was passing by in the train today, I saw you squatting down in the waste-ground and digging up the earth with your hands. What's the matter?

I: (*Silence*)

ABEL (*striding up and down the room*): A man squatting down and digging up the earth with his hands! What can he be doing? Impossible to tell. Is he attempting an experiment? Or is he in the throes of a fit? No one can tell. Are you subject to fits?

I (*after a pause*): Do you know what I'm thinking, Abel? I'm thinking that dreamers ought never to have children. Of what use are a dreamer's children to the new world? Let dreamers plant trees for the benefit of the new world.

ABEL: That's not provided for in the Five-Year Plan.

The land of observation began at the head of the bed; it began with the chair that you set near the bed when you undressed before going to sleep. You might wake early in the morning; the house would be still asleep and your room full of sunshine. Not a word. Don't stir; don't disturb the immobility of the light. A pair of socks lie on the chair. They are brown. But in the bright immobile light, you might suddenly observe, amid the brown knitted wool, some separate, mobile, variegated strands: a purple, a blue, an orange strand.

Sunday morning. I am once more treading the familiar path on my way to Natasha. An appropriate heading would be: *Trips to an Invisible Land*. With your permission, here is a chapter from these *Trips*, a chapter which ought to be entitled:

The Man Who Hastened to Cast the Stone

Shrubs sprouted in the shadow of a brick wall. I was strolling along a path flanked by these shrubs. I noticed a hollow in the wall and was seized with a desire to throw a stone into the hollow. I stooped to pick up a stone at my feet. . . . There I saw an ant heap.

Twenty years had passed since I had seen an ant heap. In those twenty years, I had of course frequently trodden on ant heaps. Very likely I did notice them, but I saw them without thinking: I'm treading on ant heaps. What happened was that the word ant heap simply detached itself in my consciousness, and that's all. The living "image" had instantly and subserviently allowed itself to be petrified in a glib and current phrase.

Then it all came back to me! Ant heaps are unearthed by lightning glances. One glance following another. There, look there! Another! And so it happened now. One after another, three ant heaps appeared.

I could not see the ants from my level; my eye only caught a certain stir of forms, which might very well have been thought motionless. Eyes lend themselves readily to illusion. I looked on and was satisfied to think that those were no ants swarming in the ant heaps, but the ant heaps themselves crumbling like dunes.

Gripping the stone, I stood at some four paces from the wall. The stone must find its resting place in the hollow. I swung my arm. The stone flew and hit a brick. A spray of dust fell. I had missed. Only then did I hear the protest of the stone, a protest which had already been voiced in the palm of my hand long before that hand had unclasped.

"Wait!" cried the stone. "Look at me!"

I had really been hasty. I ought to have examined the stone. For it was a remarkable thing, there was no doubt about it. And now it was lost in the shrubbery, in the undergrowth; it had vanished forever! And I, who held it in my hand, had not even observed its color. The stone might have been tinted lilac; and, if not monolithic, it might have been composed of several bodies; or, again, it might have been partly petrified, containing the remains of a beetle or a cherry stone; or, again, it might have been a porous stone; or, finally, what I had picked up might not have been a stone at all, but a gangrened bone!

I met an excursion party on the road.

Twenty men were marching across the waste-ground where the cherry stone reposed. At their head marched Abel. I stepped out of their way. Abel did not notice me or, to be more exact, he saw me but did not take me into consideration; like a fanatic, he swallowed me whole, without waiting for me to agree or to protest.

Abel detached himself from his flock and, turning to face it—with his back toward me—exclaimed with a mighty wave of his arm:

"Here! On this spot! Here!"

A pause. Silence.

"Comrades from Kursk!" Abel shouted. "I hope you have imagination. Use your imagination then, and don't be afraid!"

Oh! Abel was trying to shove his way into the land of imagination. He has taken it into his head, perhaps, to show these excursionists the cherry tree that was blossoming in memory of an invisible land. . . .

He paced up and down. He stopped and kicked up his leg. He repeated the kick. Once more he was trying to kick himself free from a plant which had got entangled around his ankle.

He gave a final stamp with his foot and shook off the last clinging blades. (What a number of plants in this story of trees and shrubs!)

"On this spot will soar the gigantic structure of which I told you."

. . . "Dear Natasha, I have overlooked the most important thing: the Plan. The Plan exists. But I have acted without consulting the Plan. In five years' time, on this spot, on this waste-ground of ditches and useless walls, a concrete giant will arise. Imagination, sister mine, how rash you are! In the spring, they will begin laying the foundations—and what then will be the fate of my silly cherry stone! Yet the tree dedicated to you will blossom one day in the invisible land. . . .

"Excursionists will journey hither to see the concrete giant.

"They will not see your tree. Is it really impossible to make an invisible land visible? . . ."

This letter was an imaginary one. I never wrote it. I might have written it if Abel had not spoken as he did.

"The building will be laid out in a semicircle," Abel explained. "The interior of the semicircle will be made into a garden. Have you any imagination?"

"Yes," I replied. "I see it, Abel. I see it clearly. Here is the garden. And where you are standing the cherry tree will blossom."

In the Basement

AS A SMALL BOY I had the vaguest idea of truth. This was the result of too much reading and an over-excitable imagination. I was always poring over books: stealthily in class, during the breaks between lessons, on the way home, and in the evenings, squatting surreptitiously in the shadow of our dining-room table. For books I sacrificed all the most popular amusements, such as the secret excursions to the port during school-time, the billiard-parties in the Greek Street coffee-houses, and the swimming on the Langeron. I had no friends: for who would care to consort with such a bookworm?

One day at school I caught sight of a book about Spinoza in the hands of Marc Borgman, our head boy. He had just finished reading it and was unable to resist the temptation to tell the other boys about the Spanish Inquisition. What he said had an erudite flavour, but sounded very dull. There was no poetry in his words. And I simply had to break in. I edified my audience with tales of old Amsterdam, of its gloomy ghetto, of the philosophers and the diamond-cutters. My account, based on a knowledge gleaned from books, was greatly embroidered by my own invention. But that was only to be expected. My imagination intensified the dramatic scenes, found mysterious and complicated motives and surprising conclusions. Spinoza's death, that free and lonely death, loomed in my imagination like a battle. The Sanhedrin urged him to repentance, but the dying man

137

was adamant. And then I introduced Rubens, whom I saw standing by Spinoza's bed taking a mask of the dead man's face.

My audience listened open-mouthed to this fantastic and animated recital. And, in the next break, Borgman came up to me and, taking my arm familiarly, led me off for a stroll. Before long we had become the best of friends. Borgman was not a bad type of head-boy. His powerful brain had already out-distanced our school-boyish wisdom, and he seemed bent upon the discovery of greater truths. Even we, thoughtless twelve-year-old boys, could realise that a career of unusual distinction lay in store for him. And now this brilliant and reserved youth grew attached to me because of my peculiar knack of spinning the most fantastic tales on the least provocation.

That year we had moved up into the third form. One day towards the beginning of summer Borgman invited me to spend a day at their country house. Borgman's father was manager of the Russian Foreign Trade Bank, and was one of that generation of men who were transforming provincial Odessa into a Marseilles or Naples, but he still had in him the leaven of the old Odessa merchants. Fond of the society of sceptical and affable men of the world, he avoided when possible talking in Russian, preferring to express himself in an English that smacked of the rough and abrupt jargon of Liverpool sea-captains. When the Italian Opera had come to town in April, the Borgmans gave a dinner in honour of the company. And the self-indulgent banker, the last of the old Odessa merchants, had then proceeded to carry on a vigorous intrigue with the generously-bosomed prima donna, who departed after two months, taking away with her only some memories which did not weigh too heavily on her conscience, and a necklace chosen with taste, but of negligible value.

Borgman's father was also Consul for the Argentine and Chairman of the Stock Exchange Committee; his business abilities were generally recognised. I had been invited to his house, and my Aunt Bobka was not slow to make the most of this, and soon the news spread far and wide. On the great day, my aunt dressed me up with the greatest possible style, and I caught the local train for Bolshaya Fontanka.

The Borgman house stood on a low red cliff overlooking the

sea. In its grounds, sloping gently to the edge of the cliff, a garden had been laid out, planted with fuchsias and mulberry trees trimmed into sphere-like shapes. Coming as I did from an indigent and disorderly household, this tastefully appointed residence sent me into raptures. Wicker-work chairs gleamed whitely in the foliage-shaded alleys; the lunch-table was elegantly laid and adorned with flowers; the window-frames were picked out in green; and a low and spacious wooden colonnade stretched in front of the house.

The bank-manager himself arrived in the evening. After dinner, setting a wicker armchair near the edge of the cliff overlooking the restless plain of the sea, he lit a cigar and engrossed himself in the *Manchester Guardian*. The guests, Odessa ladies for the most part, sat on the verandah, playing poker. A slender samovar with narrow ivory handles stood steaming on a table. Gamblers, profligates in secret, these dainty Odessa women in their negligently fashionable dresses fanned themselves languidly as they staked gold pieces. The sun reached them filtered through a hedge of wild vine. Its fiery disc appeared enormous and its reflection glowed like bronze on the women's dark hair. Sparks of sunset glittered in their diamonds—jewels that sparkled everywhere, in the hollow of their breasts, on their delicately tinted ears, and on their plump white fingers.

It grew dusk. A bat flittered by. The darkening sea rolled down upon the red cliff. My twelve-year-old heart was bursting with the joy and happiness of other people's good fortune. Borgman and I strolled down the furthest alley hand in hand. He told me of his intention to become an aviation engineer. There was a rumour too that his father would soon be appointed representative of the Russian Foreign Trade Bank in London and that Marc would thus be able to finish his education in England.

At home, at Aunt Bobka's, nobody ever talked of such things. I had nothing with which to repay these moments of endless delight. But I told Borgman that, though my home life was very different, yet my grandfather Levvi-Isthok and my uncle Simon Woolf had travelled all round the world and had gone through thousands of adventures. These I recounted in order; and my sense of the probable forsaking me, I conducted Simon Woolf through the Russo-Turkish campaign and then to Alexandria and Egypt. . . .

Night settled itself darkly on the rigid poplars; stars began to stud their heavy branches. I talked on and on, gesticulating. The hand of the future aviation engineer quivered in mine. With difficulty breaking the spell, he promised to return the visit on the following Sunday. And cherishing this promise, I caught the local train back home, to Bobka's.

Throughout the week I imagined myself a banker. I made million-rouble deals with Singapore and Port Said, and had a private yacht in which I sailed on business. But on Saturday it was time to awake, for Borgman's visit was due the very next day.

There was, of course, not an ounce of truth in the tales I had told him. The facts were in a way far stranger, but then I had not yet learned to respect the truth of this world. My grandfather Levvi-Isthok, the rabbi, who had been dismissed from his post for forgery, was looked upon as a madman by our neighbours and the boys of the district. My uncle Simon Woolf was unbearable because of his rowdy eccentricity, his bullying manner and his fiery, meaningless abuse.

Aunt Bobka alone was presentable. And she was proud too that I should have made friends with a bank manager's son. She looked upon this friendship as the first step in my career, and she baked a jam strudel and a poppy-seed cake in honour of the occasion.

But our great problem was how to get grandfather, with his battered top-hat and ragged bandages swathing his swollen feet, out of the way; we finally entrusted him to the care of our neighbours, the Apelhots, and I implored him not to show himself until the guest had departed. We disposed of Simon Woolf as well. All my efforts went to packing him off for the rest of the day, and I even gave him three roubles I had painfully saved up. He went off at last with his fellow-jobbers to drink tea at the Bear Tavern. Three roubles were not so easy to spend, and vodka being obtainable on the premises, we felt sure that Simon Woolf would not put in an appearance till late in the evening. Borgman would thus never suspect that the stories of my uncle's prowess were false.

That morning Bobka had donned a brown cloth dress, tightly clasping her kindly voluminous bosom. She also put on a neckerchief with black printed flowers, the one she usually wore to the Synagogue at Atonement Day and Rosh Hashanah. Then she set out the cakes, the jam and pretzels on the table, and settled down to wait.

We lived in a basement. Borgman raised his eyebrows as he walked over the uneven floor of the passage and saw the butt of drinking water standing in the hall. As soon as he entered our living room I did my best to distract him with all sorts of curiosities. I showed him the alarm clock which my grandfather had made with his own hands down to the very last screw. A lamp was attached to it, which lit up whenever the hour or half-hour struck. I also showed him a little barrel of boot polish, an original recipe of grandfather's who jealously guarded the secret. We then read through a few pages of Levvi-Isthok's manuscript, written in Hebrew on square sheets of yellow paper as large as wall-maps and entitled "The Headless Man." In it were described all of Levvi-Isthok's neighbours during the past seventy years of his life. Undertakers, cantors, Jewish drunkards, cooks come specially for the circumcision festivals and rabbis come to perform the ritual operation, such were Levvi-Isthok's heroes. They were all fantastic, stuttering fellows with bulbous noses, pimply pates, and crooked rumps.

We drank two glasses of tea each and helped ourselves to the *strudel*, and then Bobka left the room, bowing and walking backwards. With joyful abandon I struck an attitude and began to declaim the lines I valued above everything else in the world.

> "*Friends, Romans, countrymen, lend me your ears:*
> *I come to bury Cæsar, not to praise him . . .*"

Thus Antony, bending over Cæsar's corpse, begins his harangue to the Roman mob. Panting, I clutched my breast:

> "*He was my friend, faithful and just to me:*
> *But Brutus says he was ambitious;*
> *And Brutus is an honourable man.*

He hath brought many captives back to Rome,
Whose ransoms did the general coffers fill:
Did this in Cæsar seem ambitious?
When that the poor have cried, Cæsar hath wept:
Ambition should be made of sterner stuff:
Yet Brutus says he was ambitious—
And Brutus is an honourable man.
You all did see that on the Lupercal
I thrice presented him a kingly crown,
Which he did thrice refuse: was this ambition?
Yet Brutus says he was ambitious,
And sure he is an honourable man. . . ."

Brutus' face loomed through the smoke of eternity before my eyes. It had grown whiter than chalk. The Roman populace bore down upon me with a thunderous roar. I raised my arm—Borgman followed it obediently with his eyes; I shook my clenched fist, my outstretched arm pointed through the window, and I saw—my uncle Simon Woolf coming across the courtyard accompanied by the jobber Leykhach. They were carrying between them a clothes-hanger shaped like a pair of antlers and a red trunk with lion-headed spring locks. Bobka had evidently seen them too, for, oblivious of the guest, she came rushing into the room and clutched me with trembling hands.

"My pet, they've been buying furniture again!"

Borgman stood up in his prim little uniform and bowed in perplexity to Bobka. The outer door was flung open with a crash. There was a thundering of boots in the corridor and the noise of the trunk being dragged in. The voices of Simon Woolf and the ginger-headed Leykhach were raised in a deafening roar. They were in high spirits.

"Bobka!" bellowed Simon Woolf, "guess how much I paid for these antlers. . . ."

Though he blared like a trumpet, a note of uncertainty could be detected in his voice. Although drunk, Simon Woolf no doubt remembered how much we detested Leykhach, who encouraged our uncle in his senseless extravagances, which only lumbered the house with useless and inconvenient pieces of furniture.

Bobka did not say a word. Leykhach squealed out something to Simon Woolf. Then, to drown his snake-like hissing, to drown the alarmed beating of my heart, I cried out in the words of Antony:

> *"But yesterday the word of Cæsar might*
> *Have stood against the world: now lies he there.*
> *And none so poor to do him reverence.*
> *O masters, if I were disposed to stir*
> *Your hearts and minds to mutiny and rage,*
> *I should do Brutus wrong and Cassius wrong,*
> *Who you all know are honourable men. . . ."*

At this point there was a thud. It was Bobka falling, knocked down by a blow from her husband. She must have made some bitter comment about the antlers. And now the familiar, almost everyday scene repeated itself. Simon Woolf's voice stopped up all the crannies of eternity. He shouted as always on such occasions:

"You're tearing the heart out of me," he complained thunderously. "You're tearing the heart out of me to stuff your own rapacious mouths with it. . . . Work's been my perdition . . . And who has hung this millstone round my neck? It's you . . . you accursed harpies, who have fastened it there. . . ."

Heaping Bobka and myself with Yiddish curses, he gave us an assurance that our eyes would ooze out, that we should not have time to bury each other and that finally we should all be dragged together by the roots of our hair to a common grave.

Borgman had risen. He was pale, and kept looking uneasily round. Though uninitiated into the subtleties of Yiddish blasphemy, he was familiar enough with the Russian variety of curses. Nor were these disdained by Simon Woolf. The bank manager's son stood twisting his cap. His figure grew blurred in my eyes as I attempted to shout down the immense evil of the world. My own mortal despair, and Cæsar's already accomplished death, were blended into one. I was already dead but I went on ranting. Hoarse moans welled up from the very depths of my being:

> *"If you have tears, prepare to shed them now.*
> *You all do know this mantle; I remember*

The first time ever Cæsar put it on;
'Twas on a summer's evening in his tent,
That day he overcame the Nervii:
Look, in this place ran Cassius' dagger through:
See what a rent the envious Casca made:
Through this the well beloved Brutus stabbed;
And, as he plucked the cursed steel away,
Mark how the blood of Cæsar followed it. . . ."

But nothing could drown Simon Woolf. Bobka was still lying on the floor, blubbering and sniffling. The imperturbable Leykhach was moving the trunk behind the partition. Then my crazy grandfather decided it was the moment to create a diversion. Having eluded the vigilance of the Apelhots, he crept up to our window and began sawing on his fiddle, in the hope very probably of preventing the passers-by from overhearing Simon Woolf. Borgman glanced out of the basement window and stepped back aghast at the sight of my grandfather grimacing there with his blue twisted lips. He had on his battered top hat, a black wadded mantle with bone buttons, and ragged bandages on his elephantine feet. His straggling tobacco-stained beard tossed to and fro. Borgman took to his heels.

"Excuse me," he muttered, breaking away, "I hope you don't mind . . . I must go. . . ."

His little uniform and cap flitted across the courtyard.

With his departure my agitation subsided. In its place came decision and peace of mind.

I waited for evening. As soon as my grandfather had finished scrawling his hooked Hebrew characters upon the square sheets of paper—that evening he was portraying the Apelhots, with whom he had spent the day on my account—and had stretched himself out in his bunk to sleep, I stole into the corridor. Barefoot, in a long patched nightshirt, I groped my way in the dark along the cold earthen floor. From the streets, through chinks in the wooden walls, came a sharp steely flicker of moonlit cobbles. The water-butt stood in its usual place in the corner. I lowered myself down into it. The icy water cut me in two, and I bobbed up, spluttering. A cat on a shelf above was looking down at me drowsily. The second time I held out longer: the water gurgled as my gasping breath bored through it like a screw.

Opening my eyes I saw the fold of a shirt and a pair of small feet hugging each other at the bottom of the butt. My resolution deserted me once more and I got out. Grandfather was standing by the butt in a jersey. His single tooth was chattering to itself.

"My grandson,"—he uttered the words clearly and contemptuously—"I am going to take a dose of castor-oil to have something to lay on your grave. . . ."

Beside myself I screamed and plunged headlong into the water. Grandfather's feeble arm dragged me out. Then, for the first time that day, I burst out weeping; and the world of tears was so vast and beautiful that all else vanished from my eyes.

I came to myself in bed, wrapped warmly in a quilt. Grandfather was striding up and down the room, whistling. Aunt Bobka was warming my hands at her breast. I let her keep them there.

"How he trembles, our little fool, our child," Bobka said. "Where does he find the strength to tremble so?"

Grandfather tugged at his beard, whistled, and took up his pacing again. Simon Woolf was snoring painfully in the next room. He always had his fill of battles by day, and never woke in the night.

I. ILF and E. PETROV

Count Sredizemsky

THE OLD COUNT was on his deathbed.

He lay on a dirty couch and, stretching out his neck like a bird, stared through the window with disgust. Outside, a small green branch quivered like a brooch. Children were yelling at the top of their voices in the courtyard. On the railings of the house opposite, Count Sredizemsky could decipher a slogan to do with salvage upon a conventional enamel plate: "When you visit anyone, Bring back a bone!" This slogan had long revolted Sredizemsky, but just then it seemed to contain even more of a hidden insinuation. The ex-Count turned away from the window and angrily fixed his gaze on the cracked ceiling.

Sredizemsky's room was anything but a Count's room! Here hung no portraits of the robust men in satin breeches of the Empress Catherine's reign. There were none of the traditional round Tartar shields. The furniture had none of the solidity of the antique. The parquet floor lacked polish and reflected nothing. It behooved the Count, before he died, to meditate upon his ancestors, among whom were numbered many famous warriors, statesmen, and even an Ambassador to the Court of Madrid. It behooved him, likewise, to meditate on God, for the Count had always been a believer and a regular churchgoer. But, instead of all this, the Count's thoughts were directed at this moment to nonsensical everyday matters.

146

"I am dying in unsanitary conditions," he muttered peevishly. "They haven't even whitewashed the ceiling in all this time."

And, as if on purpose, he immediately recalled a certain damaging event. In 1910, when the Count had not yet become an "ex-Count," and when all that was now "ex" was still real, he had reserved for himself for the price of six hundred franks a grave in the cemetery at Nice. There, beneath the electric foliage, the Count had desired to find eternal repose. But, not so long ago, he had dispatched to Nice a jaundiced letter, in which he had stated his wish to withdraw his claim on the cemetery and to have his money returned. The cemetery authorities had politely refused his request. In their reply, they had pointed out that the money, which had been paid in advance for the grave, was not subject to refund, but that, if Monsieur Sredizemsky's body together with all the proper documentation were to arrive in Nice, the body would then be duly interred in the cemetery at Nice. Monsieur would, of course, be entirely responsible for the expenses of the funeral.

Since the Count's income from hawking cigarettes in the street was less than considerable, he had all too hopefully relied on the expected refund from Nice. This correspondence with the cemetery authorities had caused the Count much agitation and had exercised a devastating effect on his organism. After the nasty letter, in which the question of the transfer of the Count's body had been so calmly discussed, he felt very debilitated and hardly rose from his couch. Justifiably distrusting the assurances of the district doctor, he was now preparing to settle his accounts with life. However, he had no wish to die, just as a schoolboy has no wish to tear himself away from a ball game in order to study. He had, first of all, to settle a certain important and complicated matter with three students from the VUZ [1]—Shkarlato, Prouzhansky and Talmudovsky, who all lived on the floor above him.

His hostility to the three young men had developed in the usual way. The House Wallsheet [2] had recently featured a colored caricature depicting the Count in a disgusting light—with pointed

[1] VUZ—Higher Institute of Learning, i.e. University.
[2] A form of weekly newssheet, containing local news and party instructions, which is pinned up on a wall in either factories, buildings or institutions.

ears and a foreshortened body. A caption in verse under the caricature read as follows:

> *In our house that's numbered Seven*
> *There is room for all men even,*
> *You'll find here at a certain moment,*
> *As far as class goes, an alien element.*
> *What would you say, if you were told,*
> *That Sredizemsky is a Count of old?*

The verses were anonymously signed: *Three.*

Sredizemsky was frightened. He sat down to refute the accusation, resolving in his turn to versify the reply. But he could not attain to the high level of verse technique displayed by his enemies. Besides, at that particular moment, Shkarlato, Pouzhansky and Talmudovsky, happened to be entertaining. One could hear a twanging of guitar strings, snatches of song, and a constant shuffling of heavy feet. From overhead, a few exclamations reached him: . . . "Engels attacked him, but Plekhanov . . ." Sredizemsky only succeeded in writing one line of verse: "That I'm a Count I never hid . . ." There was nothing to refute in prose. So the attack had remained unanswered. The affair died a natural death. But Sredizemsky could not forget the slight. As he fell asleep, he saw three phosphorescent words light up on a dark wall, in the manner of Balthazar's *Mene, Tekle, Phares:*

SHKARLATO   PROUZHANSKY   TALMUDOVSKY

That evening in the street it grew as warm and dark as between the palms of two hands. The couch springs creaked. The Count felt no peace of mind as he lay dying. A week ago he had already worked out a plan of revenge against the three young men. It consisted of a whole arsenal of the customary domestic abominations: first, a complaint to the House Committee against Shkarlato, Prouzhansky and Talmudovsky, charging them with ruining their lodgings; second, a letter anonymously signed "A Friend of Education" and addressed to the administration of the VUZ, wherein the three students were accused of perversion and the sin of sodomy; and, third, a secret report to the militia, alleging that suspicious, unregistered citizens lodged at night in the students' room. The Count was obviously in touch with the contemporary scene. And, for that reason, his plan included yet another anonymous letter addressed to the University *cell*, containing a vague insinuation that Talmudovsky, a Party member, was constantly practising in his room a "right deviation" under the appearance of a "left phrase."

This plan had not yet been put into execution. The obstacle had been a certain skeletal figure. The Count felt its presence whenever he shut his eyes. It hovered behind the dusty glass cupboard. Mystically a scythe gleamed in its hands. Everything might go wrong: the Count might die unavenged.

And yet Sredizemsky felt obliged to wipe out the insult. His ancestors had been in the habit of wiping out insults in blood. But it was beyond the Count's powers to flood the country with torrents of Shkarlato's, Prouzhansky's and Talmudovsky's warm, young blood. The basic economic premises had changed. But it was already too late to launch this complex system of "accusations," since it had become obvious that only a few hours of life were left to the Count.

Instead, he must invent some sort of very effective and rapid revenge.

As the student Talmudovsky was walking past the house under the light of a greasy, Greek moon, he suddenly heard himself being hailed. He turned round. A gaunt hand beckoned him from the window of the Count's room.

"Me?" the student asked in amazement.

The hand continued to beckon him. Then he heard the Count's squeaky peacock-like voice:

"Please come in ! I beg you! It's essential!"

Talmudovsky hunched his shoulders. Within a minute he was already sitting on the couch at the Count's feet. A small lamp spread a dim, bronze light through the room.

"Comrade Talmudovsky," the Count said, "I am on the threshold of death. My days are numbered."

"But who counted them!" the good-natured Talmudovsky exclaimed. "You will live for many a segment of time yet."

"Don't try to comfort me. By my death I shall expiate all the evil I once caused you."

"To me?"

"Yes, my son!" Sredizemsky moaned in a devotional voice. "To you. I am a great sinner. For twenty years I have suffered without finding strength to reveal the secret of your birth. But now that I am dying, I should like to tell you everything. You are not Talmudovsky."

"Why am I not Talmudovsky?" the student asked. "I am Talmudovsky."

"No, you're not Talmudovsky in the least. You are Sredizemsky, Count Sredizemsky. You are my son. You may, of course, disbelieve me, but it's the honest truth. People don't lie when they are dying. You are my son, and I am your unfortunate father. Come close to me. Let me embrace you."

But there was no answering gush of tenderness. Talmudovsky leapt up, letting drop with a thud on the floor a thick volume of Plekhanov.

"What nonsense is this?" he shouted. "I am Talmudovsky. My parents have been living in Tiraspol for the last thirty years. Only last week I received a letter from my father—Talmudovsky."

"He is not your father," the old man announced quietly. "Your father is here, dying on a couch. Yes. It all happened twenty-two years ago. I met your mother on the reedy banks of the Dniester. She was an enchanting woman, your mother."

"What the devil!" the long-legged Talmudovsky kept exclaiming as he spun about the room. "This is sheer swinishness!"

"Our regiment," the vengeful old man continued, "the Guards regiment of His Majesty the King of Denmark, was then taking part in extensive maneuvers. But I was a great sinner. Indeed, in the regiment I was known as the Don Juan of Peterhof. I seduced your mother and deceived Talmudovsky, whom you wrongly regard as your father."

"That can't be!"

"I can understand your agitation, my son. As you must realize, a Count's life is full of hardship nowadays. You will, of course, be thrown out of the Party. I can foresee, too, that you will be eliminated from the University. And here in this house they will write verses about you just as they did about me: 'What would you say, on learning that Talmudovsky is a former Count?' But in you, my child, I can detect the noble heart of the Counts Sredizemsky, the noble, courageous and pious heart of our lineage, of which you are the last issue. The Sredizemskys have always believed in God. Do you go to church, my boy?"

Talmudovsky threw up his hands and ran out of the room, yelling, "Go to the Devil's Mother!" His shadow could be seen moving hastily through the courtyard and then it disappeared down the street. The old Count laughed and then cast a glance at the dark corner where the cupboard stood. The skeleton figure no longer appeared so terrifying. The phosphorescent words glowed again on the wall, but the word Talmudovsky was not among them. Only two surnames remained, glowing with a greenish hue:

SHKARLATO   PROUZHANSKY

At that moment a cheerful voice rang out in the courtyard:

> *Over the seas, over the waves,*
> *Here today, tomorrow yonder,*
> *Over the seas, the seas, the seas!*

It was that happy-go-lucky Prouzhansky, the *Komsomol* member, returning home from a carnival on the river. He wore tightly fitting white trousers, which gleamed in the moonlight. He was in great haste. A round tin of marinated perch was waiting for him at home.

"Comrade Prouzhansky!" the Count called out, with difficulty raising his rooster head to the window. "Hey, Comrade Prouzhansky!"

"Is that you, Vera?" the Komsomol lad shouted, throwing back his head.

"No, it is I, Sredizemsky. I have some business with you. Will you step in for a minute?"

Within five minutes Prouzhansky, stricken to the very core, was spinning about the bronze-lit room. He was as restless as if a whole hive of bees had attacked him. But the old Count, supporting his chin with his hands, which was as pendulous and soft as a purse, went on with his glib narration:

"I was a great sinner, my son. I was a dashing officer then in

His Majesty the King of Denmark's Guards regiment. At the time the regiment was taking part in large-scale maneuvers in the vicinity of Vitebsk. There it was I met your mother. She was an enchanting woman even though a Jewess. Let me be brief. She was very much taken with me. Nine months later, in the poor lodgings of Prouzhansky the Tailor, a little red bundle of flesh began to stir. This little red bundle of flesh was you—Prouzhansky."

"Why, what makes you think that the little red bundle was me?" Prouzhansky asked plaintively. "That is to say, I want to know why you think you were the father of that little red bundle?"

"That holy woman loved me," the dying man answered in a self-satisfied tone. "She was a pure soul even though a Jewess. She it was who told me who was the real father of her child. I was the father. And you were the son. Yes, you are my own son, Yasha. You are not Prouzhansky. You are Sredizemsky. You are a Count! And I, great sinner, I was known in the regiment as the Don Juan of Oranienburg. Embrace me, young Count, the last issue of our almost extinct line!"

Prouzhansky was so overwhelmed that he impulsively embraced the old rascal. Then he thought better of it and muttered sadly:

"Ah, citizen Sredizemsky, citizen Sredizemsky! Why didn't you take this secret with you into the grave? What will happen to me now?"

The old Count looked commiseratingly at his second only son, and coughed admonishingly:

"Poor, noble heart! What deprivations you will have to suffer! You will, of course, be thrown out of the Komsomol. And I hope, indeed, that you will not remain in a corporation so hostile to our class. You will be expelled from the University too. But what do you need with a Soviet University? The Counts Sredizemskys were always educated in lycées. Embrace me, Yashenka, once more! Can't you see that I am dying here on a couch?"

"This can't be!" Prouzhansky exclaimed desperately.

"It is a fact, nevertheless," the old man replied dryly. "Dying men don't lie."

"I am not a Count!" the young Komsomol protested, defending himself.

"But you are!" countered the Count.

"It is you who are a Count!"

"We are Counts, both of us," Sredizemsky concluded. "My poor son! I can tell you in advance that they will write satiric verses about you: 'What would you say, on learning that Prouzhansky is just a Count?' "

Prouzhansky departed, all askew and muttering: "So I'm a Count. Ai-ai-ai!"

The phosphorescent letters of his name were blotted out on the wall. Only one name still remained hanging there like an inscription on a tomb:

SHKARLATO

For a dying man, the Count exerted remarkable energy. He succeeded in enticing into his room Shkarlato, who was a non-party man, and confessed to him that he, the Count, was an old sinner. It became glaringly obvious that the student was the last descendant of the Counts Sredizemskys and, consequently, a Count himself.

"It was in Tiflis," Sredizemsky now plodded on in a tired voice. "I was then a Guards officer . . ."

Shkarlato dashed out into street, reeling with happiness. There was a buzzing in his ears, and the student fancied that a white sword was trailing and clanking behind him on the pavement.

"Serve them right!" the Count muttered hoarsely. "They shouldn't write verse!"

The last surname was now dimmed from the wall. A fresh ocean-going breeze blew into the room. A skeleton figure emerged from the Slavic cupboard. Sredizemsky squealed. Death hacked at him with a scythe, and the Count died with a happy smile on his blue lips.

That night none of the three students slept at home. They wandered about in the violet streets, in different quarters of the city, frightening the nocturnal cab drivers with their appearance. They were undergoing a variety of emotions.

Towards three o'clock in the morning, Talmudovsky found

himself sitting on the granite edge of the sidewalk and whispering:

"I have no moral right to conceal my origins from the 'cell.' I must go and declare myself. But what will Prouzhansky and Shkarlato say? Perhaps, they will not want to share the room with me any longer? Especially Prouzhansky. He's such a hot-tempered fellow. Perhaps, he won't even shake hands with me."

In the meantime Prouzhansky, in his now soiled white trousers, was walking around the Pushkin monument and excitedly trying to convince himself:

"In the end, I'm not guilty. I am the victim of an amorous adventure on the part of a representative of the drink-sodden Tsarist regime. It would be quite impossible for me to tell everything. . . . Talmudovsky would stop talking to me. I wonder how Engels would have acted in my place? I am done for. I must conceal it. Life would be impossible otherwise. Ai-ai-ai! And what would Shkarlato say? You've had it, he would say, you've got stuck. He's a terrible activist even though not a member of the Party. Ah, what would he say if he learned that I, Prouzhansky, am an ex-Count! I must conceal it, yes, conceal it!"

In the meantime Shkarlato, the activist, still deafened by the clanking of his invisible sword, was marching through the streets with a military step, calling out boisterously from time to time:

"What a pity he didn't leave an inheritance! Strike me blue! Father told me had an estate in the Chernigov province. Oh, why wasn't I born in the right age! Now they've probably established a *sovhoz*[1] on the estate. Ah, forward trot, black hussars, the bugles call! I wonder if I could drink a bottle of rum sitting outside on a window sill?[2] I must try that. But I can't tell anyone about it. Talmudovsky and Prouzhansky might spoil everything for me out of envy. It would be fine to marry a Countess! In the morning, there I'd be entering a boudoir. . . ."

Prouzhansky was the first to reach home. Trembling in all his limbs, he rolled himself up like a pretzel beneath the raspberry colored quilt. Just as he was beginning to feel warm, the door

---

[1] A state farm.
[2] An allusion to the drinking bout in which Pierre, Dolohov, etc., participated in Leo Tolstoy's *War and Peace* (Part I, vi).

opened and in came Talmudovsky, whose face was the dark hue of emery paper.

"Listen, Yashka," he said severely, "what would you do if one of us turned out to be the son of a Count?"

Prouzhansky uttered a faint cry.

"Now it's started," he thought.

"What would you do in a case like that, all the same?" Talmudovsky persisted resolutely.

"What silliness is this?" Prouzhansky stammered timidly. "Who's the Count among us?"

"But just in case. What would you do?"

"I personally?"

"Yes, you personally."

"Personally, I'd break off relations with him!"

"And you wouldn't talk to him at all?" Talmudovsky asked with a groan.

"No, I wouldn't. There would be no point. But why this silly talk?"

"It's not silly talk," Talmudovsky affirmed gloomily. "The whole of life depends on it."

"I'm done for, done for," Prouzhansky thought, squirming under the quilt like a mouse.

"Of course, no one will talk to me now," Talmudovsky thought. "Prouzhansky is quite right!"

He dropped heavily into the round bisquit-colored seat of the Vienna chair. As for Prouzhansky, he completely disappeared beneath the waves of the quilt. A long awkward pause succeeded. Then, in the hallway, there was the sound of sprightly steps and Shkarlato entered the room.

For a long while he stared contemptuously round the room.

"It stinks here," he announced haughtily. "Like in a doss house. I can't understand how you can live here. This is impossible for an aristocrat."

These words dealt a terrible blow to both students. It seemed to them as if a bolt of lightning had floated into the room and, swaying in the air, was about to pick a victim.

"It's a fine thing to be the owner of an estate," Shkarlato said rather indefinitely, glancing challengingly at his friends. "Mortgage it and live on the income in Paris. Pedal about on a bicycle. Isn't that true, Talmudovsky? And what do you think, Prouzhansky?"

"Enough!" Talmudovsky shouted. "Tell us, Shkarlato, what would you do if it came to light that one of us was secretly a Count?"

At this, Shkarlato took fright. Perspiration of an orange hue beaded his face.

"Well, lads," he muttered, "there is nothing particularly terrifying about it in the end. You would suddenly learn that I am a Count. Of course, it would be a trifle unpleasant . . . but . . ."

"But what if it were I?" Talmudovsky exclaimed.

"You what?"

"Well . . . what if I turned out to be a Count?"

"You a Count? What a joke!"

"But I am a Count . . ." Talmudovsky, the Party member, said in desperation.

"Count Talmudovsky?"

"I am not Talmudovsky," the student replied. "I am Sredizemsky. I am absolutely not to blame for that, but it is a fact."

"It's a lie!" Shkarlato shouted. "I am Sredizemsky."

Dazedly, the two Counts measured each other with their eyes. Then a long, drawn-out moan came from the corner of the room. That was the third Count, who had been unable to support the torture of expectation and who was now emerging from under the quilt.

"I am not guilty!" he shouted. "Did I wish to be a Count's son or a Count? An amorous excess on the part of a representative of a decayed . . ."

Within fifteen minutes the three students were sitting on a mattress as hard as cork—Prouzhansky's mattress—exchanging their experiences of their brief barony.

"And did he mention the regiment of His Majesty the King of Denmark?"

"He did."

"He spoke of it to me too. And to you, Prouzhansky?

"Of course. He also said that my mother was a pure soul although Jewess."

"The old rascal! About my mother, he also said that she was a pure soul even though a Greek."

"And did he ask you to embrace him?"

"He did."

"And you embraced him?"

"No. Did you?"

"I did."

"Well, you're a fool!"

The following day the students stood watching at their window as a yellow coffin was carried out of the house into the street. It contained the last remains of the vengeful Count. The silvered hearse, drawn by a single horse, rattled off over the cobbled street. A general's white plume swayed on the top of the passive horse's head. Two old women with strict eyes ran after the disappearing coffin. The world was well rid of a great troublemaker.

Kate

KATE was descended from a prize-winning pedigree stock recognized by all dog experts. She belonged to a modern species—that of the continental setter. Kate's coat was of two colours: she had two clear patches on her back, while the rest of her looked as if a handful of coffee beans had been spilled over a white surface.

Kate was the name I gave her. Her original masters, an intelligent newly-married couple, had called her Kitty. They had no children during the first two years of their married life, and Kitty had been like a child to them. As a result, she had spent two years sprawling on a divan in their Moscow apartment. In a short while this gun dog of excellent breed would have become transformed into a useless, pampered pet. But, by the end of the second year, the young wife found it difficult to go up and down five flights of stairs while her husband was away at work all day. As it happened, at this time, my own dog Faithful had met with an accident—he had been bitten by a mad dog; and it would be painful for me to relate now the manner in which I had to part from him. Being dissatisfied with my new, but too impetuous dog Ardent, I decided, when I heard about the setter, to take on this dog; and I persuaded her masters to let me have her. They sold her to me at a very reasonable price and, with tears in their eyes, implored me never to beat her.

I had been told by experienced dog trainers that a two-year-old gun dog could still be trained for shooting if it had not already been tampered with by an inexperienced hand. Fortunately, Kate was still so unspoiled that she did not even chase after birds. To begin with, she hunted only after flowers: on the run, she was very fond of biting off and tossing into the air a corolla of camomile. Politeness and understanding were a peculiarity of her species. It was just as well that Kate was a bitch, for a bitch is always more intelligent. In almost a single day I succeeded in accomplishing with her all that goes by the name of housebreaking. I placed a slice of white bread on the floor and, when the dog tried to get at it, I gave her a jab with my fingers and uttered a loud, "Soho!"

"You're not a dog," I added, "to be lying on a divan in Moscow."

In a quarter of an hour, I had taught her not only to refrain from snatching food without permission, but also to restrain herself from touching the morsel I had balanced on her nose.

Then I trained her to *go* and *back* by merely raising my voice, and also *retrieve, here, quiet, down.* The following day I was training Kate in a thick patch of hazel trees, where there was no game. I hid in the thickets and, as the dog sought me out, I taught her in one day the secrets of short range forest tracking. In the open field, it was not so easy. I covered the field myself, tacking like a yacht against the wind, forcing Kate to follow my example by gestures or by whistling softly. For three days I moved about in this way until all the essential training for stalking game had been completed.

Then I took Kate hunting in the swamp at a time when the snipe and the great snipe had not yet abandoned their fortified positions for the open spaces and when only the young lapwing were to be found on the spot. In Hunting Manuals it has been absolutely erroneously stated that the lapwing is bad material for training bird dogs; I myself, on the contrary, know of nothing better. The older lapwing, it is true, tend to excite impulsive dogs, but a few shots will easily disperse them. The fledgelings, on the other hand, will be found so firmly rooted to the ground that, looking like reddish lumps, they can easily be stepped on.

To begin with, Kate did not sense these "lumps." I had to find them myself and give them a shove; and only then did the "lump" become a lapwing which, unable as yet to fly, hobbled off between the tree stumps. Commanding *down*, I made Kate lie still and follow the lapwing only with her eyes until it settled down again, like a "lump," among the stumps.

"Quietly, go!" was the next command.

Kate would advance then, crouching. She did not point, but merely sniffed at the lapwing, which again took off. I then made the dog look the other way to prevent her from seeing where the lapwing had settled again. I myself watched the lapwing, and then sent the dog to cover the ground after it.

Kate did not follow the scent, but seemed to weave her way instinctively with a sort of sewing motion till she came upon the pawing. Again she failed to point, and merely pushed the lapwing with her nose. I repeated the manoeuvre a hundred times, but got nowhere; the dog simply refused to follow the scent or to point. I was feeling rather moody as I walked away from the swamp: It looked very much as if the dog had lost her natural scent after spending two years in the Moscow apartment. But there was still a chance, I thought, of the dog recovering her scent in a new environment.

The Lyakhovo swamp, where I had been experimenting with the lapwings, was about five miles distant from my house. It was impossible for me to go there very often and watch for the snipe and the great snipe to emerge into the open. But, instead, I discovered in my own neighborhood, in the vicinity of the lake, among the marsh reeds, an acre or so of marsh land, where Kate was finally able to flush two old snipe. I began daily to train the dog against these two snipe. But even this walk took up two hours of my morning time, and, moreover, I was obliged to change my clothes every time because, to reach the marsh I had to cross very soggy ground. But it was disappointing to come back always with the same result: Kate, as she pottered about the marsh, only frightened the snipe away without any profit to herself.

One day I took my shotgun with me to the swamp and shot a snipe. It fell on firm ground in the wooded part. Kate found the snipe, but she did so in the same way as she had tracked the lap-wing, weaving about until she had stuck her nose right against it. Yet there was some advantage, I thought, in the fact that she had become familiar with the scent of the bird and that I could there-fore count upon some new achievement on the following day.

It is not only the poets, I believe, who suffer the torments of creation. There is no less torment in canine affairs; and some-times at night some lightning thought would suddenly flash through my mind and give a new direction to my research. Thus, one night, I remembered a discussion, which had been printed in *The Hunter*, concerning the habits of the snipe: some writers maintained that the male snipe did not, after the hatching of the young, take any further part in daily life; others, on the contrary, affirmed that the male snipe often remained in the vicinity of the nest. Thinking of my two snipe, it occurred to me that they must be a male and a female, and that therefore there must be a nest in the vicinity. Next morning I set out for the marsh with my curiosity aroused. As Kate was nosing about, a snipe suddenly flew out. Kate stood and pointed. I moved the marsh reeds apart and there, on a stump, I discovered four snipe eggs, which were amazingly large considering the size of the snipe.

That was something. I would now be able to train the dog daily to point. I would lead her to the spot on a leash and thus would gradually develop her scent. When the young snipe would hatch out, I would catch them and hide them and . . .

How interesting it was to visit the marsh next day, but the unexpected happened. About two hundred paces, I think, sepa-rated the entrance to the marsh from the nest. As soon as Kate had come out of the bushes and had covered fifty paces at the most or some hundred and fifty from the nest, she pointed and then lead on again, approaching nearer and nearer; and how she led: tap, tap, went her slender legs, like those of a ballerina. The boots I was wearing were huge, equine ones, which had been made for me by a certain out-of-work priest, and they had been fashioned in such a homely way that I was always obliged to wind a whole heap of rags round my feet to prevent the boots falling off. But when Kate took a step, all you would hear, perhaps, would be a drop of water falling. And there was I walking along like a mammoth. My clumsiness made her stop and stare at me very severely as if to say:

"Walk quietly, more quietly, master!"

Five paces more and Kate finally pointed. I stroked her, encouraging her to advance a little further. But this proved impossible: one of my priest-made boots squelched down, and the female snipe flew out.

"Ah, ah, what happened?" Kate seemed to ask in her excitement. But she did not budge from the spot. Then I carefully allowed her to approach and sniff the nest.

I felt happy now; but, as I emerged from the marsh, I noticed that haymaking had begun in the marshes. I was informed that the mowing would begin that very evening. I could not ask the peasants not to disturb the nests, for there were many of them, and unfailingly there would be one of them who would have deliberately destroyed the nests if I had made my request. So, returning to the marsh, I cut down a few willow branches and stuck them into the ground near the nest. The result was a bush. I was now afraid of only one thing, that the female snipe might be frightened of the branches and abandon her nest. But it did not turn out that way. Next day Kate led me over the mown grass of the marsh in exactly the same way as the day before, and then pointed at about five paces from the mown down bush. The female snipe flew out again.

At this very time, only at some distance away, of course, Boris Ivanovich, the artist painter, and a certain doctor, were likewise engaged in training their own dogs. Boris Ivanovich had a French pointer; and the doctor, an Irish setter bitch. I invited them to the house on the pretext of having tea and a chat, and afterwards walked them to the marsh, where I gave them a demonstration. . . .

In brief, I blew my own trumpet. In my excess of joy, I even felt some embarrassment as I told the painter:

"It was smart of you, Boris Ivanovich, to train a pointer. It took me three weeks to train my dog."

And to the doctor I said:

"It was smart of you, Michael Ivanovich, to choose an Irish setter. You will have to work hard with him, but then you will have a rare gun dog."

Naturally, both the painter and the doctor instantly spread the rumor that I had an extraordinary ability for training gun dogs, and soon I became quite famous throughout the region.

But things are not always what they seem. Young dog lovers, hunters, newly married couples, poets should never trust in sudden happiness. They should realize, on the contrary, that this illusion is, in reality, the greatest obstacle in their path; and they should never rest upon it, but leap over it. For a week, no more, I reveled in Kate's ideal pointing, that of a remarkable pedigree gun dog. . . .

The marsh looked greener than ever after a week had gone by and the hay had been removed; and one marvelous, grayish day, when I went there again, it looked most attractive and, it seemed to me, as if a snipe might be flushed at any moment. And, in truth, the snipe was flushed just as soon as Kate had stepped forward. But she paid no attention to the snipe. Then she flushed a young snipe right from under her feet. But Kate, still paying no attention and acting as if possessed, guided me straight towards the nest. Then another young snipe was flushed, followed by a third, fourth and fifth. But there was Kate still guiding me on. And exactly as on many occasions previously, Kate stopped dead and pointed at a distance of some five paces from the nest which, when I examined it, contained only broken shells.

The nest, I thought, scented more strongly than the snipe themselves, and so I threw the egg shells away.

I flattened out the hummock, piled dry brushwood over the nest, and lighted a bonfire.

We tried again. But Kate, overturning the fledgling snipe with her feet, only guided me back to the bonfire.

By then I was convinced that this dog had no scent at all for living creatures, but worked only from memory. In fact, Kate was no gun dog, no hunter's friend and helper, no mother of quick, keen puppies; she was just a dog-actress.

In cases like this, many hunters will boast of pulling the trigger.

But I made up my mind to try and persuade Kate's former masters to take her back again, by dropping a hint as to the fate hunters usually reserve for such dogs. . . .

When the shooting season opened, I first amused myself by going duckshooting with the boys; but that was not really my favorite sport. A week later I was out shooting newly fledged black grouse. I enjoyed this, but not too much. I prefer shooting fully fledged black grouse; and whenever my dog points at some distance from them, I have to rack my brains as to where to place myself in order to cover them head on; and when I succeed in doing this, then each fully fledged black grouse in the bag is equivalent to ten of that summer's brood.

The rowan berries had turned redder and redder. The martlets had winged away long ago. The swallows had collected in swarms. The oats had been reaped. The linden trees had grown yellow from top to bottom, and so had the aspens and the birches in the swamps. There had already been two slight frosts. The potato tops had turned black, and the hunter's soul was already rent by schism: he had now a choice of either black grouse in the forest or of plump snipe in the marshes or of gray partridges in the fields.

I was trying to get them all when someone informed me:

"Yesterday Boris Ivanovich shot a great snipe on the wing."

I forgot all about the mere snipe and the partridges. I then found myself some five miles from home in the Lyakhovo swamp, on the watch for the heavy whirring flight of the great snipe. When it was reported that two of them had been shot that day, and three the next, my only comment was, "They're piling it on!"

One day, at the very height of the Great Snipe windfall, my horrible, priest-made boots had chafed my feet so much that I found it impossible to walk all the way to the swamp. To hire a horse on working days was rather expensive and, above all, I would have felt ashamed. That was the way I was made—I just could not ride to the shoot.

It was a meditative sort of day. There were golden nests in the birch trees. Then Kate walked up to me, looking rather sad and forlorn. How thin she had grown!

I felt sorry for this handsome bitch. I remembered we had gray partridges in the stubble just beyond the farmhouse; but, since they were so close to the house, I never thought of them as game and preserved them instead of shooting them. But why should I not try the dog against them, and why not shoot a brace for the table?

I walked into the field in my sandals. The breeze, as it happened, was blowing in my direction. I let Kate cover the ground; and, like a yacht, she went tacking against the wind. In the course of one of her early tacking movements, she caught the scent, jumped to one side and stopped. She stood there for a while and then leapt to one side as gracefully as a ballerina, stood again and stared fixedly at one point. After waiting a while, she began to cover the ground again, slicing into thin pieces, like cheese, all the ground between me and my invisible goal. When, after sniffing, she understood that the goal was not too far away, Kate suddenly guided me forward in absolutely the same way as she had previously done in the case of the snipe nest.

Then she pointed, quivering like a motor and restraining herself with difficulty from the temptation of leaping straight to the source of the scent.

Then suddenly! . . . But you are familiar with the crashing noise made by a huge covey of some thirty gray partridges bursting into the open. I shot twice. A brace of partridges fell a short distance away.

Kate had observed all this.

Then, finally, everything was clear to me. I had been training the dog in a forest swamp, hemmed in by bushes and devoid of any movement of the air. There, Kate had failed to understand what was required of her and had gone about with her nose to the ground. But, out in the open, the fresh breeze had immediately stimulated her ability to follow the scent, which had been deadened by her indoor life in Moscow. But now that she had understood from this experience with the gray partidges, Kate could not fail in future to flush the snipe and the great snipe in the open marshes. By this time I had completely forgotten that I was only wearing sandals and that I did not even have a crust of bread with me. How could I remember this under the circumstances! Just as I was, I hurried, almost ran, the five miles separating me from the Lyakhovo swamp.

We made our first trial on very swampy ground, in which Kate sank up to her belly. She guided me over higher ground towards a dark-looking, circular hollow, a water hole of the previous year. There, we at once flushed both a great snipe and a snipe. I had only time to shoot the great snipe. But Kate managed to flush the snipe again from its new covert. I shot the snipe too. From then on, everything went from better to better.

The Lyakhovo swamp stretched for some three miles, and the sun was in a hurry. I had reached the point of imploring the sun to halt for a moment, but that inhuman luminary insisted on going down. It was now growing dark. I could no longer distinguish the sight on my shotgun and, when I shot, it was at random.

On emerging from the swamp into the stubble, I felt a terrible pain in my foot: the stubble had bitten into the sores, for my sandals, unnoticed by me, had long ago sunk into the swamp.

After this big and excellent shoot at Lyakhovo, I happened one day to set foot in that part of the swamp, which had proved the stage of Kate's original and almost fatal performance. What a memory these dogs have! Here Kate crouched again and would have guided me to the spot where the snipe's nest had once been. But then the scent of real, living snipe conquered her passion as an actress and, stopping now and then to cut figures, she led me to one side in pursuit of the game. I had no time to shoot the snipe as it was flushed, but I kept it in sight until I seemed to see just a little funnel in the air; and when I finally shot through that funnel, the snipe fell into the undergrowth. This time I decided to send the dog to retrieve, and very soon Kate was coming back through the brushwood with the snipe between her teeth.

BORIS PASTERNAK

Troubled Days

(From an unpublished novel: The Year 1905)

KHARLUSHINA'S forebodings came true. That same night some artillery units laid siege to the Fiedler School on Chistiya Prudy. The dragoons fired several volleys at a peaceful crowd on the Tverskoy. In our locality, and in the neighborhood, barricades began to go up.

The streets had emptied. To show oneself abroad involved an element of danger. The pallid rows of buildings with their roofs, approaches and attics, stood there absently as if the space around them had shifted away and turned its back upon them.

And, at the same time, something had happened to the air! This phenomenon deserves a more detailed description. The air, all of it, from the ground to the sky, had attuned itself to the rebellion; and all of it, frosty, high and unpeopled, whirled and hummed like a copper top, which had been set spinning desperately by the gunshots and the explosions. These latter could no longer be distinguished separately. The stunned sky was entirely steeped in their quivering waves. Another sound also impinged upon the hearing: an insistent, mosquito-like droning, mingled soporifically with a gentler clicking and rustling.

A bullet smashed its way through a window-pane of the laboratory in Alexander Alexandrovich's house. Penetrating the inner

167

wall, the bullet shelled off a piece of plaster from the ceiling in
his study. We were all kept behind locked doors; the lamp oil and
the firewood were rationed, for no stock of them had been laid
in and they were now running short. It was during these days
that misfortune overtook Anna Gubertovna.

In November, between the two strikes, Alexander Alexandrovich, that lover of antiquity, had purchased somewhere a second-
hand wardrobe of monstrous proportions, the size of one of those
old traveling coaches in the days of Catherine the Great. The man
in the overcoat, who had delivered this object in a cart, carried it
in sections into the drawing room. The question was where to
place and assemble it. Anna Gubertovna was in despair at this
new acquisition. The rooms of the apartment were already so
overstacked with furniture that it was impossible to turn round.

It was getting on to night. The carter wanted to go home, and
the man in the overcoat was reluctant to walk back alone through
the streets in the frost. He neither pressed Anna Gubertovna,
nor took off his coat. This made her nervous.

Finding it impossible to select a better place, they decided in
their haste to leave the wardrobe for the time being in the drawing room, which was the most spacious room in the house; and
there the wardrobe was assembled noiselessly in five minutes by
the expert in the overcoat, who then mutely bowed himself out
like an artist who had just performed his brief piece in a long
program. "It's no wardrobe, but my coffin!" Anna Gubertovna
exclaimed, sighing whenever she passed near it on emerging from
her closet. The wardrobe was a sore to the eyes. I, too, began to
detest it.

On the evening of November 11th, Anna Gubertovna, while
trying to reach for a bundle of warm winter clothes in the darkness, placed her foot on the edge of an open drawer, gripped the
top ledge and, losing her balance, fell; she complicated her fall
by twisting her body forward while trying to preserve her
balance. She hurt her knee so badly that she lost consciousness
for a few minutes.

On the twelfth, there was a lull in the firing. Profiting by it,
they found a doctor in the vicinity who was not a specialist, and
with difficulty he was persuaded to attend her. Although the

doctor failed to diagnose any broken bones, he nevertheless admitted the possibility of a fracture and prescribed an ice compress.

Glafira Nikolaievna, puffed with pride and dignity, emerged the victor out of this sortie. Everyone questioned her about what she had witnessed in the streets, but she was reluctant to inform her equals whereas, in the sickroom, she was only too ready to explain that Skotniki, and the adjacent side streets, were blocked off with barricades. The people had abandoned them and had concentrated their forces in Verkhny Kopytnikovsky but, at nightfall, the factory workers would certainly descend and stage a battle in the square.

Alexander Alexandrovich also sent Glafira to fetch some ice; and, at the same time, he requested her not to weary the invalid with all that nonsense, because, he argued, the men of the fighting brigades were not such fools as to entrench themselves in a hole where they could be fired on from the houses of the adjacent side streets. Glafira took offense at this and pouted. As for us, we were allowed to spend a few minutes in the courtyard.

Normally, the state of affairs prevailing there would have been described as quiet. But, in those few minutes, it seemed to me nameless and inexplicable. The air, which the crack of shots had perforated for so many days on end, now amazed one by its intangible quality; and, thanks to the twilight and the sunset, it glowed as pink and smooth as the cheeks of a young girl.

This silence was suddenly broken by a conversation carried on in low tones, but every word of which could be overheard. Yerofey, our old janitor, had perhaps started it expressly for our benefit. He was chatting with Moukhrygin just round the corner, in the gateway passage. The edge of the wall hid them from us.

"There's nothing strange in believing in the Trinity," Yerofey was arguing. "People are born to it. It's one thing to practice, another just to talk. If we dip into it deeper, we'll find it is the 'semic' and the 'antisemic' who are shooting it out, some for the sake of the spring of the people's liberation, others for no good reason at all. And the masters were right in what they said about you when they called you an antisemic, and even if you are a devout man, yet you are a manifest opponent of the semic. Real living is foreign to you; you exist without any fresh air on stone premises, like slime or some sort of tree fungus, what with your cough and your tobacco and your drunkenness, but a janitor is always out in the free air and that benefits both his mind and his chest."

I suddenly awoke in the middle of the night. "Get up, we're on fire!" Tonya was shouting at the door as she dressed. "Be quiet, you'll rouse the whole house," I told her. "It's only the bonfires. They're emptying the latrines. Can't you smell the stench." I began to snore again, but I was soon made aware that something was really wrong when I was awakened again a few minutes later.

The whole house was on its feet. Doors were being banged downstairs. The shooting in the town had been renewed with increased vigor. Probably, it was the artillery. Tonya, completely dressed now, was standing over me after succeeding in shaking me out of my sleep.

"Leave the room for a minute," I told her. Wrapping myself in a quilt, I jumped on the window-sill and opened the hinged window pane. The familiar stench overwhelmed me but, having absorbed it, I ceased to notice it. It was swept clean from my consciousness by the wild and alarming spectacle I saw outside.

The sky was bursting and bellowing from the fire and the roar of guns. It was ringed by the glow of several conflagrations. One of them was blazing somewhere nearby. Voices I could not distinguish clashed in the darkness; people were running after and passing each other. Someone was summoning someone else, despatching him, issuing orders. Shattering the houses to their foundation, a squadron of cavalry galloped past along the street. Tongues of flame jerked in that direction. Then all was quiet.

I began to dress, unaware of what I was doing. Then I heard Alexander Alexandrovich thunder up the stairs. In an unusually stentorian voice he called to us from the middle landing.

When we answered, he made sure again that we were all right, and then thundered down the stairs.

We finally gathered in the dining room, wearing our street

clothes in case we might have to abandon the house. The cloth window curtains had been pulled together so that they over-lapped and a candle, propped upright with a book, stood on the dining room table.

Anna Gubertovna, a cloak round her shoulders, reclined on a sofa, her eyes rolled up as usual beneath her drooping eyelids. The whites of her eyes gleamed in bands from under her eye-lashes. Tonya dashed forward to kiss her. Anna Gubertovna, biting her lips, freed her arm from beneath the cloak and, grimac-ing from tears, began in a breathless whisper to bless herself, her daughters and the walls of the dining room where we were all assembled.

Suddenly Yerofey, as pale as death, glanced in at the doorway and called Alexander Alexandrovich outside. They were both too preoccupied to pay any attention to me. Profiting by the con-fusion, I ran out after them.

Every morning I used to leave for school in the artificial light, at the ebb of the blue winter night. As, on those occasions, the dawn now seemed to be here. Outside, in the street, someone was banging and shaking the courtyard gates. The gates were being forced.

"We ought to run to the front door and see who it is before opening." Alexander Alexandrovich had hardly finished saying this when five or six armed men, some in quilted coats, others in short sheepskin coats, burst into the courtyard. "Who's the pro-prietor here?" demanded a man in a shaggy Port Arthur fur cap. "I am," Alexander Alexandrovich replied. "May we hide here?" the man asked again. "Oh, of course! Hide here, gentlemen. In the shed, if you like. Or in the house. Yerofey, give me the keys! But, on second thought, I'm not so sure . . . there are sick people in the house."

The men exchanged glances. The foreman in the shaggy fur cap and his companion began to look round. "What's behind the fence?" the foreman enquired. "A wild neglected garden."— "And behind that?"—"Some waste ground used as a dump."— "And beyond that?"—"A network of streets giving on Dolgoru-kovsky Street."—"We shan't hide here, then?" The foreman put it to the men in a half-questioning, half-conclusive tone.—"No!"

the others replied.—"The courtyard's too small, and we should look sharp." They all laughed at that. "That's right. Let's go, comrades," their leader said, and they all rushed for the fence.— "Get a ladder, Yerofey!" Alexander Alexandrovich shouted. But the men were already on the other side of the fence.

Several minutes passed. "It's freezing hard," Alexander Alexandrovich commented, yawning.—"Hard it is. Exactly so."— "Listen, Yerofey, be careful. You have a long tongue."—"What do you mean, sir? It's deeper than the grave . . . Would you want me to put the ladder away?"—"Yes. Let's take it away together. Ah, but look at all those footprints in the snow. If we could only blot them out!"

This they began to do when they had locked the ladder in the shed.—"Walk away from the fence. You're doing it the wrong way round, blockhead!" Alexander Alexandrovich shouted. "Didn't I tell you how to do it, but you keep doing it your own way. The footprints should come from our direction and not towards us."

Suddenly the street was shaken again by the same thudding of hooves I had heard on wakening. From their speed one might have judged that the squadron would gallop past the house. But the squadron came to a sudden stop. The horses had been reined in right opposite our house. They halted, slithering and sliding.

Then I made out the thump of jumping feet, the tread of steps and the clatter of weapons. Yerofey hid behind the shed. Alexander Alexandrovich ran up the steps and stood inside the boxed doorway. Several Cossacks hurried into the middle of the courtyard, illuminated by the conflagration.

Their leather straps, and the rifles slung over their shoulders, made them look short and squat. They all seemed askew from vodka, frost and sleeplessness. Their boots slithered on the frosty ground. Their cavalry gait made them appear round-shouldered.

"Dubrovin, get five men over to the fence!" the cornet shouted. "Onisimenko, I told you to get hold of the janitor! Ah, there he is, the scoundrel! In whose service are you, you son of a bitch! Don't you know the Governor's orders? Why do you leave the gates wide open? Why, I ask you, are the gates . . .

Take this, you . . ." the cornet yelled, hitting Yerofey twice across the face. "Answer me, you wobbly-backed devil . . . Dubrovin, you'd better keep a sharp watch! When he comes to, I'll question him. I don't understand. What are you saying? Footprints? What footprints? Ah, footprints in the snow!"

Then he looked round and at once forgot about the lance-corporal. He jumped aside and pulled out his revolver.

"I'll shoot you! Don't move!" he yelled. "Hands up. Who are you, my dear sir?"

"Why did you hit the janitor?" Alexander Alexandrovich asked quietly, with a quiver in his voice.

"Don't try and teach me, I beg you. It's forbidden to be out in the streets after nine. Why are you here and who are you?"

"I'm the proprietor of this house and I've something important to tell you. But, first of all, order me to be searched. I cannot answer you when a revolver is pointed at me. My arms are getting numb."

"Your name?"

"Gromeko."

"Never heard of you. So you're the proprietor? So much the worse. You'll have to answer under the severest penalties of the law. Have you read the Governor's order? And do you realize that your gates are wide open? Just look. You can't go on like that, you can't, young man. The janitor was all you thought of when you opened your mouth. But do you know anything about him? Are you prepared to vouch for him? And that isn't all! Why aren't the people in your house sleeping? Are they uneasy in their mind? That's interesting. Why aren't you easy in your mind? Well, all right. Do you have any weapons?"

"No."

"Do you belong to the gentry?"

"Yes."

"Drop your hands, then."

"*Merci*," Alexander Alexandrovich replied mechanically and, descending from the porch step by step, set foot on the ground. "The people in the house were sleeping," he began. "The gates were bolted. Then there was a sudden disturbance. I aroused the janitor. There were several armed men in the yard. Workers."

"What workers? You must call them by their right name. Thieves, gallows-birds, the accursed tribe."

"Well, yes. Several of them . . . gallows-birds . . ." Here Alexander Alexandrovich became confused. "I realize that they had made their way from Dolgorukov Street through the adjacent properties and that they were breaking down the gates in an attempt to take a shortcut to the street yonder. I'm astonished you didn't come across them. It all happened about five or ten minutes ago. That means they must have rushed towards Skatniky."

"Now tell me, has there been any shooting from that direction in the past few days? From the neighboring gardens? Have you noticed anything?"

"No. Everything was quiet there."

"So, so. You'll answer for it, if it isn't true. All right, dismiss. Dubrovin," he went on. "You reported footprints. Let's go. Show me them. Farewell, dear sir. Remember what you risk. I'll not put you under guard. I'll always know where to find you."

They went off. In the dark depths of the courtyard words of command rang out. The Cossacks could be heard falling into step and marching out into the street in better order than they had entered. The squadron was then commanded to mount. The horses started off at a trot and, within a few strides, had broken into a gallop. The memorable thud of hooves, which I had heard in the night and which had just now stopped with such terrifying abruptness in front of our house, was now resumed with its former rhythm and began gradually to die in the distance. Everything vanished like an interrupted dream.

Glafira and Tonya were standing on the porch, tugging me by the sleeve.

"In a moment. Leave me alone," I said, trying to get rid of them, but I ended by telling them everything.

Alexander Alexandrovich could not utter a word. The enforced humiliation gave him no peace. His lips were trembling. He was, with difficulty, trying to overcome something within himself.

As soon as the Cossack squadron had moved off, he went up to Yerofey. But the latter picked himself up without any difficulty. His unconsciousness had been half-simulated. One of his eyes was slightly blackened, and a cheekbone was bleeding from where the skin was broken. We were now sent off to bed and, strange as it may seem, fell asleep immediately.

I rose late. The curtains were drenched, as with jam, in the pomegranate juice of the sunset. In my drowsy state, I had the impression that it was springtime. Moist, champing sounds were borne upon me from the outside. Sinking into the soft snow, someone was dragging something through it. It was thawing. People were clearing away the debris of last night's fusillade. And there was the same warm and nauseous stench.

Then I remembered everything. But it was the first time that I had risen at such an hour. It was a new feeling. It blurred the memories of the previous night. I liked this new impression so much that I decided to find another opportunity to get up at this hour.

They now discovered that Anna Gubertovna had an inflammation of the knee joint. She slept badly and moaned at night. If I had seized the opportunity and gone downstairs to sit by her bed, I would have profited by my right to do so . . . but I carelessly slept through these possibilities. I forget what pretext I used to this end.

The rebellion came to an end. The consciousness of its collapse, and the rumors of retribution, filled the air. There was talk of the savagery of the soldiers of the Semeonov regiment and the insolence of the Cossack pickets in the street. Then followed the period of the court martials.

Alexander Alexandrovich no longer seemed himself. Over and above the general frustrations, he was depressed by the condition of his sick wife. To bring her pleasure, he bought her some blue and white hyacinths, several branches of cineraria, and three pots of bleeding heart. When the bleeding heart were brought into the bedroom in the wake of the other flowers, she threw a fit of tantrums. It turned out that she had always disliked bleeding heart. Her husband's forgetfulness upset her. The bleeding heart were removed to the dining room.

I awoke towards six in the evening. As on the previous occasion, the day had slipped by without my knowledge and was now entirely behind me. While I dressed, the twilight thickened into the resemblance of a cloud of dust which, on departing, it had raised on the road. With insuperable sorrow, I gazed at the claret eye of the sunset as if at a glowing lantern hung at the back of a receding train. And I developed a headache into the bargain.

I descended to the dining room. There, with her back to me, stood Glafira Nikitishna, preoccupied with something or other. She had just watered a flower and was smoothing out the turned down edges of the lilac wrapper. I asked for some tea. "In a moment," she answered, watching the water gather in the pots on the window-sill and ready to wipe it up if it should overflow.

The masseuse came out of Anna Gubertovna's bedroom. Her duties were finished as of this moment. The new doctor had been horrified when he learned the day before that, for a whole week, she had been spreading pus throughout the patient's body. Glafira Nikitishna went to see her off.

In the meantime the front doorbell had sounded. "There now. She'll forget all about the tea . . ." I thought, approaching the cabinet with the bleeding heart.

Suddenly, with a blast of cold air, Uncle Fedya burst into the drawing room. I identified him from afar off by certain signs. Nervously he paced over the carpet from one corner of the room to the other. Alexander Alexandrovich came out to greet him. Talking, they entered the dining room.

Uncle Fedya was terribly agitated. The words spurted from him with such force that he spattered his beard with saliva and bellowed while, at the same time, he wiped his lips with a handkerchief so as not to lose a single moment of speech.

"You know how much I love you, Sasha," he exclaimed. "But you are monsters, all of you. The world might have been turned upside down and still you would be proccupied only with massages and with growing plants. Now prepare to face the real horror. Where is your sister Olya?"

"If you know anything about her, tell me."

"No, it's your turn first. Have you thought of her even once? Did it ever occur to you to think about her?"

"I've been looking for her for the last three days," Alexander Alexandrovich replied. "Without result so far. But that's in the order of things, and it does not disturb me. Because, as you must agree, on the day following the suppression of the revolt, and with the conditions now prevailing, to find her, as you will understand, is not as easy as weaving a bast shoe."

"Bast shoes! Conditions! You're barking up the wrong tree. That's not where you should be looking. A corpse, that's what . . . in the morgue . . . in the anatomical . . ."

But Alexander Alexandrovich had already gripped Uncle Fedya's hand above the wrist.

"Stop!" he shouted. "What's happened to her?"

"She's been killed."

"How do you know?"

"A feeling tells me."

"But . . . have you verified it?"

"Twice I've made the round of friends. There's been no sign or breath of her."

"You're a regular swine with all this," Alexander Alexandrovich burst out. "A plague on you for talking like that. Thank you for the information and . . . the sympathy. You don't care where anything blows from, whether it be from a rooted oak tree or just the movement of the wind as long as there's a noise and an impression. It might only be a dream or acorns seeding, but it's all the same to you. A feeling tells me!"

"Stop, Sasha, don't get excited. After all, in a case like this, . . . I'm not sorry that I came. I'm very glad. You have set my mind at rest. Your faith has reassured me."

"At a time when I'm literally exhausted . . . and when my wife is ill . . ."

"Ah, that knee of hers. God give she will surmount it."

"Well, of course. Your prayers will help a lot. I regret to say that I am a specialist in the natural sciences. I know all about nature and the danger of septic infections . . . but instead of helping me when I am literally torn apart . . ."

Uncle Fedya was served tea. He visited the bedroom and inspected the patient. Then he began to take his leave. On departing he said:

"I realize now why you have so many flowers here. But neither cactus nor rhododendron will help. They won't deaden *it*. This stench has got the best of us. Where does it come from?"

"On the night of the twelfth a shell exploded in a well—a sewer, I mean. You understand?"

Within two days Auntie Olya was found.

BORIS PASTERNAK

The Proud Beggar

A HOT APRIL DAY in nineteen hundred and two or three. This was evidently on St. Thomas' Feastday, before the customary May chill descended on Moscow. All around there was a feeling of spaciousness and wide audibility, which had succeeded the noisy and long-lasting Easter celebrations. The sky had not yet dried from the daylong bell-pealing with which it had been drenched during the whole of Holy Week.

I was nine years old, almost ten at the time. For the past half hour I had been idling along the Third Bogoyavlensky Street, peeping into the courtyards and gaping at the belfries. Very soon I would settle down here in Gromeko's house.* In the meantime, although a frequent visitor to the house, I was still a comparative stranger to this side street and did not know the quarter very well.

In the distance, beyond the lumberyard which the lower end of the street suddenly severed from view, a square was visible. I did not know that this was Bolshii Skotniki, which was destined to surprise me so greatly in the next two or three years, and that one of two houses on the square, the one of plain brick and many windows, was the Schepihinskie Workshops, while the second, painted ocher, was the aniline factory of *The Anonymous Society*. Nor did I know that, despite its real name, the beautiful

* In *Doctor Zhivago*, Alexander Alexandrovich Gromeko is Zhivago's father-in-law.

church with the thirteen cupolas at the upper part of the street
was popularly known as *The Perished Call You to Account*, after
the miraculous icon which it contained.

I was still lodging with Feodor Stepanovich Ostromyslenko, a
relative seven times removed of Gromeko; and shall henceforth
call him, like everyone else, Uncle Fedya. I never gave any
thought to where I stood in relationship to him. Matrena Ivanovna Belestova—or Motya—the psalmreader's daughter, who
was his young companion and who had been repudiated by her
family on that account, dignified him by calling him "protector"
—that is, a man called upon to preoccupy himself with me. As
far as I can remember, I was always with him, but I had no idea
how that came about.

Now he was at Gromeko's. He had left me in the street so that
I should be at hand if need be. I was on the alert, waiting for that
moment, but I could not figure out how I would find out.

The day before, Uncle Fedya had been summoned to Gromeko's by a letter, evidently an unpleasant one, which had been
delivered in the evening. Until then, the day had gone like clock-
work. After dinner, Uncle Fedya had taken the broken kitchen
clock apart. That was his main passion. In his day, he had taken
an uncounted number of clocks apart, but he had never succeeded in piecing a single one of them together. After scolding
me for fetching the wrong tobacco and after sending me to the
Sretenka for a new packet, he had begun to prepare his own cigarettes. Then, remembering the shaky stools in the kitchen, he had
gone there with a paring chisel and a jack-plane to fashion new
legs for them; but, leaving the job unfinished, he had only piled
up more work for Motya by leaving a heap of shavings on the
linen on the ironing board and by upsetting a jar of hot carpen-
ter's glue on the floor.

He had then sat down near the window with Max Stirner's *The
Ego and His Own*,* a really harmful book full of crude delu-
sions, according to him; but he would have grumbled about it in
any case, even if it had been the very voice of truth. In general,
the only reason he read books was in order to repudiate them in

* In which the author attacks formal social institutions as hampering the self-
realization of the individual.

front of Motya and myself. While reading, he was in the habit of humming, even though he had no ear. For some reason, he read Stirner to the tune of *In the Midst of Level Plains*, interrupting his reading with exclamations such as: "Ah, the bandit! You just wait, I'll show you!"

Meanwhile, in the courtyard, life had pursued its way. The courtyard was situated in one of the side streets between the Sretenka and the Tzvetnoy Boulevard. One could hear the canaries, which belonged to the happy-go-lucky fellow who traded them on Sundays on the Trouba, pouring out their filtered trills. The Tartars, who traded in horse meat, had received their delivery of blue horse carcasses with intelligent marble heads. A pimp from among the horse jobbers, who had recently been released from prison, was in the habit of beating up his "mamoshka," as they called her here. She would squeal provokingly and then rush out into the street in teasing disarray and, there, weepingly complain to any odd passer-by. There had been also an old bow-legged beggar woman who, indifferent to everything and, as it were, petrified from drink, had stood near an open sewer. An old woman ragpicker, with the wooden splint in her sack looking like a bony extension of herself, had treated the beggar to a goat's foot. The old hags, screwing up their eyes, had lingered on the spot, belching hoarsely, spitting and scratching their behinds; and they had stared at the round sky with its round sun, which stood right above the open sewer.

The letter had been delivered before supper. Over the pickled cucumber soup with giblets and the calf's foot jelly, Uncle Fedya had complained about all the pother of life, which had dogged him since his youth.

"All the same, it would be better for you to have an occupation," Motya had suggested shyly. "It would be more agreeable for you, and you'd find it easier to look people in the eyes. Was there anything wrong with that job at the printers for the Archives? Well, I won't mention the city school. Teaching children is evidently not your cup of tea, and, true enough, there's nothing worse than when the authorities start fishing for subversion in the ABC's."

"How does Uncle Fedya live?" I also asked myself while stroll-

ing along the Third Bogoyavlensky. Alexander Alexandrovich
Gromeko lectured at the Petrovsky Academy and wrote books
on natural history; his brother Nicholas was a Professor of
Roman Law; and his brother-in-law Kanchugin had a medical
practice. I listed every one of my acquaintances, including the
carpenters I knew, and came to the conclusion that Uncle Fedya
had mastered the secret of neither sowing nor reaping, but of
existing like the very birds of heaven, if not better.

By contrast with our quarter, the neighborhood of the Fourth
Bogoyavlensky was replete with purity and poetry. In the shade,
the sparrows hopped and twittered without a moment's rest, and
the cobblestones exuded the burned frying-pan smell of the
scorching sun. As though perspiring frequently, linden tree
sprouts hung down, festooned in strongly, even pungently,
smelling buds. And, in the church garden of *The Perished Call
You to Account*, the poplars were already in fresh leaf, looking
as if they had donned all their summer wear for the benefit of
the heat.

Below, it was still damp. Piles of light saffron logs in the lumberyard swam in the hot chocolate of black mire. Like the white
of a fried egg, the blue, white-clouded noon had been plopped
into the puddles. The whole of Holy Thursday the geese had
cackled here, vying in their whiteness with the last lingering
snowdrifts.

But now there were neither geese nor snow left. The cries of
the rooks were burning the heady white willows to ash. Hens
stalked cautiously and apprehensively about the yard. All the
neighboring yards answered the cock that was concealed behind
a stack of logs. Then the cock himself, with oil-painted head and
silken beard, seemed to choke on his crowing as on a bone and,
charred by the heat of his feathers and scattering sparks with his
tail, recovered from his singing as though easing his stomach. It
was quiet all around. And hot.

But what was that? A signal for me? Screwing up her eyes as
if about to shoot, Glafira Nikitishna, Gromeko's old maid, was
opening the French window of the drawing room with both
hands. Fastening back the windows with hooks, she leaned with

her breast and elbows on the window sill. In front of her, across the street, were the three stories of the house opposite.

"Seems you have a new maid," she said in a quiet voice in that direction, as if speaking from one box into another at Korsh's Theater. "You tell her to use chalk first, because it's a mess otherwise; she rubs and rubs, but can't wipe it clean."

The reply was lost. Moukhrigin, the upholsterer, emerged from Gromeko's basement; his personality was prematurely wrinkled from a propensity to laughter and a tendency to soulful remorse.

"Listen to them, ma'am," he said, speaking in the same direction. "One doesn't cover a roof just by raising one's skirt.* It's house painters know most about window-washing. It's not soap, but chalk that's needed most of all."

Turning the corner of the house, I passed through the yard and then entered by the back door.

Here, I found myself, first of all, in a spacious hallway with a wide triple-stained glass window. From the hallway a staircase ascended to the attic. In the courtyard in front of the hallway, a triple-trunked poplar was growing. In the summer, when it was covered with foliage, it made the windowpanes look bottle green and made them shimmer in beer-colored patches of brown heat. Peeping through the door, I caught sight of Tonya standing near the drawing-room window with some children's sewing in her hand. Her eyes were not on her work; she was listening to something.

"What are you doing here?" I asked, approaching her. Without replying, she raised a finger to her lips. Then she suddenly announced:

"You are poor now. Very, very poor. They say he's nibbled you as clean as a bush. Don't argue; I heard it myself. They say he's dissipated and squandered everything. They'll send you to a gymnasium now. You are going to live with us."

The door of Anna Gubertovna's boudoir was partly ajar. Uncle Fedya was holding it by the handle from inside. He was evidently on the point of departing. But then he closed the door

* A Russian proverb.

again, leaving a mere crack. I thought the room was full of smoke
and people, but my feelings had perhaps deceived me. The ar-
rangement of the furniture in the closet may also have helped to
create this impression.

In the boudoir, a whole shower of harmoniously tinkling glass
pendants cascaded down from the ceiling; the whiskers of creep-
ing plants hung down from bamboo flower stands; in front of the
windows translucent mica pictures were suspended on fine
chains; and over the threshold hung a rush and bead curtain, in
the streaming play of which stood Uncle Fedya, entangled.

"On top of it, he's offended!" a tigerish voice burst forth
through that hedge of reeds. "You might think he was a Kazan
orphan!"

That was the voice of Gromeko's bride, a hard coffee drinker
and a lover of fur wraps, as well as a dark-haired cigarette
smoker. Uncle Fedya could not be heard, for he was speaking in
a low voice. He was probably suggesting that I be confronted
with them. This excited a fresh storm of indignation. Everyone
was talking in one voice; it was impossible to distinguish who
was arguing what.

"To involve children?" "Don't get so excited!" "You're a
parasite!" "Not so long ago in the orphans' court . . ." "You
can have your affairs, brother, with whom you will, but children
. . ." "It's not your business, you have no fear of God." "Better
tell us what you did with the mortgage." "Bravo, Aneta! Yes, yes,
tell us now what you did with the mortgage." "Science?" "In the
interests of science?" "That's enough to make a dead man laugh!"
"Well, you're a fine druggist, aren't you!" "A distiller of anise,
are you, or of St.-John's-wort . . . Ha-ha-ha!" "You've no fear
of God." "Feodor, stop this instantly or I'll show you a thing or
two in the presence of all. You won't soon forget what comes of
whining as on the Hitrovka."* "Calm yourself, Sasha, it's bad for
you to get excited."

The voices leveled out. After the general screaming, their
calmness seemed sinister. Now something practical was being
discussed at the family council. Uncle Fedya was invited to the
round table in the depths of the room. Frequent calls were

---

* A quarter infested by beggars.

made on Glasha, the maid, to bring either tea and *petits fours* or the inkstand, which she carried in on a tray, with the sealing wax and a candle in a candlestick. The family drafted and signed some sort of document.

Tonya and I were about to walk upstairs to her playroom, but instead we remained rooted to the spot. Uncle Fedya suddenly appeared in the doorway—a gaunt pole of a figure in spectacles and long hair, a living reproach aimed at everything in the world in his gray trousers tucked into soft felt boots.

He did not notice us. Reaching the middle of the hallway, he came to an abrupt halt. Bending forward and scooping up his beard with the palm of his hand, he stood reflecting. Having resolved to say his final word, he turned back to the boudoir.

"Uncle Fedya!" we called out to him, warning him of our presence.

"Why are you here, children?" he asked, forgetting his instructions to me. After a moment's reflection, he walked into the closet; then in his absent-mindedness, he walked toward the front door but, remembering us, returned.

"Good-by, Patricky," he said in a trembling voice. "Mature here as you matured with me. The good seeds I planted will not go to waste. You're too young still to understand what has happened here, in this woman's study. The Lord suffered and bade us suffer, too. Good-by, Patrick. Good-by, Antonina. And please don't accompany me."

The following day I came to live under the same roof as Tonya.

Afterwards, when I had taken up historiography as well as literature, and when my vocation had brought me into contact with the doctrine of types, my trust in theory was uprooted when I remembered my first patron. On the basis of my childhood experience, I learned to think that every form of typicality was equivalent to artificiality, and that, strictly speaking, only those are types who, contrary to nature, deliberately aspire to become them. Why, I reflected, should we drag typicality onto the stage when it is already so theatrical in life? Uncle Fedya founded his strength upon a parody of a spiritual personality, which, having no conception of such things, he mimicked.

His own inclination for the abstract noun of neuter gender and for the indefinite pronoun he interpreted as a vein of philosophy. He saw himself as a sort of Sretensky Diogenes, and his own, in no way distinctive, dullness he regarded as an attribute of the common people.

How could this pretension have been generated? The common people lived and moved beside him—composed wholly of the craftsman, the tool-maker, the specialist in some one thing, the master and the fanatic of detail, the child of passion and the plaything of chance; but he failed to observe that they were all sharply defined, for his apprehension went no further than that watery and pompous community which he himself represented, who was not properly trained in any one thing and who remained relative, a nonentity, an everyman.

Years passed but wrought no change in Uncle Fedya. Nor did misfortune alter him. Motya paid dearly for her affection; she was obliged at one time to sell all his books, but, thanks to her neat penmanship, she eventually managed to earn a living of sorts by copying documents and affidavits.

As an amateur chemist out of Rubakin's textbook, Uncle Fedya was engaged one day in boiling some kind of mixture. For some undetermined reason, the retort exploded into smithereens. In an instant, his face had become a bloody mess. He lost his sight in unspeakable torments—both his eyes were perforated with tiny glass splinters.

During my last years at the gymnasium I did some paid tutoring. One of my pupils lived on Tzarytzin Street. After Uncle Fedya's misfortune, the Ostromyslenkos had moved to Hamovniki. I had their address and decided to visit them.

The windows of the minute kitchen, which they rented in an uninhabited apartment that was let as an office, gave on the street. From the outside I could distinguish Motya's level voice. She was reading aloud. Judging by the "first cause," the matter and the form, I surmised that the text was Aristotle in some antediluvian translation.

"Do you understand this?" I could hear Motya inquire as she interrupted her reading.

"What is there to understand here?" Uncle Fedya's voice replied. "It's arrant nonsense. The author—a respectable name, an ancient Greek philosopher; do you think I don't know? But the translator ought to be taken to task. Will you go on, please."

At this point I announced myself. They were both very glad to see me and pressed me to come in. But I still had two lessons to teach, one after the other. I promised to call again and told them that, on this occasion, I would remain in the street. In this manner, we conversed.

For a time everything went well. Uncle Fedya had changed but little. His facial wounds had healed without leaving any scars. He had grown slightly grizzled. The conversation was conducted in keeping with the warm air, our relative positions in the kitchen and on the sidewalk, and the difference in our ages.

"Ah, the years, the years!" Uncle Fedya exclaimed.

"Where have you been absenting yourself all this time? Motya, examine every aspect of him and describe him. Does he look important? Has he grown taller? I'm sure he puts on airs, the horse face. In January, you know, Matrena Ivanovna buried her father. You'd better sympathize with her."

That sentence changed everything. Motya's youth and charm suddenly hit my eyes. It would have been so easy to fall in love with her. The old fool ought not to have spoken in this way about her loss—he was no prop for her, and he was probably the cause of her grief. I felt revolted.

"The earth is filled with rumors; I know of your attempts to wield the pen," Uncle Fedya pronounced, and he proceeded to speak of these attempts in greater detail.

In principle, he approved of them, but warned me against bad influences. Under the latter heading he included everything I then adored, everything I then venerated.

In between the cut of his mustache and his beard, his lips moved, looking as self-satisfied as a couple of Astrakhan grapes. It was terrifying to gaze upon them, because their vital glow produced the impression of a seeing center in that smooth face which his blindness had drawn and pacified. He was reading his sermon to me and enjoying it as though eating dessert, and I was compelled to agree with him for fear of upsetting him.

"I wish you'd mount the steps. Just for a minute!" Motya

called out in order to put an end to my involuntary treachery.

I obeyed. Turning into the yard, I found her sitting on a step, resting an extremely bulky volume of The Holy Scriptures on her knees. Licking her finger, she was rapidly turning over the pages and, without raising her head, she gave me her left hand to shake.

"Just look at this, Patrichok, look at what I am going to show you. Just look at what I came across the other day. Ah, but where did it get lost? Here it is now. Just look."

"And there are three kinds of men," I read in the verses, "whom, in my soul, I have come to detest: the proud beggar; the rich man that uttereth falsehood; and the old man that hath lechery in his heart. . . ."

"The proud beggar!" Motya repeated triumphantly. "How do you like that, Patrichok? Right in the eye, isn't it!"

MICHAEL SHOLOKHOV

During the Retreat

From *They Fought for their Country*

THE MAJORITY of the men settled down to sleep in the yard near the shed. The woman of the house made a bed for herself in the kitchen, while the sergeant, together with Streltzov, Lopahin, Khmyz and Kopitovsky, as well as four others, lay down in a room separated by a small passage from the kitchen.

Khmyz and a long-necked soldier, to whom the nickname of "crabcatcher" had firmly stuck, talked for a long time in whispers. Kopitovsky kept blindly catching fleas and swearing in a low voice. Lopahin smoked two cigarettes, one after the other, and then grew still. After a while, the sergeant called to him in a whisper:

"Lopahin, are you asleep?"

"No."

"Make sure you don't fall asleep!"

"Don't worry!"

"You need a shot or two of vodka to bolster your courage, but where the devil's father can we get it?"

Lopahin laughed quietly in the darkness and replied:

"I'll manage without that poison."

His bones could be heard cracking as he stretched himself and then got up.

"Are you going then?" the sergeant whispered.

"And why should I lose time?" Lopahin answered without restraining his voice.

"May you be successful!" the crabcatcher earnestly exclaimed. Lopahin kept silent. Tiptoeing, he groped his way in the infernal darkness towards the door leading to the passage.

"All the hungriest men are sleeping in the house, the rest—in the yard," said Khmyz in an undertone, and then boyishly put his hand over his mouth and blew a raspberry.

"What's got into you?" Kopitovsky asked in astonishment.

"*No passaran!* He'll not get through!" Khmyz answered in a voice shaking with laughter.

He was immediately rebuffed by Akimov, a sniper of the third batallion, a bilious and irritable man, who had worked before the war as an accountant in a large construction plant in Siberia:

"I would ask you, comrade Khmyz, to be more careful with words that are precious to humanity. An intelligent young man, with ten years of schooling behind him as far as I know, and here you are falling into the bad habit of using words carelessly. . . ."

"He'll not get through!" Khmyz repeated, choking with laughter.

"What are you croaking about, you flaplip?" the crabcatcher inquired indignantly. " 'He'll not get through, not get through,' but he is advancing quietly. Do you hear the board creak, and here you keep saying he won't get through. What do you mean by won't? He'll get through easily enough!"

"Quiet there! Silence and snoring is what we need most. If hunger won't let you snooze, pretend at least to sleep."

"How can we camouflage ourselves if the belly rumbles loud enough to be heard in the street," the crabcatcher commented dismally. "These damned cannibals! Not to feed a soldier, how do you like that? In the old days in the province of Smolensk, a peasant woman would give you her last potato; but from these people you wouldn't even get a helping of snow in the winter. Their collective farm here must be made up entirely of former kulaks, most likely. . . . How is he getting on there? There isn't a sound."

"He's got within range, but he won't get through all the same!" Khmyz jovially whispered.

"The situation at the front has completely spoiled you. You are incorrigible, I see," Akimov protested in disgust.

"Hey there, stop chattering!" the sergeant whispered hoarsely.

"What's he hissing for, like a goose at a dog? He's got his own old man's business to attend to, so why doesn't he snore both ways. . . . It's no sergeant we have, but a beast on a chain."

"I'll give you beast tomorrow! You think I don't know your voice, Nekrasov? You can alter your voice as much as you like, but I'll know you anyhow!"

There was a minute's silence in the room, interrupted by a variety of snores; then the crabcatcher spoke out with unconcealed disappointment:

"He's not advancing! What's he marking time for? Oh, contagion! He'll wear the soul out of us before he gets into the line of fire! O Lord, what a lumpkin you sent! By the morning, maybe, he'll reach the passage."

There was silence again for a while, and then the crabcatcher spoke again, with despair this time in his voice:

"No, he's not advancing! Hugging the ground, is he? What's keeping him down? Has she set up barbed wire in front of the kitchen, or what?"

Finally losing his patience, the sergeant raised himself:

"Will you shut up now, you sons of Satan?"

"O Lord, as it is we're lying here as if under a German rocket . . ." the crabcatcher whispered almost inaudibly and then stopped:

Kopitovsky had clapped his outsized hand to his mouth. . . .

Several more minutes passed in harrassing expectation; then came the sound of a woman's indignant voice in the kitchen, the noise of brief scuffling, the crash of something as the fragments of a broken dish scattered over the floor; and then the door hit the wall with such a bang that the plaster fell rustling from the walls and, with a mournful wail, the fussy pendulum clock above the chest came to a stop.

Pushing the door with his back, Lopahin tumbled into the room and, walking backwards, took several quick, unsteady steps and, hardly keeping his feet, finally halted in the middle of the room. . . .

The sergeant leapt up with youthful zest and, lighting the kerosene lamp, raised it above his head. Lopahin stood there, his legs straddled. His right eye was glossily black and blue; but the left eye glittered with bright exultation. All the men lying on the floor raised themselves as if by command. Sitting up on their spread out army coats, they stared in silence at Lopahin and asked no questions. And there was nothing to ask: the black eye and the swelling lump the size of an egg, on his forehead, spoke more eloquently than any words. . . .

"Alexander the Great! Petty flea! Well, and did you have your unexpected fill?" the sergeant, pale with anger, ground annihilatingly through his teeth.

Lopahin fingered the still growing lump above his right eyebrow and casually waved his hand:

"An unforseen hitch! But, brothers, you should have seen the strength of that woman! She's not a woman, but beauty itself! I haven't seen the like of her before. A first rate boxer, a wrestler of the highest category! Thank God, I had my training beaten into me. I've got strength in my hands, I can lift up a hundredweight from the ground and carry it where you will, but she seized me by the leg above the knee and by the shoulder, raised me up and said: 'Go and get some sleep, Pyotr Feodotovich, or I'll throw you out of the window!'—'Well,' I said, 'we shall see about that!' Well, and I did see. . . . I displayed some superfluous activity, and that's it, if you please. . . ." Lopahin, wrinkling his forehead from the pain, fingered again the knobbly, purple patch above his brow, and said: "Yes, lucky it was that I hit the door with my back or the whole doorway might have come away on my shoulders. Well, do as you like, but—if I survive the war—I shall return to this village after the war and take this woman away from her lieutenant of a husband. She's a real find, not a woman!"

"And what about the sheep now?" Nekrasov asked in a dispirited tone.

He was answered with such an explosion of deafening laughter that Streltzov jumped up in alarm and, in his drowsy state, stretched his arm out for the automatic rifle which lay where his head had been.

"But will your 'find' feed us tomorrow?" the sergeant asked, containing his rage.

Lopahin, after emptying a flask of tepid water, answered quietly:

"I doubt it."

"So what were you messing about and bothering us for?"

"And what do you want from me, comrade sergeant? That I should try another pass? I prefer the German tanks. But if you are so impatient—go yourself. I have earned one bump, but she'd plant a whole dozen of them on you, that's sure! Well, shall I accompany you as far as the kitchen?"

The sergeant spat, swore under his breath and began to pull on his tunic. Having dressed and speaking to no one in particular, he said grimly:

"I'll go to the chairman of the collective farm. We shan't leave without breakfast. I can't turn up before the commander and ask to be fed at once: 'Please feed us tramps.' You just stay quiet here, I'll be back soon."

Lopahin lay down in his place, put his hands behind his head and said with a feeling of duty well executed:

"Well, we can sleep now. My attack was repulsed. I retreated in order but with some loss, and, in view of the enemy's obvious superiority, I shall not renew my advance in this section. I know you will laugh at me, lads, for a month or two—those of you who will survive two months. But one thing I ask of you: begin doing so tomorrow morning, and now let's sleep!"

Without waiting for an answer, Lopahin turned over on his side and, within a few minutes, fell into an unawakening, child-like sleep.

Early next morning Kopitovsky awakened Lopahin.

"Get up for breakfast, you petty flea!"

"What is he for a flea? He's Alexander the Great," said Akimov who was conscientiously rubbing an aluminum spoon with a clean rag.

"He's a conqueror of peoples and a menace to women," Khmyz

put in. "But yesterday, he didn't go through even though I warned you all."

"Rely on such a conquerer and you'll die of hunger!" Nekrasov exclaimed.

Lopahin opened his eyes and raised himself. His left eye looked as bold and sparkling as always; the right one, bordered with puffy purple, was hardly visible except for a glimmer through a narrow slit.

"She struck you all purple, didn't she!" Kopitov smirked, turning away for fear of laughing out loud.

Lopahin knew that his only salvation from his comrades' derision lay in silence. Whistling to himself and looking absolutely indifferent, he took a towel and a tiny piece of soap and went out on the steps. The soldiers were washing themselves, crowding round the well, and in the garden of the house some weatherproof tent-cloaks had been spread out, and upon them in close array stood kettles, plates and mugs. Nearby a bonfire blazed hotly. On an iron bar above the fire hung a large army cauldron. The woman of the house, attractively dressed, was keeping the fire going as she bent her mighty body and stirred the cauldron with a wooden spoon.

It was all like a dream. Lopahin blinked in a daze and rubbed his eyes. "The devil's own work!" he thought, but then his nostrils caught the smell of boiled meat; shrugging his shoulders, Lopahin descended the steps. Stopping by the bonfire, he gallantly bowed:

"Good morning, Natalia Stepanovna!"

The woman straightened herself, threw a quick look at him and bent over the cauldron again. A rosy flush spread over her cheeks, and red spots even appeared on her full white neck.

"Good day to you," she said gently. "You must excuse me, Pyotr Feodotovich. . . . Your bruise doesn't look good. . . . I fear your comrades may have heard the noise in the night?"

"That's nothing," Lopahin generously said. "Bruises adorn men's faces. Of course, you should use your fists more accurately, but there's nothing to be done now. And don't worry about me, it'll heal beautifully. A dog will leave no stone unturned to find a bone. But I sought you by ruse only to find a purple bruise. It's a marriageable affair we have between us, Natalia Stepanovna."

The woman straightened herself, looked at him with clear eyes, and severely knitted her heavy, auburn eyebrows.

"The trouble is you fancy yourself as a bridegroom. You believe that, if her husband is away in the army, a wife must be a bitch. So I have to show you with my fists, Pyotr Feodorovich, what we are like, and God did not stint me strength."

Lopahin squinted with his seeing eye at the woman's clenched fists and then inquired:

"I apologize, of course, for my immodesty, but tell me all the same what sort of man was your husband? Well, how tall, for example?"

The woman measured Lopahin with her eyes and smiled:

"About your height, Pyotr Feodorovich, only a little more solid."

"I'm sure you bullied him? He must have been like a brother-in-law to you?"

"Don't say that! How can you, Pyotr Feodotovich! We lived lovey-dovey!"

The woman's full rosy lips quivered. She turned away and with the tip of her handkerchief wiped a tear from her cheek, but then in a twinkling she smiled archly and, looking at Lopahin with moist eyes, said:

"There's no better man than mine in the whole world! He was a good man, hard-working and quiet, but as soon as he had his fill of vodka, he'd turn hard. But I never went complaining to the local militia. He'd start raising hell, but I'd manage him soon enough; I wouldn't hurt him beating him, but just do it lovingly, so to speak. . . . Now he's in Kuibyshev, in the hospital, after being wounded. Maybe they'll let him come home afterwards to recuperate?"

"Of course they will," Lopahin assured her. "But tell me, Natalia Stepanovna, what makes you prepare this breakfast for the whole band of us? There's something I don't understand. . . ."

"There's nothing to understand here. If you had only explained soundly yesterday to our chairman that it was your company that fought the Germans the day before at the Pod'yemsk village, why, we would have fed you yesterday. But we, women, thought

that you were taking to your heels and didn't want to defend us
from the enemy, so we got together and decided among us as
follows: such as are running away to the rear from the river Don
were to get not a morsel of bread, not a mug of milk, and might
they perish of hunger, the damned runaways! But as for those
going towards the Don, in our defense, they were to be fed with
anything they asked. And that's what we did. We didn't know
about you, that you had been fighting at Pod'yemsk. The day
before yesterday our collective farm girls had been carting shells
to the Don and they told us when they got back: a lot of our dear
ones, they said, had been killed on the other side of the Don, but
they had piled the Germans up too on the mound and they lay
there like logs in a wood stack. Had we known it was you bat-
tling out there, we'd have greeted you otherwise. Your sergeant,
the red-haired one, the graying old man, he went to the chairman
this night and told him how hard you'd been fighting. Well, I
looked—and there at dawn was the chairman hurrying almost at
a run towards my yard. 'We got it wrong, Natalia,' he said. These
aren't runaways, but heroes. Slaughter the chickens and make a
noodle soup for them, so that these lads may be well fed. He
told me how you defended yourselves in Pod'yemsk, and what
losses you suffered, and I at once prepared the dough for the
noodles and killed eight chickens and threw them into the pot.
Surely we are not sorry to part with these wretched chickens
for the sake of our dear defenders. Surely we'll give up everything if only you don't let the Germans in here! And well we
might ask how long you will go on retreating? Time you stuck
your heels in. . . . Don't let a harsh word hurt you, but it's
shameful to look at you. . . ."

"Seems we hadn't picked the right little key for your lock?"
Lopahin inquired.

"Seems like it," the woman confirmed with a smile.

Lopahin groaned with disappointment, made a gesture with
his hand and walked off towards the well. "It's bad luck I'm
having with love latterly," he grieved to admit as he strode along
the path.

MICHAEL ZOSCHENKO

An Extraordinary Incident

I SPENT my last summer vacation in a House of Rest. The director of our House of Rest had concentrated all his paternal attention upon the proper nourishment for his charges, assuming very rightly that good meals would cover many other defects in his institution.

He had attracted the services of an excellent chef, who baked wonderful pies, prepared amazing salads and fairly good hamburgers. The desserts, the skilled handiwork of this chef, always claimed general approval.

As a result, the vacationists were well-disposed and expressed their gratitude more than once to the director for his model household management and his amazing table.

One day, the director, wishing to add to his vacationists' pleasure, made a suggestion to those who had come to express their gratitude:

"With your permission," he announced, "I shall pass on your thanks to our chef Ivan Fomich, who is doing his best there by the stove. That will undoubtedly encourage him. And thus we shall achieve even better results."

Indeed, on the following day, the quality of the dishes proved even higher. And then the director, his face shining with satisfaction, told the vacationists:

"You see what zeal our chef has exercised after receiving your thanks. But oral gratitude is just a bird in the bush. I counsel you from all my heart to write a letter of praise to the chef. We shall publish this letter in our Wall Newspaper. And then we shall see what will happen."

The vacationists followed this advice. They inserted a letter with five signatures in the Wall Newspaper, drawing attention in an exuberant style to the culinary achievements of the chef Ivan Fomich.

In addition, one of the vacationists, an artist, drew a handsome frame round the letter, wreathed in ribbons, flowers and laurel leaves.

The effect of this exceeded the director's expectations.

The wonderful pies baked by our chef now literally melted in the mouth. The salads were such that even a satiated man went on eating them. And, as from that day, the dessert evoked general amazement mingled with vociferous enthusiasm.

But particular enthusiasm was displayed by one of the vacationists—a young composer, who sat at the table next to mine. To be exact, he was to be found leaping to his feet more often than eating. Some sort of hidden spring would not allow this gaunt and long-legged body to remain in repose.

At our table were also a Doctor of Philology and his wife. The philologist was an unusually lean and taciturn individual. But his wife more often than not made up for these defects.

Thus, when we were dining one day, the young composer gave vent to an exclusive outburst of enthusiasm which bordered on a nervous disturbance. He praised extravagantly everything that was served on this occasion. But when the dessert was brought in, he leapt from his chair and exclaimed, turning to the philologist:

"You must taste this cream caramel immediately! It is a miracle of the art of cooking!"

The Doctor of Philology, having tasted the cream, assented, and bowed his head to signify approval.

The philologist's wife began to explain to us the excellencies of this particular cream and why cooked creams are usually of indifferent quality.

Without waiting for her to finish her speech, the composer again exclaimed:

"No, no, we haven't yet fully appreciated the services of our chef! We are obliged to encourage this divine gift again and again!"

The philologist's wife suggested that the vacationists should make a collection and buy for the chef either a silver cigarette case or a cut of cloth for a suit. But the composer reproachfully exclaimed:

"But that wouldn't be quite it! We have before us an astounding master of his trade—a veritable artist! And we should honor him as an artist!"

The composer, having said this, began to applaud.

The other diners stared at him in bewilderment. Then the composer hurriedly made the round of the tables and in a low voice informed everybody that it had been decided to summon the chef by applauding and then to give him an ovation.

Everyone willingly agreed to this. And, at a signal from the composer, unanimous applause broke out in the dining room.

The service personnel in the kitchen did not at once tumble to the significance of this noise. First, the dishwasher appeared on the dining room threshold. The chef's assistant Fedyushka jumped out after her. Smilingly but mystified, they both gazed at the applauding throng.

The waitresses began scurrying to and fro. The Director appeared. He immediately joined the applauding crowd and called out loudly, summoning the chef:

"Ivan Fomich! We beg you to come out!"

Very soon Ivan Fomich, the chef, appeared. He was a corpulent man with a gray straggly mustache. His high chef's hat gave him a somewhat forbidding look.

Yes, of course, the chef Ivan Fomich was already accustomed to attention and success, but the ovation evidently excited and even dumfounded him by its novelty. For a time the chef stood silently on the dining room threshold and, wiping his perspiring face with his apron, stared sideways at the people around who stood there applauding him.

The applause increased in volume. The composer, rushing to

the grand piano, began to play a flourish. Then the chef Ivan Fomich walked into the center of the dining room.

On his face, which had grown pale, there glimmered now a complex scale of feelings. Pride, spiritual agitation, delight, astonishment—one could detect all these simultaneously on his countenance.

The director raised his hand and, establishing a silence, turned to the chef with a short speech. This is what he said without once faltering:

"Dear Ivan Fomich! Your predecessors had long tried the public's patience with their dubious culinary efforts. And it was only when you came on the scene that the administration was able to have peace of mind, which is the key to health. Allow me, in the name of all our vacationists, to thank you again and again for your high mastery which, like the sun, has illumined our humble House of Rest."

Then, to the thunder of stormy applause, the director embraced the chef and kissed him thrice on his mustache and cheeks.

It was now the chef's turn to make an appropriate reply. But Ivan Fomich was no master of this complex art. However, it may have been his agitation that fettered his gift of eloquence. Whether it was that or not, Ivan Fomich merely let drop a few niggardly sentences, which nevertheless made it possible to judge the noble quality of his thoughts. Doffing his white chef's hat and pressing it to his heart, he stammered:

"I tried . . . I attained . . . I promise henceforth to give every consideration to people. . . . From my heart I thank you for your interest. . . . Many thanks. . . ."

Stormy applause, music and shouts of "bravo" marked the end of this meeting between the vacationists and the chef. With a humble bow, Ivan Fomich retreated to the kitchen.

No, I did not follow the further course of events, but eyewitnesses have related with official precision what took place soon after.

At five o'clock that afternoon, the chef Ivan Fomich set out together with his nephew Fedyushka to visit some fishermen he knew in a nearby settlement. There, after drinking a great deal,

Ivan Fomich hired a rowing boat with two rowers. He decorated the boat with rugs and foliage. In the stern he placed an accordionist friend of his. To the sound of music he swept along the lake past the settlement and past numerous health resorts and sanatoria.

The chef made the whole of this aquatic journey standing upright in the boat, with his hand resting on the shoulder of one of the rowers. Ivan Fomich stood like a monument amid the rugs and the foliage. And, whenever the accordionist paused, young Fedyushka, the chef's assistant, began immediately to strum on his mandolin.

However, the no small quantity of vodka, which the chef had consumed, brought an unexpected mishap upon the expedition. When the rowers swung the boat round sharply for the second run, Ivan Fomich lost his balance and toppled overboard. His corpulent body rocked the frail boat and, shipping water, it turned over.

Fedyushka and the rowers managed to swim to shore. But the fishermen had to rescue both Ivan Fomich and the accordionist, who still held on to his accordion.

Ivan Fomich had swallowed a mass of water and, for a long time, lay immobile on the shore. The inhabitants of the settlement wished to apply artificial respiration, but he would not submit to it. Soaking wet, he hurried home together with his nephew Fedyushka. In his apartment, Ivan Fomich, as people later affirmed, drank into the late hours, ate and even created an uproar.

In our House of Rest we learned of this extraordinary incident only next day when, for morning breakfast, we were served with semolina and vulgar cranberry sauce instead of rare salads.

At breakfast, the Doctor of Philology said to us with a slight smile:

"Yes, I have always assumed that extravagant praise requires an additional moral backbone from people."

The philologist's wife began to decipher for us her husband's thought and, in the process, undertook to explain verbosely that it was necessary to praise people, that it was pedagogic and produced wonderful results. However, in certain circumstances, she added, we sometimes arrive at unexpected consequences—such as the scandalous incident with our chef. From this it was obvious that disproportionate praise contains a certain danger for weak souls.

The young composer gave expression to his agitation by explaining:

"No, I disagree with you! Even the most exalted praise can do no harm! I am more than ever convinced that our chef will excel himself once he has recovered from the accident."

That day we were served a dinner, which had been hastily cooked by some inexpert hand. Indeed, for the next five days—and that is no short term for vacationists—the dinners were of an altogether dubious quality. But, by the end of the week, the vacationists could not resist once more expressing their noisy appreciation of Ivan Fomich.

And then the young composer, as he was eating his dessert at dinner, excitedly addressed the philologist's wife:

"Just taste these meringues! Rich praise has done no harm! The honors we paid the chef have only helped to reveal his astounding mastery!"

Having also praised the meringues, the philologist's wife still maintained her opinion. She argued that extravagant praise held more danger for the inexperienced apprentice than for a first-class master of his trade. After excessive praise, the growth of an inexperienced apprentice is frequently arrested, since he might conclude that he has nowhere further to go. He is discouraged after his first failure and then seeks oblivion in drink.

The young composer leapt up from the table in order to protest, but the philologist's wife continued without pause:

"However, there is a certain danger here even for a first-class master. Immoderate praise not infrequently lulls the consciousness, nurtures arrogance and renders a critical attitude to one's work impossible. For this reason, even a first-class master—an artist of the word, let us say—will sometimes abandon his wonderful work and become a homespun predicant, a hypocrite, a hysteric or even an unstable decadent."

The philologist's wife talked long and verbosely on this theme and concluded her speech with the following words:

"Of course, such a transformation could not happen to our

first-class chef. Extravagant praise shook his spiritual balance only for a brief moment. Judging by the meringues, everything has ended to the general satisfaction. And now, evidently, we can praise our chef again, without the risk of stumbling upon unpleasant consequences."

The Doctor of Philology did not take part in this discussion, but at the termination of it, he addressed the composer in an edifying tone:

"A moral backbone, young man, is what is absolutely required in any profession, including the culinary business and particularly in music, which is so frequently accompanied by applause."

To this the young composer made no reply. He left the premises with the unstable gait of a person who has been surfeited with applause and honors.

VSEVOLOD KOCHETOV

A Conflict of Ideas

From *The Brothers Yershov*

FOR TWO DAYS the Party Organization at the theater debated
Alexakhin's play about the Okuneyevs. Almost everyone was in
favor of taking it and staging it for the coming anniversary of the
October Revolution. Yakov Yershov had won. Tomashuk and the
chief director could do nothing but accept the fact that there
was a stronger force than themselves in the theater.

"Well, stage it if you like," Tomashuk had finally said, "but
don't count on me for help. It'll be a flop and you'll play to an
empty house."

The chief director excused himself on the ground of illness and
there was no sign of him for about ten days. Those ten days he
spent entertaining a playwright from Moscow, the one who had,
as the chief director expressed it, very kindly offered his play to
the theater, assuring them that it would prove the hit of the season.

This Moscow playwright was an experienced hack rather than
a talented man. In his work, he championed no original theme
or ideas. His themes were not taken directly from the life
around him. He merely circulated in various circles in Moscow
and kept his ear to the ground, attempting to assess the social
situation and to select those factors in the situation which might
contribute to his success at that particular moment. He could turn
out a play—and he had done so—in which it was maintained that
the retreat of the Soviet Armies in the first weeks of the war was

204

attributable not to the force of circumstance, but to a deliberate strategic plan, brilliantly executed by the Soviet generals. He could also turn out a play—and he had done so—maintaining that the defeats of the early months were a disorganized retreat and depicting the generals to be inefficient and cowardly, divorced from the people, stupidly complacent and wanting in honor. He could turn out a play—and had done so more than once—in praise of the Party, in praise of the Communists. And, in his plays, he could likewise assert that the Party bred hypocrisy, leveled all men and crushed their individuality. He could do all things, because he valued nothing, had nothing of his own, nothing that was part of him; he was entirely detached, and his position at any given time was dependent on the advantage it brought him.

This playwright was familiar with what he called the "secrets of Moscow." He had no difficulty in forecasting social trends, and he now communicated these in strict confidence to the chief director with the repeated warning: "This is, of course, strictly confidential. As you realize, it mustn't go any further." He had in his possession translated copies of articles by foreign critics, of whom the chief director had never heard and who bitterly attacked Soviet literature, Soviet art, the method of Socialist Realism and, ultimately, socialism itself. The chief director twiddled his thumbs and wagged his head in all directions, but it was impossible to judge by these gestures his attitude to the playwright's information. And he confined his verbal opinion to such exclamations as: "Oho!" or "Well, well!" or "That's a bit of all right . . ." or "Perhaps we'd better have a snifter of brandy!"

Meanwhile work on the production of the new play continued at the theater. No one tried to persuade Tomashuk to participate, and the direction of the play had been entrusted to a young director, who immediately asked Gulyaev to help him with the sets.

Alexakhin, whom the first unfortunate reading of his play had rather upset, now revived his interest and once more frequented the theater.

To the surprise of everyone involved, the chief director put in an unexpected appearance at one of the rehearsals when work was in full swing. He sat down in a corner of the rehearsal room, observed, listened, and made a few comments. Then he strode to Yakov Yershov's office and declared: "You shouldn't keep your rehearsals secret, you know. I'm not retired yet." Having made this pronouncement, he turned purple and lost his temper.

Yakov Yershov coolly answered that he was very pleased that the chief director was now ready, as indeed he was, to apply himself to the new play. But what he failed to understand was the motive for this sudden change of heart. The chief director's heart was a closed book as far as he was concerned.

But even if Yakov Yershov had been able to plumb the depths of that heart, he would still have been no wiser, for the chief director would not admit certain things even to himself. With an insight derived from many years of experience in the theater and of life, the onetime brilliant actor-director had seen through all of his guest's gossip. He now saw the playwright as a time-serving hack, a man barren of ideas, an angler for success, and a man who preferred to fish in turbid waters. Wretched material, the chief director thought with distaste. All that fine talk was beside the point. And he was very relieved and pleased when the playwright took himself off and there was not need verbally to dally further on the edge of this perilous swamp. But even to himself he would not admit the real depths of that swamp. And now he addressed both Yakov Yershov and himself rather evasively: "Better reject his play. After all, we are only a small provincial theater, and we could never carry off such a production. That kind of thing is for Moscow."

It was Tomashuk's turn to feel bewildered. He could not determine the direction of the wind which had brought about such a change in his chief's attitude. He commiserated with his chief for taking part in the production and implied that it would not enhance his reputation. "Maybe," the chief director answered. "But I'll try all the same. And please don't throw a wrench in the works, and don't spread a wet blanket over everything." Tomashuk felt hurt. He was not accustomed to being addressed in this tone by the chief director. "I don't think I deserved this," he shot back.

"That's possible, too," the chief commented. "But just don't do it."

This made Tomashuk dispirited. He needed a prop now, some sensible, friendly counsel. His thoughts turned to Orleantzev, whom he had not seen since his return from Moscow, when he had visited him to convey the greetings from his Moscow friends. As an engineer and metallurgist, Orleantzev was, of course, rather remote from the world of art. But, firstly, he did have wide connections in the art world, and this Tomashuk had realized when he had paid a number of calls in Moscow bearing Orleantzev's letters of introduction; secondly, he was always excellently informed about what was going on in the higher spheres; and, thirdly, he was an able man with a wide grasp of affairs and an ability to produce results.

Orleantzev received Tomashuk in his usual amicable manner. Putting his arm round his shoulders, he sat him down comfortably in an armchair and treated him to brandy and lemon, rebuking him mildly at the same time for visiting him so infrequently.

"I've had much unpleasantness of late," Tomashuk replied by way of apology.

"Now please don't misunderstand me, my dear fellow, but here is a fact," Orleantzev explained. "I have noticed that people in the provinces attach more importance to unpleasant rather than pleasant things. Whatever conversation you engage in here always involves trouble. You people just refuse to be satisfied with life; that's your main weakness. One might think that people in the provinces were born for nothing but trouble."

"But what is one to do if there's nothing but trouble?" Tomashuk asked, and then began to explain what had happened at the theater.

"Doesn't it strike you," Orleantzev inquired after following him attentively, "that these . . . er . . . the Yershovs—that's their name, isn't it?—these Yershovs occupy too much space everywhere. A Yershov is responsible for your trouble too. Yakov Yershov? Wasn't it him you mentioned?"

"Yes, Yakov Yershov. But he's not the only one. Gulyaev is more dangerous."

"That I'm ready to admit. But I'm referring to what hits you in the eye, so to speak. There is a Yershov in the theater. At our plant, in the blast-furance shop, there was another Yershov, a Platon Yershov, who really made a mess of things. And there's one of them still left there, a young shift foreman. And there's a fourth Yershov at the blooming mill. And besides all this, these Yershovs have stirred up a wave of concentric circles which spreads far beyond the sphere you'd think was theirs. What caused the sensation at that art exhibition? A portrait by Kazokov. Why? Because it was a portrait of a Yershov. The fourth Yershov. The blooming mill follow. And the play you're finding such an obstacle? The play by Alexakhin. What's it about? Why, the Okunyevs. Just a pseudonym for the Yershovs. And the hero of that play? Old man Okuneyev-Yershov, the head of this Yershov clan."

"But where does this take us?"

"Nowhere. I was just registering a fact. What I have to say about it is this: I'm no great expert in theatrical affairs, but if you want me to help you, I can only recommend. . . . But on condition, first of all, that you will stand ruthlessly for your rights."

"Naturally, I will. I am a very active person. I haven't gone to pieces yet. I was only seeking your advice. . . ."

"Very sensible of you. Well, act we must. My assistance will take the form of a very agreeable young man, whom you must receive. He is a correspondent of the regional newspaper. Smart and understanding. We're on the best of terms. By the way, my dear fellow, a lot of people underestimate the role of the press. There are some peculiar characters among us engineers and you, people of the arts, who look down on the press and its working men. When a reporter comes to see one of those people, he claims he is too busy and tells him to come back another time. He turns the reporter away, in fact. The man who does so risks losing more than he realizes. Now take me, for example. I am always ready to postpone the most urgent affairs when dealing with a journalist. And if I have to turn a journalist away, I make a point of fixing a time with him and of receiving him properly when he comes. I've never had any bother with the press. On the contrary, I always win their backing. Do you remember? The incident of Krutilich's ordeal, the inventor they wouldn't recognize at the plant, and the director Chibisov?"

"Of course, I do! Quite to the point, in my opinion."

"Yes, but the point might have been a different one, you know, if I hadn't met that reporter myself. If some groucher or other had nabbed him first, he would have got a very different picture. And when a picture dominates a man's mind, it's not so easy to remove it. And what does a man gain by turning his back on the press? He merely hands a reporter over to other, perhaps more dishonest and unscrupulous people, and the outcome is a blast from the press against himself. Newspaper correspondents, especially the young and inexperienced ones, should be kept informed—by yourself. It's the only way to guarantee objective information and to ensure an objective account in the papers. I promise you therefore that a young man will come to interview you tomorrow or the following day. Tell him all about the situation in your theater."

The correspondent of the regional newspaper visited the theater two days later. Tomashuk primed him in detail about the affairs of the theater, arguing that the damaging effects of the "cult of the personality" had not yet been obliterated, that there was still a tendency to look at things through rosy-colored spectacles, and to stage plays with no edge or conflict to them; topical, or acutely critical plays were rejected and, on the whole, the theater was failing in its duty to the people and the Party. The manager, whose job it was to attend to the business side rather than rule on questions of repertoire, had acquired too much authority. What could a man like that know about art when he had been nothing but a trumpet player in a works band a few years ago?

VALENTIN KATAYEV

Tolstoy's Death

An Episode from *The Cottage in the Steppes*

FOR DAYS Tolstoy's death was the only topic of conversation in Russia. Many extra newspaper editions recounted the story of Tolstoy's flight from his Yasnaya Polyana estate. Hundreds of telegrams from the station at Astapovo described the great writer's last hours and minutes. The small, unknown station of Astapovo became as famous overnight as Yasnaya Polyana itself, and everyone had become familiar with the name of Ozolin, the obscure station-master, who had given asylum in his own house to the dying writer. The new names of Astapovo and Ozolin which, together with those of the Countess Sofya Adreyevna and of Chertkov, accompanied Tolstoy to his grave, were as alarming to Petya as the black lettering on the white ribbons of the funeral wreaths.

Petya was surprised to note that Tolstoy's death, which everyone referred to as a "tragedy," seemed to have some connection with the government, the Holy Synod, the police and the gendarmerie. Whenever he caught sight of the bishop driving past in a carriage with a monk sitting next to the coachman or the chief of police in a rattling *drozhki*, he was convinced that both the bishop and the chief of police were speeding on urgent missions related to Tolstoy's death.

210

Petya had never seen his father in such a state, not excited exactly but somehow inspired and exalted. His father's normally good-natured, open face had grown somehow sterner and yet younger. In student fashion, he had combed back his hair above his high, regular forehead. But, behind his pince-nez, his aged, red-rimmed, tearful eyes expressed such grief that Petya's heart ached for his father.

Vassily Petrovich Bacheis entered and placed two piles of tightly tied exercise books on the table. Before changing into an old house-jacket, he pulled out a handkerchief from the back pocket of his frock-coat with frayed silk lapels and thoroughly wiped his moist face and beard.

"Come on, boys, wash your hands and we'll eat!" he commanded with a decisive jerk of his head.

Petya sensed his father's mood. Vassily Petrovich was taking it hard: Tolstoy was not only a writer whom he adored, but also, more than that, the moral center almost of his own life. He could find no words to express all he felt.

"It's just terrible, terrible!" Auntie exclaimed at dinner. Putting down the ladle, she pressed her fingers to her temples. "Think what you like about Tolstoy—and, personally, I regard him as the greatest of writers—but his pacifism and vegetarianism are just ridiculous; and the attitude of the Russian government in this affair is quite abominable. We've been disgraced in the eyes of the world! As disgraced as by Port Arthur, Tsushima or Bloody Sunday."

"I implore you . . ." Father began nervously.

"Please don't implore me. We have a stupid Tsar and a stupid government! I'm ashamed that I'm a Russian!"

"Do stop, I implore you!" Father shouted, his chin thrust forward and his beard trembling. "His Imperial Majesty's person is sacred—above criticism. I won't allow it. In front of the children especially."

"I'm sorry. I shan't do it again," Auntie hastened to reply.

"Let's drop the topic."

"But I just can't understand how a generous, intelligent man

like you, a man who loves Tolstoy, can honestly hold as sacred
the man who has spread the gallows all over Russia and who—"

"For God's sake," Father groaned, "don't let us discuss politics!
You've got a knack of introducing politics into any conversation!
Can't we talk without getting involved in politics?"

"My dear Vassily Petrovich, you just won't admit that everything in our life is politics! The government! The church! The
schools! They are all politics. Tolstoy is politics too!"

"How dare you say that!"

"I will!"

"It's blasphemy! Tolstoy is not politics!"

"He is precisely that!"

For a long time after, Petya and his brother Pavlik could hear,
as they were trying to do their homework in the next room, the
excited voices of their father and aunt raised in fierce argument.

"*The Master and the Worker, Confession, Resurrection!*"

"*War and Peace*— Platon Karatayev!"

"Platon Karatayev is politics too!"

"*Anna Karenina*— Kitty, Levin!"

"Levin argued about communism with his brother!"

"Andrey Bolkonsky, Pierre!"

"The Decembrists!"

"Khadzhi— Murat!"

"Nicholas Palkin." [1]

"Do stop. The children can hear us!"

Petya could still hear Father and Auntie arguing in the dining
room. Some words were repeated more often than others. Those
words were "freedom of thought," "popular government," "con-
stitution," and, finally, that searing word "revolution."

"Just wait, it will end in another revolution," Auntie insisted.

"You're just an anarchist!" Father shrilled.

"No, I'm a Russian patriot!"

"Russian patriots have faith in their Tsar and government!"

"Do you have faith in them?"

"Yes! I do!"

Then Petya heard Tolstoy mentioned again.

[1] A satirical nickname given to Nicholas I. "Palka" means stick.

"Why then did the Tsar and the government, in whom you put so much faith, excommunicate Tolstoy and ban his books?"

"To err is human. They regard Tolstoy as a politician, as a revolutionary almost, but Tolstoy is simply the world's greatest writer and the pride of Russia. He is above all parties and revolutions. And I'll prove that in my speech!"

"And do you think the authorities will let you say that?"

"I need no permission to say publicly that Leo Tolstoy is a great Russian writer."

"That's what you believe."

"I don't believe it—I'm absolutely positive!"

"You're just an idealist! You don't realize what country you're living in. I ask you not to make this speech. They'll squash you. Listen to me!"

The following morning, while Vassily Petrovich was washing, combing his hair, and fixing a black tie to a starched collar, Petya had an opportunity to have a peep at what his father had been writing that night. On the desk lay an old, homemade notebook stitched together with coarse thread. Petya recognized it at once. It was usually to be found on father's dresser with the rest of the family relics, such as the yellowed wedding candles, a spray of orange blossom, a pair of his mother's white kid gloves and small bead bag, a pair of mother-of-pearl opera glasses, a few leaves of wild pear tree from Lermontov's grave, and an assortment of odds and ends, which Petya regarded as mere junk, but Vassily Petrovich thought very precious.

Petya had paged through the notebook before. Half of it was filled with a speech Vassily Petrovich had written on the hundredth anniversary of Pushkin's birth: the other half was empty. Petya now noticed that a new speech occupied this faded half of the book. Written in the same fine hand, it treated of Tolstoy's death. It began thus:

"A great Russian writer is dead. Our literary sun has set . . ."

Vassily Petrovich put on a pair of fresh starched cuffs and his best gold cuff links, folded the notebook with care and thrust it into his inside pocket. Petya watched as his father quickly drank

a glass of tea and then went into the entrance hall to don his
heavy coat with a frayed velvet collar. Petya noticed that his
fingers were trembling and his pince-nez quivering. Petya of a
sudden felt extremely sorry for his father. He approached him
and brushed against his coat-sleeve, as he used to do when a very
small boy.

"Don't worry. We'll show them yet!" Father exclaimed, pat-
ting his son's back.

"I am telling you again not to do it," Auntie advised solemnly
as she peeped into the hall.

"You're wrong," Vassily Petrovich replied in a soft quavering
voice. He donned his wide-brimmed black hat and left quickly.

"I wish to God I were wrong!" Auntie sighed. "Come, boys,
don't waste time or you'll be late for school," she added, going
over to help Pavlik, her favorite, to fasten his satchel, a simple
procedure he had not yet mastered.

The day slipped by, a short yet interminably long, dreary November day, filled with vague foreboding, furtive rumor and endless repetition of the same disturbing words: "Chertkov," "Sofya
Andreyevna," "Astapovo," and "Ozolin."

It was the day of Tolstoy's funeral.

Petya had never seen a forest, for he had lived the whole of his
life on the southern sea coast, in the Novorosiisk steppe region.
But now he had a very clear picture of Yasanaya Polyana and
the woods on the fringe of an overgrown ravine. Petya imagined
the black trunks of the ancient, leafless linden trees, and the
plain pine coffin with the withered, shrunken remains of Leo
Tolstoy, as they were lowered into the grave without priest or
choir boys in attendance. Overhead, Petya could picture likewise
the ominous clouds and the flocking crows, very like those that
swooped in the drizzly dusk over the bleak Kulikovo field.

Father returned as always from his classes just when the lamp
was lit in the dining room. He was excited, happy and deeply
moved. When Auntie, not unanxiously, inquired whether he had
made his speech and what the reaction had been, Vassily Petrovich
could not hold back a proud and radiant smile from flashing
under his pince-nez.

"You could have heard a pin drop," he related, pulling out his handkerchief and wiping his moist beard. "I never expected the young rascals to be so eager, serious and attentive. That applies to the young ladies too. I repeated the talk for the seventh form of the Maryinsky school."

"Did you have permission for it?"

"I asked no permission. Why should I? I maintain that a teacher of literature is fully entitled to discuss in class the personality of any famous Russian writer, particularly if the writer happens to be Tolstoy. Moreover, I believe it is my duty to do so."

"How reckless of you!"

Later in the evening some young people, who were strangers, called: two students in very worn, faded caps, and a young woman who also looked like a student. One of the students had a twisted pince-nez on a black ribbon, wore high boots, and smoked a cigarette, puffing smoke through his nostrils; the young woman wore a short jacket and kept pressing her small chapped hands to her bosom. For some reason, they were reluctant to go inside, and remained talking with Vassily Petrovich in the hall. The student in the pince-nez spoke in a deep resonant voice, while the young woman repeated the same sentence again and again in a lisping voice:

"We feel sure that you, as a progressive, noble-minded person and a public figure, will not refuse this humble request of the student body."

The third caller, blowing his nose discreetly, kept wiping his feet on the doormat.

The news of Vassily Petrovich's speech had somehow reached the Women's Higher Courses and the Medical Faculty of the Imperial University in Odessa, and the student delegation had arrived to manifest their solidarity and also to request him to repeat his talk to a Social-Democratic student circle. Vassily Petrovich, though flattered, was also disagreeably shocked. After thanking the young people, he categorically refused to address the Social-Democratic circle. He explained that he had never been a member of any party and never intended to join one, and that he would consider any attempt to turn Tolstoy's death into something political as a sign of disrespect for the great writer, since it was generally known that Tolstoy abhorred all political parties and had a negative attitude to politics.

"If that is so, then we beg to be excused," the young woman stated dryly. "We are most disappointed in you. Let us go, comrades."

The young people made a dignified exit, leaving behind the smell of cheap tobacco and the imprint of wet feet on the doorstep.

"Astounding!" Vassily Petrovich repeated as he paced up and down the dining room, wiping his pince-nez on the lining of his jacket.

"It's amazing how people always find some excuse to drag in politics!"

"Didn't I tell you," Auntie said. "The consequences will be serious, I'm afraid."

Auntie was right in her foreboding, although the consequences were not as rapid as she had expected. A month at least elapsed before the trouble started. A few preliminary shadows did, indeed, fall. But they were so tenuous that the Bacheis family paid little heed to them.

Then at dinner one day, Pavlik, his bright, naïve eyes fixed on his father, asked unexpectedly:

"Papa, what is a 'red'?"

"What's this, really," Vassily Petrovich exclaimed. He was in fine spirits. "It's a strange question. Red, I'd say, means something . . . something that's not, well, blue nor yellow nor brown . . . H'm, and so on."

"I know that. But I mean people. Are there any red people?"

"Oh, that's what you mean! Indeed there are! North American Indians, for example. Redskins, as they are called."

"They haven't got that far in their preparatory class," Petya interjected snootily. "They're infants still."

Pavlik did not react to the insult. Keeping his eyes on his father, he asked:

"Are you an Indian then, papa?"

"Fundamentally, no!" Father exclaimed, laughing so uproariously that his pince-nez fell off and almost drowned in the soup.

"Then why did Fedka call you a 'red'?"

"Aha! That's curious. And who is this Fedka?"

"A boy in my class. His father is senior clerk in the Governor's office in Odessa."

"Well! Fedka may know best. But you can see for yourself that I'm not red. I only turn red during the big frost."

"I don't like the look of this," Auntie said.

Soon after, a certain Krylevich, the bookkeeper of the mutual aid society at Vassily Petrovich's school, called one evening to discuss some problems relating to the Savings Bank. When they had finished talking business Krylevich, who had always struck Vassily Petrovich as a rather dubious person, stayed on for tea. He sat on for an hour and a half and bored everyone. He kept returning to the subject of Tolstoy, praised Vassily Petrovich for his courage and asked to borrow his lecture notes which, he said, he wanted to read at home. Father refused, and his refusal upset Krylevich. As he stood before the hall mirror, pulling on his crumpled, greasy cap with the Ministry of Education cockade, he said with a glib smile:

"I regret you deny me the pleasure, regret it very much! Your modesty is worse than pride."

Krylevich's visit left an unpleasant impression.

There were other minor occurrences of the same kind; for example, some of their acquaintances displayed exaggerated politeness when greeting Vassily Petrovich in the street; others, on the contrary, were unusually brusque and did not hide their disapprobation.

Then, a few days before Christmas, the crisis came.

OLGA BERGOLTZ

That Meadow

LATE ONE EVENING my father dropped in to visit me and announced that he would stay overnight.

"And tomorrow I shall take you to the Zoo," he added strictly. "Yes, yes. In the morning. Without fail."

"Well, well," I thought, "our doctor's in good form . . ."

The old surgeon, who had gone through two wars—the Imperialist and the Civil War—combined austerity and good nature with an exacting and convivial manner; he was rarely excited but, when he was, it was a rather unusual excitement. He would show himself unexpectedly petulant and carping: he would pull to pieces the way the surgical department was run (which he himself directed), harshly berate the local committee, to which "he was always being deliberately elected," criticize the district health organization and naggingly insist that I—I and no other—should provide the answer to: "Why are all these horrors being perpetrated?"

But he was also unusually concentrated and serious, tenderly recalling the terrible times of the First World War and the Civil War; he would discuss questions of international policy—"my prognosis is this . . ."—and would get very angry if his prognosis were challenged.

Sometimes he would just fool about noisily and cheerfully, clapping his hands for no reason and singing an old Nevsky ditty, which was both melancholy and gay like all such ditties:

"But Alesha had a cap of golden curls!
He sang such splendid town songs . . ."

While thus engaged, he would shake his golden-gray and still wavy head of hair; declaim fragments from Derzhavin's poem, *God,* and, as a former student from Derpt, never failed to execute (in a deep voice) the *Gaudeamus.* When in this state, he was governed by the most extraordinary desires, such as "to have another little child"; "to write a tragedy in verse"; or, as on this particular day, to drag me to the zoo—me, a responsible, adult person and one, into the bargain, faced with torturing personal complications as a member of an editorial department.

"Oh, papa," I fought back. "You just don't realize that I haven't got the time. And . . . I don't feel like it!"

"Well, well, well! Just drop these trifles. Am I your father or not? I bred you. I said I was taking you to the zoo, didn't I, and so I will."

He paused and added with significance and flavor:

"We shall see the lion. The King of Beasts."

I smiled involuntarily. Noticing this, father grew enthusiastic and clapped his hands.

"Darling little mother of mine, I'm a tractor driver!" he shouted, fooling, and then, turning absolutely serious, asked in a low voice: "Well, and how are your affairs?"

I came to life. At this time two individuals had brought a captious charge against me, and the investigation of this "affair" had already been going on for the last two months. The "affair" was a source of torment and exhaustion to me; it was a pressing thing to me; and I could have gone on talking about "my affair" endlessly, at any time of the day or night. In my mind I was constantly making endless and pathetically moving speeches and conducting bitter internal dialogues with the editor, the Party secretary and with my accusers. I even dreamt of almost nothing else.

"You know, papa," I began, "they have again postponed the final inquiry. At the last session, this woman Klimanchuk was saying such things . . . that I . . . I just simply. . . . No, I can't leave things like that! I will bring a charge against her myself, you understand! And I shall take my case to the highest instance . . . At present I am writing a fresh and very detailed comment on that particular article. In this comment . . ."

Heated and vexed, I began to give an exposition of my commentary, while father watched me attentively and absolutely soberly, interjecting every now and again his doctoral comments: "Well, well," "yes, yes," "so-so!"

"Och, how frightened of people you've become!" he suddenly exclaimed without hearing me to the end. "Och! You're all psychopaths, ladies and gentlemen. Well, all right. Go to bed now, for we'll be up and out very early in the morning. I'll lie down too . . . *I'm Tsar, I'm slave, I'm God, I'm worm.*"

"Yes, father, you lie down. But I'll sit up a while. I must do a rough draft of my charge. Not of the old one, but of the new one. About another of my articles. . . . Wait a minute, I'll fetch a mattress."

"Don't bother," father replied. "I am an old soldier. I can do without a mattress. *'He wears a three-cornered hat and an old campaign uniform.'* "

"But don't sing, papa! My head is splitting as it is!"

"Well, all right, all right! Am I your father or not? Oh, what a grave case . . ."

He lay down on the hard, very narrow couch. I made a paper shade for the lamp and sat down in front of a blank sheet of paper. I felt most lonely because father had neither listened to my account of the affair, nor taken the trouble to understand it or my anxiety, and seemed inexplicably satisfied with himself, while I. . . Yes, it was simply disgusting that he hadn't even heard me out . . . and I. . . .

Suddenly father called out affectionately and a little sadly:

"Lyalka! My little girl. . . ."

"What is it, papa? . . ."

"Do you remember when, in Zaruchevie one day, mother and I forbade you and your friend Moussia to go mushroom-picking? To some favorite meadow of yours . . . a long time ago it was. . . . But you wept so much, both of you, O Lord. . . ."

"Do leave me alone, papa. I don't know anything about *my* meadow! Don't interrupt me. . . ."

Father relapsed into silence.

For a long time I sat there, torturing myself and selecting the right formulas, fighting mentally with Klimanchuk; and I smoked so furiously that my heart beat faster. The hurt was stifling me; I was terribly sorry for myself and kept repeating in a whisper: "I'm tired, tired, terribly tired. . . ."

At dawn I fell asleep. I dreamt of some public meeting, but at the height of it I heard father exclaim:

"Lyalka, get up! Let's go to the zoo!"

I opened my eyes with difficulty: "You haven't forgotten . . . ," he was saying.

"But, papa, it isn't ten yet. Where can we go at such an unearthly hour?"

"And a good thing too it's so early. The zoo opens at ten. Get up now, look at the sunshine! Come along, be quick . . ."

Father was cheerful, brisk and unusually energetic; his face and large blue eyes looked mischievous as if he were planning to surprise the world; and all this irritated me to the point of weariness.

Wearing his old army cap, which I remembered since childhood, and his short Raglan coat that looked like a peasant woman's skirt, father hurried along the street as if he were late for a train. I trotted after him, swearing under my breath. We leapt on to a moving tramcar. Near the zoo the air had the uncitylike smell of cool autumn soil; the trees were bronze, austere and motionless, as though they understood in their stillness that the golden, lukewarm light was pouring upon them for the last time. The austere, peaceful and wonderfully tender transparency of that autumn day pricked me, like an icicle, with a very special feeling of sadness, also austere, peaceful and transparent.

"And yet I'm well on in years," I thought.

But father, voluptuously closing his eyes, sunning his face and breathing in the sharp air through his expanded nostrils, huddled and croaked blissfully:

"Ah, it's so good! So wonderful! What? Aren't you glad, my girl, that we came out? Pity Moussia isn't with us. Do you re-

member that autumn in Zaruchevie when we forbade you and
Moussia to go mushroom picking? To that special meadow of
yours?"

"Well, yes, I do. What about it?" I replied brusquely, irritated.

"Hyenas!" he commented with pleasure when we got near the
cages. "Just look at those rascals. They can laugh too. Look at
that one there—the way he's shambling, eh! And the stench of
him, oh mother. . . ."

"A typical Klimanchuk!" I said to myself, smiling grimly.

"And there are the tigers. Look at the tigers, Lyalka. Splendid
beasts, aren't they?"

"They look as if they were sewn of tiger cloth," I answered.
"They're improbable."

"You shouldn't say that. They are beautiful beasts. I like
them," father insisted. "And here are the lions. They'll be feeding
them soon (here father looked concerned, pulled out his grandfather's onion-bulb watch from his waistcoat pocket, glanced at
it and even held it to his ear). Yes, they'll be feeding them soon,
I'm sure. Well, I'll show you how they feed them."

"Oh Lord, I don't have to see it. Are we to stand about waiting here . . . for their feeding time? Look how mangy the
lions are. As if people had been walking on them. And the stupid
look on their faces. Like the Tsar! Just like Nicholas II. . . ."

Father guffawed uncertainly.

"Well, let's go now, papa," I urged. "We've seen everything.
And there's nothing to see anyhow."

"These lions are really a bit . . . off," father admitted in an
embarrassed but cheerful enough way. "But I'm sure you'll like
the bears. They're very frisky and scamper about, you know.
And then there's the aviary we must see, and the various kinds
of cows, and the bears, of course. Do you agree? And then some
other species. Eh? All right?"

"All right. As you like, papa."

We stood in front of a cage filled with birds. It gave off a
sickly smell of birds' droppings, and the water in the shallow
round basin was filthy and polluted. The birds were ranged in a
neat circle round the basin: A plump, immobile pelican was

watching a cork float in the water; beside him sat an untidy hen
with neck outstretched and film-covered eyes; behind the bend,
some kind of pernicious-looking bird with a tuft and sharp beak
stood on one leg, and so on. For some reason, all the birds were
immobile as though dumfounded.

"Our editorial board in session," I ventured at once, rather
drearily.

Father sighed heavily, but made no comment. In silence we
reached the pony pen.

"Here are the ponies," father announced. "Not too exciting,
just a smaller type of horse. . . . You won't like them either."

Something in father's voice startled me: I glanced at him
rapidly. His face looked old and disappointed and . . . yes! . . .
rather embarrassed.

"Why has he gone sour?" I asked, and then it suddenly hit me.
Father wanted me, of course, to be astonished and delighted like
a child. His idea had been not so much an outing to the zoo as
an excursion into my childhood and his youth.

And here was I being squeamish and paying no attention to
anything around: neither the golden trees, nor the amusing
creatures; but only immersed in my own dreary worries; I was
getting old. . . .

"Well, shall we go?" father muttered dispiritedly.

"Certainly not, papa. Wait, wait!" I suddenly exclaimed with
enthusiasm. "I'd like to have a look at this little horse!"

"Well, look at it," father replied distrustfully, but more gently.

"Now these creatures I like," I continued warmly, quivering
with compassion and love for my father, and keeping a sharp
watch not to overplay my part. "What a small creature it is! Why
is it so small, papa?"

"Just another species; it's a pony."

"An English pony, papa. It's better than the other one, you
know."

"It looks better. Got a good nuzzle on him."

"It's not that it 'looks,' but it is definitely handsomer. I'm rather
curious: is it comfortable to ride on? I'd love a ride. . . . In
England, they ride them, don't they?"

I could not do enough to please him.

"Why go to England? Look at the children riding there!" father exclaimed, perking up.

Actually, a pony cart was driving towards us, rattling like a tin can and drawn by a rather angry-looking, very shaggy pony. Hidden up to their necks in the cart sat four children in fluffy berets, while a boy-driver held the reins and urged the pony on. A small woolly-woolly dog with tufts of hair over its eyes trotted behind. All of them: the pony and the children, the boy-driver and even the woolly, eyeless dog, looked terribly serious, concentrated and important; and they all looked so businesslike, as if hurrying to an office or executing some responsible task.

"Well, would you like to take a trip?" father asked, winking. "I can drive you!"

"I'd love it! Only . . . perhaps, it would be embarrassing?"

"Well, then, let's go on. There's a lot more to see."

"Yes, yes, let's go. I want to see the monkeys!" I exclaimed, delighted to have taken father in. "You know, I adore monkeys. Especially the apes. I've been wanting to see them for ages."

We started off towards the monkey house. I took father's hand and, deliberately walking a pace behind, walked along with him like an exemplary daughter. Father was beaming.

"Would like me to buy you a waffle?" he asked. "A big one with cream?"

"Of course. Very much."

"Does it taste good?"

"Just marvelous!"

Actually the cream, by its smell if not its taste, reminded me of country soap, and the waffle itself showed signs of wood fiber. I masticated it, choking with disgust and dropping crumbs all over myself. Father puffed a cigarette, and the golden trees stood motionless above our bench, enjoying the last rays of sunshine. Beside us on the bench a young woman was trying to pull on a dull, blunt-nosed rubber on her three-year-old son's foot. The boy's fat leg dangled as if made of cotton-wool, and the mother, unable to fit it into the rubber, kept asking him in a tender, sing-song voice as she struggled with the foot:

"Well, Vovochka, and what shall we tell grandma about what we've seen at the zoo?"

Earnestly wrinkling his plump forehead and pursing his lips, the boy replied:

"We saw . . . a big elifant . . . a big camil . . . and a wee horse . . ."

The boy pronounced "elifant" and "camil" in a deep tone, but he piped "wee horse" in a thin, squeaky voice.

"Wonderful!" I exclaimed, finally finished with the waffle. "And now for a drink of something, papa. Only with syrup, please."

"What syrups do you have?" father asked severely, turning to the vendor.

The vendor, a woman with shining, fustian-red cheeks, answered, stressing each new brand with growing enthusiasm:

"Cranberry. Cherry! Fresh Straw!! Nectar of Tea!!!"

I selected "Fresh Straw" halved with "Nectar of Tea"—a spree was a spree! As I drank, father stared at me anxiously.

"Not too cold, is it?"

"No, not at all."

"And do you remember, Lyalka, how Moussia and you howled when mother and I forbade you to go mushroom-picking?"

I began nodding my head. He laughed happily.

"Oh Lord, how you did howl, the two of you! How you howled! For three hours on end. I kept wondering how long it would go on."

"No wonder! It was just the right sort of day. A mushroom day," I replied. "A drizzly, luminous, gray sort of day, smelling of damp fir, and that meadow was just full of butter-mushrooms, but you. . . . Well? Now, fifteen years later, you no doubt feel sorry for us?"

"Sorry . . . we were sorry for you then, too, but mother was anxious about the rain. That's why we didn't let you go."

Father glanced at me guiltily and happily. How I loved him now! I wanted to take him still further back into the past, nearer to his youth, and generous memory at once suggested a way there.

"And do you remember, papa, how we visited the zoo when you came back on leave from the German front?"

"Well?" father was amazed. "Do you really remember? You were just a little puppy then."

"But I do remember. There was a kiosk near the zoo gates— a huge golden bottle, and they sold lemonade there. And I wanted above all to see the Gray Wolf who had carried Ivan Tsarevich. . . . And I remember that wolf too! And you were in uniform. . . . And then we kept being photographed, and I was photographed sitting on your knees and holding on to your sword. And I felt terribly brave because of it. Do you recall it, papa?"

"I recall, I do, but you . . . Lyalka! Wasn't I a handsome fellow then, eh? With my curly locks!"

With a shake of his head, he quietly hummed:

> *But Alesha had a cap of golden curls!*
> *He sang such splendid town songs . . .*

"I had mustaches too," he continued. "Do you remember my mustaches?"

"Of course I do. Moussia used to say, 'Papa has a pair of tails growing under his nose.' And you kept twirling them and singing: '*My mustaches, my little mustaches, they won't curl any more, and the wench my lady is looking glum . . .*'"

"Wait a second," father cried, waving his hand. "'*She's put on her mob cap and sips her tea, and you can't get near her any more.*' That's the way it went on, wasn't it?"

"That isn't all!" I replied triumphantly. "'*They dressed the wench the uniform, and now she commands us all!*' It was a front-line soldiers' song. . . ."

Happy, laughing and rejuvenated, both of us, we approached the monkey house.

As usual, more people were gathered round the monkey house than elsewhere. Boys, blue from the chill air, were hanging over the barrier like Petrushkas, admiring with envy two macacos fight, and egging them on with advice and exclamations:

"Shove him there, give him a push!"

"Hey, you, this way! There she is on the branch!"

"Grab her by the tail! With your back hand, grab her!"

There was a couple pressing behind the cold blue boys: a miniature brunette and a young man with such huge padded shoulders that he resembled a kiosk. The girl was so excited watching the monkeys that she squealed and laughed at their antics, but, as she glanced into her partner's eyes, she restrained herself and asked staidly:

"Zhenyechka, aren't they really original?"

"Real eccentrics," the lad replied condescendingly.

But the monkeys lived their own independent and riotous life, full of labors and worries. They did not give a fig for the spectators; they were always too busy and preoccupied. One disheveled macaco was trying hard to push the trough out of the cage. The trough was firmly wedged. The macaco was pushing it now to the left, now to the right. Another macaco squatted nearby, observing attentively the efforts of its companion. Realizing that these efforts were unsuccessful, she intervened; but being stupider, she tugged the trough back. At last, the trough unexpectedly leapt out of the cage. Both the macacos were dumfounded for a moment; they grasped that they had done something wrong. Thrusting their thin, childlike arms through the bars, they began to touch the trough stealthily as if to convince themselves that this was, indeed, the same object. Beside them in the cage a gray, bearded, virile baboon was busily shaking the wire netting; gripping the netting with his tenacious fists, he would shake it and then wait to see if anything had happened. But everything was as before! The gray-bearded baboon's vanity was so fantastically, awkwardly and comically human, that I felt myself in the best of humor.

"That's one for me, fool that I am!" I thought without resentment and, glancing at father, laughed out loud.

He looked at me happily. He was now in that state of heightened pleasure and good will when a man has only one desire: to lavish that good will.

"And now I'll show you the elephant," he announced.

"The elephant! Why, let's see him quickly!"

I could now play the game easily and convincingly. To be

exact, I was no longer playing but really living this unexpected manifestation of exuberant and precious life.

"Oh, papa, what a huge animal! And just look at his ears. . . ." I exclaimed, fussing near the barrier. My childish excitement was so genuine that some haggard, elderly man, remarkably like a jerboa, very considerately allowed me to pass in front of him as if I were a tot. But even this gesture seemed to me all in the order of things.

"But just look at his tail, papa!" I forged ahead. "What a terribly disproportionate tail. And I wonder what his name is?"

"Betty's their name," the elderly, jerboalike man, informed me respectfully. "They're a lady."

Betty stood there—huge, indifferent and almost eyeless. Only her wrinkled trunk swayed from side to side; and every now and then she would displace her heavy, columnlike legs.

"If there is such a thing as fate, it must resemble Betty," I thought; and, becoming frightened at this "unchildish" idea, I exclaimed:

"Look, papa! She's picked up a coin!"

"Aha. She'll buy herself a carrot in a moment. She understands things."

"They can do real work," the jerboa man put in. "They have consciousness."

"Papa, she has bought the carrot, she has bought it! Ah, how interesting."

Father, after searching his pockets, pulled out a coin and handed it to me. It was a ten kopeck piece with shreds of tobacco stuck to it.

"Here you are," father said generously. "Buy the elephant a carrot."

Beaming blissfully, I threw the coin to the elephant. The coin flashed right under Betty's trunk, rolled rapidly underneath her monstrous body and, after spinning for a while, came to rest behind the elephant under her very tail.

"A bad throw, that!" the jerboa man exclaimed. "They won't be able to turn!"

"That's right, they can't turn," someone in the crowd confirmed as though pronouncing judgment.

"If the elephant finds the coin, my wish will be fulfilled, and everything will be all right!" I thought impetuously and grew hot: I was tempting my luck.

"She won't find it!" someone else cried out as if answering my doubts. Betty's enormous trunk was now groping along the asphalt floor. But always in the wrong place! First, it groped to the right; then near the railing, after which it paused swaying gently. This was the end, I thought! I dug my nails into the palms of my hands. Suddenly my fate, budging slowly on its terrible elephantine legs, swung its back on the spectators, stretched out the trunk and—snap!—caught hold of the coin.

"Fulfilled!" I squealed, gripping father's sleeve. "Everything will work out, do you understand?"

The jerboa man's eyes registered alarm. The crowd gasped in wonder. Only father, my father, understood *everything!*

"Of course I understand!" he growled, but I thought tears might spray from his large eyes. "Everything will be fulfilled! Well, and now, my daughter, let us go. We have seen everything. Did you enjoy it?"

"Very much! The elephant in particular!"

"Well, well, I'm so glad! And where are you off to now? To the tram? I'm going to the left. To Uncle's. Do you remember Uncle? Don't you really remember him?"

"Just a minute . . . I seem to remember something. . . . Yes, Uncle. . . ."

"Of course, Uncle—Minha Volokhin, my colleague from Derpt. H'm . . . Well, perhaps, you don't really remember him; you weren't yet born then. Why, we studied together at the University, sang *Gaudeamus* together. . . ."

Here father began to hum, though he was not at his top form: *"Gaudeamus igitur . . ."*

"What a distance we've traveled together this day," I thought, following with my eyes his old military cap, so familiar to me since childhood, and his short Raglan overcoat so like a peasant woman's skirt. And I felt very pleased with myself for having been so clever and cunning as to lead father along and give him so much pleasure; for I had walked back with him into his youth. But it flashed upon me, too, that father was also congratulating himself as he walked away on being so clever and cunning as to divert me from my worries and plunge me back into my childhood.

As it had turned out, both his youth and my childhood were right here beside us with all their happiness and light; and happiness and light were the essence of life, real life. . . . As for my worries. . . .

"They were simply nonsense, my worries," was the thought that now amazed me. "They were a burden and they hurt, but they were neither lasting, nor the chief thing. The chief thing was Life. And Life I had with me. I was glad of it and I loved it. . . . Was there only Klimanchuk in the world? Who was she anyway? There was the editor too. How patient and scrupulous he was in trying to unravel this muddle. He was a good man. . . . And the man from the communist district committee was a fair man too; he had spent the whole of yesterday trying to clarify just one point. . . . And my father, how good and considerate he was too! There were many good people! And life was where good people were! It was there, life was there!"

I spent the whole of that golden day strolling about the transparent autumn city; and I laughed, remembering the zoo, my childhood years, papa, the elephant; and passersby imagined that I was smiling at them: some showed hurt surprise; others responded by smiling back at me.

That night I saw my favorite dream. I had two fond dreams, which resembled each other. The first dream, the favorite one, was about Ouglich, the town we had inhabited while father was fighting in the Civil War, and about my walking in the direction of the monastery in which we had been installed by the town commune. My second fondest dream was about the meadow to which our parents had forbidden us to go mushroom-picking on that particular luminous, rainy day. The meadow was situated in the Novgorod government, near the village of Zaruchevie, where we had spent several successive summer holidays.

Thus I dreamt that I was walking in the direction of that meadow, as we did in childhood, along a narrow path leading through an extremely overgrown and ancient alder grove, thick with alarming and foreboding dusk and the rustle and mutter of

an unseen, turbulent stream, which swept over the darkened rust
of leaves caught between smooth stones. The dark, damp paths
wound for a long time through the dusk and the rustling of the
vigilant grove; but as soon as you had stepped beyond the last
alder tree and set foot in the meadow, you were bathed at once
in a soft and bright green light: the meadow grass was of a
tender green, and the birch trees on the edge of the grove had
had small, fine leaves; and, from there, the meadow unfurled into
a wide, wide, luminous, peaceful expanse. The meadow was
poised on the brink of a cliff, right on its sheer edge; and from
this eminence you had a sweeping view of the horizon, down
below and on every side. The gently rolling, barely-pronounced
hills spread far and wide without restraint and with meadows
and more meadows upon them, while the crowded blue forests
stood on guard in the distance. The narrow, blue ribbon of the
river wound and flashed below with just one small hut poised
above it; and this whole scene was spacious and light, so very
Russian, wise and expansive.

And if, in my dream, I never actually reached our Ouglich
lodgings, yet in these repeated dreams I always reached that
meadow where I paused for a long time; and, for a long time, my
heart drank in the beauty of those unfurled expanses; and,
afterwards, I always awoke refreshed, somehow very much at
peace with myself and reassured, because I knew now that all
this—one's own land, light and life—existed in reality as well as
in dream. . . .

KONSTANTIN PAUSTOVSKY

The Crowd on the Quay

"WHEN YOU LAND in Naples," said my daughter, a young woman prone to do unexpected things, "give this *matreshka* as a present to the first Italian girl you meet."

I agreed. For all I knew, this mission might lead to some romantic episode. And, as we know, we have all become fundamentally disused to such episodes.

Possibly not everyone can picture to himself a *matreshka*. It is a wooden, egg-shaped doll rather like a Humpty Dumpty. It is made in the image of a Russian peasant girl. The *matreshka* is hollow inside and is made of two easily separable sections. Within it you can place other, smaller *matreshkas*. If you were to show a *matreshka* to a stranger, a foreigner for example, he would hardly guess that it contained several other such dolls inside it.

Before my departure, this *matreshka* stood, in a bright crimson shawl, on top of my writing desk. She was thickly lacquered and shone like glass.

Within it were concealed five other *matreshkas*, all in bright variegated shawls: green, yellow, blue, and purple; and, finally, the smallest *matreshka* of all, the size of a thimble, in a shawl of gold leaf.

The village craftsman had endowed all these *matreshkas* with a specific Russian beauty—sable brows and blushing cheeks blazing like red-hot coal. He had shaded the eyes with such long lashes

232

that the slightest movement on their part would have been enough to shatter any man's heart.

Since childhood I had pictured Naples to myself fairly clearly and even in some detail. But when I saw Naples in reality, it seemed to have shifted both in space and color. What I had been accustomed to seeing on the right was now on the left; what I had imagined to be white turned out to be olive green or brown; and the classical smoke above Vesuvius was now entirely absent. Vesuvius had, it seems, emitted no smoke for the past two years. It was even rumored that it had become extinct forever.

One early morning our boat docked at a pier near the Castel Nuovo. A group of black nuns in white, winged headdresses was waiting on the quay. From a distance, they began hastily to make the sign of the cross and to bless our steamer.

Suddenly a stout, elderly Mother Superior dashed up on a motor scooter and shouted something angrily at the nuns. They looked round apprehensively and, trotting away from our boat, vanished in the morning haze of the Neapolitan streets. The Mother Superior roared off in their wake.

Evidently, as a result of some misunderstanding, the nuns had met and blessed the wrong steamer.

As a matter of fact, very soon after, an old limping steamer, the *Palermo*, docked beside us. A faded Italian flag drooped disconsolately at the stern. The boat had arrived from Palestine, bringing a band of pilgrims who had been visiting the Lord's Tomb.

A smell of coffee and incense was wafted towards us from the *Palermo*. Black crucifixes and bunches of prickly grass were hung on the walls of the cabins. Those were the herbs and the furze of Judea, the wooden-like plants of the desert, fodder for camels and asses.

The *Palermo*, having disembarked the pilgrims, fell asleep immediately, leaning against the pier. She sighed blissfully from time to time, ejecting puffs of exhausted steam. Clumps of thick, hirsuite seaweed dangled from her red hull, and it seemed that this ancient boat was so exhausted from its long run that it lacked even enough energy to shave itself.

But the *Palermo* was unlucky. She was not allowed even a half hour of sleep. Two tugs with lowered funnels edged up sideways to the ship and hauled her away from the pier to make room for an American boat, the *President Hoover*.

The American boat was white, long and boring. She had brought many tourists, most of them middle-aged. Over her decks wandered, waddling, brightly made up ladies in wrinkled bathing suits and dark sunglasses of fantastic shapes in the form of bats, trapezes, tropical butterflies and parachutes. The men walked about in shorts, unembarrassed apparently by their bluish, rooster-like legs.

But what was the most amazing thing of all here in Naples, where the tints of the sky, the clouds and the sea had transformed the whole visible world into a pale-blue, subtle haze and where the nights sobbed with the voices of street musicians— what was the most amazing thing of all was that these American men and women turned out to be so unbelievably stale and dull and reluctant to relinquish any of their established habits. Nothing in the world seemed capable of astonishing them. The earth, though it did sometimes deserve an encouraging pat on the shoulder, seemed to provide them with little cause for enthusiasm.

Passing through a vast Customs building with a mosaic floor of caravels, we emerged on the jetty and stepped on Italian soil, which was here paved with ordinary squared timber. Throngs of pigeons wandered about among the stones.

Policemen in white tropical helmets and white lacquered sword belts stared at us intently and expectantly. Their eyes sometimes entreated us in a way we did not understand. It soon became obvious that the policemen were thursting to be given Moscow souvenirs ("souveniro de Mosca") and, in particular, badges with views of the Kremlin. But they did not venture to ask for the souvenirs openly.

I walked out on the quay. I had not forgotten about the Italian girl and carried the *matreshka* with me, wrapped in tissue paper. For some time, the souvenir hunters plodded after me silently and reproachfully, but I eventually lost them.

I came across no girl immediately. True, I might easily have missed one, for I often stopped and stared into the depths of the side streets, which gave on the quay.

These deep streets looked alluring and mysterious. Alluring because of the fantastic interweaving of powerfully voluted columns with the black branches of yew-trees; of the screaming shop signs with the jets of absolutely crystal water from the fountains; of the winged, full-breasted goddesses on the façades of the houses with the variegated glitter of the stained-glass windows of the churches; of the striped awnings above the cafés with the giddy perfume of the oleanders. The pink oleander flowers swayed faintly in the ceaseless draft caused by automobiles. The streets, like rivers, carried to the redhot quay a cool current of air from the marble buildings.

I still could see no girl. Sadly I thought that she had perhaps managed to give me the slip. Finally, I forced myself to desist from watching the spectacle of the harbor streets and to gaze down the quay. At first the dense, blazing sunlight blinded me; then the baskets of exotic flowers, which were displayed for sale all along the quay, made my eyes dance. Then, at last, I caught sight of the girl.

On my way to the shores of Italy, I had sometimes tried to visualize the first girl I should meet in Naples. To my mind she resembled the youthful grape-picker whom Brullov has depicted in his famous painting. She had the same bluish hair, full of deep sunlight, the same mischievous eyes and smooth, peach-like cheeks.

The girl, who was now advancing towards me, was quite unlike that. She was only ten. She led a small boy by the hand. The boy kept turning round to stare at something which had stirred his imagination, and, for that reason, he walked sideways. The girl, scolding angrily, just dragged him along.

The spectacle behind the boy's back was, of course, somewhat out of the ordinary. An old donkey was being hoisted onto a small steamer (one evidently doing only local excursions—to Sorrento or Castelamarre). The donkey objected to walking the gangway, resisting with all the strength of its four legs and braying hideously with indignation. In the end, a breast-collar was attached to him and he was hauled aboard with the help of a steam-winch. This was obviously done for the pure fun of it.

The winch made an awful rattle. Steam gushed from it. The longshoremen in striped shirts whistled at and applauded the donkey, which ignored them completely.

I scrutinized the girl. She was much better than Brullov's grape-picker—incomparably simpler, poorer and more beautiful.

She wore an old black dress, threadbare at the elbows, darned, light-colored stockings and a pair of old, black espadrilles. All this black agreed wonderfully well with her gaunt, pale face and her unexpectedly bright, auburn plaits, which were carelessly knotted together on her breast.

When the girl came near me, I unwrapped the tissue paper and pulled out the *matreshka*.

At the sight of the *matreshka*, the girl stopped and laughed, pressing her smooth fingers to her breast. What she was laughing at I did not know. Perhaps at the beauty of the unfamiliar toy, which blazed there beneath the Neapolitan sun. People usually laugh like that when their cherished or comic dreams come true.

I held out the *matreshka* to the girl. She refused to take it. She ceased laughing, knitted her dark brows and then broke away in fright. Gripping her by the hand, I almost forced her to accept the *matreshka*. Then she lowered her eyes, curtsied and said almost inaudibly:

"Grazie, Signore!"

She curtsied again, raising her moist, shining eyes. I found it hard to believe that a girl could be so delighted with a trifling thing like a *matreshka*. But, at closer range, I was able to make out the gaunt collarbone beneath her dress, which smelled of tar, and then perceived other signs of antediluvian poverty. Finally, I was convinced that the *matreshka* was indeed a source of the greatest joy to this girl.

At this time I had not yet seen those quarters of Naples, which exude the evil smell of rotten vegetables, nor the northern suburbs where a pall of canary-colored, acid-permeated smoke hung above the waste grounds. Both those sections were inhabited.

All this I was to see later. For the present, Naples lay gleaming before me in a carefree fashion, returning generously to the sea the glitter which the sea lavished upon it, and answering it in kind.

The girl was still thanking me. The boy was too small to catch a glimpse of the *matreshka*, no matter how high he raised his head and strained to look. Yet, imitating his sister, he hummed below there at her knees in a deep husky voice:

"Grazie, Signore."

I bent over the boy, but at that very moment someone embraced me round the neck from the side and then looked into my face; and then I saw beside me a pair of firm, smiling lips and large joyful eyes.

A young woman, a peasant girl by the look of her, in a flounced blue skirt and with a lightweight black shawl over her shoulders, pressed her hot cheek against mine for an instant, repeating in a tender, guttural voice those same familiar words:

"Grazie, Signore!"

She was one of the flower vendors who sat on the quay. She had come running up to thank me for giving such a rare toy to the little Italian girl.

Within a moment, a variegated crowd of flower-vendors, shouting to each other, had gathered round us. They had left their stalls unguarded, piled with oranges, cheap coral, flowers, ribbons, American chewing gum and cigarettes. They all patted me on the back, embraced me, shouted words in my face; and they all had laughing eyes.

The *matreshka* was passed from hand to hand. The women gazed at it as if it were the sun itself, shading their eyes with their hands and uttering sounds of approval. They fussed round the little girl, too, congratulating her and tidying her old dress. One of the women quickly replaited the girl's hair with an orange ribbon.

The women tried in every way to enhance the girl's appearance, and they even pinned a little yellow rosebud to her dress. The little girl really seemed to bloom under their fingers.

Amid all this noise and fuss, the women seemed to be a trifle embarrassed by the presence of a foreigner, a "Soviet signore," embarrassed by the girl's gaunt face and her poverty-stricken appearance.

The crowd grew larger. Taxis, which had been speeding along the quay, pulled up. The drivers asked what was happening and then jumped out together with their passengers and pushed their way towards the girl. Longshoremen, the very same men who had been whistling at the old donkey, also began pressing from behind. Schoolboys materialized out of nowhere. They, too, applauded the *matreshka*, banging their books together and scattering loose pages to the wind. A few Bersaglieri with cock feathers in their hats jumped down from a passing army transport and joined the throng.

An old cab driver climbed up on the seat of his *veturino*, which was decorated with flowers and bells and which looked like a small traveling circus on wheels, and began in a falsetto voice to sing some kind of a song, his arms raised to heaven.

As for the little girl, she was sparkling with joy at all this extraordinary commotion in the harbor.

There was a sudden hush. I looked round. A Customs officer in a gold-braided cap and with a small toylike pistol in a white-lacquered holster at his belt, was slowly advancing upon the throng.

He walked up with great assurance, pushing the people aside. His face with a slight mustache looked absolutely dispassionate.

The officer went up to the girl, took the *matreshka* out of her hands and began examining it with creased brows. The little girl looked imploringly at him. Several times she shyly stretched out her hand towards the doll, but then pulled it away at once. The officer raised his head and examined the crowd. Dozens of vigilant eyes stared back at him in turn. With an ironical smile, the officer snapped his fingers. An indeterminate buzzing sound emanated from the crowd.

Then the officer lifted the *matreshka* above his head, exhibiting it on all sides as might a conjuror ("Oh-la-la!"), and then with a rapid, imperceptible movement, opened the *matreshka* and pulled out of it a second *matreshka*—the one in the bright green shawl.

A low buzz of admiration passed through the crowd. The officer made a clucking sound with his tongue, and instantly out of the green *matreshka* there appeared a yellow one, then a blue and a purple one. Finally, with two fingers he picked out and carefully lifted up the last and tiniest *matreshka*—the one in the gold-leaf shawl.

The crowd seemed to explode. A whirlwind of shouts swept over it. People clapped their hands, whistled, spanked their thighs, stamped their feet and roared with laughter.

The Customs officer collected, as calmly as ever, the six *matreshkas* into one and gave it back to the girl. She hugged the *matreshka* not to her chest, but to her throat, which was throbbing with happiness, and, seizing her little brother by the hand, took to her heels.

In broken French, the Customs officer said to me dryly and pedantically:

"You were a little remiss, sir."

"In what way?"

"You could have made a present of this toy to six little girls instead of only to one."

He was right, of course, about the six girls. It was because of this, perhaps, that he raised his white-gloved hand so majestically to the visor of his cap before walking away rather haughtily and disdainfully.

In substance, that is all that happened that particular morning with the *matreshka* in the port of Naples, but I must add just one more circumstance. It belongs to the category of phenomena, which may exist only in our imagination and which are the fruit of our own desires. But, despite this, they have an irresistible influence upon the further current of our days.

The little girl had run away, forgetting to thank me again. This mistake on her part was at once corrected by the peasant woman in the blue flounced skirt. She embraced me once more, pressing again her smooth, flaming cheek to mine and saying in a soft, embarrassed voice:

"Grazie, mia cara signore!"

She immediately ran away, followed by the other flower-vendors, back to the baskets of flowers, leaving behind her the somewhat bitter and viscous scent of her face upon my cheeks. It was rather like the scent of lavender.

It was remarkably persistent, this scent, for it lingered for several days and vanished only when I visited Rome for several days.

Perhaps I was so conscious of this scent because I had desired it so much.

As the train, which was ever trying to jump the rails and to crash down into the yellow gorges of the Appenines, was rushing from Naples to Rome, I peered from the carriage window at the small mountain towns, thinking to myself that my peasant girl might have been born in any one of these towns.

These were very ancient towns perched on mountain tops, crenelated fortresses, girt by dented walls. Inside them, bells tolled in gloomy cathedrals and churches, in the twilight of whose altars gleamed, perhaps, the divine frescoes of Giotto or even Raphael himself.

Out of draught-parched valleys towards these towns crawled white, winding, almost deserted roads. Here and there a donkey could be seen jogging along. The donkeys' ears were the most clearly visible. It was impossible to distinguish their slender legs, which were of the same color as the slate-gray dust.

I peered closely at these towns, into the narrow streets between the time-faded façades, at the sensational posters of the movie theaters and at the cracked marble of the crumbling fountains, at the knotted olive trees in the gardens; and, I was thinking that, perhaps, in a town like this, I was already in touch with a heart that responded to my own heart—a heart as tender and as warm as her blazing cheek. And this frank heart, I thought, would never refuse me assistance or comfort if I should ever find life particularly difficult.

I was absolutely convinced of this. And this belief helped to make my life immeasurably easier.

On the return journey, the train from Rome arrived in Naples late at night. A warm sea breeze, smelling slightly of gasoline, was blowing through the carriage window. Most of the houses along the railway track were plunged in darkness, but the control station was brightly lit and in it I saw a young man with whiskers and the face of Yves Montand sitting at the window and strumming on a mandolin.

That was my last impression of Naples.

The train stopped on the quay near our boat, which was unmoored very soon after. In the unnaturally bright light of the lamps, I was able to identify the location on the quay where I had seen the flower-vendors. I stared at it, ashamed to admit to myself that I was expecting a miracle—expecting a young country woman in a blue flounced skirt to appear on the deserted quay and to run along it in the wake of the boat, which had already pulled out and which was cutting with its steel prow through the gloom of the night and the black waters of the bay.

For an instant I even fancied that I could distinguish a vague female form in the distance. But it was only one of those light shadows, of which there were so many in this nocturnal port.

I remained sitting on deck till dawn, when suddenly the lights of Sardinia were revealed to us, twinkling amid the measureless expanse of the sea that had just begun to glimmer pale and blue.

That dawn I met with regret. I was very much aware that each succeeding day would remove me further away from my recent past and plunge me in darkness as surely and slowly as a rheostat blots out the stage lighting.

NATALIA SOKOLOVA

A Savage

THOSE WHO LOVE MOSCOW are also interested in the life
of her streets. They know that, if you walk down the Petrovka,
past the *Fisherman-Sportsman* shop (where, on the sidewalk
opposite, there is always a crowd of mysterious, strong and sturdy
fellows whispering to each other, and you can overhear the im-
pressive but, to ordinary mortals, quite incomprehensible words
such as: "floats," "flies," "lines"); past the skating rink *Dynamo*
(where long-legged, teen-age girls in slacks and sweaters go whiz-
zing by on slender blades of skates with a glint of hoar-frost on
them); past a sidestreet bearing the ancient name of "Petrovskii
Linii," (where, since bygone times have flourished well-nourished
and, far from timorous, pigeons, which are slow to rise and which
take off reluctantly under the very wheels of slowly advancing machines); past all these, and turning afterwards to the right along
the Kuznetzky Most; then, you will finally arrive in front of another shop whose speciality is to sell editions of books by sub-
scription. There, beneath the wide arch of this collectors shop, a
tightly-packed throng of book lovers is always collected; each
individual in the throng seems to have the colored spine of a book
protruding either from under his elbow or from under his jacket.

Among these individuals you will find some genuine Knights
of the Book, as well as a number of not so disinterested. Here
an exchange is going on and—why hide this sinful activity!—

242

some underhand traffic in the volumes of certain Collected Works and in duly signed receipts for subscriptions. Published books are rapidly increasing in number, but the demand for them increases even more rapidly. The result is a fever of speculation.

A tall, stately pedestrian came swinging into the Kuznetzky Most; the snow creaked beneath his white felt boots with brown leather patches. He also wore a reddish half-coat of calf fur, a wadded ear cap, a "Kiev" camera slung on a strap over his shoulder, and an army mapcase flapping against his thighs. He kept clicking his camera as he walked; and it was obvious at once that he was not a Moscow Man. Girls turned round to stare at him: the freshness and the healthy, wintry glow of his youthful face attracted them.

"Visiting Moscow?" asked a man on the edge of the throng of book enthusiasts. This character had a blue chilled nose, a frozen bristling appearance, and a turned up overcoat collar held together by a thick knotted scarf.

"I'm a Siberian!" the pedestrian replied.

"Are you interested in books?"

"Yes, you know, I'd like to get a few . . ." the Siberian answered, eyeing respectfully from above the rather sickly-looking questioner. "We're building a new town out there. Some day we shall have wonderful bookshops! With marble façades and inlaid with malachite. In the meantime," here he smiled, spreading out his hands, "in the meantime we sometimes have bears promenading down our main street." Then, with a sigh, he confessed further: "I'd very much like to get hold of Heinrich Mann."

"Heinrich? That's no good. There's no shortage of him," the man with the knotted scarf declared, looking superior. "That's not a limited edition. But take Thomas Mann, for example, that's another thing! His edition is limited to subscribers."

"But *Henry, King of France* is an excellent novel. In general, I am very interested in that period," the Siberian naïvely explained. "And in his other works too . . ."

The man with blue chilled nose paid no attention. He kept twisting the lowest button of his new acquaintance's reddish half-coat of calf fur. Then, lowering his voice confidentially, he said:

"I'd recommend you to get *A Thousand and One Nights*. There was a regular battle to subscribe for that edition. And you could always sell it again for a decent sum. Book collectors are falling over themselves to get it. It's an opulent edition. The binding is of cream and gold . . ."

"It's not the binding that will make us happy," the visiting Siberian replied, clicking open his mapcase and pulling out a private memorandum. "What I really want to buy is Klyuchevsky's *History of Russia*. And Fartouchny, our geologist, has asked for Anatole France and Hertzen, too, in eight volumes. Our doctor, Marina Dmitrievna is dreaming of Twardovsky . . ."

"You'll find Lyuchevsky in all the shops," the character retorted with a contemptuous twist of his face. "You're on the wrong beat entirely . . . But how would you like Defoe? His *Moll Flanders?* There are such passages in it! Or *The Golden Ass* with colored illustrations? Some of the illustrations, you know . . ."

The Siberian frowned. Preserving his politeness, he resolutely liberated his button from the tenacious fingers of his chance acquaintance and put his mapcase in order.

"Excuse me. I'm in a hurry," he snapped, and his downy, snow-flaked ear cap disappeared behind the door of the shop.

The man with the knotted scarf was left alone, chilled to the marrow, disillusioned and disappointed in his expectations. With a supercilious look he pursed his lips and muttered hoarsely and irritably:

"The provinces! Not a cent's worth of culture. Gray matter . . . Try and talk to the likes of him. Only a waste of time. Tfu!" Then he pronounced the final sentence: "A savage! What can you get out of him?"

FEODOR PANFEROV

Love and Art

An episode from "In the Name of Youth"

THAT PARTICULAR spring evening Tatyana went downstairs
to telephone Vassily Gagin, but some inner sense of caution prevented her from doing so; she abandoned the telephone booth and
walked aimlessly along the sidewalk of a newly constructed street,
bordered by freshly planted trees, maple, acacia and birch.

The birch trees were, like earrings, adorned with tiny leaves
and, in the light of the electric street lamps, they glistened and
glittered as though smeared with honey. The birch trees gave
their sweet, vital sap. Peonies were thrusting through the crusted
earth. They had already thrown up their leaves, which looked
like puppies pricking up their sharp, inquisitive ears.

Spring was on its way.

Spring it was that may have induced Tatyana to cross the final
dividing line. It was perhaps these birch leaves, wrapped in
rosy smoke, that made her go back to the telephone booth and
call up Vassily Gagin's studio.

At the sound of her voice, Gagin asked excitedly:

"Where are you? Where? You can't do this! I was on the point
of suicide. What sort of a joke is this! No sign of you in a month-
and-a-half! Where are you? I'll dash over to you at once!"

"Don't. I'll come myself. Wait for me," was all Tatyana replied, panting from excitement and pluming herself with female pride. "He loves me all the same. But Nikolai Stepanovich (her husband) did not seek me out, did not try to, even though he was in Moscow before he flew to England. But Vassily nearly went crazy. And what a voice he has! A voice I adore! Therefore I am acting rightly: I am drawn to a voice that is dear to me."

Telling her roommate that she might not return to her retreat that day, Tatyana impetuously dashed downstairs and, hailing a taxi, gave the driver the address:

"Only drive quickly, please," she added impatiently.

"Is there a fire or is someone giving birth?" the taxi-driver asked. "Nowadays speed profits only us taximen, for *they've* confiscated the cars from those who got disused to traveling by subway and they've put them in our taxi park. Soon there will be one of us taxi-drivers for every inhabitant in Moscow. Formerly, we just waddled at work. If you need a taxi, citizen, you can cool your heels. Drive quickly—you can wait. But now we have to chase after the citizen. . . ."

The driver was a droll type, and Tatyana, on another occasion, would have enjoyed this chatter, but now her mind was elsewhere. Vividly she pictured to herself at this very minute mounting in an elevator to the studio on the seventh floor. . . . Vassily was, of course, waiting for her downstairs. How could he possibly wait for her in the studio? They would embrace and kiss each other in front of passers-by. They would even astonish Liza, the elevator girl. Let everyone know about their love. Why conceal it? Why?

"Since we love each other, let everyone know about it." She even half-closed her eyes and lightly kissed her own arm above the wrist, the arm that had embraced him, Vassily Gagin.

Blast these militia men! Why did they hold one up at the crossroads? There was nobody about! There were stone-hearted people in the world. They did not care who was driving and where he was hurrying. They just shouldn't do that sort of thing. Just look at that militia man sitting there in his glassbox as at the bottom of a glass, staring round like a barn-owl. Can't he see that Tatyana is in a hurry to meet her beloved, whom she has not seen for over a month. She had deliberately avoided him, but today she has revealed herself entirely.

At last, they passed the crossroads. At last, there was the familiar doorway to the apartment house, where Vassily Gagin's studio was situated "right on top." Of course, this Zasolny Street would become known in the future as Vassily Gagin Street. Little Fathers! What love does to one! Tatyana had already reserved an honorable niche for Vassily Gagin in the history of Soviet painting. Little Fathers! She was ready to sacrifice herself for some future reference to the effect that "Tatyana Polovtzeva played no small part in the creative life of Vassily Gagin; she declared that she herself was ashamed to paint after such a great talent as Vassily Gagin has appeared on earth."

But Vassily Gagin failed to meet her at the entrance. "Well, he might be tidying his studio," she thought. "He was living like a bachelor, after all.

"He's an eccentric. I'll do all the tidying. I'll do it with pleasure. An eccentric," Tatyana whispered, nimbly running up the steps leading to the elevator, near which Liza was sitting on a stool.

"Whom do you want?" Liza asked automatically.

"Gagin. Is he here? Ah, Liza, you didn't recognize me?" Tatyana said with marked familiarity.

"How could I! He has heaps of women visitors!"

"You're slandering him."

"Why should I? The models come in droves."

"They aren't ladies," Tatyana was about to say with relief, but the elevator was already bumping up to the seventh floor.

Vassily Gagin, after the telephone conversation, remained sitting motionless in a worn armchair as though stricken with paralysis.

For a writer it is far more difficult to recompose a lost manuscript than to write a new version; it would probably be impossible to recompose it, for he would keep thinking that what had been lost was much superior. For some time past Vassily Gagin had found himself in the position of a writer who had lost his manuscript. He had been looking everywhere for Tatyana: at their mutual friends', amid the endless daily and evening flow of the inhabitants, in museums, at exhibitions; and daily he had also rung up her apartment in Privolzhsk. But now he was in the position of a writer, who had sought his manuscript everywhere and then had suddenly found it at home under his pillow. He had found it and gone limp from exhaustion.

He was still sitting limply in his worn armchair when Tatyana entered through the half-open door. She glanced at him and then at the setting, and her experienced eye told her that he had not been working all this time on his painting, "Morning on the Volga." Dropping on her knees before him, she took his hand and, pressing her cheeks against his palm, said almost inaudibly:

"Darling . . . what pain I have caused you! But I felt the pain too!"

He kept silent for a time, unable to suppress a slight, very slight shudder within him, even though he felt and understood that the mere contact of his hand with her luxuriant hair had already awakened in him that potent and virile force, which had compelled him to seek her everywhere during those long drawn-out days.

"Help me to pull myself together," he finally said. "Oh! How many days . . . how many nights . . . without you! My eyes went dark: I lost all sensation of day or night. I lost myself: I felt utterly depressed. As you see, I didn't even put brush to canvas."

"Darling, what have I done!" Tatyana kept saying almost inaudibly, proud nevertheless to have been able to reduce an artiest of such renown to this state. "See how much he loves me!" she shouted mentally.

"Help me to rise and become myself. Help me," he said, half-rising.

Impetuously she jumped to her feet like a startled deer and, taking him under the arms and kissing his lips in motion, suddenly found herself in his arms.

Her dress, blue as the spring sky, was torn open from top to bottom like a dressing gown. A second later it bared her shoulders, arms . . . and then, with a rending sound, the buttons of her bra flew in every direction.

"What are you doing! You're mad!" Tatyana cried out without any show of resistance, observing his clothes falling on the armchair.

The world was shut out; for an indefinite period the service bureau agreed to receive his telephone messages and Liza, the elevator-girl, was ordered to inform callers that "There is no one in the studio." She was also given some ready cash to buy wine, flowers and, for some mysterious reason, a needle and thread.

Now both Tatyana and Vassily really lost all sense of night and day. They found a nook for themselves in a small, windowless side room. Here stood a table laden now with a variety of eatables and bottles of wine handsomely set out by Tatyana's own hands. Nearby was a rather narrow couch, but upon it they somehow managed to merge into each other and this they both found pleasant.

She even admitted:

"I have never experienced anything like this before. *We* always use separate beds." She did not refer to Nikolai Korablev, her husband, by name, but Vassily Gagin fully understood who "we" were. He talked his own language:

"What a marvelous body you have, just like hot velvet!" he purred. "That's what we haven't learned yet to communicate on canvas: hot velvet. But Rembrandt possibly knew how to."

"He sensed it, touching his beloved one."

"Yes. He was a Hercules of passion," Vassily Gagin went on. "Michaelangelo gave Eve, the Mother, to the world: looking at her, you would believe that the human race really sprang from her . . . but he himself yearned for a family . . . but could not have one, like the great Tchaikovsky. Rembrandt gave the world the beauty of the female body, its hot velvet. Gave it and openly enjoyed it, imbibing this beauty as a thirsty man drinks water from a crystal source."

This conversation was conducted in the dimmed light, but outside it was very possibly daylight already.

"You have a firm, supple body," Tatyana said.

"You don't like it?"

"What do you mean! Then why would I kiss my arms when I'm alone?"

"Why indeed?"

"Because they have embraced you and now your nakedness too. I have a whole file of drawings I made of your hand. *He* once looked through that file and understood everything."

"Hardly."

"No. He is clever. That cannot be denied him. But we mustn't blot our happy isolation."

They continued to fence themselves off from the outside world. Without embarrassment they sat down to table half-naked, drank wine, ate, laughed at every trifle. Tatyana, in particular, knew how to laugh and infect anyone near her, making them laugh without knowing why.

"Oh, to live like this for years on end," she would say, bursting into a pealing laugh and straining her nostrils, the effect of which was to make her face look beautiful and imperious.

"Yes, but the world will summon us," he answered reluctantly.

"We'll descend into it—and then return to our isolation," she replied. "You will, I believe, find a corner for me in the holy of holies—in your studio—and we shall create paintings and. . . ."

"And love?"

"Yes, love."

Thus it lasted for five days.

It happens so. It happens so.

Tatyana, an intelligent woman, ought to have broken out of this isolation before now: a thirsting man may drink one goblet, another one, and then refuse a third. Vassily Gagin should have been allowed to drink one goblet only to stimulate his desire for more. But this thought occurred to Tatyana only belatedly; but now, on the sixth day, she woke to find Vassily Gagin sitting opposite his canvas of "Morning on the Volga."

"Little Fathers! He's found himself!" she inaudibly proclaimed her surprise. Picking up needle and thread, she began quickly and carelessly to repair the tear in her dress and to put her bra in order. Having dressed, she came out of the cozy little room and, stepping into the studio, caught sight of the hot and brightly dazzling spring intruding importunately through the large studio window.

"You're already . . . ?" Tatyana asked fearfully. She had wanted to say "satiated," but stopped in time; but Gagin, not understanding her question, answered rather coarsely, though half in jest:

"Must earn my bread. And the business has piled up. I've lost over a month, you know. I've neglected everything—not only in the studio here, but in the secretariat of the Artists' Union. I'm not just anybody after all, but the deputy chairman. If I go on working like this, I'll be dropped like a hot brick at the next election."

"So that's what he is worrying about, that they'll drop him," she thought. But aloud she said:

"You repent then? Lost so many days because of me?"

"Why twist things so? Don't you understand that it's time for both you and me to go back into the world. We're not living on a desert island."

"You're talking with me as you do with your empty-headed wife," Tatyana was about to reply, but checked herself again. What she actually said was rather different from what she had intended to say by way of frightening him:

"So I'll be off then?"

"Shall we breakfast?" was his only answer. "Or perhaps I'd better call a taxi."

Her nose turned pale; her eyes, gray until then, went white and, breathing hard, she cried out:

"Vassily, I'm not a model . . . not a wench."

"What's the matter with you? Lost your mind?" Throwing his brush aside, Vassily Gagin ran up to Tatyana, embraced her, and began kissing her on the lips, the eyes and behind the ear, saying: "If you wish, I'll tear your dress off again? If you wish, we'll lock ourselves up in that room forever? But the world was calling us. All right. Let's breakfast together and . . . and then we'll discuss everything."

She might have stayed, but was prevented by his tone in which one could hear: "We've had our fun, that's fine; but now we must use our heads." Forcing an affectionate smile, she replied:

"No, you're right. Back to the world it is. Call a taxi."

"Leave me your address. In the evening, at about six, I'll pick you up and we'll go to a theater."

"But aren't you afraid that the hypocrites will talk and label you a libertine: you, with a wife in the background, going to theaters with another man's wife."

"I'm not frightened of anything."

"Fine fellow, and a brave one!"

That evening . . . Little Fathers! It was like a blow with a hammer on the temple. . . . In the evening a brief note arrived from Vassily Gagin.

"That was passion, not love," he wrote. "Passion is not lasting. It passes like a famished man's hunger after a good meal. You and I had better part enemies rather than live together. Life together would be murder."

Tatyana rushed downstairs to the telephone booth. She dialed the number and, when Vassily Gagin picked up the receiver, shouted:

"Vassily! You're joking?"

He slammed the receiver down.

She dialed the number again and again. The other side was silent like the sky in calm weather.

VLADIMIR DUDINTSEV

A New Year's Fable

I LIVE in a fantastic world, a fabulous land, a city of my imagination. There wondrous things befall people, and I have had my
share of these adventures. I shall tell you something about them,
profiting by the fact that on New Year's Eve people are inclined
to listen to all sorts of fantasies.

I shall speak of time and the tricks it plays on us. Time, after
all, is boundless and ubiquitously active. In a world of fable a
watch can always be set by Moscow time. This is why I am
taking the risk of setting out on my story—perhaps some curious
person will be found who will become interested in certain
passages of my fantasy as they touch on the reality of his life.

A mysterious bird—an owl—came flying into our city. It
made a few people happier by visiting them. The first of these
was my immediate chief, the Head of the Laboratory for Solar
Research, where I work. The second turned out to be a doctor,
a neuro-pathologist and my old school friend. For the third the
owl selected me. It was a remarkable bird, that. It would not be a
bad idea to study its habits and to include its portrait in books
of ornithology.

By that time I had already published several scientific works
about certain aspects of solar light. I had a degree, acted as con-
sultant to several commissions, and was in a hurry to make a
solid reputation for myself. Modeling my behavior on that of our

venerable scientists, I learned, like them, to hold my head high; in the same way, I deliberately weighed every problem presented to me and, like them, raising an eyebrow, I gave my precious, well-pondered answer in a sing-song voice. One other trait: I grew accustomed to taking care of my expensive overcoat. We had closets in our offices and, imitating the older scientists, I hung in my closet a wooden coat hanger with my initials on it.

As a person endowed with a few modest accomplishments, I trained myself, on the advice of a certain academician, to jot down any ideas that unexpectedly entered my head. As we all know, our most valuable ideas are not those we painfully labor over at a desk but rather those that descend upon us like a gust of wind, most often when we are strolling in the street. I would jot down these ideas and then forget all about them. But our stove-woman was well aware that she could always find in the drawers of my desk magic scraps of paper which flared like gunpowder. She got into the habit of emptying my desk and using these scraps to kindle all the stoves in the laboratory.

Behind my solid exterior there lurked a naïve child (it also lurked within my chief, who had his doctorate). This chubby-cheeked child would sometimes emerge into the open, especially during those evening hours when we, the unmarried men, would settle down in our quarters in front of the TV set and goggle-eyed, immobilized, as if preserved in alcohol, stare for hours at the rapidly flashing legs of football players on the bluish screen.

As you can see, I am not sparing myself here at all. Quite consciously I am exposing, and shall continue to expose, many aspects of my character for your judgment, and I myself shall be the strictest judge. For some time past my eyes seem to have been opened—in particular, ever since that day when the owl in person paid me the first visit. The owl opened my eyes. I am very grateful to it.

For example, I saw in an entirely new light my long disputation with a certain Mr. S., a corresponding member of a certain provincial Academy of Sciences. Five years ago he had, in an article, called my well-known published work "the fruit of idle fancies." I was obliged to answer him. In a subsequent article I refuted, as if in passing, S.'s fundamental premises and threw in very appropriately, I believe, the following sentence: "This is precisely what the doctoral candidate S. has attempted unsuccessfully to prove." (I was perfectly well aware that, even though he was a corresponding member of the Academy, the degree he held was the same as mine—that of a doctoral candidate.) S. immediately responded to my attack by publishing a brochure in which, just as casually, he affirmed that I was forcing the results of my experiments into the framework of a theory, and he put quotation marks round the word "theory." Soon after, I printed a long article about my new observations on the sun, confirming the theory he had put in quotation marks and playing havoc with S.'s statistics. "The torpedo made a direct hit," was the general opinion of my colleagues. In the article I did not mention S. by name—I knew that my enemy could not withstand the second torpedo. I simply referred to "certain authors." But the battleship stood the shock and answered back. . . .

And so forth. This war, which lasted for five years, had shaken my nervous system to the roots, and not mine alone!

But let us get down to business. One morning we had all gathered in our laboratory, hung up our overcoats on our hangers and, before proceeding with our research, stopped for our usual morning chat. Our senior and most respected chief, the Doctor of Sciences, was the first to start the ball rolling. In his spare time he was a student of antiquity and a collector of stone axes, ancient coins and old books; and, in my opinion, the whole significance of his peaceful life lay in this hobby rather than in our work.

"A curious thing!" he exclaimed, inviting us to listen. "Not long ago, while deciphering an inscription on a stone slab, I discovered the following image."

He showed us a white sheet of paper on which an owl with large ears had been drawn in ink.

"I also succeeded in deciphering the inscription," the chief announced proudly. "There was a name there and words that read: 'And his age was nine hundred.'"

"Y-yes . . ." one of my other colleagues, who loved to dress smartly and to play practical jokes, said thoughtfully. "Four hundred would be enough for me. . . ."

"Why do you need it?" a dry, broad-shouldered, elderly man, who usually was silent, asked abruptly. He was sitting near me and differed from all of us by his marked carelessness in dress, his taciturnity and his incredible capacity for work. "You have no need for these four hundred years," he added. "You're in no hurry anyhow."

"I'd like you to note!" the chief exclaimed, raising his voice to make it clear that he had been interrupted, "I'd like you to note that owls of this type have been discovered at different times in various countries. In one of the deserts there stands a gigantic owl of granite. But this is the first such find in our locality. If I may boast a little," and hereupon the chief smiled broadly, "both this owl and this inscription are my personal discovery. I excavated the slab in my own garden."

We congratulated the lucky man, examined the owl once again, and then dispersed to our places of work.

"I'll make it my business to discover the meaning of this image," the chief said. "Then I shall publish the findings."

"Perhaps this hieroglyphic denotes a man who best knew how to utilize his time," I ventured to suggest.

"Possibly. But that would have to be verified."

"But an age-span of nine hundred years!" I could not restrain myself from exclaiming. "Was such longevity ever possible?"

"Everything is possible!" snapped my broad-shouldered, forever concentrating neighbor, without stopping his work.

"What do you mean?" the chief politely inquired.

"Time is an enigma," he replied even more enigmatically.

"Yes, time is an enigma," the chief said, echoing this interesting idea. He took the hour-glass from the wall, turned it upside down and set it before him on his desk. "It's running!" he commented, watching the sand. "And look at the result. Every instant of our life may be compared to a minute grain of sand, to an infinitely tiny speck . . . one that vanishes instantly. . . ."

I suddenly felt a spasm of pain in my chest. I had once experienced several months of unexpected and extraordinary love, and now that I looked back with pain upon those months, they emerged into one single instant, into a mere grain of sand dropping to the bottom of the hour-glass. Not a trace remained in my hands. It was as though nothing had even been! I sighed. If I could only turn the hour-glass again!

"Excuse me, chief," our personnel manager said, interrupting my reflections. "Where does your theory—if I may call it that —lead us: if time is a mere speck, then we have no heroic past? No sunny future?"

He was fond of loudly posing very blunt questions as if implicating a man in some horrible crime.

"My apologies if I said something amiss," our peace-loving chief replied. "But, in my view, I did not have time to formulate any theory. It's all a joke, a fantasy. . . ."

"A strange fantasy that. After all, we have a certain framework . . ."

"My dear fellow!" our perpetually busy, shaggy-haired eccentric suddenly snapped. We all turned around. "The new— what we are seeking—is almost always to be found outside the framework."

And opening his mouth (a mannerism of his), he laughed noiselessly in the face of the severe critic. This gave us a new insight into the character of our colleague.

For two years we had sat in the same office with him without having any conception of the man! We had observed only that he seldom shaved and that he flung his overcoat on a chair. We had noted that half a button was missing from his overcoat. Finally, we noticed that he did the work of four men. But somehow we had not really gotten to know him!

"You know, I think I'll tell you an interesting story," we again heard the voice of this colleague who was forever stooped over his work.

We were all astonished: it was the first time we had been so favored as to have him waste his time chatting with us! I had no idea that our conversation about longevity would stir him up so much.

"But I must first run down to the basement and start the instruments working so as not to lose time," he added, rapidly leaving the office.

"Is he a dry old stick or not?" someone asked.

"I don't think so!" our practical joker protested. "There is a lady visits him sometimes. I live next door to him. A young lady! I once bumped into her on the stairs. There she was walking along staring into space. Blinded by love."

"Do you know, he owns a unique sort of ancient watch. It keeps very precise time and has to be wound only once a year." It was the chief who said this.

"Here we are, friends!" exclaimed our graying, untidy new colleague (for we had just got to know him this very day), our work-horse, as he entered the office, sat down at his desk and picked up a logarythmic slide. "You say nine hundred years . . . but do you realize that time can stand still as well as fly at terrific speed? Haven't you ever had to wait for your girl-friend to turn up?"

"Yes, indeed," the chief said sententiously. "Time can crawl very slowly."

"It can stand still too. Do you remember the story of the scientists who succeeded in growing plants from lotus seeds that had lain buried for two thousand years in a stone sepulchre? Time had stood still for those seeds! Time can be arrested as well as pushed on!"

Saying this, he opened the slide rule and then jotted something down—he was still managing to do his work.

"I shall illustrate my statement with a story which you, regardless of its moral, will find interesting."

And, as he began, he seemed to turn towards me as if his words were destined exclusively for my benefit.

"In a certain kingdom, in a certain state—in our own city, to be exact, the following event came to pass some years ago. On a Sunday, in one of the shadiest corners of the Park of Culture there gathered some six or ten or, maybe, even a hundred well-dressed men for the purpose of engaging in some sort of conversation which they had decided to conduct in the open air. It later became known that, in our Park, there had been held for a period of two hours a—what shall I call it—a symposium of bandits and thieves who, as they themselves term it, were bound by 'law.' These fellows have their own strict rules. Any transgression is punishable by death. Those who are 'bound by oath' must be vouched for by several sponsors. Any new member of the society must have a device tattooed on his chest: just a few words to identify him at once as 'one of them.' "

"What relation has this story to our theme of time?" the chief softly inquired. "Or perhaps you have not yet finished?"

"I haven't finished. It's a very direct relation. I am just coming to the theme. The Congress of bandits, of the 'oath-bound,' pronounced six death sentences, five of which were executed. They were unable to lay their hands on the sixth condemned man because complications developed in this case. I shall tell you, first of all, who this sixth man was and in what his guilt consisted. He was the head, the president, or, as they call him, 'the big wheel' of the entire society of the 'oath-bound,' the oldest and the most cunning of all the bandits. He was sitting in some remote jail, and it was there no doubt, in solitary confinement, that the thought occurred to him that he had, in substance, done nothing in life, had received nothing, and that there was but little time left to live. He reasoned as follows: the whole meaning of a bandit's life could be summed up as the easiest way of acquiring other people's possessions, whether gold or other valuables. But the value and the prestige of possessions in human society are undergoing a catastrophic decline."

"Your bandit seems to have been a theoretician!" the personnel manager could be heard saying ironically.

"Yes, he was a serious person," our eccentric agreed. "I came to like him more and more. This criminal, who had done a great deal of harm, quieted down in his later years and began to read books. Books can be a terrific force! He read numerous books. He was in no hurry to leave the jail—he found his cell convenient for reading and reflecting, and his 'bond' brothers supplied their potentate from the outside with any book, even such as were guarded under seven seals in the official cellars. Yes. . . . And thus he realized that the prestige of wealth was catastrophically declining. Once upon a time, in the remote past, magnates and princes used to make special fishing preserves in bays for breeding moray eels. They used to feed the moray eels on human flesh—that of slaves, whom they tossed into the bay. Such a moray eel, served at a festive board, was considered a supreme delicacy. But nowadays we cannot think of such diversions on the part of our ancestors without shuddering. Once upon a time gold was an anonymous metal embedded in the earth. Then man gave it a name and a value. To have the glitter of gold on one's dress or weapons was regarded as the height of fashion. But in our days none of us would venture to appear in society with a gold chain across our belly or any vestige of gold even on a tie pin. The prestige of gold is declining. And where is the prestige involved in owning expensive fabrics? I can vouch for the fact that even the most expensive modern fabrics are finally going out of fashion. To flaunt riches nowadays is a sign of spiritual backwardness.

"What a way of dealing with material values that bandit had, if you please! It would be curious to see what will replace material objects," the personnel manager said. This story had jarred him somewhat because he was sporting just then a very expensive tweed suit with broadly cut shoulders, and his wife, on visiting the laboratory, had carried a substantial silver fox over her arm.

"What things are you referring to? There are things and things. The bandit realized this and pondered over it. He grasped that the worship of material objects was being inexorably replaced by the concept of the beauty of the human soul, which he knew could neither he bought nor stolen. You cannot make anyone love you by force of arms. The beauty of the soul is free. The soul occupied the foreground as soon as gold and velvet surrendered their position. At present, Cinderellas in cotton dresses triumph over princesses in silks. The beautiful cut of a cheap dress constitutes its main value, and that is no longer a material value. The style of a dress bespeaks the taste, the character of the person who created and who selected that style for himself. And it is no accident that many princesses, who have not lost their souls, have begun to dress like Cinderellas. And if we meet some woman laden with furs and fine fabrics, we are no longer enraptured by the lavishness of her apparel, but, on the contrary, we shy away from her as from a spiritual freak who is bent upon making a public display of herself.

"My bandit observed this. He suddenly discovered that, throughout his life, he had never possessed such 'things' as other men's approval, their friendship, true love, but had rather striven all his life towards something devoid of any real value. Something like a monetary reform had come about. Yes . . ." Here the narrator's voice grew hoarse. He coughed. "But the people, the love and the friendship, of which he was so much in need, did really exist. He, too, knew them . . . There was a woman. But he could not even appear before her. He could not reveal himself, he could not risk it.

"To sum it up, this man wrote down all his observations in a long letter addressed to his brothers, the 'oath-bound,' in which he declared that he was stripping himself of his 'rank,' joining the society of normal, working people, and that he was resolved, by some outstanding act, to gain for himself what he had hitherto ignored in life and towards which he was now drawn, as they say, with all his being. The prison authorities printed this letter of his in a special leaflet. As you can well understand, of course, this document had terrific potentialities and it was important to make the most of it.

"Now consider the position in which our 'big wheel' found himself. In the course of his life, he had been sentenced to some two hundred years of penal servitude but, owing to the confusion of the times, he had not served anything like it! He was aware that he could expect no 'reduction' from the State. On the other hand, knowing better than anyone the rules of the 'oath-bound' commune, he realized that his 'brethren' would never overlook his betrayal and that somewhere a keen knife was already awaiting him. But he felt the need of living just a few years longer in order to achieve that which had induced him to take this step. Thus, even before his 'brethren' had sat in judgment upon him, he had made his last break. He was affluent enough, and, as sometimes happens in fairy tales, doctors were available who were able to graft new skin on his face and hands, as well as new skin and hair on his head. They even did something to his voice. They were great craftsmen.

"Our bandit acquired a set of impeccable papers and became a new man. Within three years he had completed courses at two Institutes. At present, he is nearing his objective. He has conceived an important mission and would like to bestow a gift on humanity . . ."

"That's all very well," I interrupted him, because he kept looking at me all the time. "But what does this have to do with our conversation? With the notion that time can stand still and fly? Or with what was inscribed on the slab: 'And his age was nine hundred'?"

"It is directly related. The executioners are now after him. They are close on his trail. They are bound to get him. The man has very little time left. Very little *time*—do you understand? And this man is determined to relive the whole of his life within a year or two. But what would have happened if he had lived all his years in this way? His life might have added up to nine hundred years or perhaps even more."

"You have in mind, of course, the content of his life rather than its span?" the chief suggested.

"It's very clear you're not very economical with your time!" my neighbor angrily replied. "Yes, yes, yes! The content! That with which we fill the vessel of time. This should be filled only with the strongest satisfactions, with the sensations of the most potent joys. . . ."

"You're certainly laying it on thick!" the personnel manager could be heard exclaiming. "You're preaching the purest form of egoism. You want only to enjoy and satisfy yourself! But it seems to me that we also have to work for the benefit of the people. Ah? What do you think?"

"You're behind the times, that's what I think. You should be taken in tow. You assume that enjoyment and satisfaction are a sin—something you indulge in secretly within the four walls of your room. And working for the benefit of the people is your public duty. Compared with you, my bandit is an advanced man. He has tried all your pleasures and is fed up with them. He now admits only one form of enjoyment—that which you regard as mere duty."

"Tell me . . ." the chief began after a moment's silence. "How do you know all these details? This man has altered his face, his identity. . . . He is probably no fool and does not confide in the first man he meets."

"I am not the first man he meets."

"In that case, you must denounce him if you are a conscientious man," the personnel manager suddenly intervened. "You should report him. He has committed so many crimes and broken out of jail. . . ."

"Nothing would make me do it!" our colleague replied. "Nothing! He is no bandit now. He is harmless. Even useful. When he achieves his objective, he will declare himself before all men."

Thereupon he pulled out of his pocket his famous watch—a weighty bulbous instrument attached to a steel chain.

"Excuse me. I must go down and check the instruments."

On going out, he paused in the doorway.

"All of you should ponder this story. And you especially," he said, looking me straight in the face—"perhaps you will heed the experience of some people and will stop playing with toys. Perhaps you will put an end to your fruitless polemic with that corresponding member. . . ."

I had no reason to suppose then that life would link me, too, with that affair and make me its second hero, the protagonist's *alter ego!*

After about half an hour, in order to verify a certain suspicion which had suddenly hit me, I walked down to the basement and almost noiselessly opened the door behind which this man was seated amid the surrounding glitter of glass and brass instruments. The door creaked almost inaudibly, but he leapt aside so violently that he broke several retorts.

"Excuse me," I said.

"You are verifying your suspicion?" he asked me, recovering himself.

"You are very rash," I replied.

"I am not frightened of you," he answered, returning to his apparatus.

Now that I had established what I had merely suspected before, several other things (about which I shall keep silent until the right time) were at once clear to me.

A short while before this episode, I had come to realize that I was the object of inexplicable attention on the part of a certain individual. A certain shadowy figure dogged me ceaselessly through the streets of the city and watched me from a distance.

I had not once succeeded in making out my pursuer's face even though he showed no hurry to get out of sight. He (or she) usually selected dark arcades or gateways as his point of observation. Sometimes he stepped into the sunlight but, as soon as I put my hand into my pocket—to get my glasses—the fellow would stealthily remove himself behind an arcade. On several occasions, I approached those gateways or entrances where this individual, so attentive to me, was hiding, but never found anyone. Not so very long ago we had our first fall of soft, clean snow. Late one evening, as I was walking through the deserted street, I caught the sound of footsteps behind my back and, before I had time to turn round, I realized that it was my shadower (man or woman). I turned and saw something in the nature of a cape or the tails of a dress suit flashing round the corner. I dashed in pursuit like a madman and, when I turned the corner, saw merely a white deserted side-street. I examined the snow without finding any footprints. True, I later recalled noticing in the light airy snow several rapidly melting cruciform prints which resembled the traces of a huge chicken's claw.

In the basement, I recounted all this in whispers to my colleague. He squeezed my hand and said: "I have observed a thing or two myself. You must go now. I have to hurry. As you see, my time is pushing me on. Yes, and it wouldn't do you any harm to speed up your tempo. One never knows what might happen . . ."

We were working, both of us, on the same problem, but were pursuing different approaches. One of us was on the right track, the other on the wrong one. But the problem was a very important one, and even an error might help to lead others on the right path. We were investigating the way to condense sunlight. The substance which he hoped to extract would ensure months and years of bright sunlight and warmth for a remote continent whose inhabitants were strangers to the sun. The sun never lights one side of our planet. There it is always night and winter. The fact that my colleague was grappling with precisely this important problem was additional proof to me that I had before me this extraordinary bandit leader, who was in such great haste to live faster. Would he succeed in completing his plan within a year or even two?

After all, I am a person who views things soberly. I mark time year after year, pondering all the time from which angle to set off, because to begin a research project implies putting everything else aside and burying oneself in work a good ten years or so. If only we could harness the whole laboratory to the task! But the Lord be thanked that at least we have been given the go-ahead to concentrate on this idea. We had many opponents. Almost all the members of the Scientific Council regarded us as visionaries. So that was it: ten years to go. . . . How could he do the work in two years?

But, as it turned out, this man had only a few hours left at his disposal rather than two years. The next morning the hospital rang me up. The previous night my extraordinary bandit had been discovered lying all covered with blood near the entrance to our house (he lived in the same building). There were several deep knife wounds in his back. The whole of our Institute was in an uproar; they began telephoning to the polyclinic for the best-known doctors. But it was too late. By midday the Institute social workers were already telephoning the funeral parlor.

His death, which he had in a manner foretold himself, affected us deeply. For several days we exchanged expressive looks when coming to work. I proved myself a weakling. At first I gave way to panic and even lost weight. I could not bear any extraneous conversations, and for a week I concentrated on my work. But a week later, when I received the new issue of our scientific journal and spotted the name of S., the corresponding member, in the table of contents, I lost my head and became oblivious to everything except that sheet of paper dotted with printed words. Nervously I thumbed through the journal and immediately lighted upon a footnote in small print (the most poisonous attacks always appear in small print). There, in the midst of polite but venomous words, I recognized my name. Thus I fell back into my groove. Paper, paper! who ever invented you! I abandoned my research and, egged on by all of my partisans, wrote an article, putting in it not just one but three footnotes. They were intended to annihilate my enemy completely. The whole department joined in composing these footnotes. If you wished to see us at this work, may I suggest you visit the Tretyakovsky Gallery and examine Repin's famous painting, *The Zaporog Cossacks Sending a Letter of Insult to the Sultan of Turkey*. This painting depicts our entire department—our chief, roaring with laughter and holding his belly, and myself sitting at a table with my glasses on and pen in hand.

Having re-entered my old accustomed groove, I completely forgot about that individual who had shadowed me from behind corners, arcades and gateways. Following the mournful days you all know about, which had ended in a funeral, the tails of the evening dress appeared no more. I was firmly convinced that it had been one of the bandits and executioners of my now absent colleague who had shadowed me then.

But soon after the day on which I received the journal containing my letter of reply to S., my enemy of long-standing, on that very day when I left the editorial offices, my back suddenly warned me that I was the object of observation. I glanced around, but failed to see anyone. Or, rather, when I looked more carefully, I did notice in what was left of a house which workers were demolishing—I did notice in a dark corner a figure of sorts; but it vanished in an instant, disappearing behind a wall.

That very day I was going to celebrate my thirtieth birthday. I intended to invite some friends to mark this festive occasion. But now, as you can see, in broad daylight, an early shadow fell upon me.

I went home and climbed upstairs to my floor. In the communal room, where we all watched the TV set in the evenings, my comrade, the smart dresser and practical joker, was waiting for me.

"Well, shall we go on a binge today?" he asked.

"I don't feel so well," I replied. "We'll have to put it off."

"It's no good sulking on such a remarkable day. Thirty—that's a man's best year!" Hereupon he presented me with a florid necktie.

"Come, let's celebrate, eh? I'll get you loaded!" he went on in a whisper. "I've been lucky enough to get hold of some very rare wine!"

In the meantime, while talking to him, I had noticed a strange woman sitting in the far corner. She must have been expecting me for some time—I felt this in some strange way. Then she got up, took a step towards me; and I became deaf to what my comrade was saying. She was a woman of about thirty, with decidedly sloping shoulders, and very beautiful. Her beauty lay in the very individual and charming irregularities of her face and figure and, particularly, in her frank mournful eyes. This beauty was suddenly evidenced once again in her subdued, gentle voice. I at once remembered that other grain of gold dust which had long ago found its place in the hour-glass. That woman now lay forgotten and non-existent, whereas this one was bearing down upon me.

"I have been requested to give you this on your birthday," she said almost officially, handing over to me the familiar bulbous watch on the steel chain. "And this also . . ."

She pulled out an envelope from her hand-bag and passed it to me.

"It's from him?" I asked.

"From him," the woman replied.

I was about to inquire cautiously whether the man who was no longer here had succeeded in discovering the true love of another, the love which it is impossible either to buy or to steal. But I did not have the time. She read the question on my face and, with a gesture of her hand, stopped me.

"That came to pass, it did," she whispered.—"It is still so. And it will be so! But he was not sure . . . I played a game. You understand how it is? . . . But when they let me into the hospital, I shouted to him for a whole hour: 'Yes, yes, yes!' But he did not hear me."

I lowered my head. My poor friend! I understood it all.

Having placed the watch in my pocket, I accompanied the woman downstairs and then returned.

"That's the woman," our smart dresser said in a low voice. "She used to visit him. She never noticed anyone else. You might try to stop her, but she kept right on as if she would go right through you. Love had blinded her."

And then he added, laughing: "She noticed you, though! Look out!"

I retired to my room and tore open the envelope.

"This letter will be passed on to you if I am killed," wrote my no longer existing colleague. "You are very talented. I am writing you because you know more about me than the others and because you may, perhaps, set a greater value on time. Life yields herself to us only once, and we must drink her without stopping. In great gulps. We must seize what is most precious. And what that is—I have already discussed with you. It is neither gold nor finery. I should like you to live and experience great joy. You must remember the lightless continent where millions of people are now living. May the day on which you receive this letter prove to be your true birthday. . . ."

I did not read the letter to the end. Suddenly, in a flash, a powerful, happy thought interrupted me. "I am happier than he," is what occurred to me. I still have half of my life ahead or even two-thirds. I need not hurry. I have time for everything."

At that moment a dark solid mass blotted out the window. It must be the house-painters swinging their scaffold up to the fourth floor. Turning over a page of the letter in order to continue reading, I went over to the window, nearer to the light. "But what would house-painters be doing in the street in wintertime?"—I suddenly understood. I raised my eyes and shuddered violently. Outside, on an iron ledge beneath the window, sat a huge shaggy-eared owl with gray whiskers and—what was even stranger—it looked distorted as though carved by some primitive man. It was my owl. I was seeing it in the flesh for the first time. With all my strength I waved the letter at it: "Shoo!" This made no impression.

An idea suddenly came to me, and I began to sweat from pain and fear. Phew! With difficulty I recovered my breath and wiped my forehead. The owl sat immobile on its perch, vertically like all owls. I took another deep breath, wiped my forehead, and left the room. I don't recall how I found myself in the street. It was freezing out. Where was I to go? Yes, that's it! I'd visit my old school friend, the neuro-pathologist, a man of experience and creative bent. My case would interest him, and he would attend to me.

In the lilac dusk, I strode quickly along the boulevard, and almost at once became aware of a hopping step in back of me. I glanced around. Someone now stood behind the nearest tree. I could distinctly see a shaggy ear and an unfurled wing. The owl was as tall as I!

The doctor was busy. For a long time I sat near the white door of his office and could hear someone inside pacing up and down with rapid, regular steps. At last, the door swung open and my old school friend appeared in a white gown and a white cap pulled down over his brow. He looked thin and pale from too much night work.

"How goes it?" someone shouted.

"Still the same!" the doctor cried, his face twitching nervously. He did not see me. "Again no result!"

I stood up. The doctor slowly became conscious of his surroundings. He noticed and recognized me, then held out his hand.

"If it's a social call, you're out of luck!"

"It isn't."

"Well then, let me examine you." He took my hand and looked at the tips of my fingers. "How old are you?"

"Thirty . . ."

"I forgot that we are contemporaries. . . . What's worrying you? Is anyone persecuting you?"

"If you only knew who it is! A very odd fellow. You'll laugh when I tell you."

"I know him. Would you like me to show you? Come in here. . . ."

He took me into his office and made me look out of the window.

"My owl!" I whispered. There it was outside.

"Not your owl alone!" the doctor explained. "Mine too. Let me see your hands again. Yes, yes . . ."

He moved to his desk and turned his back on me for a while. Then he turned around.

"Sooner or later, you'll find out about it. You might as well know sooner: you have only a year to live."

The floor suddenly collapsed under me. I would have fallen if my friend had not supported me and put me in a chair.

There are people, I know, who are not afraid of death: those heroes have nothing they must protect. I confess I shook with fear. When I complete my task, then I can die. But not now!

"I don't believe it," I whispered.

"Get out!" he suddenly shouted. "You are stealing my time! I am ill myself. I have only a year and a half left!"

However, he stopped me in the doorway and said almost as though he were reciting it:

"It's an old disease, and it mostly affects talented people. They get it in an acute form. People with soured characters ail quietly and die imperceptibly."

"And you haven't yet discovered any cure?"

"We have discovered a great many things. But we haven't learned to cure our patients yet. Still we have discovered a thing or two."

And then he uttered the following enigmatic words:

"He who sees the owl distinctly is already half-saved."

Then he banged the door behind me.

"Do I see it distinctly? I must make sure," I thought.

Then, in the silence, I suddenly heard a very precise ticking: the watch, the bandit's present to me, was doing its job and meticulously counting off the seconds. Hearing the clear ticking, I pulled out the heavy steel bulb, inserted the ornamented key and wound the spring. I turned the key some twenty times until it finally would not turn any more. That was all! The watch was now wound for a year.

"I must hurry! I must organize my life," I prompted myself. For the first time in my life I was driving myself realistically, that is to say, cold-bloodedly.

The clean frosty evening greeted me with gay lights, the noise of cars, and the distant glimmer of stars.

"I shall meditate and gaze at the stars," I decided. And the starry skies seemed to descend toward me as if to give me a better view of this majestically infinite spectacle.

"Very well then. Flesh will rot. Let it rot. But thought, thought! Must it perish too?" I closed my eyes.

"I shall not perish," my thought declared in the dark. It was calm, unlike one's emotions. "Look about you," its voice said. "The world of civilized men is only a few thousand years old. How long do objects manufactured by men last? Machines, furniture, fabrics—all these fall to pieces within a few decades. How did we manage to collect all the things around us? Very simply. We first collected ideas: the secrets of smelting metal, the formulas for medicine, the mystery of hardening cement. Burn all the books, destroy all craft secrets, let a few dozen years pass for them to be quite forgotten, and still mankind will start again upon its ancient road from the stone axe. And your son— not your grandson—having dug up a cogwheel which you had made in your youth, will begin worshipping it as a divinely created miracle."

From an invisible loud-speaker above the city came the resonant and limpid strains of a waltz. I did not know the composer. And I even did not seem to hear the music: it was not a full orchestra, just brass; not the brass, but the strings; not the strings, but the sound of my feelings. And when the woodwinds raised their song, when the wood began to sing, it was clear to me that these were firmly locked desires singing gently inside their narrow box—desires that were strictly confined within the boundaries of my short life.

"You wish to live," my anonymous composer told me. "Look at the effect upon you of a few little notes, which I left behind me a hundred years ago after my short and very onerous sojourn among men. Listen; the man who is allotted little time, loves life more passionately and fiercely. It is better not to have but to desire than to have and not desire! I loved life passionately and I am passing on this love to you."

"But listen now," he continued, lowering his voice. "In my brief life I experienced no great happiness. And you? Has a grateful man ever shaken your hand—shaken it so hard that your heart was shaken out of its place? Have you ever seen at close range a pair of eyes filled with tears of love?"

These thoughts stunned me. I had never experienced anything like that. I had loved, but I had never yet seen such eyes. I knew no great friendship, had not earned the gratitude of men. . . . Lowering my head, I no longer heard the music, and the city lights grew dim around me. But one thing I did hear—the lively ticking. It was the watch, the bandit's present, doing its work, counting off the time, my seconds: "You have your whole life before you! A whole year! You have just been born! You are younger now than you were! Run fast towards your work! Everything is there—your friendship and your love!"

I broke into a run, leapt into a taxi—fast, fast to the laboratory! —and the taxi driver, shifting into high gear, looked around with amazement at his extraordinary fare.

Leaving the taxi waiting at the entrance, I dashed in and mounted the stairs. In the corridor, beside the hot stove, the old stovewoman, her head drooping, had fallen asleep. I shook her awake.

"Quickly, hand me all my papers! Those I gave you this morning! There was a basketful this morning . . ."

"You should have thought of them earlier!"

At this I groaned and reached for the burning ash of the stove.

"I burned them all, I did." The old woman explained. "They burned well—only your papers burn so well. It made me feel warm, as you see. I even fell asleep."

"Tick-tock, tick-tock," said the bandit's watch in my pocket. Clenching my teeth, I opened my office and began to carry out boxes of apparatus into the street towards the waiting taxi. I had decided to open a branch of the laboratory at home and to work nights. I could earn the highest gratitude of men, but I had not yet even made a start!

When I appeared, holding a box in each hand, on the threshold of our bachelor quarters, a few men had already gathered in the communal room near the TV set, idlers all of them.

"So, it's been decided—we are postponing the celebration!" the practical joker said to me.

He was fiddling with the television knobs. Football players' legs began to flash on the screen. The spectators froze. Their eyes, dilating unnaturally, became fixed. I heard the ticking of my watch and understood: if our TV set were to continue to work uninterruptedly for the next two thousand years, these five men would go on sitting in this way without a break—and they would be preserved for their descendants like the lotus seeds.

I moved several people, together with their chairs, out of my way, and I carried all the boxes to my room. I then dismissed the taxi.

My owl was still perched in the same place outside the window. I was calm now. The owl was well lit up by a bright lamp in the room. Did I see the owl distinctly? I went to the window. For a while we stared at each other. Then the owl walked back and forth along the iron sheet—exactly as owls walk on a branch in the zoo. It bent over, raised its yellow, triple claw, which looked as if it had been covered with wax drippings, and, like a hen, it quickly, very quickly, scratched its beak with a hind claw. Then it quieted down, perched itself vertically, and fixed me with two metallic circles—its eyes. I could see my owl very distinctly!

Then I pulled myself together again and began quickly to open the boxes and to arrange the apparatus. Within five minutes my room began to glitter with glass and chrome. It had become a laboratory.

"Will I have time?" I thought. "I need at least ten years."

I tried to remember some fragments of the ideas which had been burned at various times in the laboratory stoves. I attempted to jot them down again, but nothing came of it.

"This would have reduced my work by half!" I even banged the table with my fist.

At this moment I noticed on the floor the bandit's note, which I had dropped earlier in the day. I had not had time to read some of the lines, and it was these lines that now stared at me from the floor.

"I can be of use to you. Did you grasp what was told you about a certain bandit? Then ask the woman standing before you, and she will give you the notebook in which I secretly copied all your ideas—those which you had been throwing into the stove for the last two years. I intended to make use of them myself, for you did not need them."

"Where shall I find her now?" I shouted, failing to finish reading the note again. Then I suddenly noticed the words: "Her telephone . . ."

In a few seconds I was standing, like someone in a fairy tale, amidst a group of people who looked as though they had been drugged by TV, breathing regularly, although their eyes were wide open. Placing the telephone on the shoulder of one of them, I dialed a number. After a few rings, I heard the sound of her voice.

From that moment another chapter opened in my new, brief life. It began with a misunderstanding, for which only I was responsible.

"You should pick up the receiver at once!" These words burst from me before I had time to realize my rudeness. "Where is the notebook? Why didn't you give it to me?"

"You didn't ask for it," the voice replied. "You didn't even read the letter. And the note said: if you. . . ."

"It's obvious you set no value on time," I burst out again. "Forgive me. . . ."

The receiver was suddenly silent.

"Why don't you speak?" I roared again. "The notebook, the notebook!"

"I am coming," a soft, caressing voice replied.

When I heard her footsteps, I suddenly realized that I was waiting not only for the notebook. From the very instant I first saw that woman, I felt gently and imperceptibly drawn towards her, just as a floating twig is drawn from afar towards a waterfall. Was this not a second grain of gold dust that had come near the throat of the hour-glass only to fly over it in an instant? "Well, go on and fly," I thought. "These things do not exist for me any more. . . . For, my beauties, don't you love to be pursued long and stubbornly, and how right you are. And you above all, for you have not yet forgotten him for whom you shouted: 'Yes, yes, yes!' And you will hardly forget him, for how could my not-so-distinguished person exclude from your memory that exotic, improbable man with the borrowed face? I am dead to love. I am non-existent."

At this point she opened the door and entered—a small, gentle beauty with sloping shoulders. "I love you!" everything alive in me shouted. I realized that, in my new life, my childhood was over and early youth had begun. But then I heard a chilling peck at the window. I did not even glance at it: everything was immediately clear.

Barely greeting the woman, I snatched the notebook from her hands, turned my back on my guest, opened the notebook and saw the designs, plans, notes and calculations—they were identical with those which, over a period of several years, I had freely strewn about and burned. I thumbed through the notebook. Aha! I now needed eight, not ten years! I would work at the Institute and at home, and that would give me two more years. I would arrange things so that experiments would be conducted in several directions at the same time. Day and night!

"What's the hurry?" the woman asked, noticing my haste to connect the wires and plug in the apparatus.

"I have very little time left . . ." I replied, then stopped myself. "Life is short, and there is a lot of work. I am in a hurry."

I plugged in every piece of apparatus, and gay little flames kindled in the flasks and the retorts, transparent bubbling rivulets ran along the glass tubes, and rare earth samples began to melt in the crucibles.

My owl slumbered outside the window, its head under its wing. To remove my last doubt, I decided to verify something.

"What is that outside the window?" I suddenly asked the woman, pointing to the owl.

At these words the huge bird raised its head and blinked rapidly, very rapidly, the yellow lenses of its eyes. The woman went up to the window, pressed her face against the glass and shielded her eyes with both hands from the light.

"There's no one there," she said, smiling. Suddenly she stopped talking. She began to scrutinize me closely, and bit her lip as though astonished by some new discovery. "There is no one there," she repeated. "But did you see anyone? Are you being watched?"

"No is no," I avoided answering her directly.

Then, all of a sudden she—she!—asked a question. It was her turn now to surprise me and drive me into a corner.

"Why did you change your room?" she inquired.

I was dumfounded. I tensed up, but made no reply. I was already living under the authority of a new discipline. I began to turn the handle of my calculating machine; I had to make certain calculations. The woman watched me without taking her eyes off me.

After about an hour she could not contain herself any longer: she laughed quietly.

"You might as well tell me where you are rushing."

"Where? A certain man—you know whom I mean—has probably told you already where *he* was rushing . . ."

"He told me . . ."

"Well, I am rushing there too. I have lived a whole lifetime and accomplished nothing. But I can contribute something to mankind. I shall have no rest until some grateful man shakes my hand so hard that my heart will be moved from its place. I shall work for him. He will come—and that will be a happy day for me."

These words must have pleased her. She was silent for a while, then said:

"Why do you waste time? That is so unlike you. After all, you own a new, a perfect calculating machine."

That was news! Some new gadget! Again I did not answer her. Then she took me by the hand and led to the door.

"What now?" I asked, stopping.

"Don't waste time," she said, mimicking me. "Don't be afraid! I can gain time for you."

She dragged me off to another apartment—to the one where my extraordinary bandit friend had lived a month ago. She pulled out a key, unlocked the door of his room and turned away, suppressing a smile. But I beamed: the room was full of the newest and most expensive apparatus. It was exactly what I had needed. I began to examine and play with the apparatus, completely forgetting about my companion.

"Aren't you ashamed!" I suddenly heard her say. "You're pretending never to have seen these things!" She was off again.

"What do you mean?" I asked.

"You should at least have visited your colleague," she replied evasively. "Perhaps you never saw this either?"

An unfamiliar, large, white flower with a pungent smell was growing in the aquarium, on the window sill. The woman made me approach it. She seemed to be testing me. And then I suddenly remembered.

"It's a lotus. It was grown from the seed which lay in the sepulchre for two thousand. . . ."

"That's it," she cried triumphantly. "I give you A-plus. And have you seen this?"

She handed me a calculating machine of the most modern type —such as I never even dreamt of possessing. This device could replace a whole staff of mathematicians armed with simple calculators.

"May I take this thing?" I could not resist asking.

"You are wasting time!" she exclaimed, raising her voice, mimicking either the bandit or myself. "Yes! Yes! Yes! All this is yours. You can take all the apparatus! Even the lotus!"

It seemed she was annoyed by something.

"Well, yes, of course," she suddenly said musingly. "He altered his face, his voice, he had to change rooms too. So that no one should know or say anything. . . . And even friends. . . ."

I should have pondered these words! But as I have said, I was then under the authority of a new discipline, which had turned everything I thought upside down. I dismissed her chatter with a wave of my hand.

In a single night I had made a huge stride in my work. I proved the validity of my abstract premises. At this rate, I would attain my first concrete results in about eight months, and then I should be able to involve the whole Institute in my cause. All the skeptics would have to give in.

Oblivious of everything around me, I arrived next morning at our laboratory. In the doorway I heard a commotion. It seems that my steadfast opponent S. had already written a reply to my article!

"What an operator!" our chief exclaimed ironically, and each of his words was greeted with a wave of wild laughter from his colleagues.

They were all grouped around my desk, the chief roaring with laughter, holding his belly. This perfect picture lacked only the author with the pen behind his ear, that is to say, myself.

"Well, dear competitor, it's up to you now," the chief said, placing the newspaper clipping on my desk.

But I astonished them. I did not even begin to read the article of that S., who now struck me as a very naïve and in no way dangerous eccentric. He no longer inflamed me: another fire had been ignited. I waved him away like a mosquito. I must add, getting ahead of my story, that this S. continued for a long time afterwards to print articles, especially for my benefit. In one footnote, he wrote that I was shamefully silent; in others, that I was wearing the blinders of reserve, that I was hiding in the bushes, that, like an ostrich, I had buried my head in the sand. He crowed from afar and flapped his wings like a cock, trying to provoke me to continue the battle.

Seeing me push the clipping aside, my colleagues exchanged glances.

"Can this be you?" asked the amazed practical joker. "Just look at him! He hasn't even shaved! Friends! He has tossed his overcoat on the chair! Well, well . . . Two buttons are missing from the coat! Doesn't he look like a changeling? There's something about him that reminds me of that . . . the one who used to sit here beside him. . . ."

And he glanced expressively at the bandit's vacated desk.

True enough, my character had changed drastically. I had become a different man. I had all at once forgotten the mannerisms of the established scientist; I stopped speaking in a singsong voice; I stopped playing around with trifling problems. I was floating all the time in a kind of frenzied half-dream. Greed for life had awakened within me and, strangely enough, what a change I felt in my conception of pleasure!

What did I enjoy now? I kept gazing at her all the time. She fitted splendidly into my room, having brought with her a folding bed, and she worked day and night with the apparatus. I don't even know when she slept. And I found delight in gazing from afar at her as she sat at the table; I admired the distinctive curves of her head and neck—those of a young mother bending over her child.

And I continued to dream, watching the lines of her head, her neck and her sloping shoulder, that lightly-curved, affectionate arch, by which alone I could have always recognized her; I wanted her to turn around and look at me. She always sensed my unspoken command and, when she turned, she would press her chin against her shoulder. But some perpetual question always disturbed her and, after looking intently at me, she would resume her work.

The question tormented her. She resolved to test me again. We had established a certain rule: if there was a break in the work, we made a point going somewhere for an hour or two—to an exhibition, the opera or a concert. But one evening, having set the automatic instruments and plugged in the heaters, she put her arm in mine.

"We have some free time. A whole hour. Will you make me a present of it?"

I thought it over.

"Well, all right. I'll make you a present of it."

We went out into the street. She dragged me off somewhere, and I found myself walking with her through some dark alley. Then suddenly she asked me:

"Don't you really remember this walk?"

I was tired of all this and did not hide my irritation:

"I'm glad you are becoming less formal. It should have happened long ago. But I beg you to stop your strange game; you've been playing it for two months already, and I don't understand anything. This game is a waste of time."

"Where are you always hurrying?"

At that moment I saw in the shadows behind the street lamp the dark shape of my owl, and its glittering, rapidly blinking eyes. I stopped. I was about to show my companion those two eyes, but I remembered she would not see them anyhow.

"Where am I hurrying to?" I decided to tell her everything point blank. "All right then: I have less than a year to live."

My words overwhelmed her. I seemed to have said the one

thing that was needed to produce the explosion. She stopped me, stepped in front of me and, cupping her hands, held them under my chin. I saw at close range her eyes filled with tears.

"If you are convinced that you have less than a year, then why are we deceiving each other here?" she whispered.

I was about to say something but she put her fingers on my lips.

"You are *he*, of course you are!"

I guessed the truth.

"You think that I am—*he* . . . your former man?"

"Stop tormenting me . . . Do you remember how you used to hide from me the first time? Why are you punishing me?"

"But I am another person!" I yelled. "Look—I have different hair, a different face. Nothing has been changed in me. I have no scars. All this is mine!"

"You had no scars either the first time. But I guessed right. I guessed at once! Now tell me why, when I called on you with the letter and the watch, you suddenly changed the expression on your face and asked: 'Was there love?' You wanted very much to find out. I saw through your naïve cunning." She laughed. "If you only knew how glad those words made me!"

"I shall soon part from you forever," I said.

"We shall never part. I shall find you even if you run away from me again and change not only your face, but everything about you."

"I have less than a year to live. That is definite."

"I don't believe it. You have been saying that for so many years!"

"But *he* said that, and he was murdered."

"They didn't kill him! You're smart. You've thought of everything! And you ordered me to hand over everything to your double—to yourself. You're a cunning one! They will never get you. . . ."

"Ah, the devil! What nonsense this is. . . ."

He must have always cut her short like this too. She laughed.

"I won't speak of it again. Even then you didn't like it. Today you are even better than you were. You are gentler now, you smile so wonderfully! And you speak so beautifully about the man who will come . . . I have wasted so much time! Why did I allow myself to play games with you as if I were only seventeen! If you want me to, I shall say that word you wanted to hear. Yes! Yes! Do you hear? Cry out that you hear me!"

"I hear," I whispered. I could no longer fight against the current. The twig was racing towards the waterfall. "Which *me* do you love best," I asked, "the one who was murdered or the one beside you here?"

"The one here!"

I was loved. I saw the eyes. I had only to turn my head slightly to the right to meet two stars glistening with tears. Now I occupied the place of the departed bandit. The days of my youth had now been transformed into an early maturity.

The doctor's diagnosis proved correct: five or six months after consulting him I began to feel ill. In the middle of a bright summer I took to bed.

Apologetically I informed my gentle, distraught, love:

"Do you know, my dear, I find it hard to walk. You'll have to take over today while I shall stay in bed. Turn on the radio."

She turned it on. At once we could hear a loud howling, and through the roar of magnetic storms the fading voice of our dark continent. They were working out there, mining coal or growing cabbage under artificial light!

"We must act more energetically," I said. "We must hurry."

The bubbling rivulets ran ever faster through the glass tubes and the flames flared brighter.

In rainy September, we completed our work on one of the installations. I was in bed, feeling so weak I could hardly raise my head.

"Open the first copper container," I said.

She opened it.

"An error," I heard her say gently. "We have here only a small lump of reddish coal."

"No, it isn't an error," I answered calmly. "It's merely a variation. Everything has been checked in the other installations. But we can exhibit this lump of coal. . . . Call the fellows. Call the chief. . . ."

They entered, walking on tiptoe as people do when visiting the sick. I had never let them in before; and now on entering my room, which had become transformed into a laboratory, they halted near the door and began to look around them. They did not know what to think of me. Everything amazed them: the walls scribbled over with formulas and the furniture scratched with a nail—I wrote on it too—and the glitter of the apparatus, from which light puffs of warmth reached them.

Then they caught sight of me. My appearance must have surprised them, and they moved with even greater care. Only the practical joker, who did not take his eyes off my companion, whispered something to the chief.

"Give them the report," I said.

And she, like a true scientist, gave them, within ten minutes, a report on our work and showed them the small lump of coal which refused to cool.

This lump of coal astonished everyone, the chief in particular. He was the first to advance solemnly to shake my hand. Then all my colleagues began to talk and rushed pell-mell towards me, seized my weak, thin hands and began to shake them. And I felt as if my heart might burst at any moment.

"From today on, we are all joining in the work," the chief announced. "The whole laboratory!"

From that day on, two of our colleagues were on duty in my room day and night and, in addition, the laboratory kept us informed every day by telephone. The project went ahead rapidly.

In the icy month of December, my companion opened a second copper container, in the presence of my chief.

"Again an error," she told the chief softly. "This is even worse —this lump of coal is quite black."

But I heard her.

"This error has been accounted for," I said, barely moving my lips. "Go on with the work. Faster."

I had an acute sense of hearing. I heard the chief whisper, covering his mouth with his hand:

"A third error will be the death of him. . . ." Then he added loudly: "H'm . . . I suppose it would be better to transport the third installation to our laboratory. There we shall conduct the experiment more rapidly and accurately."

"I have confidence in you," I replied.

Thus my wife and I were left alone in our quiet, empty room, the two of us—and the owl, too, which had very cunningly managed one day to squeeze into our room through the open vent and which was at present either slumbering on the window sill or wandering under the table, pecking at the floor with its beak. My wife—she had really earned that title—sat beside me as we softly reminisced about our brief youth.

On the third or fourth day I felt worse.

"Please open the window," I asked.

"My dear, there's frost outside. Do I have to?"

"Open it, open it," I whispered.

My wife approached the window.

"What's this? Spring in December! Can you hear? It's thawing in the street, and there's a fly just awakened beating against the window pane!"

"Open it!"

At first she opened the vent, then flung open the whole window, and into the room, together with the warm spring breeze, there burst an extraordinarily pleasant and remote music. It flowed over the city, now fading, now gathering into a mighty wave. I listened to it without realizing it was the telephone wires playing and spreading all over the world the tidings of man's victory over cold and darkness. From time to time this music was accompanied by a solemn buzzing sound that faded in the distance—those were the planes flying over the town with a precious load. They were carrying the very first springtime to the dark continent. But unaware of this, I felt very low; I had grown extremely weak; and I waited for my colleagues to bring me some good news. Moreover, the owl alarmed me: it was walking near my bed in a state of strange excitement, shaking its feathers and flapping its wings. There is nothing harder than to part with life if one has not yet brought to a conclusion some project essential for mankind and depending upon our own efforts.

Then drowsiness overcame me. Somewhere the staircase hummed, doors banged, hurried steps shuffled. But I did not hear this. I heard only the doctor's voice, that of my old school friend:

"He's still alive!"

He sat down by my head and with trembling hands began to unscrew a copper cartridge.

"Faster, faster, tell me!" I wanted to cry out.

And I finally did, because my sickness had left me.

A dazzling drop quivered in the doctor's hands, drowning the entire room in sunlight. I knew about it long ago; I had dreamt of it. Shutting my eyes, I had often seen it even when I had just begun to install the apparatus. But now I could not look at this too resplendent, little sun. I got up from bed, staggering on my feeble legs. My companion ran to support me, but I stopped her with a gesture of my hands and walked the length of the room by myself. I even stamped my feet! My wife, radiant and unbelieving, leaned against the wall.

"Thank you, doctor," she whispered.

"What for? He triumphed over his *own* death. He, himself, discovered the medicine! It is *his* own light!"

The staircase hummed again, doors banged and a whole crowd of people burst into the room. Here were my colleagues and a multitude of others whom I did not know. I was surrounded; someone shook my hand. My chief pushed his way towards me.

"You have managed, after all, to put time in its place," he said by way of congratulation. "In antiquity they would have drawn an owl beside your name! You once suggested the hypothesis that the hieroglyphic might be . . . Do you remember . . . ?"

"But do you realize it has been confirmed," I replied. And I reflected that I had really put time in its place. I had lived a whole lifetime in a year. And how many years still lay ahead—a whole ocean of time!

Whom should I thank for this? I glanced at the window sill where my owl always used to sit. But it was not there. There was only an aquarium and, in it, a lotus blossom. But outside the window, very far away in the pale blue-green sky some large bird was flying towards the horizon, ponderously flapping its wings.

The ocean of time splashed at my feet. I stood on the shore, ready to begin my life anew, and the mysterious waves of the future fell at my feet, one after another, and then retreated beckoning to me. Tomorrow I shall be swimming far beyond the horizon. I felt somewhat frightened: for a year I had been accustomed to the constant presence of the owl. Could I manage to live without its injunctions? Would not this mighty ocean, which was expecting me, become transformed into a rivulet I could step over without even noticing?

Here I remembered the watch, the bandit's present. At once I felt chill with fright: I could not hear the watch.

I grasped the chain . . . Ah, yes! The watch had stopped. A year, a whole year, had passed. I must wind the watch again!

I pulled out the watch, inserted the ornamented key and turned it twenty times. Then I felt the resistance—the watch was going. It had started for the New Year.

VLADIMIR TENDRYAKOV

Two Characters

from *Three, Seven, Ace: A Novella*

HUNDREDS, perhaps even thousands (who could count them!) of tributaries, streams, and stubborn rivulets filtering through the compost of fallen leaves and heaped pine-needles, and forcing a path for themselves through the tree roots, carried water from the rusty old swamps into this large river. For this reason, the river in days of rain and sleet had a very particular tint—not just of lead, but of old and long exposed lead.

The river always ran high. Sandy shoals near the riverbanks were rare. Describing capricious loops, the river flowed through a wild, uninhabited region towards the Arctic ocean. And day and night down the river itself flowed a mute procession. Day and night logs floated down the river.

Their journey was not easy. The shoals (they are to be encountered on any river, even a high one), the quiet shallows, the broken edges of the banks—all these were traps for the floating wood. Unhurriedly, the current moved slowly onward. Many of the river pilgrims could resist no more. Swollen with water, huge logs would sink at one end, leaving only top jutting out of the water. But obstinately the log would continue to push on and crawl forward, dragging its heavy nether extremity along the bottom of the river until, finally weighted down, it would settle to the bottom. There, in summer, limp eels would hide beneath it, and it would gradually become covered with sand and silt. But other pilgrim-logs would float on further and further until they got caught in the jaws of the sorting base. There, the men rolled them out of the water, and sorted them: this lot, earmarked for building, would go to the saw-mills; that lot, to the paper-mills; this one would do for pit-props in the mines; and that, which had resonance, would go to making musical instruments. Entered in books and ranged in stacks—a new lease on life awaited those who had managed to reach their destination, while the deceased were buried in oblivion.

Thus flowed this Northern river—a great artery for floating logs. In places, it changed its lazily austere character for a raging temperament; and it seethed among the boulders, splashing and carrying flocks of yellow foam. Here were the rapids. There were several of them along the course of the river. The biggest of all were the Ostroshni rapids.

To be precise, there were two rapids here: the first was known as the Big Head; a little lower down, some two hundred yards or more was the Little Head. There was constant, never-ceasing agitation above the huge, submerged boulders, and an endless roaring in the moist air.

Right opposite the Big Head a very small settlement was spread out—five houses in all, including a small store, which traded bread, sugar and canned goods.

The forest pressing the houses up against the riverbank, the gray sky, and the river seething over the rapids. . . . This river was the only means of communication, and once a week along it a boat delivered provisions.

The five houses constituted Dubinin's log-rolling station. Its population consisted of thirty-two persons: twenty-five workmen-loggers, a cleaning woman, the storekeeper Klasha, the truck-driver Tikhon, three girls serving the dining room, and Master Dubinin himself—the boss of the station.

A scatter of logs floated down the river, jostling each other crowding closely in the creeks, and getting stuck in the shoals.

Each morning the loggers with gaffs and hatchets would enter their boats and row off to their checking-points. Logs caught in the bushes would be rolled back into the water, the creeks would be cleared, and the shoals cleaned out. . . . The population of that small station had no other purpose but to see to it that the endless procession of logs down the river should never be interrupted.

Master Dubinin lived in his office. His bunk stood beside a wobbly table on which he wrote out his orders. A telephone hung on the wall.

Dubinin was neither tall, nor broad-shouldered; his gait was slow and rolling. The loggers, all of them hefty fellows who spent whole days rolling logs, spoke unanimously and respectfully of his strength. "He can bend a couple of elms together for you," they used to say.

They finally pulled the drowning stranger out of the rapids. Then they laid him on a bunk in the dormitory.

His head had fallen back on the pillow, his unshaven chin jutted up, a vein quivered under the bristles near his Adam's apple, his eyes were closed, his thin arms were stretched out alongside his body, his fingers were listlessly bent—his hands limp. It was hot in the dormitory, and a blanket had been thrown only over his legs, so that his flat, ribbed chest showed bare, and on it was tattooed: "Years pass, but no happiness."

The loggers crowded round, interchanging remarks in low voices:

"He's been a jail-bird, one can see that. See how he's prettified himself: 'No happiness . . .'"

"He's happy enough here. If Leshka hadn't turned up on the river bank, he'd be feeding fish."

"He's got a grip on him to have come out of these rapids."

"Been in more than one fix, that's clear."

Then Yegor Petukhov, who had a trunkful of rubles under his bunk, said in a worried way:

"An unreliable type. He might get at our goods . . . clean us out."

"He's not worrying about your trunk just now. You can sleep easy tonight."

Dubinin, his hands thrust deeply into his pockets, his chin pressed against his chest, was scrutinizing the unexpected guest from under his cap, pulled down low over his brow.

He saw the scraggy neck and the Adam's apple, the wearily outstretched arms, the sodden pair of rough shoes thrown under the bunk, and the tattoo! Dubinin chewed his extinguished rolled cigarette, and continued to stare; and the more he stared, the stronger was the pity he felt for this stranger.

If you met a fellow like that on the road, you'd walk straight past him without another glance. Did he have any relatives? Was there anyone in the whole world who would show any sincere, heartfelt compassion for him? If it hadn't been for that floating log, he'd have disappeared, leaving no name, no ripple even of vague pity for himself, nothing at all. Here he was, having just eluded death, on a strange bunk, among strangers who stared at him with unceremonious pity. . . .

Dubinin with difficulty tore his gaze away from the tattoo on the man's gaunt chest.

"I say, lads, which of you undressed him?" he asked. "Any documents on him?"

"There were. All soaked. We put them on the stove to dry. Fifty rubles he had on him too—he's not rich."

"Hand them over!"

Dubinin carefully took the documents and, shouldering the workers, went out.

Dubinin had been a logger himself, but now he was a master-workman. Alexander Dubinin had lived a modest life. It hadn't been rich in events, this life, nor clouded over with tragedies, and he had not even been at the front. Nor had he learned to read books, and they kindled no noble urges in him; he had discovered no lofty ideals for himself and was not aware (or, if he was, then only vaguely, by hearsay) that there existed in the world men of great soul who had faced the stake for the happiness of others, had endured torture, and had obliged posterity to hear their voices through prison walls.

He had simply been a logger, and then a master-workman—that was all.

Alexander Dubinin lived a life of everyday chores: he had to attend to everyone getting his fair share of work, a just share of the wages, a good helping of food in the dining room, a clean dormitory, and a change of sheets every week.

Five houses, which the forest pressed close to the river as it roared over the rapids—this was but a small sector of the boundless world. Here men labored, and their labor was heavy. But this tiny diminutive settlement opposite the Big Head Rapids was nevertheless a happy enough sector in its own way. The rather morose, taciturn man, who walked about the settlement with a slightly rolling gait, was the lawgiver of this sector.

Back in his office, Dubinin carefully spread out on the table the rescued man's sodden documents. Some of them had turned into a handful of paper pulp. The passport was better preserved. The passport was there—that meant its owner had legal status.

With the point of his Finnish knife, Dubinin parted the stuck pages of the passport and read: "Bushuyev, Nikolai Petrovich, born in 1919." Something had been stamped at the end of the passport, but the ink had run, and one could only surmise that the owner of the passport had been sentenced and had served his prison term.

The man on the strange bunk, alone among strangers, his whole appearance expressive of weary inertia, had given death the slip. . . . This man must have had behind him a tangled, uncomfortable life. Somewhere in his youth he must have apparently desired to grasp at happiness—a tawdry happiness such as could be bought for the price of a ten ruble note. For that ten rubles he had thrust his hand into somebody's pocket, had been caught, and dragged off where need be. Assuming that he had been let off the first time, he had still found no happiness. He had still to seek it. He had sought it. . . . The years passed, and still no happiness. . . .

In the morning, after the workers had scattered, Dubinin looked into the dormitory. The bunk, on which the uninvited guest had slept, was already tidy.

"He's got guts. Off already. Gone tramping again? But I've still got his passport, he can't get far without it. . . ." Dubinin set off to his office without haste.

The house containing the office was the only two-storied building in the district. The ground floor contained the office and a room where lodged Tihon Mezayev, the truck driver, and his wife Natya, who cleaned the dormitory.

On the floor above was a recreation room with radio, a shelf of books, and a table covered with a spread of faded fustian. Here in the evenings the loggers gathered to listen to the radio and to play dominoes.

As he passed the staircase leading to the recreation room, Dubinin heard a male voice quietly singing to a guitar:

Why do some men lead a fantastic life,
A life full of intoxicating dreams,
While life to others is a horrid strife,
Forever filled with grief, despair and tears . . .

Dubinin went up. In a clean shirt, borrowed from a broad-shouldered logger, his scrawny neck projecting miserably from a much too-wide collar, there sat the stranger with a guitar propped on his knees—a guitar which hung for many years unused above the radio.

Why are some men successful
In avoiding the blows of fate . . .

On catching sight of Dubinin, the man leapt to his feet.

"Best of health to you, little chief," he greeted Dubinin with forced glibness.

The man had a narrow face, shifty eyes and, when he smiled, his small, closely set teeth looked jagged.

Dubinin dropped into a chair.

"Sit down, what's your name . . . Nikolai Bushuyev. Let's have a chat."

"That's right—Nikolai Petrovich Bushuyev in person. I'd wanted to hit it lower down the river at Tormenga, but blew in here instead. My excuses for not warning you to meet me . . ."

"Stop fooling. Where are you from?"

"I'd been working at the lumber camp."

"And ran away?"

"The boss there was no good. Didn't think me human, you see. 'You,' he'd say, 'after your stretch, you're a criminal element, a swindler, just dregs.' We didn't hit it off in character, as you might say."

"Was it just a matter of character?"

"And what if I'd had to fall back on my old ways because of that snake. Keep clear of sin, I said! I'd earned two hundred rubles and I didn't even take them."

"What were you in for?"

"For a job, as they say. And I don't deny it. If you done a job, you done it."

"A drunken business?"

"God forfend!"

"Stealing?"

"We won't particularize, little chief. But I'll say one thing: I'm done with it all."

"Is that so?"

"Believe it or not, but I'm not twenty any longer. I don't feel much like going on playing the cossack-robber."

"And where were you born? Why did you take up work at the lumber camp and not go home?"

"My home's under my hat. My home's where I put it on."

"And you feel no tug to visit your native parts?"

Nikolai Bushuyev's glassily flittering eyes were lost beneath his eyelashes, and for a second his pale, unshaven face became immobile, hermetic and dull. A chance question had arrested his flow of forced glibness.

"What's the point?" he asked after a pause. "I know what it's like to go back home with empty pockets."

"But I've heard they work in jail too and come out with money."

"There was a little rustling in my pocket, but I lost the sound of it playing cards in a train with a fellow. . . ."

Dubinin sat solidly in the chair, his jacket open, his cap pulled down over his eyes, scrutinizing Bushuyev with his habitual, rather morose calm.

"And where now?" he asked.

"Where? To Tormenga. I'll find work there at the sorting base."

"Do you have a specialty?"

"I'm an all-rounder. I've stubbed up tree-stumps, dug holes under foundations, felled trees. . . ."

"That means no specialty!" Dubinin shifted in the chair and

turned away. "Now listen," he said to one side, "you can stay with us. You'll work here like everyone else. Every logger here willy-nilly knocks off a couple of thousand a month. You have no family. Food and clothes will come to about five-hundred of the whole. In a year you'd save fifteen to eighteen thousand. Then— you could either stay on or beat it. I'm saying this having pity on you, the fool. If you don't like it, we shan't detain you or implore you to stay."

"And why shouldn't I like it? All right, let it be with you then. It's all the same to me where I mark time."

"Mark time? No friend, you'll have to work. You don't get paid money for marking time. Don't hope to ride on somebody else's back. This is rather a remote place, and the militia are a good way off. We keep order here ourselves. You've seen our lads. They can get the feel of anybody's bones. And you can't run away either—there are forests and swamps all round. Even the local inhabitants don't stray far. There are only three ways out of here: to the lumber camp where, it seems, they wouldn't welcome you very fondly; to the villages, where you'd be noticed at once; and then down the river to the log-rolling stations. I'd only have to telephone, and they'd hold you as long as was necessary. Mark this on your nose—you'd better not try anything here. I'm taking you on not so much because I trust you, but because I have no fears—you just can't spread yourself here with us. That's how it is, friend."

MAXIM GORKY (*1868-1936*)

Maxim Gorky was born in Nizhny Novgorod (now Gorky). His real name was Alexey M. Peshkov and he usually signed his correspondence thus. After his difficult childhood years, he got to know provincial Russia at first hand by tramping over it. But as a writer he became famous under his pseudonym, first, as the author of the short stories which were collected and published under the title of *Sketches and Stories* (1898) and, secondly, of the play *Lower Depths* (1902). The latter was an immediate international success, as were also his stories. In these works Gorky revealed a new aspect of Russia, and thus introduced a new subject matter into literature. Many of the characters in these early works were taken from low life—they were tramps, hoboes or fallen men and women, in fact the inhabitants of Skid Row. In depicting them, Gorky combined realism with touches of romanticism and, while depicting the beast in man, he also sought to discover ennobling human traits in their characters.

A man of tremendous energy and application, Gorky also led a rich and active life, and always spent a good portion of his royalties in helping people, launching newspapers, journals, reviews and publishing houses, as well as on helping financially the cause of the anti-Tsarist Revolution. He was involved in the 1905 Revolution, after which he left Russia, stayed for a year in the USA (1906), and then lived for seven years in Italy. He played an active part in the 1917 Revolution, but became critical of the Bolshevik seizure of power and their drastic methods. After helping many intellectuals and writers to survive the rigors of the period, and after encouraging and materially assisting many new writers, he left Russia in 1921 and settled first, in Germany and, then, in Sorrento, Italy, where he lived until 1933. As from 1928, however, he periodically revisited the Soviet Union and, having come to an agreement with Stalin, became the "Father" of Soviet Literature. It was during this period that his novel, *Mother* (1907), which he did *not* consider to be his best work at all, became widely disseminated as a "Soviet classic." As an author, Gorky hardly touched the Soviet period except in polemical and educational articles. His last major work, *The Klim Samgin* cycle of novels treats of Russia from 1880 but stops in 1917. In between this and his early work, he had written a mass of varied and often remarkable stories, novels and plays, as well as a number of outstanding autobiographical works (*Childhood, Among People, My Universities*), and portrait sketches of Leo Tolstoy and Lenin. Gorky's *Collected Works* were published in the 1950's in thirty volumes. In many ways, Gorky's life and work were the main bridge between pre-Revolutionary and Soviet literature.

The Nightingale is an early story of Gorky's, which had never found its way into any of his books. It was re-discovered and printed in the Soviet Union in 1957, and here it is rendered for the first time in English.

ANDREY BIELY (*1880-1934*)

ANDREY BIELY is one of the most original and interesting writers and novelists of the twentieth century. His work—over forty volumes of it—has been obscured from the attention of Russian, English-speaking and other readers, by a campaign of vilification not only on the part of Stalinist critics, but also by the usual type of "anti-modernist" critic who fails to understand him and finds him "too complex." His work is, of course, the antithesis of the so-called Socialist Realism, which has been the official Soviet doctrine of criticism since 1932; nor does his work appeal in general to those who dislike either Proust or Joyce. Fortunately, Biely's *Petersburg* has recently been published both in New York and London. Two of his other works are due to be published here in the near future.

Andrey Biely is the pseudonym for Boris N. Bugayev, who was born in Moscow as the son of Professor Bugayev, a noted

Mathematician and Dean of the Faculty of Science at the University of Moscow, who figures in his son's works as Prof. Letayev. Andrey Biely had an extremely broad and varied education in philosophy, mathematics and philology at Moscow University and abroad. From his early youth he was in a position to meet many of the outstanding men of his time. At the turn of the century, his interests had become mainly literary and philosophical. By 1910, he had published a book of verse and four prose *Symphonies*. These latter were symptomatic of the new "musical atmosphere" which was permeating the arts. With Alexander Blok, he became one of the leaders, exponents and theoreticians of the Symbolist movement, but his greatest contribution lay, perhaps, in his aesthetico-revolutionary treatment of the novel. This can be observed in his *The Silver Dove* (1910), *Petersburg* (1913), *Kotik Letayev* (1922) and the *Moscow Cycle* (1926-34), to single out only some of his principal works. His fiction has not been re-printed in the Soviet Union since 1935. Yet, as Boris Pasternak has said, Biely's earlier works "had created an upheaval in the pre-Revolutionary taste of his contemporaries and had given rise to the first Soviet prose."

In *Kotik Letayev* (published in 1922; written in 1915) Biely has depicted the impressions and sensations of the external world upon a boy from a pre-natal stage to the age of five. Here mythological interpretation, the confusion of identities, and the intrusion of both reason and objective reality, all play their part. The rhythmical structure of the book and its language approximate to states of being. Biely, it should be noticed, uses his own willed system of punctuation to stress his rhythmical structure. Like Apollinaire in his *Calligrammes*, Biely also plays with visual effects of structure. His irony and sense of comedy are also very evident as in the "Pompoul" episode of *The Gropings of Cosmoses*. His identification of characters with inanimate objects is a device he has taken from Gogol, but Biely has pushed it much further.

EVGENYI ZAMYATIN (*b. 1884-1937*)

EVGENYI ZAMYATIN was born in St. Petersburg and educated as a shipbuilding engineer. In 1915 he was sent to England in connection with the building of an ice-breaker. He had, however, begun to write fiction (*District Tales*, 1911). He also wrote a book of satirical short stories about England, *The Islanders*. In the early years of the Revolution, he turned entirely to writing. But he also helped to instruct some of the younger generation of Soviet writers in writing techniques. He became a member of the Serapion Brothers, an independent grouping of talented writers, who objected to regimentation. He was a modernist in form, style, and ideas, and rather "western" in appearance, manner and persuasion. The turn of his mind was ironical and satirical and, apart from his many stories, he is the author of *We*, a satirical novel of the future society which anticipated Huxley's *Brave New World* and Orwell's *1984*. A new paperback edition of *We* has recently been published in New York. *We* was never printed in the Soviet Union and its publication in 1930 in Czechoslovakia led to attacks on Zamyatin. As a result, he departed from the Soviet Union and lived abroad in Paris from 1931. *Mamai* is a story constructed in the 1920-modern manner. It deals ironically with the living problems of the difficult early revolutionary days as they had to be faced by the inhabitants of St. Petersburg. Zamyatin's approach blends symbolism, realism and abstraction.

VSEVOLOD IVANOV (*b. 1895*)

As AN AUTHOR, Vsevolod Ivanov was another of Maxim Gorky's "discoveries." Gorky had encouraged this remote provincial, first, by correspondence and, then, by more direct assistance and advice in Petersburg. As from 1921 he became one of the more interesting Soviet writers, beginning with such books as *The Partisans, Coloured Winds, Skyblue Sands*—all collections of short stories and novellas. He was also the author of *Armored*

Train N 14-69, which was dramatized and staged in Moscow and Paris. As an early member of the Serapion Brothers, Ivanov acquired more polish, and an imaged, modernist technique in his short story writing. In his early stories, he contributed a new subject matter—by describing partisan warfare in Siberia and Soviet Asia. *The Desert of Toub-Koy* is a good example of this type of story, combining as it does structured lyrical prose, vivid realism, and the analysis of naïve psychology—that of the Siberian peasants, which had rarely been described before. In writers like Ivanov and the early Fadeyev, hitherto neglected areas of the larger Russia become the subject of exploration.

Vsevolod Ivanov was born in Turkestan, and his early life had been difficult and highly adventurous. He wandered a great deal through Sibera and the Asiatic provinces and, at one time, set out on foot to India. He tried every occupation from being a circus clown to a typesetter. After he became established as a writer, he tried other themes and, perhaps, lost some of the vivid realism which had characterized his earlier stories. When he published his *Mystery of Mysteries,* he was accused of "Freudism and the propagation of unconsciousness." In the early 1930's, he wrote *The Tales of Brigadier M. N. Sinitzin,* which dealt with the campaign of collectivization in Turkmenistan. He also wrote a novel about World War II, and has lately been working on a novel about the new Siberia.

ALEXANDER GRIN (1880-1932)

Alexander Grin, pseudonym for Grinevsky, is a most unusual Russian writer. He is quite unlike anyone else. He is almost a "myth." As he once said, "Between 1906 and 1930 I heard so many strange things about myself, I began to doubt . . ." The legend about Grin has grown up partly as a result of his somewhat elusive personality and life, and partly also as a result of the strange character of his stories, which are utterly un-Russian in their conception and atmosphere. Grin has indeed defied all the tenets of Russian realism and, in the Soviet period, his attitude and work has appeared "alien to new themes and ways." His work is informed with a deep love of life and independence. It is, of course, romantic in feeling, and evokes the enchanted atmosphere of the fairy tale. Grin deliberately transforms his environment, creating an imaginary landscape and an ideal, romantic world of characters, who always bear French- and English-sounding names such as Gray and Asole, Harvey and Daisy. The characters are always imbued with heroic passion and the sense of adventure, and there is usually in the background a feeling of adventure on the high seas, as we can see in *The Eloquent Goblin.*

Alexander Grin's life was not easy, and his work was often neglected. During the Revolution, he fought in the Red Army, contracted typhus and then found himself in the street. But Maxim Gorky came to his rescue, and he spent his final years writing in the Crimea. Of late there has been a revival going on of his work. Apart from his numerous tales and stories, he is best known for his tale *Crimson Sails,* out of which a ballet was made in the 1940's when it first played at the Bolshoy Theater in Moscow. He also wrote the *Autobiographical Tale* which appeared in 1939. His story *The Eloquent Goblin* (1925) was first printed in 1957.

VERA INBER (*b. 1890*)

VERA INBER, poet and short story writer, is another literary figure from Odessa. Her father was the head of a Mathematics publishing house and her mother a teacher of Russian. She began writing verse in school. In 1912-14 she lived in Paris and published three books of poems in the then modernist vein under the titles of *Melancholy Wine, Bitter Pleasure, Frail Words.* Back in Russia, Vera Inber had to readapt herself to a changed environment after the Revolution, and her second literary life began in Moscow in 1923. She has described this period of her life in her autobiographical novel *A Place in the Sun* (1928), which was published in France, Germany, Poland and the Scandinavian countries. She had written some of her best prose in the 1920's, and Maxim Gorky at the time had praised some of her stories.

She was not much in evidence during the thirties, but re-emerged after the siege in Leningrad with a book of poems, *Pulkovo Meridian,* and her *Leningrad Diary,* for both of which she was awarded the Stalin Prize in 1946. She also wrote an autobiographical tale, *When I was Small* (1953). Vera Inber's *Selected Works* in three volumes appeared in 1957. These contained poetry, stories and articles, and included those stories of the twenties, like *Maya,* which had not been available in print for over thirty years.

ALEXEY TOLSTOY (*1882-1945*)

ALEXEY TOLSTOY was born of a landowning gentry family in the Province of Samara (now Kuibyshev). His father, who belonged to a side-branch of the Tolstoy family, was no close relative of the Leo Tolstoy. His mother was a Turgenev by birth; she separated from her husband and later married again. Alexey Tolstoy was brought up by his mother and stepfather. By 1907, he was living in Petersburg, where he first began to write verse, but he soon concentrated on prose. He established himself as a leading, young writer of the neo-realist school. By 1919, he had written a number of short stories, novellas and novels such as *Rastegin's Adventures, The Lame Gentlemen, The Eccentrics,* and *Nikita's Childhood.* Many of his stories have as their background the Volga region, and the rather rougher and more "crazy" type of Volga landowner. One gets the impression from these early works that the old landowning order is going to seed. In retrospect, Alexey Tolstoy is always happiest in works of reminiscence and history. He is a deeply Russian writer and a realist to the core. Though he spent some years abroad after the Revolution, he returned to Russia from Paris and Berlin in 1923 without much Western baggage except, perhaps, a few attempts at science fiction, of which the story *Aelita* (1924) is the best example. In the Soviet Union, apart from completing his novel trilogy *The Road to Calvary,* he began to concentrate on historical subjects and especially on the life and times of Peter the Great and Ivan the Terrible. He was working on the last volume

of his *Peter the Great* when he died. His plays on the Ivan the
Terrible theme had already been published during World War II.
Alexey Tolstoy's story *The Viper* was written in 1928, but it was
printed posthumously in 1957. It treats of the "destructive"
period of the Civil War and the difficulties of settling down to
"constructive" work.

BORIS PILNYAK (1894-193?)

BORIS PILNYAK (real name: Wogau) was the son of a doctor of
Volga German origin. He finished his formal education in Moscow and began writing in 1915. His prose was influenced by
Andrey Biely's work. His novel, *The Naked Year* (1922), about
the early years of the Revolution at once made him famous. The
novel was complex in structure, stark in descriptions, and in it
Pilnyak also attempted to give the Revolution a historical background by drawing parallels between the ruthlessness of the
bolsheviks and that of Peter the Great.

As from 1927, with the publication of his novella, *About the
Unextinguished Moon*, in which he referred to the dubious circumstances surrounding the death of Frunze, he became a butt
for the critics who declared that he had committed a "crude
political mistake." After a time, he was printed again, but he committed another "mistake" in 1929. In his short novel *Mahogany*
he gave a grotesque description of a number of "left" communists who had been expelled from the Party in 1921. Since no one
would print this novel in the Soviet Union, Pilnyak sent it to be
published by Petropolis in Berlin. The fat was now really in the
fire, and only Maxim Gorky was able to extricate Pilnyak for a
time. His next long novel *The Volga Flows into the Caspian*
(1931), which incorporated most of *Mahogany*, also angered the
critics. Although he published some further works, Pilnyak finally disappeared in the Stalinist purges of 1937. It was reported
that he was shot. But in any case, the year of his death has not
yet been revealed, though this has recently been done in the case
of both Babel and Mandelstam, who had "disappeared" about the
same time. Pilnyak's story, *With Earth-Soiled Hands*, was written

in 1928 and published in Berlin in 1929. His work has not been reprinted in the Soviet Union since his disappearance.

ILYA EHRENBURG (*b. 1891*)

ILYA EHRENBURG, poet, novelist and publicist, has been for some time already an international figure. He has the knack of keeping up with the times. As a poet, he is less well known but, as a novelist, he has a keen eye for the public situation, and is therefore topical—a chronicler, indeed, of certain political moments in both international and Soviet history. His quick literary reflexes are not necessarily shallow. He has had a great deal of international experience and patience, and these have saved him from many nasty situations. Born in Kiev of a middle Jewish family, educated at the First Moscow Gymnasium, politically minded by the age of fifteen, arrested briefly in 1908, he then left Moscow for Paris. There he remained on and off until 1941. Though favoring English tweeds and a pipe, Ehrenburg has absorbed everything Paris had to offer, including the early Picasso and Modigliani of the Rotonde days, World War I in which he served as a correspondent at the front, and the entry of the Germans in 1940. He went back to Russia in 1917, but re-emerged in 1921 with his satirical novel, *The Adventures of Julio Jurenito*. Within five or six years he became, however, an advocate of the new Five Year Plan policies as well as a satirist of European capitalism. Returning to the Soviet Union in 1941, he rapidly became a leading publicist and anti-Hitlerite satirist for *Izvesta* and *The Red Star*. His sense of the topical has never deserted him as his later novels *The Fall of Paris*, *The Thaw*, and *Storm* have demonstrated. Lately, in 1960, he has also published a very interesting book of reminiscences, *People, Years and Life*. In this, he reviews his life and the people he met in Russia and Europe, and he often writes with critical detachment and welcome candor. Indeed, Ehrenburg has played a useful and important part since his return to the Soviet Union, for, as one of the few "Europeanized" Russian literary men left, his influence in art and literature has been educative and directed against narrow provincialism. His *Merry Paolo* is a story in the lighter vein.

YURY OLESHA (1894-1960)

YURY OLESHA, the author of *Envy* (1927), a novel, of various short stories such as *The Cherry Stone* (1930) here included, of plays like *The Conspiracy of Sentiments,* and of fantasies like *The Three Fat Men* (1940), was one of the subtler, brighter and more independent spirits of Soviet literature. He combined humor, irony, fantasy, and subtle psychology to treat of the dilemma of the "superfluous intellectual" under the Soviet regime. In *Envy* he opposed the romantic dreamer Kavalerov to the massive and efficient Babichev, party man and the head of the Sausage Trust. Their antithesis is based on completely different sets of values: a world of sentiments and feelings versus one of ruthless efficiency. *Envy* naturally provoked discussion and polemics. Olesha's talent was eventually sacrificed too, for very little of his work has appeared since the late thirties and he spent some years in exile. He was back in Moscow after 1953, but very little new work of his has been published to date. It is to be hoped that an edition of his collected works will soon reveal some more stories by this fine, imaginative writer, who died within a month or two of Pasternak.

ISAAC BABEL (1894-1941)

IT HAD BEEN KNOWN for the past twenty years that Isaac Babel, one of the best short story writers of the Soviet period, had fallen victim to the purges of 1937-38. Nothing definite was known about his fate. Rumor said that he had either been shot or imprisoned. His work had not been republished. But since 1956, there has been a Babel revival. His works have been reprinted and, in 1959, in a brief, and very unsatisfactory biographical note about him, it was officially admitted for the first time that he died on March 17, 1941. However, no details were provided, and the biographical note leaves an amazing gap in his life between the year 1935 and that of his death. However, we must welcome even his partial resurrection. It is also interesting to note that both Ehrenburg and Paustovsky have recently given us descriptions of Babel in his middle and earlier period respectively.

Isaac Babel was yet another Odessa writer. His father was a Jewish trader who made his son study Hebrew, the Bible and the Talmud. He also mastered French and read authors like Maupassant. He finished the Commerical school in Odessa and began writing at the age of fifteen. By 1916 he was in touch with Maxim Gorky, who published some of his early stories in *Lietopis*, a monthly journal edited by Gorky. Gorky then advised him to stop writing for a while and to "study life." For the next five years or so, Babel plunged into the vortex of life, the Revolution and the Civil War. Then he re-emerged as one of the most original of the younger Soviet writers—a writer of incisive realism, vivid style and imagination. As he has said himself, "It was only in 1923 that I learnt to express my thoughts clearly and concisely. . . . I date the beginning of my literary work to early 1924 when the review *Lef* published my stories: *Salt, The Letter, Dolgushev's Death, The King,* etc. . . ." Most of these stories were included in Babel's *The Red Cavalry* (1927) —a sequence of short, intense and vividly realistic stories of the men involved in Budyonny's cavalry campaign during the Polish war of 1920. The book immediately attracted attention to Babel's literary qualities, but at the same time it made him enemies. Budyonny, the Red Cavalry commander, took a dislike to the book which, he thought, gave a "distorted image" of his fighters. At one stage, Gorky felt obliged to intervene and defend Babel's work as a literary accomplishment. Significantly, *Red Cavlary* was recently reprinted in the Soviet Union. Among his other works, all of permanent literary interest, are *The History of My Dovecot, Stories of Odessa.* These were mainly stories of his youth in Odessa. He has also written a play, *Sunset. In the Basement* was first published in Russian in 1931.

ILYA ILF (*1897-1937*) *and* EVGENYI PETROV (*1903-42*)

THE STORY of Ilf and Petrov is really the story of their collaboration, which lasted only ten years (1927-37). They were both born in Odessa. Ilf fell ill and died in 1937; Petrov was shot down in a plane in 1942 when returning from besieged Sevastopol. Ilf's real name was Faisilberg; and Petrov's, Katayev—he was the brother of Valentin Katayev, the novelist. Ilf and Petrov met in Moscow in 1925 and began their collaboration two years later. They were both wits and humorists, and became the outstanding satirists of their generation. Their first book, *The Twelve Chairs* (1927), was a highly entertaining satirical novel of the *Nep* period. This was followed by *The Golden Calf* and then, after their visit to the United States, by *One-Storied America. Count Sredizemsky* (1930), the story I have included, was first printed posthumously in 1957 in the Soviet review *Youth*.

MICHAEL PRISHVIN (*1873-1954*)

As A RUSSIAN WRITER, Michael Prishvin is rather special and unusual. He is an observer of nature and a hunter, and is quite as happy in studying a spider in its own environment as in training a bird dog. A bird dog is what he writes about in the story, *Kate*. In fact, he is steeped in nature lore and the life of the deep countryside. He prefers the short story or even the shorter meditative piece, though he has written a few novellas and an autobiographical account of his youth entitled *Kurymushka*. Since *The Black Arab* (1911), he has published many other books of short stories such as *In the Land of Fearless Birds* and *By the Walls of an Invisible City*.

Michael Prishvin was born in the village of Kruschevo in the Province of Orlov. His original profession was that of an agronomist, and he had studied in Riga and Leipsig as well as in Russia. But he gave up this profession and began writing in 1905. He had a hard time in the early years of the Revolution, when he was expropriated from his small house and estate and had to part from his favorite hunting rifle. However, he finally persuaded Lunacharsky, the original Commissar for Education to give him permission "to gather folklore." This enabled him to keep in touch with the countryside and go on writing as well until, with Gorky's help, he was able to establish himself as a "Soviet writer." After his death, his *Collected Works* were published in 1957.

BORIS PASTERNAK (*1890-1960*)

THE LIFE AND WORK of Boris Pasternak illustrates the great difficulties under which some Russian writers have labored since the Revolution, and also to the spiritual strength of some of them. As a result, Pasternak's contribution in bulk is not as big as it might have been, but his *Doctor Zhivago* is undoubtedly a great spiritual work, a book of life, rather than a novel in the ordinary parlance. There has been some misunderstanding on this point. At his death, Pasternak was engaged in writing a play on the root question of the Emancipation of the Serfs in 1861. His reassessment of the relations between the Russian intelligentsia and the Russian people would have been extremely interesting and significant to read.

Boris Pasternak was born in Moscow. His father was a well known portrait painter; his mother, a pianist. The family were close friends of Leo Tolstoy. Pasternak had an intensive education in the classics, music and philosophy. He had studied under Scriabin and under Professor Cohen, the philosopher, at Marburg (1912); but, in the same year, he finally decided to devote himself to poetry and literature. His first book of poems, *Twin in the Clouds*, appeared in 1915. His fourth and fifth volumes, *My Sister, Life* and *Themes and Variations* (1923), which established his reputation as an outstanding lyrical poet, appeared already under the Soviets. His poetic star rose steadily until 1936, by which time two editions of his *Collected Poems* had been published, apart from many other single volumes. Then his star declined—officially. No new book of his poems was published in the Soviet Union after 1945, though he was occasionally included, with big gaps, in anthologies or magazines up to 1957. The same applies to his pre-Zhivago prose—*Tratto di Apelle* (1915), *Letters from Tula, Aerial Ways* (1924), *The Childhood of Luvers* (1918), *The Last Summer: A Tale* (1934). After 1936, however, Pasternak began to write novels. One of them was entitled *The Year 1905*. He had already written a long poem on this subject of the first Russian Revolution in the late twenties. Several self-contained episodes from the novel were published, among them *Troubled Days. The Proud Beggar* is another episode from a novel. Both episodes contain characters that later reappeared in *Doctor Zhivago*, which was finished in 1954-55. In fact, we may conclude that many of the characters and situations from his unpublished novels of the 1930's served as a basis for the later novel, which finally made him internationally famous. It is incredible but, alas, true that this great lyrical poet should have been deprived of the fruits of international recognition as expressed in the award to him of the Nobel Prize in 1958.

MICHAEL SHOLOKHOV (*b. 1905*)

MICHAEL SHOLOKHOV is officially regarded as *the* Soviet novelist. He offers a strong contrast to writers like Pasternak or Olesha. As Konstantin Simonov has recently written, "For us, Sholokhov has the same indisputable standing in literature as Eisenstein has in the cinema or Shostakovich in music." However, Sholokhov is no mere stooge; he is a man of independent views and, as a novelist, interested profoundly in character and all its psychological complications. As a matter of fact, most of his heroes have been involved in the dilemma of choice, and have wavered in their loyalties and decisions. He has devoted rather more attention to the man shot in doubt than to any black and white presentation of reality. As a novelist, he is a psychological realist somewhat in the manner of Leo Tolstoy, but his depth and range are more limited. In his novels, he has been concerned mostly with the trials of his native Don Cossacks. He depicts a

world of violence—that of the Cossacks in World War I, the
Civil War, the period of enforced collectivization and, finally,
World War II. He has been accused of overdoing descriptions of
brutality, but he holds to his view of reality. In addition, he has
developed a sense of comedy. He has qualities which raise him
above being just a regional writer of the Don Cossack region.
His language is colloquially varied and deceptively simple.

Michael Shlokhov was born of a Russian father and a
Ukrainian mother in the Veshensky Cossack settlement of the
Don Cossack region. His education was interrupted by the
Civil War. Except for occasional trips to Moscow and abroad,
he has lived all his life in the place of his birth, and his work has
been consistently devoted to the characters and the landscape
of this locality. His literary activity dates from 1923, and his first
collections of short stories, *Stories of the Don* and *The Azure
Steppe*, both appeared in 1926. For the next thirty years he has
concentrated on a more grandiose project—a cycle of epic
novels dealing with the life, sufferings and joys of various Cossack
families in the Veshensky region, all this in the background of
political, social and international events. The period he has described has been one mainly of violence, but the horrors and
emotional conflicts are occasionally relieved by vivid descriptions of landscape and outbursts of Cossack humor. His characters, though mainly simple people, show a rich variety of personality and social standing. He is austerely realistic in portraying
the bolshevik as well as the anti-bolshevik. Sholokhov's cycle of
novels began with *And Quiet Flows the Don* and *The Don
Flows Home from the Sea* (1925-39), and then continued with
Seeds of Tomorrow and *Harvest on the Don* (1930-59), which
are concerned with enforced collectivization in the year 1930.
After *World War II* Sholokhov has continued the cycle in a
novel, *They Fought for their Country*, parts of which appeared
in 1959. *During the Retreat*, an episode from this last novel,
shows Sholokhov in a humorous mood. Here the Don Cossack
villagers begin by withholding food from a retreating detachment of hungry Red Army men because they are retreating before the Germans. After an amusing amatory interlude, the real
object of which is food, the difficulties are finally resolved.

MICHAEL ZOSCHENKO (b. 1895-1958)

MICHAEL ZOSCHENKO was born of a gentry family. He graduated from Petersburg University and then served as an officer in World War I, in which he was both wounded and gassed. In 1918, he volunteered for the Red Army. After being demobilized, he joined the Serapion Brothers group of writers and published his first work, *The Tales of Nazar Ilyich*. In these *Tales* Zoschenko combined humor with tragic motifs, but in subsequent works his tone became lighter. Zoschenko soon established himself as the leading humorist among Soviet writers and has published over twenty volumes of stories. He has been much published in England. His work has not escaped criticism and accusations of being "bourgeois." His worst moment from this point of view came in 1946 when, after having been violently attacked three years previously for his book *When The Sun Rises,* he was severely taken to task by Zhdanov for his "harmful activities" as an editor of the review *Zvezda* and for the publication of his "anti-Soviet" story *The Ape.* He was practically ostrasized for a time. It took a while to live this down, and there is a gap of his published works between 1946 and 1953. After this, Zoschenko was back in print; and his story, *An Extraordinary Incident*, was published in 1957. It is also included in the representative *Stories and Tales* (1960). Zochenko's genius lies in depicting in rich colloquial speech the frustrations of naïve or eccentric small men.

VSEVOLOD KOCHETOV

VSEVOLOD KOCHETOV, a poet and novelist, was born in Leningrad. He came into literary prominence in the middle 1950's. He had originally been a metal worker by profession and is thoroughly acquainted with working class conditions in Leningrad and also managerial problems. Like Dudintsev, he is interested in, and takes as his subject, the industrial milieu, and analyzes the play of forces centering round changed methods of production and the application of new inventions. His characters are usually old and young workers, managers, party executives and, occasionally, intellectuals. He has also been concerned with Soviet careerists and the type of mentality that tries to undermine the main line of Soviet development. Though an upholder of the main line, Kochetov attempts a psychological description of many different elements on the Soviet scene, and his novels, *The Zhurbins*, and *The Yershov Brothers* are highly topical descriptions of the conflict going on within Soviet industry after Stalin's death. In *The Yershov Brothers* (1958), Kochetov has described the uneasy debates and conflicts that took place in 1955-57, the period of so-called "Revisionism" and of the Hungarian revolt. Kochetov treats of the ideological strife between the opposing factions. In his novel, Orleantzev is the chief villain both in the industrial front and in the sphere of ideas while the Yershovs are the positive heroes. This polemical novel, of which *A Conflict of Ideas* is an episode, contains many frank discussions of the impact of western ideas, which seemed to threaten the stability of Soviet life. The novel provoked a big controversy, which lasted through September and October 1958.

VALENTIN KATAYEV (*b. 1897*)

VALENTIN KATAYEV, the brother of Evgenyi Petrov, was the son of an Odessa schoolteacher. He was one of a number of Odessa writers, who made a reputation for themselves in the last thirty years. By 1932, Katayev had already won international recognition with his satirical novel, *The Embezzlers* (1927), his comedy *The Squaring of a Circle*, and his industrialization novel, *Speed Up, Time!* He is a writer of great ability, a realist by preference, and a disciple of Bunin. He has written many short stories, but in the past twenty years he has also concentrated on a partly autobiographical sequence in fiction form, of which three volumes have so far been published: *A White Sail Gleams* (1936), *For Soviet Power* (1949), *The Cottage in the Steppe* (1956). In 1947 he was elected Deputy of the Supreme Soviet and, in 1958, he was finally admitted as a member of the Communist Party.

As a writer, Katayev dilutes his realism with touches of humor and whimsy, and he is good at sensitive description of children. In *The Cottage in the Steppe,* from which the episode of *The Death of Tolstoy* is taken, Katayev describes the schooldays of an Odessa boy, Petya Bacheis, whose father is a schoolteacher who gets dismissed from his post because he ventures to give a talk to his class about "that great Russian writer Leo Tolstoy," then out of favor with the authorities. The boy later goes with his father on a trip to Europe.

OLGA BERGOLTZ (*b. 1910*)

OLGA BERGOLTZ's father was a doctor of medicine, and she was born in Petersburg. In 1930 she graduated from the Philological Faculty of the University of Leningrad. For the next two years she was a correspondent of *The Soviet Steppe,* a newspaper in Alma Ata. Then for the next three years she edited the Komsomol page of a factory newspaper in Leningrad. In 1941-44 she stayed in Leningrad and experienced the siege of the city by the Germans. During this period she made many speeches and broadcasts, and also wrote many sketches, children's books and verse. In 1951 she was awarded the Stalin Prize.

Olga Bergoltz began writing in 1930. She is mainly a poet and short story writer. Her first book of poems, *Verses,* appeared in 1934. She has published poetry and stories ever since. Among some of her later works are *Leningrad Diary and Poems, Selected Works* (1954) and *Lyrics* (1955). In her story, *That Meadow,* printed in 1957, she describes with gentle humor how her father helped against her will to dissipate her worries in the editorial where she was being unjustly attacked.

KONSTANTIN PAUSTOVSKY (*b. 1892*)

KONSTANTIN PAUSTOVSKY, a contemporary of Boris Pasternak, has assumed increasing importance as a writer in the late 1950's.

Born in Moscow, the son of a railway statistician of Cossack origin, Paustovsky was formally educated in Kiev, where he finished the classical gymnasium in 1912. (This period is described in his *Distant Years*.) His first story had been printed in the previous year. He was at Kiev University until 1914, when he transferred to Moscow University, but World War I interrupted his studies. He first became a stretcher bearer on various hospital trains which evacuated the wounded from the front. Then, in 1917, he began working as a newspaper correspondent. That year he began a novella, *The Romantics*, published in the 1930's. He later served in the Red Army and spent 1919-21 in the region of Odessa and the Caucasus. In Odessa, he made the acquaintance of Katayev, Babel, Bagritzky and Ilf, all of whom became prominent within the next ten years. To this period of his life he had devoted his latest autobiographical work, *The Time of Great Expectations*. After returning to Moscow in 1932, he became an editor in *Rosta;* but with the publication of his *Kara Bugaz*, a book about "the liquidation of deserts," he abandoned office work and devoted himself wholly to writing.

An inveterate traveler, Konstantin Paustovsky has said: "Almost every book of mine is a journey. Or, more exactly, every journey is a book." The most varied regions of the Soviet Union figure as the background for his fiction. After 1945 he also traveled in Czechoslovakia, Italy, Turkey, Greece, France, Holland and Sweden. As he once said, "Every writer has his own way of living and writing. As for me, I need two things for fruitful work: to travel and to concentrate."

His increasing reputation is based largely on his later stories and autobiographical works, in which he has attempted to reconstruct not only his personal experiences within the historical framework of his times, but also to express them with all the freshness of his youthful enthusiasms and impressions. As he has said, "Since childhood, I have wanted to see and experience everything a man could see and experience. This did not happen . . . life did not seem so full of events . . . until I began to remember. Then, one remembrance evoked another . . . and so an uninterrupted chain of reminiscences is formed, and life began to look more varied than I thought."

Paustovsky's later work is notable for its sensitivity, freedom and humor. Apart from stories, he is now mainly engaged in completing his autobiographical cycle, of which four volumes have so far appeared to date: *Distant Years* (1947), *Restless Youth* (1955), *The Opening of an Unknown Age* (1956) and *The Time of Great Expectations* (1960). He has also written *The Golden Rose*, a work about the writer's craft. His story, *The Crowd on the Quay*, the result of a visit to Naples, was first printed in 1957-8.

NATALIA SOKOLOVA

NATALIA SOKOLOVA was born in Leningrad, and was educated at Moscow University. She has specialized in Russian and Soviet Art. She is a corresponding member of the USSR Academy of Art. Natalia Sokolova is also branching out as a writer. She recently published in the review *Znamya* (Nov. 8, 1960), a number of short sketches and impressions under the title of *Greetings, People!*, which are both amusing and informative. The present piece, *A Savage*, apart from its humor, throws some light on the demand in Moscow, and in the Soviet Union, for books, especially certain more limited editions for which readers have to subscribe in advance. As we can gather from Sokolova's account, there appears to be some black market activity going on in this domain since the demand for these books in Moscow seems to be as great as that for theater tickets for "hit" shows in New York.

FEODOR PANFEROV (*1896-1960*)

FEODOR PANFEROV died in August 1960 after a long illness while his latest novel, *In the Name of the Young*, was still being published serially in the review *October*, of which he was the chief editor. On his sickbed, he was working till the last moment on yet another novel.

Panferov was of peasant origin and was born in the village of Pavlovka in the Saratov region. He became prominent as a Soviet

The UNIVERSAL Library

writer with the publication of his four-volume novel, *Bruski* (1930-37), in which he described the transformation of a village community as a result of the Revolution, Civil War, and then collectivization. He was originally somewhat of a "rough diamond" as a writer. Panferov had, however, a certain vital power and grasp of his subject. He had continued to write novels steadily and, after 1953, continued to tackle controversial themes.

In *Meditation* (1958) he set himself the problem of dealing in terms of fictional characters with the critical situation in Soviet agriculture, a situation which had been discussed at the September 1953 Plenum of the Central Committee. In this novel, he analyzes realistically the human, economic, and official factors involved in the backward state of some of the collective farms. In his last published novel, *In the Name of the Young*, he deals with a more complex picture of Soviet reality. While studying the psychological complications and the objective difficulties of an important hydraulic construction work going on in the Volga region, he also takes one of his main characters, Nikolai Korablev, on a visit to England, which he satirizes in some aspect; and he also describes Korablev's domestic difficulties. Tatyana Korablev, the wife, is a painter who betrays her husband and turns to modern art. The combination of "modernism" and domestic unhappiness proves too much for the old bolshevik Korablev, who takes to drink and finally commits suicide. The realism of this conclusion makes the novel rather unusual from the point of view of Socialist "Realism."

VLADIMIR DUDINTSEV (b. 1918)

VLADIMIR DUDINTSEV is one of a generation of Soviet writers, like Kochetov and Tendryakov, who have come into prominence after 1953. He was born in the Ukraine and studied at the Law Institute in Moscow. During World War II he served in the army and was wounded on the Leningrad front. His early verse and stories were first published in children's magazines. Then, after the war, his poems and stories began to appear in the major literary reviews. His first published collection of stories was entitled *The Seven Heroes*, and most of these stories were concerned with war themes. Later, he turned his attention to characters involved in Soviet industry, and he was particularly interested in the difficulties, which inventors and scientists face when trying to push their new ideas through the crust of self-interested minds, the bureaucracy and established career men. Thus his first novel, *Not By Bread Alone*, published serially in 1956 and in book form in 1957, immediately became the object of controversy. The debate turned largely on whether Dudintsev was distorting the conditions of Soviet life and keeping to the tenets of Socialist Realism. This controversy made Dudintsev internationally known, and his novel was published in many countries, including the U.S.A. (1957). More recently Dudintsev published *A New Year's Fable* (1960), a story on a similar theme, but more humorously and fantastically conceived. In it is a symbolical Owl, which is somehow reminiscent of the Raven in Edgar Allan Poe. In the above works, as well as in his story, *The Mad Boy*, Vladimir Dudintsev has shown himself to possess some originality of approach, and it will be interesting to watch his development as a writer.

VLADIMIR TENDRYAKOV

VLADIMIR TENDRYAKOV is one of the younger prose writers to make a name for himself in the fifties. So far he has been the author of rather long stories and novellas, most of them centered in somewhat remote parts of the Russian countryside. Tendryakov's background is on the whole rural, though it sometimes includes a landscape being transformed by machines. His characters are usually average types, "small men" rather than "exceptional heroes." This portrayal of the "ordinary man" has all the force of discovery in the Soviet situation. The interest in the "small man," remote from great events, uninvolved in proving anything, and having his weak side as well as his strong, a character once reserved for the "comics" like Zoschenko, is a new trend in Soviet literature and has caused some discussion of late. Some Soviet critics regard this trend as a betrayal of Socialist Realism—the

theory *par excellence* of predetermined "aims." T[hey com]plain of a "diminution of ideals."

In a previous novella, *The Miracle Worker* (195[?]) [he] had treated of the psychological effects of the disc[overy of a] lost miraculous icon upon various people in a rem[ote village;] in *Three, Seven, Ace* (1960), Tendryakov is concer[ned with a log]rolling camp in the far Siberian north. Here, Dubi[nin, head of] the camp is confronted with an unexpected stranger[, called] Bushuyev, on whom he takes pity, but who underm[ines the discipline] of the camp through gambling at cards. Dubinin is n[ot only led] to kill Bushuyev, but is also falsely held on suspic[ion of appro]priating Bushuyev's "winnings." The extraordinary [quality of] this novella, of which we have suggested the atmosp[here, we have] been unable to give the full flavor here because [part of it] is the complete absence of any ideological premis[es ...] Tendryakov is not just an "adventure" writer; he is [deeply in]terested in character and human frailties.

writer with the publication of his four-volume novel, *Bruski* (1930-37), in which he described the transformation of a village community as a result of the Revolution, Civil War, and then collectivization. He was originally somewhat of a "rough diamond" as a writer. Panferov had, however, a certain vital power and grasp of his subject. He had continued to write novels steadily and, after 1953, continued to tackle controversial themes.

In *Meditation* (1958) he set himself the problem of dealing in terms of fictional characters with the critical situation in Soviet agriculture, a situation which had been discussed at the September 1953 Plenum of the Central Committee. In this novel, he analyzes realistically the human, economic, and official factors involved in the backward state of some of the collective farms. In his last published novel, *In the Name of the Young*, he deals with a more complex picture of Soviet reality. While studying the psychological complications and the objective difficulties of an important hydraulic construction work going on in the Volga region, he also takes one of his main characters, Nikolai Korablev, on a visit to England, which he satirizes in some aspect; and he also describes Korablev's domestic difficulties. Tatyana Korablev, the wife, is a painter who betrays her husband and turns to modern art. The combination of "modernism" and domestic unhappiness proves too much for the old bolshevik Korablev, who takes to drink and finally commits suicide. The realism of this conclusion makes the novel rather unusual from the point of view of Socialist "Realism."

VLADIMIR DUDINTSEV (*b. 1918*)

VLADIMIR DUDINTSEV is one of a generation of Soviet writers, like Kochetov and Tendryakov, who have come into prominence after 1953. He was born in the Ukraine and studied at the Law Institute in Moscow. During World War II he served in the army and was wounded on the Leningrad front. His early verse and stories were first published in children's magazines. Then, after the war, his poems and stories began to appear in the major literary reviews. His first published collection of stories was entitled *The Seven Heroes*, and most of these stories were concerned with war themes. Later, he turned his attention to characters involved in Soviet industry, and he was particularly interested in the difficulties, which inventors and scientists face when trying to push their new ideas through the crust of self-interested minds, the bureaucracy and established career men. Thus his first novel, *Not By Bread Alone*, published serially in 1956 and in book form in 1957, immediately became the object of controversy. The debate turned largely on whether Dudintsev was distorting the conditions of Soviet life and keeping to the tenets of Socialist Realism. This controversy made Dudintsev internationally known, and his novel was published in many countries, including the U.S.A. (1957). More recently Dudintsev published *A New Year's Fable* (1960), a story on a similar theme, but more humorously and fantastically conceived. In it is a symbolical Owl, which is somehow reminiscent of the Raven in Edgar Allan Poe. In the above works, as well as in his story, *The Mad Boy*, Vladimir Dudintsev has shown himself to possess some originality of approach, and it will be interesting to watch his development as a writer.

VLADIMIR TENDRYAKOV

VLADIMIR TENDRYAKOV is one of the younger prose writers to make a name for himself in the fifties. So far he has been the author of rather long stories and novellas, most of them centered in somewhat remote parts of the Russian countryside. Tendryakov's background is on the whole rural, though it sometimes includes a landscape being transformed by machines. His characters are usually average types, "small men" rather than "exceptional heroes." This portrayal of the "ordinary man" has all the force of discovery in the Soviet situation. The interest in the "small man," remote from great events, uninvolved in proving anything, and having his weak side as well as his strong, a character once served for the "comics" like Zoschenko, is a new trend in Soviet literature and has caused some discussion of late. Some Soviet critics regard this trend as a betrayal of Socialist Realism—

theory *par excellence* of predetermined "aims." These critics complain of a "diminution of ideals."

In a previous novella, *The Miracle Worker* (1959), Tendryakov had treated of the psychological effects of the discovery of a long lost miraculous icon upon various people in a remote village. But in *Three, Seven, Ace* (1960), Tendryakov is concerned with a log-rolling camp in the far Siberian north. Here, Dubinin, the boss of the camp is confronted with an unexpected stranger, an ex-convict, Bushuyev, on whom he takes pity, but who undermines the morale of the camp through gambling at cards. Dubinin is not only forced to kill Bushuyev, but is also falsely held on suspicion of appropriating Bushuyev's "winnings." The extraordinary thing about this novella, of which we have suggested the atmosphere, but have been unable to give the full flavor here because of its length, is the complete absence of any ideological premises. However, Tendryakov is not just an "adventure" writer; he is seriously interested in character and human frailties.

The UNIVERSAL Library